MIDNIGHT CALL AND OTHER STORIES

Midnight Call
and Other Stories

Jonathan Thomas

Foreword by S. T. Joshi

Hippocampus Press

New York

Some of the stories in this book appeared in earlier form in *Stories from the Big Black House* (Providence, RI: Radio Void, 1992).

Acknowledging: Angel, with love, for staying with me on this long, chancy trip; Paige, for setting me in the right direction; and Leslie, for the gracious benefit of the doubt.

Published by Hippocampus Press
P.O. Box 641, New York, NY 10156.
http://www.hippocampuspress.com

Cover art © 2008 by David C. Verba. Cover design by Barbara
Briggs Silbert. Hippocampus Press logo designed by Anastasia Damianakos.

First Edition
1 3 5 7 9 8 6 4 2
ISBN: 0979380693

Contents

Foreword

We hear frequently of some new "discovery" in the horror field, but all too often these seemingly promising writers fizzle out into comfortable mediocrity. Aside from the genuine "finds" of the last several decades—of whom Clive Barker, Thomas Ligotti, and Caitlín R. Kiernan are perhaps the most noteworthy examples—there are any number of others whose initial brilliance has not been followed up by consistently meritorious work. But there is reason to hope that Jonathan Thomas may be different.

This writer, while far from young in a chronological sense, is still unknown to the readers of horror, fantasy, and science fiction, for his one previous venture—the slim and eccentric collection *Stories from the Big Black House* (1992)—apparently received virtually no distribution outside his native home of Providence, Rhode Island. Moreover, in recent years Thomas has adopted a significantly different approach to the crafting of horror tales, one that draws upon the established classics of the form while in no way diminishing its own originality in conception, execution, and diction.

Every tale in this collection, long or short, exhibits Thomas's deep reading in the work of Blackwood, Lovecraft, and M. R. James; but at the same time, Thomas's dynamism in plot-weaving and his pungently satirical prose testify to a prodigious fund of creativity and a fine eye for observing the little absurdities of life in the twenty-first century.

One of the most remarkable features of this collection is a simultaneous variety and unity: variety in length (ranging from 500-word vignettes to 10,000-word novelettes), in subject matter (from the caveman primitivism of "Damn the Wheelwright" to the chill of a nineteenth-century Vermont winter in "In the Wake of Bridget" to the suburban contemporaneity of "Ariadne's Hair"), in mood and genre (from the melding of psychological and supernatural horror in "Eben's

Portrait" to the jaunty science fiction of "The Christmas Clones" to the wistful fantasy of "Awakening of No Return")—but also unity as expressed in meticulous craftsmanship and a distinctly cynical vision of human foibles and societal ills.

We have not heard the last of Jonathan Thomas, for he is already amassing stories for a second collection, and a novel is in the works. His ability to lend distinctiveness of treatment to many of the time-tested tropes of horror literature (reaching back to myth and folklore as well as to previous literature) may carry him far in a field that has always been most effective when it simultaneously looks backward and forward.

—S. T. JOSHI

Eben's Portrait

The Finsters were the oldest family in Marston Hills. Their house, a mock palazzo of clapboards and clunky gingerbread under beetling eaves, sat like a beached crate on the high ridge. The paintlessness and rot afflicting the walls bespoke the decades-ago demise of family mills and fortunes, as did the morose, tarpaper feel of the riverside town below the ridge. The Finsters did not get out much anymore.

Several years ago I had resorted to Marston Hills for low-rent studio space in former factories. And never had I seen or heard tell of a Finster at large.

But somehow they knew of me, which was as curious as anything else about this note, typed on an old manual whose misaligned ribbon fringed grey letters with red:

> Miss Levasseur,
>
> We thought you might like to come up to the house and try your hand at painting Mr. Finster, our patriarch. We hear you are very talented, and we would like to pay you.
>
> Please try to reply before two weeks, as that will be the time when old Eben should sit again.
>
> We look forward to hearing from you.

A girlishly deliberate hand had signed Claudia Finster and added a phone number.

Curiosity gave me reason enough to call. Besides, grateful as I was to Marston Hills for posing no distractions, my friendlessness there had grown tiresome. Why not get to know the Finsters?

An unidentified male Finster and I worked out a time for me to visit. He was slow on the uptake, as if unused to chatting, let alone making decisions, over the phone. He suddenly blurted, apparently the very second it occurred to him, Did I charge just for coming over and talking? I said painters weren't like lawyers. After a pause he said, "That's good."

En route to the house I nearly crashed. The two-lane road out of town twisted uphill past rundown bungalows and sparse woods, behind which vistas of the valley kept breaking through. It was a cold bright fall afternoon and the colors made me look, postcard-cliché or not. Next thing I knew, the car was bouncing wildly. The road had changed from blacktop to deeply rutted dirt. Just ahead a log blocked the way. I stopped with inches to spare.

It was a hefty-looking maple trunk, but budged some inches at a poke from my foot. A harder kick sent bark flying and showed rotten wood porous as Styrofoam. The clean-cut base of the trunk still rested on its stump, and it was heavy but manageable. In three tries I had pivoted it off the road.

The Finster palazzo was the end of the road. I parked next to a dusty '50s Mercury in a grassless patch beside the house. A woman waiting on the front steps introduced herself as Claudia.

Claudia was slight. Her face was white as her hair, which was done up in a home perm from the Kennedy era. She wore a shapeless faded housedress. She squinted.

I explained how the fallen tree had delayed me. She said, "Marsden did that. He's very shy. He hates the idea of strangers snooping around. I told him to put that old tree to one side for you, but I guess he didn't get to it." End of topic.

We sat in a high-ceilinged living room off the front hall. Staying focused on Claudia was hard. The room was choked with generations of inventory. The floor was a maze of armchairs, armoires, chests, and escritoires. Hancock chairs surrounded a folding card table groaning under photo albums and ropebound bundles of dime novels. In cupboards, Maori exotica enjoyed no pride of place over gumball machine toys. Virtual Babels of Staffordshire plates and Fiesta ware and Revere pewter let only a transom's worth of light through grimy windows. Somewhere in the room a clock ticked. Dust and mold already made my throat tickle.

Claudia was explaining, "Eben doesn't really get around anymore. But he's still very much head of the household. I don't know what

we'd do without him. He came up with our tradition of doing his portrait, back oh I don't know when. And every ten years he insists on a
new one. It's a fascination of his, he says, to see what changes and
doesn't change in a man. He keeps the pictures around himself always,
so your work would be in a place of honor."

"I'm anxious to meet Mr. Finster, if he's free."

"You mean today?" Claudia seemed taken aback.

"It would help me plan how to work when I came back."

"I'm sorry, but Eben isn't one for socializing. He likes me to make
these arrangements myself. And at his age, we respect his whims as law."

"So are you his daughter?"

"Oh no!" she gasped with mock horror. "Do I look that old? I'm
his granddaughter."

"I'm sorry, Ms. Finster. I just have no idea how old Mr. Finster is."

"I understand. So what is it you've brought with you?"

I unzipped my portfolio. The length of time since my last figural
work had forced me to rummage through old undergraduate exercises.

"You know, I don't usually do portraits," I felt safe saying once
her face showed approval of my student work.

"So you must do still lifes. Eben sits very still most of the time."

Rather than explain what I did, I just let her flip the pages and tell
me it was all very nice. While rezipping the portfolio, I asked, "So
where is the rest of the family?"

"Oh, they don't have to be here for this. I don't like discussing finances in front of them."

That sounded like my cue. I took a deep breath and named my
price.

Claudia looked aghast but neither haggled nor made any excuse to
comparison shop. Instead she said resignedly, "My, I guess paintings
have gotten more expensive like everything else." She perfunctorily
scheduled my next visit and stressed I not be late. After all, it was only
one afternoon of my time.

No ma'am! But a finished portrait in one sitting? Why yes, that's
the way it always was. Eben didn't have the strength for more. Hadn't
for as long as Claudia had been in charge.

So we left each other with misgivings, whether over time or
money, and mine only grew in the next days. With every thought of

the smothering clutter, the dust, the hated quiet in an apparent house full of people, and the kind of "shyness" that blocks roads with trees, the burden of returning felt heavier and heavier. Even that brief exposure to the Finster air had been enough to give me a sore throat. If only I had quoted anything like the real-world going rate for a portrait, Claudia might have balked and let me off the hook. But finally my crying need for any kind of money forced me back up the hill.

The appointed day was drizzly and raw. Sure enough, the tree barred the road again. The wet bark was slick, and when something dark moved near my feet, the log slipped from my startled grip and crashed. It just missed my feet and landed on whatever had surprised me. The wet crunching sound made me shudder. Unnerved already, I managed to swing the tree to the roadside and looked back, ready to flinch away. But it took a few seconds to identify the casualty as a box turtle, unmoving of course, shell broken into mosaic pieces, within a widening halo of blood. I felt bad, and even worse at perversely imagining I'd killed some all-too-appropriate pet of Marsden's.

Back in the car, I flashed to some Lillian Hellman I'd read ages ago. Dashiell Hammett, she recounted, had tried killing a big mean snapping turtle. Nearly beheaded and left for dead, it had astounded them by crawling hundreds of feet back to its pond. Hellman thought that said something about the tenacity of life. She might have had the same thoughts looking at the Finster palazzo.

This time Claudia ushered me into the kitchen. The scent of soap powder and bacon grease seemed to rise from every surface. Fruit flies hovered over three bulging garbage bags under the window next to the sink. The newest appliance was a toaster. On the counter beneath paneless cupboard, the screen was bright on a portable TV, but a picture never appeared. We sat at a maple table from whose top someone had been flaying discolored contact paper. I didn't bother mentioning Marsden's roadblock this time.

Without asking my preference, Claudia mixed us each a plastic mug of instant coffee, black. Then she explained, "The room upstairs is all ready for you. You can go on and get set up. We'll bring Eben in a few minutes." I sipped the bitter lukewarm brew and she made herself clearer. "You can take that up with you. I have to start making lunch now."

I gathered my materials and left the token of Yankee hospitality on the table. Claudia instructed me to go up the back stairs as I left the kitchen, and it was the first door on my right. "Don't you want your coffee?" she asked as I trudged out. I said no thanks. "Oh well, someone will drink it," she said.

The house was silent as I climbed the unlit steep stairs. At the top I caught my breath and listened. Down the hall of closed doors a toilet flushed. I waited a minute, but nobody came out.

The first door on the right opened onto a southwestern exposure, bright enough despite dust caking windows. This room was bare. The varnished floorboards had been swept clean. They creaked with every step. The floor sloped none too subtly between doorway and windows. Heavy pine spray scent made me take short breaths.

No sooner was canvas on easel than doors began to slam and hushed talk filled the hall. Only Claudia's voice came through clearly. "Now Grandfather, don't you fret about it. I know the name sounds French, but she isn't any foreigner."

Claudia entered, pushing Eben in a wheelchair, while half a dozen Finsters milled in around them. The others didn't register at first. Not with Eben at arm's length. Shock and nausea hit me at the same time. Eben must have been dead some decades, judging by tea-colored mummy skin, eyes at the bottom of well-deep sockets, mouth gaping open, cobweb strands of shoulder-length hair, arms like grape vines rattling loose in Depression-era morning jacket. A fresh white orchid graced his mauve lapel. The pine spray made scant dent in mildewy odor.

"Miss Levasseur!" Claudia called. "Say hello to Mr. Finster! Or he'll think you're one of those snooty artists. His ears aren't what they once were, but he can still hear you."

It was all I could do to move my lips a little.

"If there's one thing we know," Claudia was declaiming, "it's how to keep what we have. And keeping dear old Eben with us has kept us a family. What would we do without him?"

Was this a joke? I tried to smile.

"I don't know if I can do this," I whispered, still unable to look away from the cadaver.

"It would mean so much to him if you would," Claudia pleaded. "He so looks forward to this. I promise, we'll leave you alone until you're done."

I swallowed. Whose throat was drier, mine or Eben's?

The family began to chime in, Yes, do stay and paint Mr. Finster, please, he'll be so disappointed, it's only once every ten years. It felt like the Finsters were closing in.

I looked into their faces at last. None was under thirty. Sandy blond hair, babyfat cheeks, shrew eyes, mushroom-white complexions reddening with excitement as if Christmas were coming and nobody had better try stopping it. In the deep little eyes pinpoints of light flickered ominously, as if eyes were windows onto revelers within, running with torches in hand. By all appearances this had been too close a family for a long time. And to paraphrase some poet, love was strong as death where the old man was concerned. Don't touch me, any of you!

"All right, all right, I'm painting him!" I cried, shaking like a rabbit.

"Ah, good!" applauded Claudia. "We'll leave you two alone now." She turned and waved the others out ahead of her. They seemed anxious to get going. As she closed the door, Claudia remarked, "They're very fond of him, but he seldom joins us. He can't stand too much fussing at his age."

What did I think I was doing? I swallowed, still so unsteady that taking a step back nearly made me sick. Okay, forget the niceties. Never mind lighting, positioning him, positioning myself. Just paint. Get some kind of likeness done.

My mind was numb as my hands went to work. After a while it got easier. I didn't think about what I was doing, while at the same time, presence of mind resurfaced. A morbid smile rose and fell when the good advice occurred to me, Don't bother doing anything to flatter the subject.

After all, if the Finsters wanted a portrait of a rotting corpse, that was their business, wasn't it? I mean, that must have been all they wanted of me, right? All sense of time deserted me, though as this last question kept recurring I grew more and more nervous, painting faster and faster. Did clouds dim the light or was it late already? The dirty windows made it impossible to tell. Meanwhile the mildew stink thickened, as if it were a sweat that Eben was giving off.

From the hall came occasional giggling, running footsteps, doors slamming. Amidst all that racket I couldn't fear they were lying in wait for me, but some giddiness in their tone put me more and more on edge. Neither staying with Eben nor confronting the noise felt like tenable courses. Then the hall was quiet a while, in which time I felt persuaded that the painting was finished. Let me just pack up and get within reach of the front door before anything else happened.

It was relief simply to turn away from Eben and his portrait, to kneel and replace paint tubes in box, soak brushes in turpentine. When my back began to ache, I stood up and stretched. Something from behind had caught in my belt. Startled, I lurched off-balance a second. There was a rattle.

Reluctantly I turned. What the hell? Eben had pitched out of the wheelchair. He was sprawled on his stomach, one arm extended toward me, his chin on the floor, deep-sunk eyes raised toward me. Vibrations must have toppled him, my footsteps on the sloping floor maybe. His finger may have hooked over my belt, but he couldn't have reached for it himself. Still, I panicked. I left everything on the floor and burst into the hall.

A Finster man and I almost collided. Maybe he had been listening, or maybe about to knock. His quivery cheeks were red. He breathed heavily through open mouth, glistening saliva smeared around his fleshy lips. His piggish eyes were fixed on mine, with hostility or surprise I couldn't tell. He wore nothing but a tattered white towel tied around his boyishly chubby middle. This was Marsden, I presumed.

"Ma!" he hollered. "The painter's done with Pa! Tell everybody to stop!" He ended on a resentful note, but as he kept staring at me, he began to leer. "If she didn't hear me, maybe we don't have to stop."

All at once I understood what I was about to become an intimate part of. I screamed and ran down the back stairs. Claudia was at the kitchen table. Still in a shapeless housedress. She looked startled at my entrance. Her matronly reserve brought me short. One of us had to say something. I couldn't help voicing what first came to mind. "Did he call you Ma? Did he call Eben Pa?"

"Oh, I admit it may not be conventional," Claudia sighed. "But who else is good enough for us except ourselves? And it's only every ten years. When Eben gets his portrait. Those are his orders."

"Eben's had an accident," I stammered. At the same time I heard more than one set of steps pounding down the stairs. Whatever was coming was nothing I wanted to see. I bolted out the front door and to the car, which thank God started up right away.

Through overcast, the pale wafer sun still rode high. Had only an hour or two passed among the Finsters? Finding the tree back in place didn't surprise me. No pursuit reached my ears, but I wasted no time hoisting the log to one side. And when I started back to the car, a trail of blood caught my eye and led across the road, to something as unnerving as anything else that day. The mashed turtle couldn't have survived. But it had crossed the rutted dirt and was halfway into the grass, entrails stringing behind splayed-out shell, trembling hind legs trying to heave forward. Never mind tenacity of life. Now I wondered, what was life, and what was will, and did they always coincide? Should I stop the turtle once and for all? No, leave it alone, just go, get away.

Anxiety like voltage in my belly kept me up all night. In the morning I went to the studio, groggy, unable to do anything, trying not to think. A lost day. A knock on the door made me jump.

No one was expected, but in my unmindful mood I answered. I didn't see anyone at first, but my paintbox and easel were at my feet. I looked down the gloomy corridor. A boy, a very puny ten-year-old perhaps, was keeping his distance, just waiting to make sure I got the delivery. His blond hair was crewcut, and arms and legs were bowed like twigs, as if arthritic. His eyes were pink. "Aunt Claudia said for you to take that stuff." The words rushed out as if he'd rehearsed them.

"Where is Aunt Claudia?" I asked.

"Out in the car," he said and ran back to her, away from frightening people and places not of the Finsters.

Inside the box all my supplies were in order, and on top of them was an envelope. It contained a check for the agreed amount and a note. The note was what decided me on fleeing Marston Hills that week, without leaving a forwarding address. Typewriter and ribbon were the same as before:

Dear Miss Levasseur,

You left in such a hurry that we never got to wrap up our business. Enclosed please find a check, and our thanks once again. You did a beautiful job! We are all very happy with the likeness, including Mr. Finster. He was also quite taken with you, which got us to thinking, maybe it is time to admit some fresh blood into the family. I know Marsden likes you.

Anyway, if you want to come up again, just give us a call. Or if your work is keeping you in the studio, maybe we'll drop in on you one of these days. And please don't be upset at Mr. Finster putting a little scare in you. It was just his little joke, and he hopes you like orchids.

Cordially,
Claudia Finster

I didn't know whether to laugh or cry. Either route might lead to loss of self-control. Orchids? What was she talking about? Then I thought back to that tug of Eben's dead finger on my belt. I had been at loose ends ever since, and far from observant. But now I checked the dungarees I had taken off last night and put back on again this morning. In the back pocket was the broken, sticky flower Eben had worn in his lapel. I threw it on the floor as if it were some white crawly thing. Sly old Eben! I stamped on his little gift, and stamped again, until it wasn't white, or flower-shaped, or anything.

The Weird Old Hole

No second thoughts about anything. That was a cornerstone of the Bicklehams' compatibility. And lately it had proved a godsend. Especially in the cellar, doubt would have made their irksome task unbearable.

Whatever they picked up, whatever they stuffed into garbage bag, every step they took, dust mushroomed into their faces. Sooty, moldy, caking in their nostrils, parching their lips. Madge's eyes had a faraway look. As if above it all. But she scrunched up her nose and sneered at every whiff of decay. Drew worked grimly. A little lightheaded from taking too many shallow breaths. Every so often, tight-set lips gasped apart as if to vent profane annoyance. But he always refrained. And more than once really did look up, more through the ceiling than at it, as if seeking divine forbearance. Otherwise, the Bicklehams were locked on course. Proceeding on autopilot.

Nothing old appealed to them. Another cornerstone of their compatibility. Into the rented dumpster went Civil War uniforms, train schedules from 1942, a four-foot-high Victrola full of 78s, a ton of pre-color photo *National Geographics,* oval portraits in rococo gilt frames of someone's grandma, a battered sousaphone, eyeless teddy bears, leather horsewhips, a potbelly stove. And all these made no dent in the total inventory.

Rust was so thick on iron that it stained hands gritty red. Dry rot caused wooden things to concuss into dust on being gripped. Fungus had fused bundles of books together, and on paper surfaces had created pastel pink and blue islands and coastlines.

Much else was discarded that had to be valuable. A shame, a waste, in some eyes. Not that the Bicklehams cared. No need for whatever money some noxious artifacts could fetch. Out with the old. Make it all new. That was their manifesto.

The whole house had been a handful, of course. Given their pick, they wouldn't have moved here at all. But with the kids grown up and out, Madge wanted to ditch the heavily taxed property in noisy, smelly town. And reclaim the elegant yet simple country life of her childhood. Hence when a friend at the State House clued Drew to a rustic charmer for next to nothing, price was the overriding factor. After all, even the best kept-up address would've needed remaking to their taste. This was just a notably onerous specimen.

County records classed the place as a "lightning-splitter" and took no better stab at a date than "before 1820." The roof was steeper than a chalet's, and the front door cleared the roof line by scant inches. To augment the second floor, topheavy-looking dormers like a row of caskets erupted from the shingles front and back. And into this already unwieldy arrangement some addled Victorian had crammed squiggly gingerbread around doorway and windows, under eaves, inside pointy gable ends. For a net effect of something long-sunken, hard to recognize beneath barnacles and coral. Historic, sure. Unique, without question. Scrape off the crust, Drew had quipped on first sight, and maybe we'll find a house in there. Of course, that had to wait until the inside belonged to them and not to the ages. Meanwhile, the rickety little barn next to the house would serve for a garage, till they could get around to flattening it.

So without second thoughts impeding them, they had traded the community where they were pillars (if they did say so themselves) for a squiredom in isolation. Theirs was not the only house on the plain, but seemed so because woods hid the others, every few acres up and down the ancient road that meandered to meet haphazardly platted homesteads. Behind their house, mountains seemed to loom, but miles and miles of forest and foothills intervened. No threat of avalanche whatsoever. And seclusion from the neighbors was probably for the best. Not likely the Bicklehams' kind of people.

The old blood that formed the local population, the old mountains staring down, the home that still needed Herculean work to keep from seeming old, good grief! If old was a well, nobody would ever have heard Madge and Drew's cries for help from the bottom. Their sole relief entailed driving an hour to the church of their choice. Well, their parents' choice really, and their forebears on back. But that distinction never weighed on them. Church for the Bicklehams was not some-

thing old because it was essentially the people, people with whom they
had in common the articles of faith, at least.

For now, though, they were entrenched in filthy cellar. As remote
as possible from spirituality. The rear wall, the mountainward one, almost in reach at last. Their single biggest obstacle, a green steamer
trunk. Padlocked, and upon it, a stenciled name to which they paid no
mind. At each end, a badly worn leather handle. Madge and Drew each
grabbed a handle and lifted, stumbling toward the stairs. On breaking
contact with the floor, there came a pop as of a cork from a jug. Then
both handles snapped and the trunk thudded to the floor, before the
popping sound could make an impression. The Bicklehams eyeballed
the trunk a few seconds longer, as if expecting more false moves from
it. Then Madge blanched and cried, "Oh my God!"

The trunk had been just wide enough to cover a hole, as perfectly
round as a full eclipse. And had they done anything other than sidle
away with the trunk, one of them could have fallen in.

"Do you think it might have been a well?" Drew suggested.

"Some kind of sinkhole maybe?" asked Madge.

Gaping into the Mariana darkness told them nothing. Madge im-
pulsively struck a match and dropped it into the pit. They both tensed
and gasped at the tardy thought of combustibles within. The flame cast
no glow. And no sooner was match in hole than it fell sideways. As if
deflected. Or sliding down an elbow pipe. Some weird kind of draft?

Drew shone a flashlight downward. But the beam disappeared like
the match. No help at all. The Bicklehams couldn't make head or tail
of it. So they refocused their attention on being thankful that no more
of the floor had collapsed under the weight of the trunk.

Indifferent to the contents of the steamer, they slaved up the stairs
with it and heaved it, still locked, into the dumpster. And then
knocked off for the day. They changed into fresh sweatsuits, and Drew
got the Weber going by the back door. The evening was comfortably
cool. Too early in the season for mosquitoes. Madge savored the view.
Of oversized back yard. Former cornfield, perhaps, gone to seed long
ago. The wall of forest at bay. No fences. Just how Madge liked to remember the place where she'd grown up. Even if, on deeper reflection,
there had been a fence, and she could hit it with a ball from the back
steps. But why be too clinical and tarnish childhood memories?

The cellphone on the windowsill rang. Madge and Drew did double-takes. Few friends from town had their number yet. And they didn't have enough meat if surprise guests "happened to be in the neighborhood." A long day of hard work and breathing toxic dust must have gone to Drew's head. Made him peevish. With phone still a foot away from his ear, he barked, "Hello?" Aiming at brusqueness. Wishing at times like this that his voice was deeper.

"Can you hear me?" came perfunctory reply. Coarse layer of static. Lousy cellphone reception! The voice sounded electronically distorted, every word ending in Doppler effect.

"Who is this?" Drew demanded, more miffed than ever at the level of cellphone service around here.

"Thanks to you we became your neighbors."

"What?" The Bicklehams exchanged dubious glances. Lousy or not, the connection was loud enough for Madge to hear from where she stood.

"What were you thinking to break down the barrier? Our pets jumped through. We want them back." The voice had grown more heated. Till the distortion sounded like a power drill being turned on and off.

"You must have the wrong number," Drew said with overweening deliberation. Started to break the connection.

"Don't you dare hang up!" shrilled the voice. "This way to reach you is uncertain, but it is certain that you are who I meant to reach. What is the expression you have? One man's flooring is another man's wall. Send back what is ours." The line went dead before Drew could protest that the caller couldn't possibly have the right party. That he had no idea what the caller was talking about. But maybe crank calls belonged to the downside of country life. Between cabin fever and in-breeding, weren't there a lot of nuts in the boonies? Madge might have mentioned this aspect of the wilderness before convincing him to take the plunge! Meanwhile, it looked like she was trying to use x-ray vision on the opaque screen of trees. As if worried that the woods might be stocked with trouble.

From bed that night they heard a curious sort of wind. It neither rattled foliage nor whistled through eaves, but was strong enough to jingle utensils and roll condiment jars back and forth on the barbecue. The cellar window that they hadn't latched flapped up and down. Reproachfully, Drew thought. But why think that? Must have been because he was so tuckered out. And after this stressful day, it would have taken more than funny breezes to keep the Bicklehams awake.

Morning sun through dormer window made Madge happy to open her eyes, throw off the covers. As it had been in childhood. As if the intervening decades had been cancelled out. Or as if yesterday's drudgery were in the dim past. For life to feel fresh again, that was what she was doing here. Drew was downstairs already. And could that be him below the window, fussing and groaning like that? How unlike him, and how crude, to spoil this pristine hour!

She found him squatting among the ruins of the Weber. Wind damage? No way had mere wind snapped off the hood and flung it aside. A bear, a catamount? Why would they have twisted the legs into crooked corkscrews? But beast it must have been to wrench the grill loose, for it had been licked shiny clean. As had also happened to mustard jar, relish jar, and somehow even the long-necked bottles of balsamic vinegar and marinades. Madge picked up the mustard jar. Extraordinarily slick with slobber, it flew from the gentle squeeze of her hand. Shattered against their home's shale foundation.

Drew had been silent since she'd come out. Reacted to this latest breakage with only a mournful sigh. The nice Ekco fork and spatula had been chewed to ribbons, and everything was dotted with apparent tooth marks. What animal could stand biting metal? And weirdest yet, the briquettes, which had been white-hot last night, were gone. Barring mythical fireproof salamander, what could have filched them?

Madge glumly set to collecting shards of mustard jar. Sun glistening on more slobber crisscrossing the cellar window gave her pause. Uh-oh. Wind had been flipping that window open and shut all night. God help them if those brutes had gotten into the house!

"Do you think whatever did this could have been the 'pets' that crank caller yesterday was yelling about?" Drew asked. How could she know? Then again, if she was so conversant with country life, maybe she would have known if backwoods loonies kept things like Komodo dragons for pets. He'd pictured himself out here with his golf clubs. Perfecting his form. Lord of the manor at leisure. No one around to make him self-conscious. Now how likely was that, for wondering what species of eyes were gleaming from behind the trees? As for

Madge, the foundation stones had her undivided attention. Spacing out was among her least endearing tendencies. Finally she muttered, "We really have to lock that cellar window tonight." What did that have to do with his question? No point talking till she was of a mind to listen.

The Bicklehams committed their barbecue wreckage to the dumpster. Then topped it off with the rest of the cellar junk, giving the weird hole wide berth. Done by noon, and back in accustomed harmony. At least in terms of immediate plans. Vacuuming and scrubbing down the empty dungeon came next. But they'd had it. Well, church was in a couple of days. Surely someone there would know who to call, who was used to nasty work for petty cash.

Meanwhile, much unpacking awaited. Especially in the kitchen, what with the demolition of the Weber. Madge and Drew were still living mainly out of boxes. Which by the dozens they flattened that afternoon and crammed into dumpster. Maybe the local recycling program picked up cardboard. But the Bicklehams firmly believed that recycling was for hippies. Drew phoned the dumpster company and arranged for pickup the next morning, and Madge remembered to go down and shut the cellar window good and tight and bolt it.

About the same hour as yesterday, the phone rang. Madge was washing dishes in the sink and yearning for that someday soon when they'd install a dishwasher and otherwise modernize the kitchen. She wanted simple, not primitive! She was happy for excuse to turn off the faucet and listen, till she realized that lightning had indeed struck twice.

"What do you mean, we've blocked the way?" Madge felt her skin crawl, as it always did when crazy people approached her for spare change. They'd moved here to avoid just this sort of imposition! "They tried to get back in? Where? When? What do you mean it's too hard to explain? No, I am not stupid. But you might feel that way if I have this call traced. What's so funny? Hello?"

Drew was glaring red-faced at the impudent phone. Holding it at arm's length. All faces, Madge assumed, must grow ugly as Drew's did in the grip of high feelings. Generally this semblance of circuit-overload was work-related. He'd inherited a steady old cash cow. Wholesale and distribution of fur coats. But when a client vamoosed and could not be lured back by Drew's best deal, only heroic efforts prevented unseemly words and behavior. Good thing such business was mostly over the phone! Madge went back to washing the dishes.

After bedtime the wind returned, and like last night skulked low to the ground, skittering around in the dumpster like something with claws. Drew could see nothing out back through the window. But agitation from that phone call smoldered just below the surface. The least little intrusion could set it off, rob him of sleep. He turned on the air conditioner full blast. Crawled back under the blankets with the positive thought, What comfort we buy with technology!

Pounding at the back door made for no gentle awakening. The Bicklehams had overslept. Nestled a little too deeply in the comfort of technology. Harsh voices were calling.

Three guys from the dumpster company were in no joking mood. "If you think we're pickin' this stuff up for you, you're nuts," said the one with the brightest muscle shirt, by way of greeting. Madge and Drew, in bathrobe and slippers, peeked over the workmen's shoulders. Their jaws dropped. Speechless, they sidled by the workmen and shuffled around in a daze. It was like the scene of an explosion. With dumpster at ground zero. All over the yard, drawers of clothing were strewn. Vases were reduced to mosaic tiles. The potbelly stove was crumpled like a ball of foil. The green steamer trunk was stuck at an angle into the ground, like a downed missile. Culling each last fragment from the lawn would take forever. As if the past were in revolt against being evicted. Preferring a kamikaze approach to remaining on the land.

"We didn't do this," Drew said.

The workmen shrugged.

"It was some kind of animal," Madge insisted, hearing a hint of shrillness that she didn't like.

Drew prevailed on the poker-faced crew to come back that afternoon. Wait till tomorrow, and the same mess or worse would be likely.

Okay, okay. They'd be back. Though whatever befell the Bicklehams one way or the other was obviously no problem of theirs. Uppity tradesmen!

Disgusted as Madge and Drew were to be handling so much detritus all over again, and to interact with the upstart trash-haulers later, at least they had church the next day to look forward to. But therein too, letdown awaited. For two Sundays they'd secluded themselves in the back pew. Reluctant to mix till they had more to go on. During today's

service, though, they conferred in whispers not about who most resembled them, but who looked most open to blue-collar proposition.
Only to get short shrift from everyone they asked. As if nobody
needed extra money. Or did work like that. Or knew anyone who did.
What, did they need formal introduction to the whole congregation
before they could talk one-to-one business? Madge had to exercise
iron forbearance when one big frowzy hausfrau couldn't seem to take
her eyes off Madge's stylish peroxide perm. How dare someone so
coarse question Madge's choice to be all the woman she wanted to be!
Even the minister, when they presented themselves and their request,
acted like he'd been put on the spot. Cleared his throat, came up with
nothing better than someplace that rented industrial vacuum cleaners.

Well, if they rated cold shoulder from their own denomination,
what could they count on from the locals at large? What the heck, they
rented the equipment. Fetched it on Tuesday. By which time no new
destruction had befallen. But first thing that morning, Drew had
tromped out for a few practice swings. One hand shielding eyes from
harsh rising sun as he went. At the very last second he shied from
plunking his golf bag onto a new feature of the landscape. The size and
shape of a beehive. Some monstrous fungus? But black, with a texture
of tar flecked with mica. Faint contours implied former phase as a fat
snakish coil that had sunk under its own weight. Was it dung? When
Drew bent closer, stench dizzied him, but it was chemical, like that
stretch of so-called "meadowland" on the Jersey Turnpike. What could
have tolerated the diet implicit in such an end-product? And, shoot!
The grass was already burnt yellow all around this thing. Worse yet, a
few dozen more of them had popped up between here and the woods!

This new development brought no comment from Madge. As if it
was beneath her to do more than stare out morosely for a minute, and
only because Drew raised such a ruckus. So what did he expect her to
do about it? Didn't they have enough to deal with, without him digging
up more stuff she didn't understand?

The Bicklehams opted for lunch before tackling the basement.
Some nice bruschetta, penne salad. The phone rang. Now what, when
they were revved up to start working?

Static loud enough to fill the kitchen informed Madge whom Drew
was about to talk to. He was grimacing already. "How dare you dump

your refuse on us?" they both heard. Ashen Drew let the caller rave
away. "And still you do nothing about our pets! What do you suppose
them to eat over there? Unlikely anything that agrees with them. Adding the insult of your rubbish to continuing injury, what are you trying
to make happen? Are you there?"

When Drew begrudged a yes, the line went dead. Madge wondered
if he'd stand like that till his arm seized up. She lugged all the equip-
ment from the car herself. Several trips later, had it all in the cellar. By
then, thank God, Drew's circuits had cleared. "Let's get started!" he
announced. What good in mentioning she already had?

Jumpsuits and filter masks, like outerwear for another planet, really
emphasized the grey lunar desolation of the cellar. Drew manned deafening dry-vac, while Madge sudsed up the walls and took wet-vac to
them. In half an hour, dry-vac suction had weakened. Too bad he'd have
to risk contaminating the upstairs to get the bag dumped out. Or would
he? That funny black hole in the middle of the floor ate matchsticks and
light. Why not dust? Drew put the motor in reverse, and the bag's contents shot back through the hose and into the pit. After a minute,
though, Drew's smile faded. In remembrance of lunchtime crank call.
Accusing him of dumping refuse. But if this specific outflow had caused
the complaint, then effect had preceded cause by almost an hour! Impossible, yet Drew had disposed of nothing else all day. And where did
that hole lead, anyway? Drew swiped his foot against the off switch.

His thoughts were rushing where he'd rather they didn't, but no
anchor or oar could save him. The caller's "pets," who else could have
vandalized Weber and dumpster? Even if that first irate message about
broken barricade had arrived hours before the actual breakout? Imagination had always seemed a crutch for feeble intellects. He hated circumstances that allowed *Star Trek* or *The X-Files* to make any sense.
And so Drew primarily felt resentful at having to admit that the phone
calls were coming from somewhere in a different time zone. Where it
was at least an hour in the future. And that forms of life from over
there were loose here. And that the point of entry was in the Bicklehams' own cellar. What had the caller said? "One man's flooring is another man's wall?"

Madge wanted to know what was wrong. Madge, whose feet were
even more firmly planted on the mundane ground. How to voice these

patently crackpot thoughts? His lips moved, but no words came. Eyes continued downcast toward the weird hole, into which he wished he could consign this moment. Then she said, "If some kind of animals came out of this tunnel, I guess we should try leaving the window open for them tonight. Drew? Are you listening?" Drew, for once, was less than comfortable with their thinking in synch. Crackpot was still crackpot. And the voice of reason was what he craved.

That night in bed they heard sirens. Smelled smoke. But from-miles-away faint. Nothing to them. At least not till next morning's big local news, of arson at a roadhouse. Some dozen miles down the road from the Bicklehams. Dead-of-night culprits had set off propane tanks outside, a grease fire inside. No suspects, no motives. But the stink of industrial chemicals hanging over the charred timbers ruled out an accident.

Some old dive was no loss, Madge and Drew agreed, but what if their grill had used propane instead of charcoal? And God forbid they should have a forest fire out their back door! To neither of them had it occurred that a mere human firebug could be guilty. Drew wrote "Let's talk" on the notepad by the kitchen land-line phone. Was half-way to the cellar door when the phone rang.

Drew stopped short, arms aloft. As if someone had grabbed the back of his collar. He turned and answered the phone. Heard, "Hello, it's about time. I can guess what prompted you. They had to piss sooner or later. The elements on your side withstand it poorly. You are lucky not to be homeless."

"We're leaving the window open so they can get back in." Drew felt like a traitor to normalcy, holding up even that much of the con-versation.

"You are obligated to do more than that. They are too busy run-ning wild right now. We will talk later." Click.

A fruitless exchange. But on the bright side, what a relief that he hadn't had to say any more. He reread the paper in his hand. Looks like he'd better send the message for which he'd already gotten a reply! He saw no point in wondering what would happen if he didn't. Or about the light this all cast on how things worked in the grand scheme.

The ambition for now was to be through with the rented equip-ment. And thus dispense as well with major reason for frequenting the ever more sinister cellar. By mid-afternoon, though, Drew had started worrying that the roar of vacuum cleaners might carry to the other side. Making the moody party over there grit his teeth at yet more exasperation. Drew worked faster. Not to be considerate. He just hated feeling self-conscious.

And supposing sound carried both ways? If he spent some time with ear to the floor, what would he hear? And learn about the other side? He didn't want to be curious, but that was something he couldn't seem to help these days. Anyway, scant hope for this house as a home if noises from the void made their own cellar too scary to use.

Done at last, both Madge and Drew loaded up the car to go back to the rental place, but Drew asked Madge to drive by herself, because he "had to stay down a while longer." With that combo of evasive eyes and forceful tone to discourage further inquiry. And could she please pick up some supper at Boston Chicken or something? She entreated him to stay out of trouble and then left. What else could she do when he was like that?

The shadows were long when Madge put the car in the barn. Drew was still in the cellar. She tiptoed halfway down to check on him. He was in the same state in which she'd see him, the next few times she looked. Sitting on the floor, with knees drawn up and arms looped around them. Right beside the hole. One gentle tilt and he'd go cannonballing into the unknown. He'd have passed for catatonic had he not been facing a different way each time. Toward the pit, or the window, or straight ahead. At some point she must have absentmindedly turned off the cellar light from upstairs. And now dusk was making the kitchen dark as a reflection in a blank TV screen. She didn't know if he'd want the cellar light back on or not. All too likely that a sudden change in surroundings would set him off when he was in one of these brown studies. Madge found herself staring for who knew how long at the light switch. Wishing Drew would call and simply tell her what to do.

Drew was aware of Madge futzing around upstairs. Had noted in passing when she'd turned off the light. But he was bound to hear what he could hear, till Madge or nature called. The silence from the pit came to feel willful. Mocking. And incidental homey sounds became louder, more distracting, the harder he concentrated on listening to the pit. Startled, he had to look when a robin twittered at the open window. When the water heater whooshed and flamed on. When ceiling timbers creaked as the house went about its seemingly endless settling. Sneaky nightfall caught him unawares. Left him wondering where his feet were.

So faint were those first long-awaited sounds that it took him a minute to realize he'd been hearing them. Growing audible at excruciating snail's pace. Resembling foremost the clacking of a blind man with his stick. Nothing fearsome about that, but because it had to be something else and Drew couldn't imagine what, his tension escalated. At last he could hear without having to strain. At which point, in that narrow gap between pants cuff and sock, what felt like a feather stroked his skin. Maybe it was a little spider, maybe only a draft. No matter. Drew yelled and rolled away from the hole. Scrambled as fast as cramped-up limbs allowed up the stairs, toward the meager light from the kitchen. Halfway there, he heard Madge scream.

She wasn't hurt. But he'd never seen her so white. Her back to the fridge, and staring toward the window above the sink. The only light, from a lamp on top of the fridge. Did she even know that he'd been yelling too?

"It got dark just now, so I couldn't see out the window after I turned the light on," she explained. Of no mind yet to move from favored spot. "I heard something scratching around below the window, like a skunk or something. I went over to look, and then two big eyes were right on the other side of the glass. They were bright orange. Like fire. And then they started getting closer to each other and then moved apart, as if that was how they focused. They kept doing that, and then they moved apart and all of a sudden around each one a whole circle of little eyes opened, like a wreath. But after I looked for a second, I realized they were teeth. And then I screamed, and you came back up."

"It's gone now. So maybe you scared it as much as it scared you," Drew remarked. With a short-lived grin. Just trying to lighten the atmosphere a little!

"How can you joke about this?" Madge wailed. "I could have been killed!"

Drew clammed up. Decided there was no point telling what had happened to him. He was forming second thoughts about leaving that cellar window open tonight, but no way was he heading back down there himself. Neither of them had anything to say. Stewing in the juices of mutually exclusive experiences. They microwaved the takeout Madge had retrieved that afternoon. Ate without talking. Watched sitcoms all evening, without laughing. Their one comfort at bedtime, the option of thinking that maybe their senses had played them false, after all.

They had no such comfort on surveying the back yard next morning. The black hives had undergone meltdown in the night. Instead of dotting the landscape, blanketing it. The entire lawn was a loss. Even if the tarry mess decayed away, the grass was cooked, the soil poisoned. Talk about impacting property values! And far worse, they had to handle this themselves. Outsiders might link this chemical reek with that from the roadhouse fire. That couldn't put them in a good light, could it?

Drew scrawled, "Call them back! How can we plug the hole?" Sprinted into basement, chucked message into undiscovered country. Intent on acting before the phone rang, as this business of effect preceding cause got on his nerves.

In that respect, at least, the Bicklehams lucked out. Presumably people were late sleepers over there. Drew and Madge stared helpless as rising sun freed corkscrewing vapors from the goo. Till a heavy mist hung over the yard. And the smell invaded the kitchen, right through closed windows. For diversion, Drew dwelt on how best to persuade Madge that they had to unload the property, somehow. Thus rendering him deaf when the phone rang once, twice. And then, too late! Madge had it!

"Hello?"

Drew winced. She was almost simpering. Like waving a red hankie, begging the wacko to charge.

"So you do me ongoing wrong, and then you make demands. Very reckless!" Remarkable, Drew realized for the first time, how well that staticky voice carried across the room.

"Then why don't you tell us what to do?"

Drew still debated grabbing the phone, lest Madge screw things up.

"You are not the same speaker as before. You would be the female? Are you the better thinker than the male?"

"I don't know." That question had obviously caught her off guard. Was she on the verge of blathering? "Can't you tell us how to block the hole up?"

Derisive laughter. "Of course you cannot. Not unless you can atomize everything within your sight. It is no hole really, but interaction between the lay of space on your side and mine. How mountains relate to flatlands exactly where you are. And much else you would not understand. What you call plug was made by time. A result of no change. No disturbance in the structure around it. Especially of objects close by. Once a thing was added, it was never moved. A cumulative effect of stronger blockage the longer things stayed put. Until you."

"We can't fix it?"

"Time has to fix it. And stasis. Those alone. You can only put weight and more weight on top of the interaction. And hope for the best. Here I can make a patch of something repellent. But that too is no guarantee. Does any of this sink in?"

Madge bit her lower lip.

"Ask about sending the animals back!" Drew hissed.

Nothing metaphysical about how to do to that. A trail of blood! For all the caller cared it could be their own, or from anywhere. As long as they had enough to color a path from truant pets' likely stomping grounds to the hole homeward. And the Bicklehams had to spill the blood after dark, when the pets would be afoot, to ensure fresh enough scent to carry a ways. Only remember, no obstacles en route! The caller would do the rest.

Altogether cut and dried, wasn't it? Drew, however, chafed at the sense of being a flunky. The course of events too much out of his hands. Here, in the house he'd paid for, under the roof where he had his wife and possessions. Sell the place, clear out, surrender in effect? By God, no! He had to assert himself. Make this place more his. He looked up Vinyl Siding in the Yellow Pages. Called every listing, arranged for a rep from each to come give an estimate. The first would drop by in a couple of days. The gingerbread, the clapboards all had to go. Drew wanted it smooth. As plain as possible. First surgical strike toward effacing from the premises all signs of aberrant, non-Bickleham personalities. Whether from the past or the cosmos.

"Drew, what about the yard?" Madge was trying her hardest to sound deferential. No idea any more of what pushed him beyond critical mass. "Do you think anyone will ask how it got that way?"

He shrugged. "Not if it isn't that way by then." He couldn't let her bog him down with insolubles. First things first. He took a twelve-pound chuck roast from the freezer. Stuck it in a baking tray, stripped off the shrinkwrap, set the tray on sunny countertop. Added a few calves' livers for good measure. And then had all day to consider the blackened lawn. But the upcoming evening loomed too big to see around. Nothing more useful could go on, he contended, than the meat thawing out.

Madge funneled nervous energy into unpacking and organizing. While Drew got good and sick of local TV. If not soaps and cartoons, then tedious '70s cop shows and '60s Westerns, for God's sakes. *Lassie,* even. Now there was a good dog, never needed buckets of blood to make him come home, Drew caught himself thinking. And hastily changed the channel. Was cable even available out here? He'd see about that, once the vinyl siding was up. Install a satellite dish, at the very least. And get online, resume running his company as soon as possible, which he knew he could do better from here than his subordinates could do on site. Instead of spending more time like this, fidgeting through such pressing issues on the five o'clock news as foreclosure for the Grange hall, the soaring cost of artesian wells. After seeing the same stories on every station, he was almost looking forward to doing the creepy caller's bidding.

Speaking of which, Madge concurred that waiting till total darkness was foolhardy. The roast was minus its icy gloss, and its icky juices had risen level with the raw liver. The Bicklehams broke out the crummy track shoes they'd worn while cleaning the cellar. Made sure their flashlights worked. Drew rummaged a meat fork from kitchen drawer. For plucking the solid bulk of their bait from the tray without sullying fingers. And also for a token sense of protection. Already it was duskier than they would have liked.

They set off at a medium jog, wary, on edge. Often glancing aside, behind. Half expecting something to spring from peripheral vision any second. Destination, the woods. No other stomping grounds hereabouts! Had they let themselves for a split second conceive of the barn as a hideout, they wouldn't have dared park there. The Bicklehams blazed a trail around the zone of ruined lawn, over which sulfurous fog still lingered. That was to the right of them, and to the left, the crude stone wall and briars bordering an abandoned orchard on the adjoining property.

From the outset, Madge felt like she was in a lose-lose situation. A day of unpacking had kept her mind off the ordeal at hand, but now she was tired, and shaky with anxiety. Had to pause a lot and steady her legs. But when she did, taking deep gulps of tainted air, she grew queasier. And Drew pulled too far ahead. Making her run that much harder to keep up. When finally the stone wall ended and nothing but woods spread before them, twilight had made way for night.

They slowed down as if through thickening air. Stopped as soon as trees surrounded them. Jittery, with the sense of being out of their own domain. Drew set down the tray. They hurriedly turned on flashlights. Pointed them at their own feet. Didn't want to know what was around them.

Madge now recognized that the uppermost task had become getting home in one piece. Singlemindedly, she got going. "Hold on!" Drew harangued her. "Help me here!" He was crouched over. As if halfway into a deep-knee bend. Flashlight projecting from between clenched knees. He jabbed fork into the lumpish roast. With both hands around fork handle, hoisted meat over edge of tray, onto forest floor. "Pick up the tray!" he whispered. "Drip a little blood over the side as we go along!"

Drew stood up. Kicked the roast a few feet ahead. Madge bent over, one hand viselike around the flashlight, the other raising the tray a few wobbly inches. She sloshed a goodly Rorschach blot over the side, stopped with alarm when the slippery liver was on the verge of joining it. "Stand up!" Drew demanded. "And be careful, we have to make that last!"

Stress was making him so tyrannical! Not that she had any alternative to following orders. Incipient chill was already making it clammy inside her jacket. Rising breeze was rattling leaves. Madge and Drew froze for an instant. From back in the trees, that long, whistly surge of air could have been the wind. Or else something taking a deep, thoughtful sniff. Then nothing, for as long as the Bicklehams held their breath. Time to move!

Drew's next swift kick sent the roast rolling out of the woods. For Madge and Drew to be out in the open again, that sufficed for a slight but needful sense of accomplishment. Had they not been in fear of their lives, the next several minutes could have seemed a grotesque game. In which the goal was obvious, but with slim chance of victory if the opposing players so much as showed themselves. The Bicklehams' beams, like outsize canes for the blind, pointed the way. Drew would kick the sticky hunk of meat, which had assumed a coating of twigs and leaves, and then spring after it. Behind him, Madge would splash a little more from the tray and strive to catch up. At which point she couldn't help lighting a wider arc than she wanted. Moreover, they were far from "coloring" their route with blood.

But halfway measures were more than enough. Avid, gurgly inhalations had become impossible to mistake for nocturnal breeze. Whether off in the orchard, or the thinning mist of the blackened field. Did they have one pursuer or two? At a distance or closing in?

In Drew's peripheral vision lurked a patch of white. Too hard to tell if it belonged to something the size of a wolf, or the size of a lion. Meanwhile, a faint patter of rain was wafting from the field. The acrid fumes were condensing in the cold. Inflicting alien microclimate on already-blighted meadow. Drew kept trying to shed light on the skulking thing, with the same irresistible perversity that had made him listen in the cellar, that had forced him to acknowledge what the cellar really contained. No matter how quickly he shone the beam, though, the whiteness was always off to one side, as if it could refract itself from place to place. He never saw two of them at the same time, and he thought he glimpsed fuzziness around the edge like fur, but in the chemical rain the whiteness glittered like chrome.

Finally, stone wall veered away at right angle to follow orchard frontage. The green swath at their feet widened. Home stretch! Madge began to feel more stouthearted. She'd also been spying the furtive white cloud, whenever she tossed more blood and her beam swung wild. And now it floated above the V-shaped corner. Where it might not be able to sidestep so nimbly. Right or wrong, she obeyed the impulse to snare it with light. Gotcha! It was heaving itself over the top, braced on big three-clawed feet, like those of a T-rex, or maybe like something from an evil Dr. Seuss. But it didn't rise via hunched shoulders, bent elbows. Instead, gleaming kinky white torso was flowing like a column of smoke, or like a worm. This she could absorb in a second, along with the impression that this wasn't the same one she'd seen from the kitchen. But of the face she could tell nothing, because there was nothing she could relate to a face. At least not until flashlight glare riled its target into displaying like a crested lizard, except this was a halo of spikes, coppery, pulsing red. And from the chaotic flesh at the center unrolled a long tongue like a frog's, which let fly from its tip a black droplet that burst at Madge's right foot. Igniting the grass instantly, and the toe of her shoe!

Wailing with panic, Madge pried off her right shoe at the heel with the toe of her left shoe. Dashed after Drew, who hadn't even turned to see she was falling behind! For a second she hated him as much as she hated the monster behind her, this whole horrible situation, the cuts and bruises rapidly mangling her foot. Not till she was at his heels again did she notice how little was left in the tray. Most of the blood going overboard these last headlong seconds. A lot of it onto her jacket. And the liver had also been ejected.

Madge realized she must have been wailing all along, because Drew turned around long enough to gape at her bloody shirt and yell, "Are you crazy?" No time to say any more! They were down to the last hundred or so feet. And then what? Dear God, please make sure Drew had some plan! And whatever else happens, please don't let me soil myself!

From right behind them, a mighty thud, a brief aftershock. And again. Compelling them to take a peek. Just as a very heavy white cloud slammed into the ground on all fours, the way a fox bounced upon mice in the snow. Were these terrible pets at play, or hunting in earnest? Not that it made any difference, should the Bicklehams stumble! "Drop the tray! Lose the jacket!" Drew yelled. "Don't slow down!"

Madge cast the tray over her shoulder. Unzipping the jacket, she heard something like an overactive metal punch, making short work of the tray. And afterwards a frustrated outburst like the belling of a stag, answered from afar, then repeated from nearby. By this time the jacket was off and gone. Madge heard it start to rip, then combust, sending a pale white flicker ahead of her.

Drew was wheezing like a broken-down jalopy, but still racing for his life. Still jamming foot under frayed hunk of meat and launching it for all he was worth without missing a step. Madge could hardly keep up for the pain in her bare foot. Imagined she must have looked like Quasimodo lurching along.

The house was close enough to bathe them in glow from the kitchen window. But home was no source of comfort now. From cellar window came what could have been the screams of a baby being killed. It went on and on, echoing as if from inside a big steel drum. Something fatted being slain to feed the prodigal pets? Counterproductive to focus on that right now!

Something hooked the hem of Madge's T-shirt. The fabric resisted, ripped, threw her staggering into Drew. Even as he took lightning aim and put the roast through the open window with the side of his foot. Score!

Drew grabbed Madge in the midst of her knocking him off-balance. Shoved her toward the back door. "Get inside!" he screeched, with more fear than he'd ever shown before. Between the screaming from the cellar and the menace at their backs they were befuddled for a second, all turned around. Long enough for them to glimpse a bulky white blur stretch like a concertina, become narrow enough to snake through the window.

Next thing they knew they were sitting in the kitchen, windows locked and doors bolted, shades and curtains drawn. But ordeal far from over. No escape from the caterwauling beneath their feet. Several times the noise faded away, seeding a glimmer of hope. And then took up again, like a mean-spirited car alarm. Madge and Drew sat numb, slumped low in their chairs. Ready to believe this would go on forever. When it did cease and hadn't resumed for a while, relief came as purely bodily reaction. The Bicklehams simply went limp, as if electricity animating them had been cut off.

Through the blear in his eyes, Drew was gradually aware of the red light blinking on the answering machine. Might as well see what this is! His thinking on autopilot. And his expression, in Madge's opinion, like a zombie's. He stood up, swaying a second before trudging ahead. My God, Drew, let it wait! But no, his finger depressed the playback button, slid off. While he stood inert, Madge gawked at the new stain on his sweatpants. If she wasn't mistaken, it was bossy Drew, high-and-mighty Drew, who had soiled himself! And she was so utterly spent that she didn't care that this was what she chose to zero in on.

"Can you do nothing right?" bellowed the voice on tape. Of the only one, come to mention it, who had ever phoned them at this house. "Where is the other one of my two? This has been my least desire, but now I must extend myself to your side and retrieve him myself. Come to the point of interaction after you hear this. I am waiting. And take care to provoke me no more. Remember that you do not have to speak for me to understand you when we are near. The ice you skate on is thin already. Is that not an expression of yours?" Click. End of final message, the machine added.

Drew was dead tired, but this actually suited him. The sooner they settled this once and for all, the better. He sighed more deeply than he thought he ever had before, like a tire going completely flat. He ponderously embarked toward the cellar, seeing himself as an old hulk being towed through a silty harbor. He told Madge to come on. Afraid that she might be giving in to one of her obstinate spells.

"Are you going to change clothes first?"

What was she talking about? Oh, forget it. Enough to put one lead foot in front of the other. "Come on," he repeated.

She didn't want to! Hadn't they been through plenty for one night? Why did he have to listen to that stupid message in the first place? She wanted to scream at him, but had no energy for it. Instead, she dragged herself after him, following the stain below his belt, hardly seeing the rest of him.

He started down the dark stairs.

"Aren't you going to turn on the light?" she asked.

"No," he mumbled, locked on course. "Don't think we'd like it. Don't think he would, either."

"Your kind of legs cannot be practical if they are always so slow!" boomed the expected voice. Still with that toy microphone distortion. "Be aware that I can do this with or without your help."

The Bicklehams stood side by side at the foot of the stairs. Squinted into the meager light that straggled past them from up in the kitchen. What rose from the hole seemed like a towering finger, crooked toward them. With a texture like beech bark, but otherwise featureless grey. They didn't see it move, but suddenly its faceless peak was hovering inches from their faces. How big was this thing? wondered Drew, averting his eyes toward the hole from which alien flesh was still emerging. And then he saw the black clawprints that the caller's pet had tracked in from the ruined field.

Don't offend it, Drew cautioned himself. Don't think anything at all! Let it do all the talking! Or else, he got the distinct feeling, this would become a predator-prey relationship. In this unbelievable moment, his sensation of reality had never been more vivid. But what was Madge thinking?

She could scarcely stay on her feet for fear and fatigue. She hadn't wanted to come down here in the first place. Drew wanted to be in charge, so let him do the thinking! This was all on his head. How much longer could she stand to look at this thing? It was obscene! And worse, it smelled old. Really old, like mildewed sheets. No, like rocks so old they crumbled to the touch, filling lungs with ancient, unclean dust. She had never smelled anything so old, and there was no smell she hated more in the world. She scrunched up her nose.

The faceless thing stopped wavering between them. Homed in on her. "So!" it rumbled. A pucker indented the place where a face should have been. And from it oozed and dribbled a fluid thick and clear like glass, that sizzled when it hit the floor. "I will not have your help, then!" Had neighbors lived any closer than a couple of miles on either side, they would have heard the Bicklehams for the next minute or two. The Bicklehams, in any case, drowned out the caller's afterthought, "At least not your voluntary help."

The man from the siding company drove up next day. At first he wondered about that rotten manure out back. Whoever sold them that must have been laughing like a maniac afterwards. Stupid city people! Stupid and unreliable! Where the hell were they? He knocked, he hollered, in front and out back. He caught sight of a car through a crack in the barn door. Finally he saw a thick zigzag of the manure, all gloppy as if it had been melting or something, entering an open cellar window. Shouting through the window, trying to peer into the darkness, got him nowhere.

He found a flashlight in his van. Shone it back and forth down there, kneeling well to one side of the gunky stuff. It stank down in the cellar too. He held his breath and poked his head in till he had to exhale. Saw nothing in that time, except for a round spot like a manhole cover, but glossy like an old slug trail, with red smears and white flecks all over it. And what couldn't really have been bunches of hair. Looked like the biggest, ugliest clogged drain he'd ever seen. Repellent! He figured he'd had enough of this place. Damned unreliable yuppies. Probably just wanted to update the house and resell it at a hefty, gentrifying profit. Well, he'd bet that nobody was going to touch this property for as long as that yucky spot lasted in the cellar. And luckily, he was right.

The Returns of Johnny Mapleseed

The roar of the lawn mower woke me. It was 3 A.M., of course. I would only have been surprised had the clock read otherwise. Laura hadn't budged from the position in which she'd last been asleep, as if wishful thinking would let her lapse from waking nightmare back into dreamland.

Lurching to the window I yelled, "Hey! Stop that!" Johnny Mapleseed mowed on, oblivious. As always, he had started around the edge of the yard, spiraling in toward the center. I knew he wouldn't make it all the way. What should have stopped him for good the first time would do its stopgap work again. I, however, was too fed up to wait and lobbed a hairbrush at diligent, flour-white Johnny. It sailed right through him and cartwheeled across the lawn.

The corner of his mower bumped the towering oak that canopied half the yard. Instead of passing through, he and the phantom mower disappeared, along with the phantom racket.

"Did throwing Mister Hairbrush make you feel better?" Laura asked, voice dismal with the hour, and sticky with sarcasm.

"Well, at least it shows the neighbors we're trying to do something," I mumbled. To either side of our house and across the street, upstairs lights were winking out as if the noise had been their source of power.

"They have a lot of nerve letting that go on every night for a week," grumbled someone from no place in particular, not forthrightly addressing us, but loudly enough to guarantee that we heard. It was that kind of a neighborhood. Polite society.

Johnny Mapleseed was doing something unlikely after his death, just as he had done unlikely things in life. Years before an uncle had left Laura his imposing Georgian Revival home, girlhood visits recalled to her a Johnny no whit different in behavior or appearance. Johnny, on the other hand, gruffly denied any memory of her.

Nobody knew how he managed the rent on his basement apartment, but the fame of his sideline had earned him his nickname. Door to door he would go, offering to pull all the maple saplings that crowded under hedges and in neglected crannies. A slight, slump-shouldered man with hard-set poker-face, he reminded me on first sight of a pillbug, and he labored tirelessly for hours, vindictively grunting and sneering at his uprooted victims. If a taller specimen proved too deep-rooted, he would yank away leaves and bark, point at the remaining slick yellowish stalk, and gloat, "The least I can do is humiliate the damn things." He charged by the sapling, keeping tally out loud during the operation, then laying his harvest before the customer like a cat dropping a dead mouse at her owner's feet. He announced the count and the cost, and if he saw no immediate move toward payment, he would begin an officious, one-by-one recount of each and every sapling.

Johnny seemed to follow some single-minded, private standard of professionalism, in disdain of the careerist affluence around him. Never wasting a glance at the unattainable wedding-cake mansions that dominated the neighborhood, Johnny on his rounds kept his eyes on the curb, on a constant, pouncing quest for pennies and dimes. He struck me as the ultimate small-profit, quick-returns businessman.

One trash night many months ago, he'd found the mower and rehabilitated it himself. It both revolutionized his business practice and led him to early demise. Johnny must have qualified as the last casualty of that really bad icestorm last February. We had found no damage to our monstrous, certainly antebellum oak after the storm or in succeeding months. But Johnny merely nudged the trunk with his mower, not even during the first mow of the season, and down came a massive, cannon-barrel bough. Johnny never knew what hit him. Distant cousins from out of state bore away the body, and tree surgeons blamed a hairline crack and longstanding internal rot. Johnny had both lived and died by herbicide.

We felt bad and guilty, even if not blameworthy, but Johnny never gave us the chance to miss him. The night after his bodily remains left, we were flabbergasted to find spectral Johnny and the grinding of his ghost mower.

I went out to find my hairbrush and met one neighbor yet to settle in. Barney, who lived behind us, was holding on to the wide-spaced slats of the picket fence between our yards, like an indifferent prisoner. In truth he was a cataloguer at the university library, and to spice up work he reveled in the most obscure occult and mystic tomes in the deepest, darkest stacks. For him, our predicament came as a welcome 3-D extension of his rich life of the mind. He alone among our neighbors openly acknowledged what couldn't possibly be happening here, even if it was ruining everyone's sleep.

"His poor spirit's on perpetual playback," Barney opined by way of greeting. "Doesn't know he's dead, is capable only of the motions of mowing, truly the chains he forged in life. Nothing matters but whatever was weighing on his mind in his last moments. And if we don't figure that out, we may never be rid of him." I felt like I'd been collared by some would-be David Attenborough of the spirit world. I gave him a look half-hopeful, half-murderous. He hastily consoled me, "Just be grateful that ghosts in this culture are ethereal and basically harmless. Did you know, for instance, that in medieval Norway, ghosts had bodily form and stalked around killing farmhands and livestock? *Aptrgangrs,* they were called. Afterwalkers. If Johnny were one, he'd probably go running over people's gardens and pets and siphoning gas out of neighborhood cars to fuel the mower. It'd be like Handyman of the Living Dead."

"Granting you all that," I said, "what do we do? Our minister won't perform exorcisms and refuses to take me seriously. He suggested the ghost would lose interest if we put down Astroturf. And if we sold the house, my conscience instead of Johnny would start haunting me. Besides, if he blames us for what happened, he might keep following us from house to house."

"Seems to me you're up against a pretty traditional psychic phenomenon, in spite of the modern noise element," Barney said reassuringly. "Three A.M. has been the standard e.t.a. of ghosts for centuries. What's more, Johnny was a classic example of the most likely personality to end up a ghost. He was obsessive, fixated on petty details, routine-bound, and stubborn. Whether someone ultimately grows up to be a ghost through some genetic quirk or through acquired habits of mind, I'd say Johnny has you to thank for helping him fulfill his destiny.

There now, no use groaning about it. We either figure out what's troubling him by trial and error. Or you let me try exorcism."

When I decided that exorcism at least offered immediate success or failure, Barney lit up like a kid with a new bike. It just so happened he'd been boning up on exorcism techniques from around the world. He promised to avoid trampling any local religious sensibilities by using a ritual so foreign that only Johnny, hopefully, would get the point. I felt as if I'd played right into Barney's hands, and Laura agreed. "If you didn't see fit to talk it over with me first," she announced, "then I'll just happily stand by and let the boom lower where it may." Not that I blamed her.

At 2:50 the next morning, Barney was setting up on the lawn. As we approached him I winced, and had no desire to look Laura in the eye. Barney carried a smoking censer, was encircled by fat candles, and wore a bright-striped Tibetan vest and pointy, earflapped cap. Behind him, from a boombox came Tibetan monks chanting basso profundo, punctuated by cymbals and droning horns. Before we could ask if he was kidding, Barney crowed, "Johnny sure won't be expecting this! Probably kayo him clear over to the Other Side."

As it happened, Barney's preparations had readied him for everything but the reality of the situation. Johnny appeared punctually and bore down full-tilt on Barney, who suddenly stood dumbstruck, censer dangling limply from his hand. There was a blinding flashbulb burst of collision and Johnny, roaring mower and all, was gone.

After a momentary daze, Barney dropped the censer and strode, ignoring us, into the garage. The monks droned on, a welcome but all too fleeting change from engine racket, for in seconds our own non-ectoplasmic mower drowned them out. And here came Barney, with Johnny's stoop and poker-face, pushing our machine. Laura gave me an acid look, which I evaded by rushing over to scoop up boombox and candles. Otherwise Johnny-within-Barney would have charged right over them, even as he made a loud bump in the night against his nemesis oak and, at last, went on to finish the job that had finished his life.

We entertained hopes of Johnny's soul finding release in the center of the yard. But when the last grass was cut, Johnny paused glassy-eyed as if something were rewinding inside, and then he returned to the edge of the yard and mowed it all over again. He treated us to needless encore after encore of the job. When he ran out of gas, he refueled from our can in the garage. He replaced the oil too, when that finally ran low. "At least he's taking good care of the mower," Laura pointed out. From the eastern sky came gray, then pale morning blue.

Through the night, all up and down the street, lights had been turned on and despairingly off. Everyone around us must have considered it déclassé to call the police, and nobody was daring one-on-one confrontation with a household proving more and more conclusively that it didn't belong in this neck of the woods. From a safe distance, people glowered as they dragged themselves off to work, more rumpled than usual. I felt confident the Neighborhood Association would convene a special tribunal against us for the transgression of excessive lawn mowing.

Only one break entered Johnny's pattern of action. When the gleam of a penny in the driveway caught his borrowed eye, he let the mower idle and, with the look of Dracula toward a laceration, snatched up and pocketed his lucky catch.

"Did you see that?" Laura asked. "I'm not going to tell you what I just thought of. You'll be too embarrassed if you don't come up with it on your own." Her eyes were wide with inspiration, and then so were mine.

"That's it!" I exclaimed. "What else could it be?" And we had Barney to thank, without whom there would have been no conduit from the waking world into Johnny's private, disembodied own. I dashed into the house and emerged just as Johnny was pausing slack-jawed between mows. Now was the perfect time. I presented Johnny with the twenty-dollar fee I had owed him for a week. I only hoped he wasn't keeping track of every time he'd done the yard since his demise.

No, the grim resolve on Barney's face relaxed into tranquil satisfaction. Maybe he was relieved at the chance to forgive a mounting grudge, and as a small businessman by his own lights, whose business was one with his life, he could not close down without the books in balance. Just like the big kids on the block, he was loath to forfeit whatever tokens of respect or iota of dignity the world owed him. He didn't even count the bills I handed him. It seemed to be purely the thought that counted. He stood for once with unstooped shoulders and wore a grin bespeaking a fulfillment I could only envy him. Then he made his flashbulb-burst exit from Barney's co-opted body.

Laura was rubbing more than glare from her eyes, and I could hardly swallow past the lump of sentiment in my own throat. It didn't take much to make some departing souls happy.

Meanwhile, Barney was blinking and gawking confusedly at our rumbling mower. A collection of fives and ones was fluttering from his loose grip. I told him, "For an *aptrgangr* you were pretty nice. Now why don't you stop wasting gas and put the mower away?"

As often happens with people, we didn't really get to know Johnny Mapleseed until after he was dead. This case was only unusual in our gaining the knowledge so first-hand.

Fingers of Stone

The girl wanted to rotoscope me. Bet she got the idea from my gloves. White gloves I always wear. Naked on the model stand or not. Nude, especially, I look cartoonish.

What's rotoscoping? First she films me going through motions of her choice. Then she traces my film image frame by frame onto animation cels. And voilà, I am a cartoon. Not the first time it's happened to me. There were some Germans, back before the war. But that's footage you'll never see. Nazis disposed of it, and them, as degenerate.

This girl, Flora. Met her in the campus coffee house. This was her Senior Project. But not the foremost thing on her mind, apparently. Saw me pick up blistering-hot coffee cup with my stiff gloved fingers. Asked if my gloves were insulated. I told her, Never be a model. Told her my fingers were ossified from too much holding still over the years. Occupational hazard. Irreversible and progressive. She seemed to believe me. Never got around to saying a word that day about her project. Just where and when to show up. I got the idea she was winging it.

Made it up to her when filming started. Told her about Lugosi. How Disney had rotoscoped him for *Fantasia*. How I'd posed for night classes Lugosi had taken. And how Lugosi had described his own modeling experiences. That modeling was such a paradox. You apparently bare yourself, but it's pure deception. Mere surface area. Who you are, a mystery behind generic impression of being a taboo-buster, i.e., naked and blasé about it. Most students, teachers know the night watchman better than their models. Never did meet Lugosi, of course. But ideas, whatever their merits, sound better coming from dead celebrities.

Flora asked, Had I always been a model? No, I used to be an artist. Oh, and the problem with the fingers ended that? I was glad, for her sake, that she hadn't bought that model's malady story. Then she asked, Was I married or ever in love? As if she sensed that something bridged those two realms of my life. Quite the paranormal piece of insight, scarily so, if she hadn't just been prating along aimlessly. So I started telling the truth. To pass the time. Why not? It was as unlikely as what I'd been making up.

In my artist days, I told her, home had been the Ligurian coast. The Italian Riviera. Back then, an obliging place in which to lose oneself or time or anything else that dogged the mortal scent. Coastline accordioned into numberless crinkles, each enfolding villages unnamed on maps. Each village hugging hillside too steep for motor traffic, and looking like Mediterranean versions of sets from *Doctor Caligari*. For work I trucked quarry stone down the few glorified goat-tracks of roads to citybound rail connections. Discreetly withheld some slabs for my own after-hours sculpting. A taxing life, but good, and I knew it.

I rented a farmhouse above a village. Most nights I sculpted. Some I went down to the village. Ostensibly to drink alone. But really, of course, to meet others also sick of solitude. Sex and love seem as one at remote enough a social orbit, don't they? Sort of the way self-destruction can feel like transcendence.

Flora stopped me. Asked if I had a problem dealing with women as people. Told her it depended on the woman. So ended the conversation that day.

Then again, I'm an ideal example of how objectifying a woman can work against a man. After all these years, wondering at first sight of every woman if it's her. Mirror of my chronic uncontrite desire. Even had to look at Flora twice at first (but no, she was a little too short, way too freckly). I alone have been the worse for my feelings. And as for my object of passion, make no mistake, she's still out there. Corrupted by memory but not time.

Next day I felt like talking about Stephanie. Who, down in the village taverna, acknowledged me only by drinking what drinks I sent to her table. Her paleness like that of Ligurian locals. Leading me to think she disdained foreigners. Until I saw she always sat alone, never talked to anyone. Just signaled the bartender to order or settle up.

She always wore dark glasses. Big round lenses. And a kerchief over every last hair of her head. What I sent she drank, never looking up. Giving me no in to catch her eye. Leaving me too many ways to picture her shooting down unwanted Yankee advances. But the way she drank. Impossible for me to turn my eyes away. As if, while depriving herself of more sociable gratifications, she had decided to wring every drop of pleasure from each self-indulgence. All too enticing to me, in some moth-to-flame way. Nightly for a week I withstood her aloofness. Then I got fed up.

Viperine's a regional specialty. The liquor, clear. In the bottle, a snake. Drowned, pickled, jaws agape. Old men call it medicinal. For her, a double-shot. Cure for rudeness. Bartender delivered it. With usual thumb-back gesture toward me. Which she ignored as usual. She regarded glass a second, as if idly curious that it wasn't one more of the same. Then, shrugging, she drank. Profound anguish ensued. Her long pretty face puckered. Darkened like an olive. Sultry mouth went tragic mask. Her table scraped forward. She stormed over. Everyone stared. As if a crack in the world were heading their way.

"What were you thinking to give me this?" she hissed. Shaking empty glass in my face.

"It worked. You're talking to me." Murder in her face. Anger that made my throat tingle. And then surprise on her face as if I really should have been dropping dead. Then she seemed to catch herself. Sat down.

Glared at me through those big lenses. Everyone watching us. I ordered viperine. Drank half and shrugged. "Tastes like walnuts."

"It has bad associations for me. Now, why should we talk?"

"You must want to. You could've just slugged me and walked out."

"I was here first."

Got her a drink more to her liking. Watched spellbound as she emptied it. Couldn't stop imagining making love to her, with her ravishing appetite. This was not romance. But prove that this wasn't what the smitten hero felt in medieval poetry.

After her drink we talked, at last. She had been in this village some years. Kept to herself. Tolerated few advances. Had made no lasting friends. Had previously been someplace else for some years. Had moved from place to place a long, long time. Was older than she looked. Lived on old money. The Mediterranean was home. As specific as she got.

Told her I was a sculptor. "Oh, really?" Told me the idea of investing so much work into the making of a statue always fascinated her. Why did I? What to say? To make what I saw mine? Because they were so hard for anyone to throw away? She wanted to see my work.

Next evening, she visited. Had to ask myself, Did she want to play patron with that old money? What better pretext for a relationship? She wore the glasses, the kerchief, and a black dress, calf-length and airy. Lugged a ribbon-tied shoebox. It seemed heavy.

She kind of prowled among the work. I poured her some grappa. She held out her glass for more a few times. Abstractedly. There was Woodrow Wilson with boulder, reprising Sisyphus. Cerberus fastened to the ankle of Mark Twain. An eagle pulling on the liver of a shackled Pancho Villa. "Bad form to mock the dead," she commented. "Otherwise well on their way." Where? "The best sculpture should beat taxidermy at its own game. Keep a spark of life inside." She undid the shoebox. "See?" Inside, a life-size ferret. Basalt. Detailed down to every bristling hair. Standing on hindquarters, front paws outheld, snout sniffing air. Gorgeous if you liked critters.

"Verisimilitude as an end is a ball and chain," I said.

"No other end holds up over time."

"I suppose, if you're talking a couple of thousand years."

"If you're not, then you haven't made the commitment. Art is no more than creating something of lasting value." Of value to whom? Oh, never mind. Did not want to waste time wrangling.

Where'd she get the ferret? Anonymous work. Indeterminate provenance. Last couple of centuries, or millennia. Important purely as example.

We drank some more. She offered to help. Advice on verisimilitude. To capture truer stance, moment. Who did she think she was? Then again, did I want her or not?

We talked sculpture a while longer. We were standing side by side, almost touching, at a pause in the discussion. Then coiled together and kissing. A move that felt as involuntary and natural as electrons leaping from orbit to preordained orbit. Stephanie's long-repressed wants surfacing. Doubt in her eyes only when catching her breath. And then, never for long. Her appetite, which I found irresistible, was as strong as I'd expected. She bid me only, "Don't take off my clothes. No!

Don't touch my glasses. I'm self-conscious."

Oh really? Almost made me laugh. But how much did my own idea of myself, for instance, agree with anyone else's? If she saw no conflict between sexual abandon and upholding a dress code, where would arguing get me?

Flora said I asked too many rhetorical questions. It had been a long afternoon of cowering, flinching, shielding gestures. Strain and pain. While she circled me with the camera. Made me nervous somehow. As if I were under siege. "Funny in a way, isn't it?" she said. "You used to make statues. Now you make a living playing statues."

"And while we're being so frank, what a stereotypical male-female dynamic we share. My freedom of movement effectively knotted up by the strings of your mysterious self-interest." I grinned good-naturedly.

That Flora. No sense of humor. Or love of debate. Said she was late for an appointment. I had to leave.

Went downtown, myself. Needed a drink. Saw Flora some distance behind. Maybe she really did have an appointment. My bar of choice had Italian leanings. Grappa, fernet, strega. No viperine. Took a booth. Watched myself drink in mirror over the bar. Caught myself eyeing all women who walked in, out, waitressed. Made me self-conscious. Decided, safer to watch them via mirror. Obsession becomes the mate you've lost. Imparts sense of mission beyond eating, shitting, sleeping, working days away. If she were around, this might be the place. Murky, marginal, minding its own business. There, she was tall enough but too into leather. That one was Cambodian. That one too busty.

Now what the hell? Someone new at the bar. Had to do double-take. Her face in profile. Dark glasses. Hair under silk shawl. My heart beat faster. She was too short. Wasn't she? In the mirror, saw her look my way. And again. My dead fingers itched. So did my wrists.

She came over. Crisis of confidence made her steps wobble. Started turning doorward.

"Godammit, Flora, sit down," I called.

Sat across from me. Too embarrassed not to.

"Don't apologize," I said. "Just never do anything like that again." What a dilemma for self-righteous youth. I was an obvious sexist swine. But she was in the red-handed wrong. And I was mad. She just sat there. "Now tell me what this film of yours is about."

"Well it's like about escaping fate. Like about a fatalist trying to convert to free will."

"That's the theme. That's what you think it's about. What actually happens?"

"Uh, I'm not sure yet."

"You old enough to be in here?"

"If nobody asks, I am."

I bought her a grappa. She didn't like it. Hers half-full when mine was gone. I stood, she followed suit. "See you tomorrow," she said.

Next day, back to work. Like nothing had happened. Like the morning after the disgraceful office party. Flora asked what there was to Stephanie besides sex. I said don't underrate sex.

Especially these days, what pretext for involvement is more often resorted to, and at the same time so officially disdained? Seems if you call it chemistry, or attraction, or even a crush, you can get away with it. But try outright claiming sex as basis for compatibility, and you're labeled a Neanderthal. So much for the sexual revolution. The prudes have the moral upper hand, no contest, only they call themselves p.c.

But sex with Stephanie, all-consuming as it was, always retained its curious taboo. Naked was okay for me. But she, always clothed. With kerchief and glasses. Why? Why never eye contact? "That's how you know I like you. Lots of species are like that. Eye contact signals aggression." Rang untrue to me. Always wondered, just who was I fucking? But who was I to begrudge anonymity?

Meanwhile Stephanie's guidance made me formidable. And resentful. All advice about work underway felt right once I gave in. She knew the life inside my images. Better than I did. Better than a surgeon would. Where was her wisdom from?

She had moneyed connections. In old places. Istanbul, Mykonos, Cairo. She sent photos of my work. They sent offers.

All I wanted was becoming mine. So easily. But then, Stephanie liked to dictate. "Only the living have souls," she decreed. I had to pick subjects among the living, from newspaper, magazine clippings. Einstein. Al Capone. G. B. Shaw. I felt compromised. Undermined. But dared not fight and risk losing what I had. Dark glasses and all.

Seaside one Sunday, asked why her eyes were so sensitive. What doctors had said. She shrugged. Called the invention of dark glasses miraculous. Nothing to take for granted. Hundreds so long in hiding, for whatever reason, could rejoin life. Then she saw a scorpion crawling toward me on the seawall where we sat. She reached across me. Picked it up by the tail. Flung it to the sea. Could have sworn she'd been stung. "I'm not allergic," she assured me.

How to answer that? For no good reason blurted out, "Were you ever an artist?"

She turned my way. My throat tingled as after her viperine. "And now you try changing me to your image." Me changing her!

Best to switch subjects. Asked what future we had together unless she were more open about herself. What had gotten into me?

"Now is all the future we have. Who I am is not subject to change. I am not a force for change. Altogether the opposite. I do not try to change you. Only make you more yourself."

"According to your idea of me." Felt panicky. As if I were that poor scorpion, out way over his head. "You've done so much for me. Much more than if you didn't care. And since you do care, at least try meeting me halfway." How was she making me say all this? Cast into the deep, with no idea how to swim. "Nothing will last with me or anyone else if you have to see others on your own terms. No one's the same as you."

"That much you understand."

After this, deathly afraid of losing her. Of having opened the first crack of widening rift between us. And as my need to hold her grew, so did my need to know how her eyes made her who she was. So presumptuous, so insightful. Could never be the artist on my own that she was making me. Unless I learned what she was keeping from me.

"So you put the pressure on and she took off," Flora opined. "Men never learn."

"But when a woman wants a commitment that's different."

"Of course it is. She's not in it just to get something out of a guy."

No, I would not get into this. Nor would I walk out. Needed more amenable talk. "All this time," I went on, "our love life saw no letup from day to day. At sunset she'd lead me to my room. Or she'd be waiting there. She drew the shade, the curtains. Took me in the dark, with her glasses and clothes on. And always like she was so ravenous. She was never there when I woke up next morning."

"How ideal." I could either talk on or get mad.

"Out of the blue, Stephanie commissioned me. To do her. 'Death arouses curiosity,' she said, 'but no death wish. Carve me the likeness of my death to look at and that will be enough.' Wanted a reclining pose. With hooded cloak and blindfold."

Had never been to Stephanie's. No idea where she lived. But there waited the stone she wanted to use. There I would work. A little place to one side of the village. Alone on a headland. Restored fisherman's shack. Drapes benighting one room. In it, accumulations of fossils, bones, statuary fragments, stone-age artifacts, life-size stone animals. In same rock as ferret. The other room was whitewashed, airy, bright. Nothing in it but marble block and a divan for her.

Gave me pause about Stephanie's guidance. And about the rest of our involvement. All to prepare me for this? Didn't care about her professed Gothic motives. But felt unnerved, wondering if her interest in me would end with completion of her statue.

"And you thought she was using you for your body." Where in hell was that demure, gullible Flora I'd met in the coffee house?

"I'm taking a break."

And it was in the coffee house that Flora found me. Sat beside me. "Look, I never speak so freely with people I'm not comfortable with."

"I see there's much advantage in gaining your trust."

"You know, I've figured out some more about the script." She wanted to portray me as a sculptor. Who falls in love with some face in a crowded bar. And tries to make her his by sculpting her. First try, bad likeness makes wrong woman appear before him. He smashes statue and woman disappears. Tries twice more with like results. Tries again, likes how it's coming, then sees his feet are turning to stone. Works more hastily, sees his legs are stone. Works faster and faster to finish before he is petrified. As last chip falls, his tools drop from fingers of stone. Woman appears, sees statue that was him and falls in love.

"I'm not posing for you anymore. You can tease me but I won't stand for being mocked." Got up and left.

Never should have told her anything. Damn her for reducing my life to an undergraduate fable. If only she hadn't told me. It was like she'd peeked through my misery's keyhole. Filmed what she found.

But how to undo what she'd done? Legally, no way. Talk to her?

My mood was not conducive to negotiation. No right move I could see myself make. Stuck on the spot.

Went to bed early. Phone rang soon afterwards. Flora. I said nothing. She said, "Look, you kinda left me in the lurch. I'm not done filming. Are you there?" I said nothing. She could talk if she wanted to. "I didn't know you were really walking out. I thought you were kidding." Told her, Well, I wasn't. "I thought Stephanie was like everything else you said. Just something you made up."

"Sorry you thought so."

"Look, I didn't mean to hurt your feelings. Suppose I gave you co-authorship credit on the finished story?"

"My life is not a college project."

"I'm not even sure what you mean or why you're so upset. What do you want me to do?"

"Scrap the whole thing as far as I'm concerned."

She finally agreed to revamp the story. I would see it before filming resumed.

Never did tell Flora the last of what happened with Stephanie. Little left to tell. Never sculpted past day one. Started at dawn. Harder to work every minute. Sight of her lying there, and me constrained by work-in-progress not to touch her. Drove me wilder and wilder. With each chisel hit, had to fight urge to throw down my hammer. All this time, no telling if Stephanie was asleep or awake. Still as a reptile. All day.

Dusk eased in. She said, "Keep going till it's dark."

Could see no reason for her to want me to go on for so long. It seemed only that she wanted this over with as soon as possible. So as not to prolong our affair.

Put down hammer, chisel quietly. Climbed onto divan. As I had climbed into my own bed so many times with her waiting there. Go ahead, cut short our days together. But you have your priorities for that time. And I have mine.

She raised her blindfolded head. "What are you doing?"

"What we always do this time of day." Except this time it was dim, not dark. No drapes on these windows.

"Are you crazy?" I went to stroke her face. She pulled her head away. Blindfold caught on my fingertips. Hood slipped back. I caught a glimpse of hair that, once freed, began to move. Like snakes. Hair that was alive.

In amazement looked to her face. As if for explanation. Eyes terrified me. Instinct made my fingers cover them. Green eyes, lidless, vertical slits for pupils. She squirmed to one side. Me still straddling her. She refit hood and blindfold. My fingers already numb. Greying. To basalt. Like the ferret.

"You're . . ." Didn't say gorgon. Suddenly hit me, might not be the polite term.

"I trusted you!"

"I've done nothing to you."

"More than you know. And nearly killed yourself. Be glad you were so quick. Or you'd have lost much more than your fingers. You fool. I was letting you sculpt me. I was letting you make me yours, as you put it once."

"Look, I don't care who you are. I still love you. Maybe that will matter when you're not so angry."

"I can't stay here anymore. Go, get away from here. Find something new to do with your life. As I've had to, often enough. Give yourself a settled existence. Something I can only envy you. Now go before my blindfold slips again." I left. Didn't want to see those eyes again, deadly or not.

Returned next morning after a sleepless night. Stone fingers not worst of my losses. She was gone. House empty. Fossils, statues, bones all gone. Only chisel-bitten stone remained.

Fingers affected me most as reminders of her absence. They also forced me to quit my quarry job. And stop sculpting. For money, took up modeling. In defiance of her. She bid me lead a settled life. Instead I've worked my way around the world. From school to colony to atelier. Never daring to presume that I'd find her, or not find her. With nothing better for a lead than her affinity for statuary. My livelihood, a literal-minded parody of being settled, stable. Letter of her wishes, but contrary in spirit. A sculptor who can't sculpt is a statue. And a man who can't love again, what is that?

Ironically, the hardening in my fingers radiated as durability through the rest of me. Granting me more time in which to cross her path. I don't seem to be pushing 100, do I?

Flora called tonight. Come on over. Sure her new story could in no way dovetail with my life.

"Had a friend help me write this," she said. "It's a lot more abstract now."

She showed me storyboards. Homeric type with mirror for shield blocks attempt after attempt of gorgon to stare him in face. Gorgon finally meets own reflection. Turns to stone. But then man throws down mirror. Looks in it. Turns to stone himself. Face in glass is that of leering gorgon.

I stood powerless to move. As if in trance. Short-circuited. Aghast, numb. There was a knock at the open door. Silhouette of woman in shadows. Tall, thin, with midlength skirt. Kerchief on head.

Tingling set in all over me. As it had so long ago with fingers. Hard to move.

"What's happening to you?" Flora cried.

That other woman was in the room now. "You're not . . ." I said slowly. Had a good look now. No, of course not.

"What are you talking about?" Flora was panicky. "This is the friend I mentioned. Who helped with the rewrite. She said she wanted to meet you. You thought she was Stephanie?" Flora bit her lip. Something clicked in that way she had. "You thought Stephanie was a . . ."

I could still nod. Still see. But through thickening film of grey.

"My God, he's turning to stone!" the friend shouted.

"Listen, there's no reason for this to happen to you. Whoever Stephanie was, she just had something wrong with her eyes. She couldn't have done that to your fingers. And my friend isn't Stephanie!"

Her voice seemed to come from behind a wall. "Stop changing!" Found this funny. Tried to crack a smile.

"Not . . . changing. Becoming . . . more the same."

"Stop doing this to yourself!"

Might as well tell slate to be mud again. Could feel my heart creak to a halt. How long had it been pumping dust? Never found Stephanie. But at least looking has given my life some meaning. Some passion. Poor Flora, will you ever be able to say as much? Believe it or not, I'm smiling on the inside.

The May Day Melée, Explained

A part-time job at the campus library pays the bills. Part-time is plenty.

Among my coworkers, I alone seem inclined to say, Thank God for the students. Without them, the staff would have only each other to turn against as subjects for gossip and badmouthing.

Take the May Day Melée, for example. For a week before it happened, we all knew that art-major libertines were plotting a "secret" May Day debauch, and debate on the likely depth of its depravity lent workplace conversations some much-needed spice.

My first reaction was an incredulous snicker. How soon our own student years are forgotten: sophomore ringleaders whipping up would-be Roman orgies, bedsheet togas and all, in coed dorms, with attendees just sitting around, Inglenooks warming in hand, too uptight to start anything. More power to these kids if they got anywhere! Not that I condone frat-boy lewdness, of course.

May Day, meanwhile, connoted celebration of the sacred rather than the vulgar. To any self-respecting library worker, Saturday's raison d'être should have been obvious, but maybe I'm alone here in constantly gleaning facts on the job. May Day is what's left of Beltane, high holy day of ancient Celts, with feasting consecrated to renewal and fertility and all the promises of spring. What wasn't to venerate there? And bogus as undergrad notions of Iron Age rites likely were, the organizers' hearts seemed to be in the right place. Spiritual priorities are all too often lacking in this consumerist decade. My coworkers, nonetheless, were fixated solely on voyeurs' visions of group grope.

That Friday afternoon as I trudged home, the sun peeked between horizon and woolly overcast and gave my street an alien grey glow. I've been a contented Wheeler Street tenant for years, since grad school in fact. Amidst the densely populated historic district, here alone is preserved a pre-urban atmosphere. Apart from my building, there are mostly woodsy lots or overgrown backyards of the mansions one block above and below. And the eerie light that day was perfect, since May Day is preceded by Walpurgis Night which, like Halloween before All Saints' Day, constitutes the haunted dark before the rosy dawn. Or so I've read.

On my right, a chain-link fence paralleled the street for a block or so. Behind the fence towered a crowded row of hemlocks, and beyond them a pitiful howling started up, so piercing that I winced. At a gap in the trees, a gate in the fence hung open, and I beheld an uphill slope of tousled grass and helter-skelter rocks. A slab fit for Stonehenge took up the middle of the yard, and staked there like a Judas goat was a gangly pup, maybe half-husky, half-lab. He trembled at the end of a thick old rope that served as both collar and chain, and I surmised he was abandoned. Whoever owned the gingerbread colossus looming over us surely would have used a more upscale tether, and if they were home, how could they have ignored this pathetic racket? Whether he was their dog or nobody's, the lure to be humane was overpowering.

My trespass into the yard met with no response from the house, but with whining from the dog, up on hindquarters and paddling his forepaws in midair. The rope was knotted to a railroad spike, and the spike was anchored between the slab and one of the three knobby rocks on which the slab rested. The pup could well have gotten loose elsewhere and been snared while bounding through the yard. Slipping the spike off and drawing the rope out of the gap in the stones was easy enough, apart from the dog springing up to lick my face. I urged the dog to come on and flicked the rope like reins, exhilarated and jittery as if pulling a heist. After all, the pup wasn't actually wearing a sign that said "Take me."

Decking the kitchen floor with newspaper, scrounging up old sleeping bag for a dog bed, and reshelving low-lying knickknacks at safer heights took till sundown. Nighttime muggings are a fact of life on my back street. So rather than trot out to the market for dog food, I shared franks from my supper with the pup, who growled happily while he chewed.

I soon learned he was housebroken, but this was a mixed blessing. Whenever I started dozing off, in front of the TV or in bed, the pup scratched at the door, eight times before I lost count. And instead of midnight discretion, he choked on the rope in eagerness to sniff around the murkiest, rankest overgrowth out back, all the best places for someone to lurk. He darted hither and yon as if after a scent, maybe expecting his lost master to pop out of the shadows. Still, after leaving his mark, any homesickness he felt rated a mere backward glance or two as I led him inside. So ended Walpurgis Night.

May Day began early, when cold mutt nose poked me awake. My first thoughts consisted of second thoughts about impulsive pet rescue, based on a look at the dawn hour and all the dog-related work ahead.

Living simply has always been my stubborn ideal, to find contentment in low rent, modest income, a few friends (mostly out of town), a decent stereo and a portable TV. Lack of romance is an issue, but I trust that destiny will deliver a soulmate, if she exists, to the library. Meanwhile I'm proud of what I'm happily living without—car, computer, credit card, checking account even. If my niche for working social change has never occurred to me, at least I'm not part of the problem, of squandering natural resources, of pointless status-seeking, of media brainwashing. The best you can do in this world, I always tell myself, is set a good example and hope someone notices.

But with one kindly act, my frugal ways were in upheaval. Dog food would be the least of it. Leash, collar, toys, a vet within walking distance, then shots, neutering, heartworm pills, obedience classes, all made me want to run as from a landslide. The commitment, the expense tempted me to flyer the neighborhood and flush out the previous owner.

Instead, I split my budget for the week between supermarket and pet supply store. I felt trapped in what may have been a new dimension of liberal guilt. After all, back in dim prehistory when we domesticated our "best friends," they could never have conceived of what they'd someday have to deal with: traffic, lawn chemicals, so much else for which nature had never prepared them. In making these animals ours, we made them our responsibility. How could I remand the pup to someone of proven carelessness? In for a penny, in for a pound, such was moral obligation. But what a drag, if one little pup forced so many changes on me that my last two decades would be reduced to a waste, a joke.

I shut the dog in the kitchen while I was out. On my return, he was still snoozing on his back, ears stretched out like batwings, fore-paws folded, but on hearing me he rolled over, barked, and sprinted to the back door. And with that, a pattern was set for the rest of the day. The dog reacted to any show of attention with a demand to go out, but he was too cute for me to get seriously annoyed. His fur was mostly white, with a red tip at the end of his thick tail, and big brown rings around his eyes. When he romped through darkening rooms at twilight, swinging his squeaky toy like a shillelagh, his white fur seemed luminous, and his eye rings accented the impression that he wore a ghost costume. Since dogs reputedly live up to their names, calling this one something like Baskerville exerted only momentary appeal.

For tonight's witching-hour dog walk I was energized rather than uneasy, as if under influence of a full moon. Distant drums and cheering sounded like a halftime show. Enough people were evidently out and about that indulging the pup sounded harmless enough when he perked up his ears and begged to investigate the noise. I assumed that all the scents en route to the corner would distract him, and then he'd come home quietly. Instead, the ruckus became louder at the first side street, as if a door had been opened. The mutt pulled at the leash trying to head downhill, and when I bent down to pick him up, he sprang forward, out of reach. After half a dozen tries, he and his crafty eyes won.

One block below, we turned onto stately Tillinghast Street. I was hustling to keep up with the pup, who pattered along without sniffing the ground, as if following some familiar line of sight. The brick side-walks were deserted; apparently the night was in ferment only where we were bound.

We traversed the parking lot beside Eat at Joe's Sandwich Shop. According to legend, on the site once stood a hotel where Poe stayed and drank whenever passing through town. Behind the lot, we fol-lowed a footpath that descended through Japanese bamboo to the mouth of a disused train tunnel, a former mile-long detour beneath this whole side of town. How cool, in my own salad days, discovering this tunnel had been, as if I'd stumbled on the ruins of Babylon.

A whoosh of heat and sunny brilliance made me squint and startled the pup against my shins. The roar of onlookers drowned out the roar of newly lit bonfire upon the tracks in front of the tunnel. Rattles, torches, and plastic skulls on sticks shook in the hands of amateur satyrs, devils, and witches. Others cheering at the blaze wore papier-mâché heads of goats, birds, the sun. Down the tracks from the direction of downtown, brandishing a huge club that must have been balsa, strode a likeness of the ancient Cerne Abbas Giant, the priapic Hercules cut into the chalk of an English hillside. I shivered in empathy, for the air still had a biting chill, and this young god wore only a bulbous mask that most resembled Munch's "The Scream," a short leopard-skin cape over one shoulder, and a monstrous Styrofoam dildo. He squatted gratefully and rubbed his hands by the fire, despite the nuisance of dildo clunking the side of his head with every shift of his weight. Here was the much-touted student debauch, boldly announcing "Beltane" to any receptive ears. And where better to honor the quickening Earth than in a tunnel, cozying right up to the chthonic, as it were? What a great party!

But then a string of firecrackers went off, panicking the pup into bounding this way and that, trying to yank his head free of the collar. To my disappointment, Hercules must have been the culprit. He was braying and—God knows where his ammo was stashed—about to cast another volley into the flames. Oh well, I sighed, there's one in every crowd.

Before the dog could work loose, I gave him some slack and he dragged me into the tunnel. Inside, it was loud as a disco, with music and chanting and laughter. Over a hundred kids were inside, many around little campfires, as far back as I could see. The pup was calmer in spite of the din, and snuffling around everyone and everything, maybe on the scent of his past master. This stirred mixed feelings in me, but I let him proceed. People said Hi to the dog and playfully roughed his fur, while me nobody noticed, far away at the business end of the leash.

To witness this splendid gathering without taint of corporate intrusion or profit motive felt encouraging, liberating even. I fairly swaggered as I toured on. Youth with antlers were banging on congas, beer and wine were free for the taking in a cauldron full of ice, and a willowy blonde all in black was adorned in little blinking Christmas lights. Why couldn't I meet a girl like that? In the deeper recesses people had seemingly been partying longer, carried to the rear by the flow tide of newcomers. Some were dancing freeform to toy horns or pennywhistles, and some more unsteadily to the stricter tempo of British folkrock, Fairport Convention maybe, on a boombox. Back here, the masks were off and joints were making the rounds. "Hey, see if the old guy wants any," someone said, and a tap on my shoulder preceded glow-tipped contraband before my eyes. I said "Thanks" and partook, passing it to the outheld hand of a goateed Asian with druid robes and cardboard sickle. There I paused in case anyone cared to chat, but the discussion stayed in its self-absorbed loop. Old guy, indeed. The most spent celebrants sat indifferently with feet in the nasty standing water between the railroad ties, or with backs against slimy granite wall.

On these ragged outskirts, this seemed less a reenactment of Beltane than an excuse to dress up and get wasted. The organizers hadn't even seen to so obvious a prop as a May Pole. Anyway, would that I'd taken another toke, myself. Meanwhile that full-moon restlessness, that air of the kettle about to whistle, overlay all. Upon gazing clear back to the glowing mouth of the tunnel, the party on the whole looked like the see-through model of an organism with very lively metabolism. The partygoers were cells of what was assuming a life of its own.

The students really had arrived at the spirit of Beltane, hadn't they? My intuition had suddenly grasped what common ground lay here and among our ancestors. This holiday marked our apogee with some force or presence outside daily access, neither good nor bad but simply, well, pagan. And its hunger drew it to celebrations, where it took possession of the festivities and sated itself by influencing the celebrants to sate themselves. Or so I conceived at the time.

The dog stood loyally by me and, unlike the kids, knew enough to keep his paws out of the gross water. He started barking in the general direction of the entrance, where two campus rent-a-cops in baggy uniforms rubbernecked and did double-takes. They accosted some students outside, who only shrugged. This goaded them into more macho posturing and heated words. Whatever was said brought Hercules on the run, club and dildo aloft. His mere presence was enough to send would-be authority packing.

For Hercules, true to simpleton form, out of sight was out of mind. He lapsed into carefree batting practice, swinging his club at traprock from the tracks, hitting occasional line drives too close to his protesting classmates. I, on the other hand, was worried about real cops on the heels of the wannabes, and the pup sagely cooperated as I reversed course. Appreciably more were in the tunnel now than on our way in. Though the merriment was unabated, the going was like that on a rush-hour subway platform. I steered via the cauldron, deciding that a beer in my uninvited hands was better than down the drain once the law came rousting. I had taken my first big swig when the dog growled and his ears flattened back. A second later, my less sensitive hearing also picked up sirens, which crescendoed harshly and then cut out. Nobody else reacted to them.

Three patrolmen, in helmets and leather, stood hands on hips at the entrance, silhouetted by the bonfire. One bellowed into his bullhorn, "Clear this tunnel! You are hereby ordered to clear this tunnel!" I needed no convincing. Chugging fast, I urged the mutt forward, sure of momentary escalation. The crowd near the entrance had discreetly thinned, but around me no one was listening, attention perhaps held, unconsciously or drunkenly, by a higher power.

The cops moseyed in, trying to impose their notion of order. Amidst this freedom of expression they moved skittishly at first, as if a bomb might go off, but then fell back on a show of strength as preferable to being at a visible loss. One cop yelled at an antlered drummer cross-legged on the ground to stop. The drummer looked around the blissful scene and asked, "Why?"

The frustrated cop kicked aside the drum and made a grab for the sticks.

"Hey! Those are mine! What are you doing?"

When the kid pulled his sticks aside, the cop hoisted him by the tasseled jerkin and dragged him out. This met with raucous disapproval from the surrounding attendees. Another cop, brandishing his nightstick, was backing slowly from half a dozen partygoers demanding the return of a papier-mâché devil head. He dropped the head and squawked into his radio, and of what I heard, the word "satanic" evoked my last laugh of the evening. The word "backup" made me push harder through the throng.

Too bad the police were altogether unschooled in the meaning of the day; maybe then they wouldn't have indulged force or panic. But unlike the straw men of campus security, here were state-sponsored egos with more on the line, while the partiers, doing no one harm, no doubt felt unfairly put upon, their rights and rites violated. The cops were like a virus invading an organism, but were the vital spots of this organism in our familiar three dimensions?

As the pup and I pressed on, the pot, the beer, the adrenaline, and snatches from *The Golden Bough* conjoined to illuminate me. To these neo-pagans, full of holiday spirits in more ways than one, wouldn't these cops, so set on venting authority, seem to be posing as kings? And what awaited those who dared be king for a day? Oh for tinder of wicker to stuff these pretenders in, for a Beltane offering as we used to make, to an appetite unsated till the offenders were reduced to ashes. Yikes! What wavelength was I picking up?

We still had far to go, when multiple sirens warned of a further dozen cops, who moved in without waiting for their call to disperse to have any effect. They now had the full attention of two hundred kids bent on confrontation, on overthrowing these men who would be kings, while I, bent merely on getting out, may have been pushy unto rudeness. Ideally I sympathize with artists, but it's never been reciprocated, and as for the cops, I somehow bring out the school bully in them. My survival instincts shrilled, The hell with 'em all, just don't hurt the puppy!

Hercules let out a rebel yell and bounded with wildly flapping phallus up to a trooper, balsa club on high. The cop spared an instant to gawk at the dildo before he broke Hercules' expressionist head open with a real club. That was the signal for general battle. Students flung stones, drumsticks, plastic skulls, handfuls of mud, whatever was at hand. The cops more methodically cudgeled and pepper-gassed all in their path. I hoped the girl with the Christmas lights would escape unscathed, even if she would never have given me the time of day. The dog, who'd brought me here in the first place, was whining miserably. I bent to scoop him up, and just then a cop who'd sidled up to me took a swing, missed, and lost his balance. One of the kids I distinctly remembered shoving a minute ago toppled the cop by bouncing a bottle off his helmet. "Thanks!" I exclaimed, unsure if I were addressing the kid or the dog, and if I were protecting the dog or vice versa. How I'd acquired him had been on the weird side, after all. In accepting responsibility for the dog, from whom had I accepted it?

No cops stood between us and the outside, as I threaded past bloody-headed kids huddled and groaning, or crawling confused on all fours. The cops, of course, would justify all injuries in the name of clearing the tunnel for the kids' own safety.

Whoa! Troopers lurked beside the threshold, and busy as they were gassing anyone within range, I overheard references to "that old guy" and "ringleader." Uh-oh! Compounding my angst, the dog wriggled loose and popped free of my arms. He landed by a cop's feet, got his jaws around the Styrofoam dildo just lying there, and pranced toward the fire. "Drop it!" hollered the cop, and I was forgotten while a couple of officers tried stomping on the trailing end of the leash. He was too fast for them and me and, with a hard wag of his head, cast the dildo at the fire as he galloped by. I kept going, but the cops stopped to rescue the dildo, as evidence if not trophy. The bonfire marked the edge of combat. In the darkness beyond, neither cop nor student had thought to stray. Good puppy!

I turned and caught my breath. In a few seconds the donnybrook had jumped from bad to worse, and we two couldn't have been luckier. Students who'd vacated at the first three cops' arrival had fetched reinforcements, rallying at the edge of the parking lot above the tunnel entrance. They were raining down sticks and stones and bricks torn from the historic Tillinghast Street sidewalk, and they felled one cop and sent others reeling. A call for more help went out from troopers stumbling through the bamboo and dodging barrage as they tried gaining the hill and their cars. The kids now fleeing the tunnel had mostly friendly fire to contend with. Averse to watching the melée worsen, I led the pup to where the tracks met a trestle, where another path snaked down to Underhill Street.

What? More sirens? I snatched up the dog and merged with the shadows of the trestle as about ten more squad cars sped by, screeching to a halt in the parking lot of the firehouse a block ahead. For these cops to connect me with the altercation seemed unlikely, but why give them the option of thinking about it? I stayed put until they formed a club-wielding phalanx spanning the nearest side street up to Tillinghast, and marched away. Then I trod softly to the side street beyond the firehouse, while the tired puppy yawned often and needed encouragement to go on.

Everything so far still left me unprepared for new developments on Tillinghast. The police ranks were slowly losing ground, like a line of seaweed inched up the beach by a rising tide. In the middle of the student mob, two cop cars had made scant headway before all their windows had been smashed. The crowd continued rocking the cars back and forth, to meager tactical advantage since they'd been abandoned. From alleys between majestic Georgian mansions and from windows of quaint old row houses, guerrilla showers of stones and asphalt chunks and the historic bricks nailed officers from the sides and behind. Too bad the first cops hadn't left well enough alone back in the tunnel!

Before expansive mayhem blocked our way, the pup and I dashed across Tillinghast and started toward Wheeler. Halfway up, I turned and tarried long enough for two especially disturbing turns of event. First, two cops had handcuffed broken-masked, naked Hercules and were prodding him down the street I'd just climbed. One cop had the Styrofoam dildo under his arm. Maybe the cops were a needful, if unwitting, part of the spectacle after all. Maybe with his he-man posturings, Hercules was really the doomed king for a day. The Beltane presence had come to seem cruelly amoral, rather than benignly pagan. Here was the staunchest booster of the holiday, and him alone did I see taken into custody, the sacrificial goat.

The second troubling moment was when the beleaguered cops entered my line of sight. The endmost cop looked toward me and nudged his neighbor. Again I heard reference to "old guy" and "ringleader" and something about "apprehend." They both turned my way but before either of them could take a step, a length of storm pipe crashed into them. Did I look like a neo-pagan provocateur? Maybe so. In any case, constabular minds were made up. I grabbed the dog and took breathless flight to Wheeler Street and home.

Newspaper accounts, of course, were full of police heroism in the face of drunken, lewd delinquency. I gathered that the mob lost steam and scattered after the arrest of Hercules, which made perfect sense to me. Poor zealous dupe! Cops and journalists alike voiced bafflement at how the night had gotten so out of hand. The role of cops as catalyst never seemed to enter straight and narrow minds.

As for my own role, maybe somebody had to see and understand the proceedings for them to satisfy the Beltane presence. Otherwise, the dog had barged into my life and drew me to the fracas for no reason, and those twenty-four hours were too weird for me to buy that.

Meanwhile, on the off chance of bumping into any cops who might have seen me at the party, I've shaved off my beard. And wouldn't you know it, nobody at work has shown the first sign of noticing. Not that it matters. What with the puppy to care for, I'm forced to comb the wider world for a position more lucrative and hopefully agreeable. Such has been the reward for my Beltane participation.

As for the tunnel, mere weeks later, the nervous city fathers sealed it with an iron gate like something out of *King Kong*. Considering what had really been conjured back there, I can't help but regard such a barricade as naïve.

Doctor Farrell's Goddesses

The erotic dreams intensified, my second week housesitting for Dr. Farrell. I had no idea what in waking life could have been inciting them. Dog days were underway, and the hellacious heat and humidity reduced sex to the last thing on my mind. It was all I could do to drag myself outside and tend the garden, all thirty or so square feet of herbs and greens. Apart from garden and houseplants and the security of Farrell's possessions, which held little obvious interest for burglars, my presence seemed to serve no compelling purpose.

The professor's bungalow was out of town, in that *terrain vague* which looked suburban or rural, depending on the side of the road you faced. Woodlots separated the house from its neighbors, and over the backyard fence was Rooseweldt Woods, a state park. Days could pass before I sighted anybody; and since I had no car, provisioning myself meant trudging a half hour to the bus stop and stockpiling all I could, between two bags and a backpack, at the A&P five miles away. The professor was in Europe for a month, avowedly combining vacation with a Classical Studies conference. He would be unreachable for the duration, but in his stead, he assured me, I could call myself "king of the domain."

So for company, I had only my dream-consorts, few of whom I would have chosen in the flesh. The majority were too old for my taste, not quite elderly, not hags certainly, but with crow's feet and laugh lines and sagging under the chin. None resembled anyone I had ever met. Their thick hair was still bright blonde or red and black, but their features seemed too big for their faces, goggle-eyed, almost cartoonish, and there was something dumpy, slovenly about most of them. They offered me the likes of bread or apples or wine, and with little more ado their come-on was aggressive, smothering, though more in hindsight than at the altogether erotic moment. I always awoke unrested, ornery, for which day-and-night mugginess could plausibly take the blame.

Throughout July the dreams filled more and more of my nights and stayed with me by day. In the fourth week, three dream-lovers at once were common, one young and two older, all three scratching, nipping, ganging up with a passion that would have panicked me except in a dream. The recollections, in fact, were oppressive enough that I tried gaining some distance from them by exploring the woods.

Under the trees and around the lake the heat felt much less spiteful, and I wondered about myself for staying mostly housebound all this time. Where the trail around the lake crossed an oak glade dotted with boulders, the Department of Parks had raised a sign, explaining that the "Victorian romantic" Merritt Rooseweldt had preserved his acreage out of "reverence for nature," supporting himself with a modicum of logging and the sale of wild roses abounding beside the paths. The state, to which he had bequeathed it all "for the public betterment and enjoyment," named the site in honor of him and the "rose veldts" that served as a kind of living rebus for him.

The sign did not advance the popular local rumor that Merritt's woods, for reasons kept to himself, were "right" for rearing scaled-down Stonehenges and bogus "druidic" altars; apparently these had all come to ruin, or had been dismantled by wild-card Merritt himself. In fact, glacial erratics loom wherever you look, but only the most credulous can find signs of ancient handiwork among them.

To my surprise, though, I happened on a kind of stonework I'd never heard about in these parts. I was about to leave the lakeside path and climb the slope to Farrell's back fence, which I could easily scale. Just beyond arm's length in the water stood a stone the shape and size of a miter. Toward its peak was a circle, too nearly perfect for a product of erosion. I scrambled down the bank for a closer look, and more faintly within the circle was a cross or plus-sign. So it was definitely a petroglyph, and even if it fell short of being dramatic, finding it made for a moment of wonderment. Who could say if the carver had been Algonquin or Merritt himself or a modern fisherman marking a favorite spot? In any case, by dint of this find I now felt more like a part of this place, as if Farrell's purview were a little more my own.

That night, I wondered if the rock would be visible from the bedroom, the rearmost room upstairs. The window overlooked the garden, behind which was a little round pool, allegedly for frogs that ate garden pests. Around the pool were three Deco-era metal lawn chairs, in the shade of a far-reaching weeping willow. Beyond the tree was the fence. I turned off the bedside lamp and gazed out vacantly while my eyes adjusted to starlight. When they focused, there were three women in the lawn chairs, two middle-aged matrons flanking a younger one. They wore ankle-length peasant dresses and the kind of broad-brimmed sunhat unpopular since 1971. They were looking up at me, through the swaying willow branches between us.

After the initial shock, my housesitting reflexes kicked in. Who the hell did they think they were, acting like they owned the place? I tore on out the back door, but they were gone, visible neither on the road out front nor in the park out back.

I was feeling my worth as a watchdog if nothing else, when the judgmental looks of the women, so unlike the expected demeanor of trespassers, came back to haunt me. I wasn't afraid of the women themselves, I told myself, but what had they wanted here? I dismissed as crackpot any connection between them and my dreams. Then as I started up the stairs to bed, the lights went out.

I was spooked all right, and less confident about laying this on coincidence. But the women would have had slim chance to sneak in the back while I was out front, and the front door had stayed locked. In any case, I groped through the gloom until I found a flashlight in a kitchen drawer. Power failures were common enough in a heat wave, with every air-conditioner in the county working twenty-four hours. But I didn't want to err on the side of having to restock the fridge tomorrow because of a blown fuse tonight.

Fusebox was presumably down cellar, but I doublechecked to no avail. Finally I pondered a padlocked door, hung without regard to the height of the frame, and far from square with it. The door was flimsy enough that locking it was less a deterrent than a form of "Keep Out" sign, and where else but behind it could the fusebox be? Against the possibility of no power for the duration, breaking the lock and replacing it before Farrell's return seemed an acceptable breach of the honor system. After all, was I "king of the domain" or not?

On a workbench in another room were mallet and chisel, and opening the door proved as easy as starting a lawnmower. The first thing my beam hit was the fusebox, and flipping a circuit-breaker was all I had to do. The room smelled as much of incense as of earth, and on pulling a light cord dangling at room center, I found myself in what seemed grotto as much as study. A grinning man-in-the-moon paper lantern encased the bulb that hung from the ceiling. It cast a yellow pallor on the rickety plank walls beside me, the fieldstone wall before me, the packed dirt floor. And though Farrell seemed unlike the sportsman type, a hefty rack of antlers was fixed to the stone wall, its shadows like a pattern of ominous fissures. Bright pushpins stuck sheaths of notepad sheets to one wall, half hiding it like an amateur shingling job. Against the opposite wall stood an old mahogany bookcase, a glass panel fronting each shelf. Instead of the upstairs floor-to-ceiling rows of Loeb classics and scholarly studies, a good two hundred bindings here referred to Neolithic, Bronze Age, Celtic, and Germanic Europe, with particular attention to pagan myths and cults, from *Golden Bough* and *White Goddess* on. And directly below the lantern was a tabletop desk, taken up largely by a planning calendar, with scribbling under almost every date. A censer shaped like a coiled snake sat beside the calendar.

At first perusal, the calendar made me sorry for Farrell. Weekly notations of "Chemo," through the last few months up to his departure date, came as a shock. A clear-cut violation of privacy was on my head, but retreating from the calendar brought me within reading range of the notepad sheets. The top line of each page read "Matres Comedovae," "Matres Griselicae," "Matrones Aufaniae," and other names, if high school Latin were trustworthy, of mother-goddesses. Below each name was a list of places, French and German mostly, and next to each place was written "Cures Recorded" and a number. In parentheses beside each number were noted "eye, spine, arm, lung," and other body parts. These Latinized versions of apparent barbarian goddesses seemed to have presided over healing shrines, at which satisfied devotees must have left testimonial inscriptions or gifts.

My eyes wandered back to the calendar, but now I was moved to unease. Farrell had plotted his "vacation" itinerary on the page, and all were places listed under names of goddesses. In desperation for a cure was Farrell going pagan, and if so, how far? From beneath the redoubtable classicist was emerging a subterranean self of less overt behavior and beliefs.

A third look at the calendar added confusion to unease. Farrell's return flight was supposedly August 1, but the center of a big red X fell left of the line, into July 31. Maybe careless haste had misplaced the mark, but why should this have been the one item not neatly centered under a date? Then again, Farrell had no reason to misinform me about his schedule.

The word "Lughnasad," whatever that meant, had been penned with the usual deliberation on August 1 itself. I puzzled over it, until the apparent stirring of underground draft brought me what must have been a whiff of Farrell's incense, with a curiously fresh element of roses.

How long had I been down here? Especially in light of my recent gatecrashers, I felt duty-bound to head back up and do my watchdog job. On my way out, though, a note, tacked to the inside of the door like some thought-for-the-day, caught my eye and lingered with me: "The Gaels drove them below, and below is the same whether here or there, the call is heard as clearly—M. R."

That night, my dreams had definite trysting place for the first time. The usual threesome seduced me behind the house, under the willow, and for once a feeling of dread rather than arousal prevailed.

This, along with the usual morning funk, stayed with me through a listless breakfast. Last night's real-life visit by three women similar to those in my dreams disturbed me more in glaring sunlight than in drowsy midnight hour. But more disturbing was the nagging urge to learn how I fit into whatever Farrell was up to, to violate his sanctum again for information.

Wearily, I raised my eyes to the kitchen window, out to where the nocturnal adventure had begun. This time, a dog had strayed into the yard and was digging in the primroses fringing the pool. He was some kind of big white hound, with red spots and ears. I hollered at him and ran outside, but by then he was gone. A few plants were squashed or minced around the dog's shallow crater, but about this I could be philosophical: with all else on Farrell's mind, coming home to this much damage after a month posed no calamity.

Meanwhile, the sun was hitting the water just right, letting me see all the way down. Not a frog in sight. Nor had any muck built up on the bottom, which was formed of a single slate disk. On this had been finely chiseled three robed women surmounted by a rose, all surrounded by "Ad Matronas, Farrellus," with additional words buried under little stones. Kneeling, I submerged one arm to the shoulder, gritting my teeth against the cold until I brought up one of the stones, which had been polished smooth except for a petally irregularity on one side. Cupping it in my palm felt good before I realized it was an exact model of a kidney, with what must have been malignancy protruding. I shivered and flung it into the pool. It settled back among some few dozen just like it.

In anthropology classes I'd read that remoter corners of Christendom still fashioned crude votive offerings of afflicted body parts to local saints, along with prayers on potsherds begging for cures. Here in the suburbs the practice was showing its ancient roots. I was feeling queasy, and the coldness of the water hadn't left me. I stepped away from the pool and its appeal to the "matriarchs," out of the willow's shade, and into the sun.

At that second there was a crack like thunder, and a crash so loud it dizzied me. Where I'd just been standing, alongside the pool, was a massive willow bough, looking at that point like a major portion of the tree, and many times bigger than what would have sufficed to kill me. I walked trembling like a nonagenarian back to the house.

I sat at the table and finished my cold black coffee, gazing without focus out the window. In me was neither the strength nor the authority to have the bough removed. With a sickly grin I wondered if I'd courted this by assuming Farrell would come home to nothing worse than uprooted flowers. In any case, the last twelve hours spelled too much, too soon. Now, out of fairness to Farrell, I had to invade his sanctum, in quest of any kind of enlightenment to dissuade me from forfeiting my post and a month's pay. After all, July was almost over.

Still feeling shellshocked, I reentered the cellar, whose chill in my shaky condition numbed me as I sat poring through Farrell's books. References to "Lughnasad" were plentiful, and reading into them some meaning for myself, I feared that my mind had grown as susceptible to suggestion as my body to the cold. Lughnasad was a Celtic harvest festival, and indeed celebrated on August 1. Its pretext was the mythological marriage of sun-god and mother-goddess, and the yield of grain, held to be the fruits of this marriage, was honored by the sacrifice, whether in effigy or the flesh, of a "Corn King." Ideally, this king was dispatched three ways at once, "triple-killed," to ensure placation of the triple-natured goddess, though on this day her role as reaper won out over those of lover or mother. In any event, propitiation was a wise way to start August, which had been considered unlucky and unhealthy in general.

No denying it: Farrell, in apparent terminal straits, had invested faith, and mileage and money as well, in the graces of long-buried deities to grant him remission. Still, no matter how deep into fantasy desperation had pushed him, connivance on his part to make a sacrifice of me smacked strongly of paranoia.

On the other hand, arguing from Farrell's seeming premises, I'd been subject to the attentions of his "Matronae" while both asleep and awake. Not an hour had passed since they'd tried making a victim of me themselves!

If Farrell had been after a fatted calf, it's true that he couldn't have done better than me. I had no local family, no love life back in town. I would go back to no prearranged employment or even address, comfortable in the routine of crashing with friends till postings for sublets and campus temp work resettled me. Months could pass before I was missed. Sinking from sight would send no ripples, nor even inconvenience anyone. Suddenly three decades of the easygoing life had come to feel burdensome. In me, of course, as much as anyone else, was some expectation, however unfounded, of making a name for myself. Short of criminal scandal, though, where were my prospects at this late date?

At my age, Farrell had secured his doctorate, a publishing career, academic rank. No doubt we had each gone to our baccalaureates with comparable possibilities; but now I seemed to squint up at the heights he had already reached in his twenties. Housesitter was foremost on my list of accomplishments. I envied Farrell and admired what he had made for himself, though on any given day, a house and position and submitting to regular hours were not priorities. But hold on a minute! This paragon of respectable scholarship was trying to kill me, perhaps, and if not, he had still quit the well-lit path for some very shadowy sidetrack. And odds were that he was a goner. None of this, though, helped make up for the indirection of my own life.

With cold, creaky joints I rose from Farrell's desk, craving the sun I'd been shunning for weeks, but still in confusion over how to prepare for Farrell's return. The note on the door obliged me to pause. The note had been attributed to "M. R." Merritt Rooseweldt? Who else? Facing the bookshelves, I focused from spine to spine, seeking potential source for the quote. Why not see if Merritt had some advice? On the bottom shelf, a thin binding read *These Are My Woods,* followed by the name "Rooseweldt."

Apparently everything Merritt had needed to say fit within 100 uncut pages, large print, via vanity press in Maine, date of publication 1890. As for Farrell, bibliophile or not, it must have been his red pen circling passages.

Presuming these would be of most use to me, I copied them on scrap paper, and have them still: "While I have these woods, I have something of the old ways, and they have me . . ." "The doctors had as good as signed my death certificate, but I have outlived them all. Nature's blessings have made mockery of medical prediction, and no doubt health shall continue to come of calling these woods home . . ." "Old forces of the Earth, cloaked in whatever personalities the ancients perceived, feel near at hand, manifest almost, in these configurations of woods and lake and boulder-crowned ledge. One can well imagine, and almost wish to undertake, assemblage of Druid monuments in the groves and overlooks." Maybe rumors of dolmens had stemmed from this or another such casual mention by Merritt. Here, at least, was the inspiration for Farrell to come and petition divine cure. My mind roved back to that miter-shaped stone at the lake, and I wondered, had its carving been the work of Rooseweldt or Farrell? And what, apart from restored health, had prompted Merritt's claims of pagan gods hereabouts? If nothing else, these woods held long-term attraction for the desperate and gullible.

As for me, no plan beyond replacing Farrell's padlock had yet surfaced. A hardware store was at the same plaza as the A&P. Was further reprovisioning in order? For the first time in a while I figured out the date. Good God! It was July 31.

Despite the heat and my haste to catch the next bus, the cold in me would not be dislodged. The dappled sun through the bus window was hot but made me shiver. Only two explanations could account for this lingering chill. Was I coming down with something, or was I being poisoned? Either way, the icy pool and the drafty cellar could have lowered my resistance to the point of feeling ill effects. And if Farrell were out to kill me, sugar, salt, or some other staple could have contained some slow-acting agent. Farrell's return tomorrow made the onset of symptoms today all the more suspect. But would my concerns turn to nonsense on airing them with anyone? It would, at any rate, have been my first conversation all month.

I was glad no clerks offered assistance in the hardware store. At first, though people were loud and near, their words came across as gibberish. Something in my head seemed to need recalibration before I could speak or hear. Even after my tumblers of perception had fallen into place, as unceremoniously as ears popping on a plane, a sense of dissociation made me feel I was foreign or among foreigners. While I waited with new padlock in the checkout line, the old cashier was telling his old customer, "A damn shame, but no surprise. One or two every summer by this time."

"Yep. Couldn't have been napping more than a minute, but I open my eyes and there are the lifeguards, doing that human-chain thing hip-deep in the water. Always too late by then to do any good. I heard the kid would've been eight this week."

"Glad mine are all grown up. Too bad they can't just close that beach down. It's treacherous, that's what it is. Bottom suddenly gets deeper, or the water gets too cold too fast, nobody really knows."

At last it sank in that they were describing the far end of the lake that lay beyond Farrell's fence. With or without Farrell, Rooseweldt Woods seemed to demand annual sacrifice. A fresh wave of cold overtook me, and to my relief the cashier took no apparent notice of what felt like obvious trembling.

On the bus back I felt hemmed in, besieged, one step from defeat. It behooved me to assume the worst, to term any other course foolhardy. I looked out the window to try dispersing my malaise. Coming up ahead, in by no means wild country, was a deer-crossing sign, of a stag rearing in a yellow diamond. I blinked, and on second glance the sign read "Yield." The thought persisted that perhaps a month alone had been too long.

No reassurance was waiting back at the house. Rather, the door swung open at my approach. How could I have been so careless? An unlocked door was the cardinal housesitting sin, but backtracking through that feverish blur before catching the bus was impossible. No, I needed some faith in my own basic competence. I must have locked the door. So had Farrell made the early sneak-return I had half expected? Who else could have made an unforced entry, except the three potentially supernatural women from last night? No visible change greeted me in the kitchen or anywhere upstairs.

Padlock in hand, I heard nothing below from the topmost cellar step. Going down took subjective ages, between stopping to listen and trying to be soundless. I felt prepared, ready in spirit at least to face something, and a perverse letdown set in on meeting nobody all the way to the sanctum. The last door as I pushed it felt charged, as if with presence behind it, or anyway with my certainty of a presence.

But only one more unaccountable sight was waiting. From the rack of antlers on the fieldstone wall, a bunch of dry brown roses hung upside-down. They faded harmoniously into their background, but still, how could I have missed them twice so far? At the same time, if this were some offering to his goddesses, Farrell should have known better than to post them where they would announce his return to me. But why would the women have left the bouquet, unless their game all along had been to warn rather than menace me? Sparing me, on the other hand, seemed unlikely when their hunger for victims knew no scruples about drowning children.

I stared at the roses. To Rooseweldt they'd meant livelihood, a symbol for himself, a token of his long life and rejuvenation. They probably meant life and rebirth to Farrell too, but judging by the stones in the pool, the spread of petals also connoted his terminal growth, brought to divine attention in hopes of trading bad organ for good. A dead bouquet could bespeak either Farrell's stronger plea for remission or a favorable reply. For me the roses held no apparent grace, and on taking stock of myself, wintry numbness was in my fingertips, and weariness was pressing heavy upon me. Replacing the padlock felt pointless now. I dragged myself back upstairs.

At this stage, my last hope seemed to consist in my having been delusional all along: nervous strain and not poison dictated my leaden, shivering state as I crawled on up to the bedroom. Maybe so, but why take a needless risk by eating? And Farrell had flat-out declared his homecoming on August 1, but against any surprises I propped a chair up against the doorknob. Then I pulled a quilt from the cedar chest at the foot of the bed and lay down. Come what may, no foul play would make sense until Lughnasad proper, so I set the alarm for midnight. Finally, I drew the covers up to my chin. A little nap would help fight off whatever was assailing me.

Sleep at unaccustomed hours often brings wild, vivid dreams, but these were even more exceptional for going on and on, and for the constant awareness that I was dreaming. This was no help, though, as flight reflex forced me to bolt and bound and hide and bolt again, endlessly, while being hunted through the woods by Farrell. He had quiver and bow, and though he drew the bowstring he never shot, as if he foremost wanted to drive me somewhere. I was naked save for a crown of antlers, too tight on my brow for yanking off. After covering breathless miles to get merely from the house to the lake, I turned from staring stupidly at the miter-shaped stone back to forest canopy's black shadow. Within, nothing but Farrell's unblinking eyes were visible, round and bright, green and cold, doomed and unforgiving.

I woke up panicky. Slippery and reeking with sweat from head to toe, I threw off the covers. The alarm hadn't roused me; it was only 11:45. A cross-breeze from the window led my sight to the door. It was wide open, the chair beside it. Stock-still in shock at this, I listened. A car engine, wincingly loud in the country night, was idling in the driveway.

No lights had been on when I lay down, and whoever had moved the chair had kept the house dark. The new arrival had to be Farrell, and clean getaway under darkness was possible by leaving through one door while he entered by the other. A scent of roses like an invisible trail cut through my own ripe odor as I tiptoed downstairs, all the while picking the sticky cloth of my shirt and shorts off my skin. A surge of arousal had coincided with my first whiff of roses, but this I blamed on adrenaline in my hour of stress.

On the bottom step, I heard the front doorknob rattle. I scurried through the kitchen, hearing Farrell call, "Hello?" And then I cried out as my careless elbow sent a skillet crashing off the stovetop, as Farrell shouted my name and grumbled, "Where the hell is he?"

All at once I realized that maybe, just maybe, Farrell had left an ambiguous return date on his calendar pending earlier or later connecting flights. But to me, of course, he would give only the later date, to ensure home protection till he was back.

Sensible as these considerations were, they came too late to slow me down. Sooner safe than sorry, I was disappearing over the back fence just as another crash, as of a whole drawer of silverware, reached me.

A second slam of the back door announced Farrell in pursuit, and since it wasn't in him to jump fences, headstart advantage was mine while he dashed the long way around. But which way would he come? Running the wrong direction now would put us on collision course. From no certain place came huffing and breathless swears and rustling of leaves. I took off straight downslope, across the path, toward the lake.

I knew this was an ill-starred direction, but whichever way I tried to veer, moonlight up ahead shone briefly on a swatch of white shirt and a length of stainless steel. More than one Farrell appeared to be after me. I stopped short, arms windmilling once, twice, to steady me as I gaped down at my moonlit reflection. The chase to the water's edge, which had filled hours of dreamtime, was over in waking seconds.

The miter-shaped stone stood almost within reach. A wreath of roses, like those adorning sacrificial bulls in ancient friezes, was coiled on top of the stone. Fluttery motion to my left caught my eye. A bald old man, tall and gaunt as a mannerist icon, was waving me away and crying, "Shoo! Shoo!" It made me feel like endangered wildlife, and the old man was just how I'd pictured Merritt himself, back from the dead or from somewhere mapped only in myth. I did as he directed, until seconds later, heavy, skidding footfalls turned me around. From this distance, Farrell and the apparent Merritt were dressed alike. Red-faced Farrell, seemingly at the end of his tether, gave no sign of noticing "Merritt," but looked my way instead, starting to speak without slowing down. Whatever he was planning, the steak knife in his hand would go unused.

A loop of woody root growing out of the steep slope caught Farrell's foot. As he flew headlong, "Merritt" thrust lightninglike with a blade that could have been the twin of Farrell's. I heard the knife punch in and Farrell began to shriek, but his momentum carried him headfirst, with a sickening little popping sound, into the miter stone. I shut my eyes, then had to open them again or lose my balance. While they were closed, rose scent grew thick in my nose, and my sense of arousal doubled, whether in response to the perfume or the violence I couldn't say.

And in that time, "Merritt" had vanished and in his place were the three women, sunhats and all, looking at me as from disdainful height. Farrell lay face down in the shallow water, wedged between miter stone and water's edge, triple-killed by stabbing, concussion, and drowning. The oldest woman's face turned haglike when she grinned wide and reached with a snake-headed staff to lift the wreath from the stone and drop it on Farrell. As she did so, her moon-faced, big-boned companion told me, "You are no King of the Domain, little pretender." Between them, the young woman, with pleasing but big, horselike features, merely smiled, with what seemed both enticement and taunt. So they meant neither to warn me nor harm me; to use me was all. Farrell was who they wanted, and under the weight of the roses he sank from sight, in water that was no more than ankle-deep. When I looked up again, the women were gone, and my feeling of arousal was fading away.

What more to tell? Of course I stayed on in the house. I may be no king of the domain, but nobody has come to oust me. And the women may come back yet, whether in dreams or flesh, we beggars and house-sitters can't be choosers.

Anyway, what should I do away from here? If nothing else, Farrell taught me the futility of worldly striving. Look at all he had going for him, yet with one bad card, a diagnosis you could sum up on a cookie fortune, the whole deck was stacked against him. Might as well remain housesitter for a man who's a man no more.

Now I suppose you want me to "come downtown" with you, if that's still the expression. Very well, but I honestly don't see why you're making so much fuss over someone who'd be going or gone by now anyway. And besides, you'll never find the body. Why not? Because Farrell's here with me. There's been no murder; he's not dead. He turned up next day in his sanctum, and I've kept him in this shoe-box ever since, in the event of inquiries such as yours. You can see it's him, look at those bright green eyes. No mistaking them. His prayers were answered. He's healthy again. I, for one, have never heard of a snake with cancer.

Some Days Before Shadow Damsel

October 4

Found a crow unconscious down in the graveyard. Some asshole kid must've winged him with a beebee. Dragged old squirrel cage of Granddad's from barn attic onto screened-in porch. Crow can mend there in peace. Except for Ma. "What's that damn murder-bird doing here?" she demanded. Her name for crows. From allegedly seeing them stand on sparrows and peck their eyes out. Glaucoma takes its toll, but Ma can still i.d. birds. Unfortunately.

Nonetheless, crow stays. One repercussion of disease is that Ma no longer always has last word. Another is that I'm stuck here either until her medication works, or forever. Curse of an only child. Is there a bright side? Sure. Ma's a widow. Coming back here would've been all the worse some years ago, when Dad, bitter with all his debilitations, had still been around.

October 9

For several days the crow has huddled immobile, morose. Wings folded tight as if glued down. I've been sitting with him when not doing chores, errands, finances, all under Ma's milky but exacting eye. To persuade him I have his best interests at heart, I maintain reassuring monologue. About the weather (Indian summer in full swing), Ma (all the more ornery in hardship), our view from atop Bluestone Hill (second-growth woods, narrow road zigzagging past cellar holes of defunct relatives whose land we inherited, family plot containing those relatives, and beyond, flimsy tract houses of a bedroom "community" along the road that services the outside world). To me, crow makes no reply. From indoors, though, I hear him and cronies calling back and forth. Maybe with mutual solace, maybe discussing crow news.

So will crow rehab join the list of noble but lost causes my life has comprised? Solar power, hemp for industry, banning lawn chemicals, these and more afforded me brief careers in the aptly termed nonprofit sector. Still, the hell with banking or p.r. or any of those spiritual poisons Ma tried prescribing for me (of course, if I had been stuck with a straight job, Ma would've been minus a live-in caregiver; has she ever thought of that, I wonder?). But as for the matter at hand, will the crow just mope himself to death? Or at best, fly away neither knowing nor caring that without me he'd have been catbait? A waste of raw burger and leftover chicken, as Ma proclaims whenever she hears me open the fridge.

October 12

Progress! The crows must have decided I'm in their corner. For a few days they've frequented the gravel around the porch. Hopping about warily, but disinclined to fly unless Ma dimly catches their chessboard movements and storms out waving a broom. Happily, we must seem less alike to them than they to us. Seeing me alone never deters them from hanging around. Then again, maybe they imagine I'll scare up enough burger for everyone.

October 15

My sulking ward, with a show of nonchalance, started preening under one wing. Lightly at first. And then probing hard till a beebee plinked onto the cage floor. We looked from it to each other. "Away we go," I prophesied.

October 16

Was brushing my teeth this morning when a barrage of crowcalls rattled the windows. Instantly Ma was hollering, "Emmett! Emmett!" in that tone that always makes me want to scream, "Shut up!" Instead, I yelled, "Wait a minute!" Spraying the mirror with toothpaste foam. I let it stay there. Not my fault, dammit!

The crow in the cage was sitting on a crossbar, flapping impatiently. A dozen others were cawing from branches and the roof of the porch. Ma no doubt feared murder-bird onslaught à la Hitchcock and hung back in front hall. I opened porch door and cage door, and out scudded the bird. They all took wing to apparent reunion in some crows-only setting. I felt a bit abandoned and sighed.

By suppertime Ma had regained sangfroid enough to resume giving me predictable grief. Just like me to waste time on that no-good murder-bird! And what was I going on about with him all day? Told her crows were reputed to be oracular. Gifted with the second sight. I was just trying to get his advice. Oh, really? And what pearls had he cast? "Oh, the usual," I tried joking. "Avoid junk bonds and follow your heart." Well, so much for having a conversation, she harrumphed. So much for having a sense of humor, I said to myself.

Downhill from there. Maybe if I weren't so flip, she scolded, I'd be married or at least have a girlfriend. Dinner half-eaten, I abruptly cleared my place at the table. No use arguing that every relationship since high school had been scuttled by that eventual, inevitable intro to the folks. Even without Dad's forthright flatulence and ghastly cigar smoke, Ma was formidable enough, between hair-trigger temper and pathological refusal to let in fresh air (dating from our purchase of an air-conditioner twenty years ago).

But even had home and folks been more presentable, I had to admit my overriding inadequacy as a "good catch." Genteel poverty now, no prospects in sight. Nobody I'd want would likely want me. Love me for myself, we all say. But has that self ever been separable from solvency?

Returned to dining room for Ma's dishes. She sat stiffly. Hands in lap. Eyes downcast. Looking severe, but saying nothing. Seemed to have stopped eating at the same time I had. Not one to back down from a snit. Not without reciprocating. Then again, poor Ma! No remedy for disappointments in an only child.

October 17

Halloween in the offing. As foretokened by leaden overcast, brown leaves rattling on the maples, depressing five o'clock sunsets. This time of year, Bluestone Hill comes into its own. Even though it's always spooky around here. Ever since I could remember, phantom footsteps upstairs, phantom knocking on the back door. Just the house settling, Ma and Dad always said. Ball lightning during summer cloudbursts, notorious for dropping in via chimney and bouncing wildly from room to room until shattering against a wall. And in spiritualism's salad days, my great-grandfather and some confrères summoned something that bypassed them and instead shook the bed where skeptic great-grandmother was trying to nap; finally, the frustrated entity gave up on her (she had reportedly repelled it by snarling, "You don't exist, so get out of here!"), picked up great-grandfather's séance table, and dashed it to the floor, giving him and his circle a thrill that cured them ever after of table-tipping.

A century later, I am no less a product of Bluestone Hill. A coalescence of the local color. After putting up with some hours of Ma's tight-lipped sulk last night, I went to bed half-guilty, half-annoyed. Regarded the evocative bedroom shadows, unchanged since earliest memory, thrown by toy chest, dresser, curtains, lamps. Skulls leered, spiders reached out, beasts crouched. But none budged, no matter how long I stared.

If I weren't so flip I'd have a girlfriend, eh? Had that been how I'd lost the last one? How long ago had that been? Her face had grown vague, interchangeable with that of other exes. A longing for love or sex overtook me. Not worth splitting hairs between the two, here in the emotional outback. Where neither stood a chance of materializing. My eye still roving among the shadow images stopped short. In the jumble of my clothes on bedside chair, a striking new likeness seemed to return my gaze. A thin face, nose and chin almost cartoonishly long and sharp, round eyes set wide apart. A cajoling smile. Almost witchy overall; bemusingly female. I wondered how kissing that extraordinary face would feel. But of course it kept its distance as long as I stayed awake.

October 20

Vacuumed first thing this morning. Then to clear my lungs of churned-up dust, stood out back surveying swamp and forest from atop the weatherworn outcrop that gave the hill its name. Missed the crow. Wondered how to fill the gulf of idle hours. Heard glass breaking and ran homeward.

Ma was in the dining room. Had tried asserting her independence in the worst way. Despite her prohibition on ever opening windows, unquestioned ritual dictates: screen windows shall be lowered and storm windows put up every spring, and screen windows shall go up and storm windows down every fall. In attempted fulfillment of which, Ma had fumbled a storm window, stubborn and warped, out of its tracks. And to its destruction on the gravel driveway. Ma had sat down and was crying softly, every so often railing, "Shit, shit, shit."

"It's a big waste of time, but let me do the rest for you," I sighed. Proceeded without further ado. What more to say? And how awkward just to stand around while Ma emoted.

"Do you think I'm too old?" she called after me.

"Too old for what?" I replied without stopping. Her question made me squirm. Without my knowing or wanting to know why.

Afterwards, took a cardboard box and disposed of the broken glass, all pieces obligingly within the fallen metal frame. Big kris-like shards, modest crescent moons, little triangles. With brush and dustpan cleared rhinestone-sized bits off the gravel. Anything smaller escaped among the pebbles, telltale sparkle dulled by the day's grayness. Then realized that my eyes were searching within my own shadow, in the way they had within the shadows of my bedroom. What was I seeking? That face again? Was alarmed that a bunch of wrinkles in fabric had made that strong an impression on me. How hard up was I?

Got to my feet. A crow stood with the box between us. His blinkless look shifting from the contents to me. Must have swooped in while I was focused on glass-picking.

"Nothing for you in there," I said. "Bad for crows. If you're craving hamburger, I'm sorry. Empty pockets."

He took this in stride. Must have been the crow in my care, because he hopped one step closer to me and proclaimed, "Away we go!" Then he took off. Was that supposed to mean something? Oracular bird, indeed. Merely repeating my words to him? No, such a Bluestone Hill thing to say must have meant something more.

October 21

Should be spooked but I'm perversely carefree. Last night in bed, the customary lurid shadowscape met my inspection. And though my bedside jumble of clothes was altogether different, the shadow damsel was there again too. After my initial surprise, as irrationally entrancing as before. And as coyly unwavering, for as long as I stayed awake.

This morning Ma asked if I knew what day it was. Tuesday? Best I could do. Ma was indignant. How could I have forgotten Dad's birthday? Every year since his death, Ma had doomed a pot of geraniums by transplanting it down by the grave. And had I refused to honor this duty of sentiment, Ma would have risked pneumonia and broken limbs to stumble down the hill herself. But that face of shadows was still on my mind. Enhancing my mood. Justifiably or not. So off I went, affably.

In the graveyard, mission accomplished, I stood up and brushed crumbled leaves and dirt off my knees. The whole point of commemorative flowers was lost on me, since I had to believe that the soul or spirit or whatever had better to do than watch its former husk rot away. Especially Dad, who'd held no perceptible love for his own body or for life in general. And if Dad's unbodily essence was off exploring the cosmos, then who was supposed to enjoy the geraniums, in that brief time before they froze?

Surely not the damn kid whose empty box of beebees I kicked as I loitered among the tombstones. Maybe from this box had come the ammo that had felled my only local friend. When I was a kid I'd never strayed outside the yard. Deterred by parental tales of crazy people in the woods. And now who did this delinquent think he was, trespassing on my family property, where I hadn't dared go at his age? And flouting his disrespect for life in the unofficial sanctuary of my own land? Let me catch him, I'd show him crazy people in the woods!

Behind me, near enough to hit with a Frisbee, was the chain-link fence that marked the back perimeter of tract housing. Offputting as the march of suburbanization was, backyard floodlights had probably saved the graveyard from vandalism. Bristle as I might at gun-toting brats.

Names on stones from recent decades were largely unfamiliar. No close family, ours. But deeper into the past, on into the 1700s, the more I knew. Courtesy of a great-aunt (buried elsewhere) who'd filled my boyish head with ancestral lore. Quaint names, prefixed "wife of" and "daughter of," faint with weathering and framed by lichen, rang distantly with old associations. Yes, I'd fantasized about what they'd looked like. That they'd been pretty. That their pretty ghosts had appeared in attic or cellar. And that they'd been subjects of whatever amorous daydreams a seven-year-old could concoct. Uninhibited, in the sense that nobody had acquainted me yet with the concept of "incest."

And from latter-day vantage, much could be said for a ghost lover. To whom else would lack of affluence, lack of status, lack of worldly ambition mean so little? Pregnancy not an issue, nor physical deterioration. As I trudged back up the hill, shadow damsel came to mind. Looked forward to seeing her again.

October 28

Aloof but consistent. Unvarying in detail every night, no matter how my clothes are piled on the chair. As if she's superimposed on the spot. Her presence soothes even as I grow more anxious for closer encounter with her. Scientific curiosity urges me to hide my clothes one night and see if and where the face would surface. But why trifle with, why risk destroying, what I have of her? Especially as hers is the only heartening influence on the homestead, much as the convalescing crow had been.

Asked Ma if she wanted me to buy Halloween candy, should any of the suburban kids venture up the hill. "Hell no! We pull all the shades and turn off the lights in the front rooms." A truly Yankee Halloween tradition.

Nonetheless, I wouldn't feel right without carving a pumpkin and stuffing a leaf dummy. Paying proper respects to my favorite holiday. These things I did faithfully as a kid. And even though this house, neighborless back then, had seen no trick-or-treating, Ma used to indulge me with store-bought costumes and masks for around the house.

This afternoon, buying groceries at the plaza included a pumpkin for myself. Afterwards, seeking inspiration for a jack-o'-lantern face, was thankful that Ma never threw anything out. Knew exactly on what shelf in the closet in spare bedroom my masks would still be stacked. Big-brained orange Martian, bristly outraged werewolf, leering Viking with horned helmet. Fondly cradled the brittle eggshell plastic. But more impressive was an over-the-head gorilla mask of flaccid, markedly unstable polymers. Leprous holes marred cheeks and forehead, and further gashes came of peeling the mask from the shelf, to which it had fused. Decay had made this the prize of the bunch. Much scarier than it had been when intact, and what's more, it was the only item that still fit an adult face.

The Martian, though, was best suited for pumpkin carving. En route to the porch with pumpkin, newspapers, and knife, I passed Ma watering the plants on pantry windowsill. "I can do this myself again!" she announced. "Haven't spilled a drop! That's good, don't you think?"

"Let's hope so." I didn't really know how good it was. And didn't want to raise false hopes by adding to premature enthusiasm. Told her I'd be out making a jack-o'-lantern.

"That's what you did when you were a kid!" she yelled disapprovingly. Without answering, I pressed on.

Sat cross-legged on the papers. Unmindful of the lengthening shadows. Cut what seemed a semblance of buggy round Martian eyes, bulbous nose, lipless grimace. Done at dusk, I fetched candle and matches. Stooped and lit candle within hollow pumpkin, stood up to let sudden dizziness clear. Squinted bewildered. Knew what face I'd put on the pumpkin. But candlelight cast onto newsprint the wavering face of shadow damsel. As if favoring me with surprise visit. Or checking up on me for some reason.

Resounding pop of a beebee gun distracted me. From the graveyard, all right. Possessed by righteous wrath, rushing to keep up with my resolve, I bounded upstairs. By chance I was wearing black denim jacket and jeans. Perfect! I stashed gorilla mask under jacket. To Ma, fixated on talk radio in the kitchen, I hollered, "When you want dinner?"

She professed to be in no hurry. Told her I'd get started shortly. Left it at that. So she'd harbor the illusion that I was still somewhere in the house.

Halfway across the yard, a voice from above startled me. Crow sat on tree limb overhead, whole body dipping like a seesaw with every caw. On seeing he had my attention, he croaked, "Away we go!" Inscrutable mission accomplished, he took off.

No time to dwell on that now! I barreled down the hill. Shunning the road. Zigzagged from tree to concealing tree. A stone's throw from the graveyard, started glimpsing a chubby nine-year-old with baggy pants, garish nylon blazer, a buzzcut. He was sitting in virtual fetal position, legs drawn up, his back against the iron railing. Every few seconds, renewing the nimbus of cigarette smoke around him. His gun propped up beside him.

Night was falling fast. Wind herded dead leaves across the ground. Impeccable conditions for sneaking up. On with the gorilla mask. Took a deep breath and sidled from behind the last tree. Tiptoed over.

Here was exactly the kind of obnoxious little bastard who'd become an obnoxious adult bastard. Chance of a lifetime, to strike a blow at boorishness! Adrenaline egging me on, I threw back my arms and shoved the brat onto his face with a force almost as surprising to me as to him.

"Don't move!" I barked as he began turning his head. "Don't look at me! I got your gun."

In truth I hadn't. Grabbed it while he sprawled unmoving. Breathing hoarsely. "Don't move, you little shit!" I savored saying that. Aimed at the ground next to him and pulled the trigger.

Bang! The kid understandably couldn't help scrambling, with a glance back as he stumbled into a headstone. From my side of the fence I lunged and growled, brandishing the gun by the barrel. Even in failing light, my half-rotten mask got a screech out of the kid. "And leave the dead in peace!" A good afterthought, but didn't occur to me for a few seconds. Not sure he even heard it.

The gun I swung over my head and down against the rail. The stock broke off with a dull clang. Left the pieces there.

Exhilarated, made my furtive way from tree to tree back uphill. First thing, mask was restored to shelf. Ma, still glued to radio, gave no nod of greeting. As if I'd never left. Proud as I was of traumatizing the little crow-shooter, had to psyche myself for possible inquiries re the attack. Throughout edgy evening, rehearsed the lie that I'd been housebound all along. But phone and doorbell never rang.

October 29

Slept as well last night as could have been expected. Which is to say, hardly at all. A lot of lingering excitement had to fade, and worries of legal repercussions. But that was the least of it. After tossing and turning for hours, rolled over to face the extra pillow bunched against the wall. Found her face an inch away, in pillowcase folds. Blinked in confusion, yet rallied swiftly and thought, Why not kiss her, she's right there, what's the harm? But on refocusing, she was gone.

My bulging eyes darted back and forth. Till motion at the window diverted me. Was a draft stirring the curtains? In any case, wrinkles in the faded cotton indicated her face, and more. Slight flares of breast and hips, indent of waist. Torso bisected where the curtains met. Arms stretching toward curtains' lower corners. Gentle billowing of fabric made the arms seem to beckon. Or did they bid me open the curtains?

The second I sat up, shadow damsel sank away. I dashed over to part the curtains, wondering if she'd be on the other side. But I surveyed only faint moonlit lay of ledge and swamp. Then into earshot came talk and laughter. Not from anywhere in sight.

Put on pants and shirt, and padded past Ma's room to the study at the front of the house. Downhill, no doubt in graveyard, minuscule red lights bobbed like fireflies. Cigarettes or something else, not that I cared what. Voices, a little louder from here, were young, male. Of unknown number. Apparently, homeowners nearest the graveyard weren't around. Had shadow damsel wanted me to break up the party? Forgoing mask this time, I got shoes and jacket. Slipped out back door and stalked among the trees. Without plan, or anything more in mind than resentment at more trespassers already.

Halfway there, heard a bottle break, with whooping and laughter afterwards. Raucousness gave me pause. Rather than move closer, I cut across hillside till I found a maple whose double trunks separated conveniently at eye level. Affording me a clear line of sight to the intruders.

My wavering nerve shorted out. Four big, bull-necked high school jocks were blundering about the gravestones. Well en route to leaving vomit as well as broken glass behind. Too many of them and too big for me to chase out. Odds strongly favored my getting clobbered. What had my unbodily friend expected me to do? Or maybe I'd done it, by realizing that my position, here or anywhere, was untenable and could only get worse. The bullies were too strong and numerous. Whether individuals trampling on my values, or corporations burying my causes. Any preemptive strike on my part was more than offset by those whom I dared not challenge. I was slinking safely back up the hill. But where to go from there? Unseen, unheard, unsuspected by those I'd thought to disperse, I was as good as a ghost already, wasn't I?

Back in the house, took to my bed. For subjective ages, looked from curtains to pillow to clothing at bedside, and thought, What the hell, come and get me. Haunts that we both were, of one kind or another. Why not, with nothing to hold me here since Ma, after all, said she was getting better. But shadow damsel wasn't going to make it so easy for me. Withheld herself, for as long as my eyes ransacked the room.

And all today, stumbled around in a fog. Giddy. Knowing how ridiculous it was to feel lovesick. But that made no difference. Was her conspicuous absence after my foray meant to make my mooning worse?

Late afternoon, drew skullish face on a paper bag and rummaged up old clothes. Then raked together leaves in the front yard. Stuffing for the traditional Halloween dummy. Kneeling on the lawn, shoving leaves into shirtsleeves, I was still fixated on how to bring shadow damsel out of the shadows. If she were real at all, then appearing on the verge of Halloween must have had some bearing on whatever she was. Ghost? Devil? From college days floated a line from an old folk-rock tune: "For tonight is Halloween, and the faerie folk ride . . ." Was she the Queen of Faerie? That was a lot to hope for. In any case, Halloween would bring us together, if any time would. Provided I could do my part on the conjure front.

Greatgrandpa hadn't been our only amateur medium. In my own childhood, Halloween usually included spooking myself reading Poe or Bradbury or "true" Hans Holzer ghost encounters. A goggle-eyed, sensitized state would ensue for a few days. Wherein I believed myself a lightning rod for the occult if I dwelt on it for over a second.

And in high school I "went public" with this talent. Inveigled my few misfit friends one foolhardy Halloween into hearing me read scary stories in barn attic. An ideal setting, between wind rattling windows and the clutter covered with dropcloths. And beyond my flashlight, pitch darkness cut off escape by the stairs. Sitting hunkered in a circle, my friends made free with wiseass remarks at first, but as they began following my words, they quieted down.

Everyone "knew better," but group mood still grew edgy. I was near the end of a Bradbury weird tale. Of a bedridden boy whose dog literally wakes the dead. As the dog in the story began baying, revenant in tow, howling started up somewhere outside. We had no dog. And there were no other houses down the hill yet, so no other dogs were at hand. But I stalwartly read on, till nervous giggling made me look up. Someone told me to cut it out. A slow, steady knocking was coming from unseen wall. Which I'd heard and dismissed in passing as some-one trying in too obvious a way to be funny. "You're not doing that?" I asked all around. Nobody was. I shared in the general urge to bolt. For the sake of dignified retreat, I wrapped up the last few lines, and we cleared out as soon as my flashlight located the stairs.

Whatever our receptive mood had aroused took weeks to calm down. My folks kept complaining of lights in the barn that no one had turned on. And the sporadic knocking of nobody at the back door continued until I vowed out loud never again to enter the barn at night.

Happily, the barn plays no needful part in my ghost-raising. The cellar, for instance, was always too spooky to accommodate boyhood Halloween readings. Day or night, the least little creak from dark recesses was enough to send my young legs flying back to the safer surface world. Where better to try and draw my immaterial girl out of the void?

This resolved, I blinked and looked around. Unreasonably surprised that I was still kneeling in the yard. And proceeding on autopilot to stuff the leaf dummy. All limbs, firmly packed. Cuff ends knotted up. Skull-faced plastic bag had ballooned into plausible likeness of a head. I stood up in the gathering murk to appraise my handiwork so far.

This time, crow presence in peripheral vision failed to surprise me. He stalked over to the plastic bag head. With sudden spread of wings like opening a cape, he lunged. Destroyed magic marker eyes in a few decisive pecks. Paused long enough to croak, "Away we go!" Then grabbed the bag in his beak and took off. Dumping leaf brains in a loose swath. I couldn't help reading this as an ill omen for my adventure in conjuring. But never considered letting it stop me. Even if I now felt aversion to working any further on the scattered body parts around me.

October 30

Whoever it is whose image I'm receiving, I suspect that she or it "adjusted" me last night for the sake of better signal. In rather the informal fashion of kicking the TV set. Was brushing my teeth at bedtime. That coarse connect-the-dots of hardened toothpaste spray caught my eye for the first time in weeks. No heat of the moment lingered there any longer. Suddenly noticed that the stuff didn't really look very nice, did it? On the edge of the bathtub, a sponge was weighed down by a bowl of soapbar nubs that Ma claimed she wanted to use but never did. With damp sponge, squeaked the mirror clean. But in putting the sponge back, my wet hand slipped with the bowl.

Sending soap shards across the tiles, under the sink. Took this in stride and bent under the sink, reaching for an errant nub. "Emmett!" cried a voice. In need, but not pleading. All around me, but from nowhere. My head bobbed up and cracked against the sink. "Shit!" I yelled.

Got all the stray soap in hand. Mashed it with vengeful palm into the bowl. Then stood up slowly and waited for the ache and throbbing to subside. Rasped "Shit!" a few more times for good measure.

Went to bed feeling like my eyes were jammed a teeny bit to one side, that one ear was lower than the other. Mischievous shadow damsel! Who else? Even if nothing marked the voice as especially feminine. Even if the amount of personality that carried hollowly across the dimensions were merely that of switchboard operator, of newscaster. Kept asking myself, Why the hell play this trick on me?

On cue, an answer. Chill breeze hit my face. Raised goosebumps beneath the sheets. No weak household draft, this. And with it came scents. Of ripe earth, low tide, old piss. Nothing out of the ordinary to be seen. No sign of shadow damsel in cloth or clutter. But my bump on the head seemed to have opened the door a crack between her environment and mine. And based on that, her impulse to emigrate was understandable. I wanted her and I wanted to help her. These urges were hopelessly mixed together. So what? As the strong air from elsewhere kept blowing in, its effect was relaxing. Despite unsavoriness. Sleep seemed the right thing to do.

Woke up this morning plagued by the question that always besets me, usually sooner than later, in a relationship. Would she cease wanting me as soon as she had me? And did she really have any interest in me beyond my usefulness to herself?

These considerations persisted in hovering nearby, even when Ma came up with her most distracting, offbeat behavior yet. Late afternoon, she called me into the dining room. From God knew where, she had produced a stack of my childhood board games. Her medication really must have been helping her vision. She'd picked out "Sorry." Had set out board, cards, pieces for two players.

"Do you remember how we used to play these games all the time?" Ma asked. Outwardly chipper, but failing to hide a beseeching undertone. "Back every night practically, when your bedtime was 8:30."

"Yeah, I remember," I said. Lump forming mysteriously in my

throat. Partway from nostalgia, but more because there was something pathetic going on. "Back when I was six or seven, I guess."

Ma pulled the chair nearest her away from the table. "Here, sit down and play. Like we used to."

What had come over her? Two days ago she'd accused me of being childish for carving a jack-o'-lantern. And now this?

Sat down. Went along with her. Saying little, afraid I'd start crying. Was this how best she could think to make things better between us, the way they had been when I was a little kid, but not since? Maybe feeling sorry for her was the next best thing to getting along with her again. Maybe a first step in the right direction. I won after a close game. And even if we didn't talk much for the rest of the day, we didn't fight about anything, either.

After supper, took a shower. Which shadow damsel made the most of, not to end my doubts about her, but certainly to sidetrack them. As soon as I turned off the water, the air grew cold, of course. But stark influx of earthy smell made me pause. Found myself hoping for something; unable to say what, exactly. I slid back the shower curtain. Steam had condensed into roiling chaos of thick mist. In which something moved. Drifting, toward me. Here was what I wanted, wasn't it? All the same, trembled and had difficulty holding my ground. Her naked form, according to my narrow gaze, was defined by clinging droplets. But I could see through her as easily as through the rest of the mist, and her face was as featureless as weathered wood. Her arms were stretching out to clasp me.

Still standing in the tub, I weakly raised my arms at the elbows. At the last second, imagined her skin taut like that of a balloon. Or that she would pass right through me as an icy wave. I wanted to feel her around me. But braced myself, jaws clenched, in case of painful surprise.

She floated like a jellyfish past the side of the tub. I took one involuntary step back. Her body pressed full-length against mine, her face closed in on mine, her hands reached back to spread across my shoulder blades. I felt coolness upon my skin, but she was warmer than the cold air around us. Then, instead of feeling flesh or anything solid, I became acutely aware of countless tiny droplets, which had formerly given her shape, running more slowly than gravity would have had it down my back, over my lips, down my chest and below. Each drop felt alive, provocative. I must have closed my eyes without meaning to, as I now found myself opening them. With no face, weatherworn or otherwise, before me. Nothing at all of her, nothing unusual, was to be seen. But I still felt the last drops of her hanging from body hair and then rolling off my ass, down my legs, across my feet, reluctant to drain away, almost tickling. No matter how gratified I felt, couldn't help realizing that this was a tease. A manipulation. Meaningless as a token of good faith. But effective, in that she had given enough of herself to outweigh any other considerations. And though nothing had happened to satisfy me in any conventional way, still, I was satisfied.

Went to bed feeling more alive than I had since coming back here. Could have had the enjoyment of myself, but held back out of a certain conviction (which had always been right in bygone relationships) that consummation was just around the corner. For tomorrow was Halloween.

October 31

First thing this morning, Ma broke that bond of sympathy she had forged between us only yesterday. I woke to what could have passed for ballpeen onslaught on my windowsill. Followed by a thud that shook the wall.

I lurched out of bed and pushed aside the curtains. Just as a big black shadow sprang from view. And another thud, right below the window, made me skip back. From somewhere on high, I heard, "Away we go!"

I threw on pants and ran downstairs. Sure enough, Ma was misusing improved vision by lobbing rocks at my friend the crow, who'd been making noisy bid for my attention.

"What are you doing?" I hollered from the porch, shirtless and teeth chattering in the cold early light. Ma had been about to let fly with another stone.

"I'd like to kill that damn bird!" she fumed. "He was trying to break that window!"

"No he wasn't! Why must you talk that way?" I scolded. "You were the one about to break a window!"

The crow, meanwhile, was watching us from gable end. When our eyes met, he repeated, "Away we go!" And finally flapped away.

"Taking my side against that murder-bird's," Ma muttered. Flung down the stone, disgusted.

Later in morning, hung up wash on clotheslines down cellar. We'd always had a washing machine. Same one, in fact, as far back as I could recall. But a drier had always been deemed too extravagant. And so the week's laundry, the bulk of it Ma's, went up in a cold, damp quadrangle around the spot I felt would be most apt for the evening conjure. This room had a window but seemed most deep-set in earth because it was farthest from the stairs. Here I always felt closest to fight-or-flight response to the unseen, even with sunbeams bursting through the window. Yes, this had to be the trysting place.

Standing under bare light bulb at room center, I scanned the white cotton surfaces around me, but shadow damsel did not emerge from incipient wrinkles. What better time to encourage me with a beckoning glimpse? Was sobered into wondering if maybe nothing would happen later. If maybe I were just up to my eyes in self-beguilement.

A round of knocking from the wall destroyed this line of thought. Briefly took me back to that crowning moment of high school séance in the barn. Then I snapped back into the present. Relieved to recognize the banging of crow beak on windowsill.

I saw the crow in silhouette, blinding sunlight behind him, in what showed of the window between two drying bed sheets. A second later, a fall of water, followed by enameled basin clanging against ground, sent crow scurrying. From what sounded like the second floor, Ma shrilled, "And stay away, goddamn murder-bird!" So far I'd been a willing, if uncomprehending, receiver of crow advice. And had found Ma's attitude disagreeable at best. But now I heard myself yell out the window, "Stop trying to save me!" And felt embarrassed. Not at Ma or anyone overhearing me. But because only this instant had it occurred to me that maybe all the crow was after was a handout. As days in a cage had taught him to expect.

Still, suppose crow and shadow damsel partook of nothing more unusual than the extent of my boredom here? Halloween was my favorite day all the same. And too many years had passed in which I hadn't managed any kind of observance. On Bluestone Hill, though, what better did I have to do? Even if female semblance had never enticed me, the cellar, scary stories in hand, would have been my inevitable destination. Right?

Only at dusk did Ma acknowledge it was Halloween, by enacting her plan to give the house a dark and deserted face. Restricting light, my jack-o'-lantern included, to the kitchen. Cooked what Ma wanted. A can of corned beef hash and a side of boiled broccoli with Cheez Whiz. Would have lobbied for a more memorable meal on this night. After which perhaps everything would be different. But Ma hadn't seemed so cross in days. Stabbing at her food. Chewing spitefully. Her glower fixed upon the portable TV at the other end of the kitchen table. Apparently absorbing the action on the screen.

"Ma, your medication still working all right?"

"Not as well as before. Not today."

"When's your next appointment with the doctor?"

"Next Monday!" A sharp outburst. As if it were none of my business.

Nothing more was said that evening that could have passed for conversation. The same person who'd wanted to play a children's board game yesterday had no comment on the pumpkin head glowing on the counter.

The clock over the fridge read eight. Trick-or-treaters were increasingly unlikely. But Ma refused to let down her guard. Voiced a preference for being cooped up in bed rather than in the kitchen, and went on upstairs.

The field was mine! With Ma none the wiser as to my agenda. I felt like the adolescent I had been when last living at home. Sneaking off on missions of transgression, behind authority's dormant back. To do nothing worse than watch Late Show horror classics at near-inaudible volume on a school night. Or try a nightcap of the old man's assuredly horrid cheap German wine (no harm, maybe improvement, and never any paternal suspicion when water replaced wine). Not till now, on the brink of middle age, was I getting around to the grand teenage coup of secret assignation.

Left candle to gutter in the pumpkin. Fetched flashlight and Poe. Had chosen safe bets for spooking myself. "Premature Burial," "Facts in the Case of M. Valdemar." "House of Usher" for backup if necessary.

Was giddy with a trick-or-treater's sort of anticipation. Except that I abstained from thinking about what I was going to get. Insofar as prediction felt foolhardy. Opened the cellar door quickly to keep it from creaking. Then tiptoed down the stairs, though they of course creaked no matter what. From upstairs had not turned on any lights down here. Wanted nothing to dilute the dead-of-night atmosphere. What point in doing this halfway? Flashlight was sole guide. Grimaced with certainty that Ma couldn't be trusted to keep fresh batteries in this thing. But too late to think other than, So far, so good.

In my throat, a hot, tingling sensation. Made taking a deep breath difficult. How my flesh informed my mind that a fight-or-flight situation was indeed in progress. My feet kept moving. On autopilot. Stepping soundlessly, as seemed incumbent on me, through rooms as soundless as vacuum. Past washing machine, past furnace, past stacked-up firewood for a fireplace we hadn't used in decades. Then through the doorway into the back room. Where laundry seemed like curtains around a bower. Whiteness of cotton dazzling in the flashlight beam. In my efforts to tread softly, my feet had come to feel heavy. As if I were on ocean floor or in some condition already other than earthly norm.

Crossing the perimeter of damp wash I gave a start, primed for some surprise. But nothing was waiting. Slowly lowered myself to the cold cement floor, paying especial attention to the back of my neck, as if I were moving into position for some coup de grâce. I took note of the overhead lightbulb. In case of trouble, I wanted something to which I could resort immediately, and if not the light, then what? A way to keep panic or paralysis at bay, that was foremost.

Flashlight in left hand, book in right. With its spine between my knees. My splayed fingertips holding the pages down. I began to read. In no time at all, acutely aware of the sound of my voice. Loud, grating against the silence. But as I read, the silence more than held its own. Soon became oppressive, as I listened in vain for extraneous sounds. Of the house settling, the furnace kicking in, the wind hitting the windows. When nothing kept happening, the silence took on the status of a presence. Catching and swallowing my voice as soon as it passed these impromptu curtains. And why presume that such flimsy walls could keep the silence out? Silence, after all, was what I had felt doomed to, ever since my nighttime retreat from the family plot.

"Premature Burial," with its lengthy preamble about "true" live interments, felt all too apt down here. Then one after the other came the phrases, "the silence like a sea that overwhelms," and "our hopeless portion is that of the really dead." Echoing my recent sentiments, text seemed like a signal bounced back from some outermost space to let me know that someone was out there. Far be it from me to care if these perceptions would have seemed to anyone else like warning signs of schizophrenia. Of closer concern to me was the scent of ripe air, as odd now as it had been in the shower. Conveying to me that events had been set into motion. And though the ending of "Premature Burial" was anticlimactically happy, the very last words warned, "sepulchral terrors cannot be regarded as altogether fanciful . . . but they must sleep, or they will devour us . . ." This was actually good for an erotic charge. As maybe to be expected in an evening already so bereft of good judgment.

On to "M. Valdemar." And though the story (of a man mesmerized on his deathbed to retain awareness after death) held no sexual interest whatsoever, my hankering for shadow damsel increased, as tidal odor grew thicker. And a chill began sinking into my hands and face. As I realized that a flow of air had been bearing down on me. But from where? Everything on the clothesline hung as still as ever.

I read on without trying to follow the story. Sounding the words without comprehension. Perceiving only that the cold draft from nowhere had broken down into narrow streamlets that were licking my ears, my neck, my wrists. Cold but pleasurable.

And into the tidal scent had come an element of smoke. As if of roasting meat, and then of burning paper as well. But from sound of any kind I remained cut off. Till that point in the story when "there issued from the distended and motionless jaws" the voice of the deceased M. Valdemar, which seemed to come "from a vast distance, or from some deep cavern within the earth." Sounding no less remote, I heard, "Emmett! Something's on fire! You trying to burn the house down? Where are you?"

"Down here!" I called. Reluctant, resentful. Not budging yet. Not wanting to know right now if I had set the house on fire.

Creak of cellar door opening. "You left the candle lit in that damned pumpkin! And it scorched a big hole right through the side! There's smoke and melted wax all over the counter!" With a click, light from the stairway broke in, wan as 5 A.M. To my dismay, rather than simply deliver a message from upstairs, Ma had to clamber down with it. "What are you doing down here anyway?"

In the middle of that question, something started knocking on the wall. Startling me, taking me all the way back to high school séance. Then I snapped almost all the way back to the present. To what had been going on this morning. The crow again! And this time, by the sound of it, loath to let up until the window broke. So unnatural, for either Ma or a "murder-bird" to be up at this hour! I took red-faced offense that on all sides, I was surely about to be thwarted.

I said nothing aloud. But my desire to be rid of whatever stood between shadow damsel and myself seemed to erupt into something outside as well as inside me. As if words just spoken were hanging in the air. No longer audible but lingering as obstinate vibrations. Or as the spark to set off chain reaction.

What followed was predictable at first. Crow beak shattered glass, while Ma, standing at the doorway with the clothesline between us, demanded, "Emmett? You in there?" Then she squawked or maybe the crow did as it flapped in and over me, barely clearing the line. I heard something about "murder-bird." Not surprisingly. But one broken pane couldn't account for the cold draft turning into icy gusts. Or for my ears popping as if from change of altitude. Then with thunder-crack and storm roar, the bedsheet in front of me flew at me like a hatch being blown. It smacked me onto my back and dropped over me like a net. The wind drove it down against me. Getting me more snarled up, the harder I tried freeing myself.

I could hear nothing meaningful. Due to rustle of smothering linen as much as the hard wind from elsewhere. And I was too busy fighting the sheet to be afraid, or shocked, or sorry yet. Garbled voices, of crow, of Ma, of the wind, no telling which was which, swept in and out of hearing. Surprise, anger, distress, violation, all or none may have been tricks of the ear.

Then my ears popped again. And the wind was gone. But the silence was not as it had been. No longer oppressive, it had become the expansive silence that takes charge after conflict or disaster or death.

Someone whisked off the sheet, the instant before I could do so. There stood Ma, and as I sat up, my eyes were drawn to the dead crow that she was holding by its broken neck.

Now, for the first time, I felt horrified. "Ma, you didn't have to kill it!"

"Your mother didn't kill the meddling bird. I did." No quaver of age, nor any tone of conciliation. "Your mother is where I was. Now nobody can interfere with us. Isn't that what you wanted?"

She knelt beside me. With a suppleness beyond anyone of Ma's years. And as shock began setting in, since no other course was apparent to my mind, I could hardly feel the wrinkled, big-veined hand that ardently took mine. As if from far away I heard, "Happy Halloween, darling."

In the Wake of Bridget

June 1816 began with a frozen well. Soon the cold worsened, and the fields were thick with frozen blackbirds that bounced like stones on being kicked. Next a foot of snow covered the valley, but it was dry as bone meal and all blew away, along with the blackened flowers on the apple trees.

Come July, the hapless farmers throughout Vermont were making bonfires of dead cornstalks to warm what corn still stood. Rumors flew that frosts had felled the wheat in Massachusetts, and then all the way down to Pennsylvania. Oats meant for horses became oatmeal for man, for the first time in our hills. Calves sickened from the blue milk that came of the cows' skimpy fodder.

In August, people were down to boiling nettles and wild turnips, and shooting scrawny possums and squirrels for stew. As of September, no place in Vermont had seen rain in two months, just more dry, fleeting snow. Only root crops survived, potatoes the size of chestnuts, finger-length carrots, radishes like buttons.

With December, the churchgoers prayed even harder than during the last war with England. But their appeals were misdirected, and though I could have corrected them, the truth, like any other beast of burden, needs both exercise and rest. Drought and freeze came in the wake of Bridget, and beyond setting the circumstances down and off my chest, no good could come of a public airing.

The first of February 1816, when this business began, marked the first anniversary of losing my wife and boy to the smallpox. Else that date would never have stuck with me, of one more solitary evening on the farm. Running the place single-handed afforded me no time to think during the day. But nights, bygone prospects haunted me till all hours: I had almost attended Dartmouth and escaped the hardscrabble way, but my parents both died of the yellow fever within a week, and the farm fell to me as elder son. My brothers stayed on till I married, and then they bolted to make something of themselves in Burlington and Montpelier. With Bridget came and went my one hope for better. No other woman, before or since, could get beyond the deep ruts that the smallpox had dug in my face.

A change in the weather had made that February night as white and thick as milk. South wind rattled the shutters and worried rain from a heavy overcast, and turned crusty old snow into fog and whipped it around. Where the ground left off and the air began shifted at every step. Earlier, gales had budged the barn door a little and soaked a sheaf of rushes meant for rebottoming some chairs. I had set the rushes to dry before the hearth, and at bedtime I moved them to the back hall. That was when I heard frantic scratching at the door. When I opened up a bit, in blew a fusillade of rain and an old tabby cat.

Instantly the cat was purring loudly and arching against my shins. She resembled none of the neighbors' cats that I knew, but neither was she at all wild. Well, maybe a mouser, and a little company of sorts, was in order here. Casting her into the downpour would have been cruel. While she lay on her side in the rushes, I rummaged up one of my wife's old nightshifts for extra bedding. She started kneading on it immediately. I shut the hall door and slept with the peace of the virtuous.

Clattering pans and dishware woke me at dawn. Visions of the cat amok in the kitchen brought me on the run, but what greeted me downstairs was a woman, wearing the nightshift, and cooking flapjacks. "Your tea is on the table," she said.

Before I knew what to say about this intrusion, she explained, "Yours was the door I found open after being caught in the rain. Everything of mine was wet through, so I put on what was offered."

Keeping one eye on this stranger with my heavy fry pan in hand, I checked the back hall. It was empty of both cat and wet clothes.

"What happened to the cat that was in here?" I called.

She fixed her wide eyes past me and into the hall and replied, somewhat archly I thought, "There is no cat."

She went back to greasing the pan, and I resumed watching her. Her every movement was flealike, as if on hair trigger, and taking my eyes off her for any time made me nervous. She was short and girlish, and her long dirty-blond hair was in perpetual disarray as if from winds produced by her own turbulent motions. Her cheeks were wide and her lips full, but her nose was blunt and small, like a thimble. Her face overall conveyed coarseness, but that restless vitality also made her face radiant, appealing to look upon.

"Sit! Your tea will be cold," she warned. Her voice rose and fell strangely, and I asked if she were from Canada, or maybe down South.

"From over the ocean" was all she told me, then or ever.

The only name she used was Bridget. She professed that with no family anywhere, she had no last name. Debating her logic seemed incautious while she held the pan, so I asked where she was bound.

She confessed to owning no plan beyond finding work, and remarked that a man alone like myself must have occasion for an able body.

No straightforward reply seemed wise yet, so I pointed out, broadly indicating the nightshift, that my wife had died of the smallpox.

She fingered the fabric carelessly and said, "That cannot harm me." Then with a startlingly swift approach, she slid a couple of flapjacks onto my plate. True, I had never tasted better, but this only rendered the moment more perturbing, as I knew that all I had was a little stale flour, although the servings, a half dozen at least, just kept coming.

After breakfast, Bridget set about cleaning the kitchen, urging me to get a jump on the chores that must have awaited. Again I verged on rebuking her for assuming a place in the household, since I was far from sure about wanting her in the house at all. But sometime after midnight the wind turned northerly again, and dawn reflected dull blue off the ice that encased the landscape out the kitchen window. A mere walk to the barn would be no fun; real travel posed danger to life and limb.

And thereafter how could I have sent Bridget away, having declined to do so right then? In those first weeks at least, Bridget's presence of itself brightened the gloomy homestead. And beyond that, she seemed a miracle-worker of sorts. When Bridget milked the cows, they gave three times their usual. She loaded the market-bound wagon with more cheese than should have fit in the larder. She produced butter from the churn as easily as water from the well. What seemed to be the way of it that winter was the way things finally did come to pass: I was getting my whole summer's yield, and more, in advance.

Bridget always demurred from going to town with me and was

never about when neighbors put in a rare appearance. When spring brought my three hired hands to help with the planting, Bridget spied on them from behind curtains all day. Afterwards I tried sounding her out, asking if she were ashamed to be seen with me and my pox scars. She blushed and cried, "I am not here to cause talk about you." I had to accept that, or else chase after her as she flew out the back door. So began her first night of disappearing till the small hours.

No doubt Bridget was kindly disposed toward me, but she still cut an imposing figure, so I shied from prying into her nocturnal whereabouts. Maybe she didn't want to be seen keeping apparent company with me because she had a swain in the vicinity; good for her! She seemed no easy mark for local rakes, and I had no worries about her virtue.

But then the hands brought news of some beast killing a man at the far end of the valley. My chief concern was for Bridget on her supposed trysts. I said nothing at first, as I knew she was already forewarned. I had glimpsed the curtains stirring during the men's report.

As for the killer, the valley had been clean of wolves, catamounts, and bears for decades, and the condition of the body suggested nothing familiar. The man's flesh had been chewed off in a straight line from mouth to crotch, and the body was milk-white, bloodless.

Then one night, I chanced to see Bridget steal out from the yard. She wore my wife's clothes, since she had no others. For working around the house this was fine, but for any other purposes I was still a little ill at ease. Almost in a crouch, she was darting toward the woods, on a pressing errand that bespoke nothing of love. Afterwards, Bridget's abrupt manner became offputting to me again, even if the import of her midnight rambles had not yet been forced on me. My nervousness must have showed, for she took steps that night to allay it.

Without troubling to clear the supper dishes, Bridget uncorked the bottle of port that my brother in Montpelier had sent some Christmases ago, on reserve for a special occasion. She insisted that May the first was a special occasion, a grand holiday where she was from, when people counted their blessings and made changes for the better. I was peevish at her for taking liberties with my one luxury article, but what was done was done. My first drink in ages tasted glorious, and my second even more so, once it occurred to me that my new prosperity made barrels of port affordable.

How much liquor could fit in a bottle? Bridget poured us each a third, then a fourth. The port, like the milk, seemed inexhaustible in her hands.

She also made a pretense of pouring herself out, while really speaking only of me. I made her sad, she said, a marriageable man in his prime, so kindly and capable, languishing alone, without close companionship. She gazed at me, somehow pitying and enticing at the same time. I snorted and told her I was fine, but where a second ago I was all smiles, now I was choked up and fighting back tears. Suddenly my year of solitude seemed like a century. Did I reach for her hand or she for mine? She pushed her full glass of port at me earnestly, as if my best interests were at stake. Tilting back the glass tilted the balance inside me back toward gladness.

Bridget contended that I deserved every enjoyment of life, that all the dreams I had forgotten could still be mine for the remembering. All I needed was her. Somehow she had moved from across the table to standing behind me, resting her chin lightly on top of my head, her hands moving around under my shirt. I slid the glass away, shrugging off those worries about Bridget that eluded me at the moment anyway. Nothing about her struck me as coarse then.

I woke up when Bridget rolled out of bed to fix breakfast. I could not recall ever feeling such contentment, and miraculously none the worse for drink. That alone should have given me pause, but I felt too good to care yet that I had become a man apart in more than years of lapsed churchgoing and smallpox scars. Loving Bridget had been like my name on a contract, severing what little connection with people I still had. This was soon impressed on me.

Sharing my bed was no deterrent to Bridget's midnight absences, but our new intimacy did make questioning her all the more awkward. She either did not know or care that her comings and goings woke me, and that news of a death sometimes followed.

After the help reported a fourth killing, Bridget stopped me in the parlor. I felt cold and fidgety, and unable to meet her eyes. She asked why I wasted money on those men, when she was all I needed for the farm to flourish. I mumbled something about getting the men some water and scurried along. She called after me to please send them home.

Maybe I should have listened, and saved a life. But if I had, the depredations might have gone unchecked. And as for Bridget, my benefactress, my only friend, should I have warned her that the whole valley was up in arms and ready for her? Come midnight, the bed creaked as she got up. At dawn I found her in the kitchen, pressing rags to her bloody shoulder. She said she had had "an accident in the barn" and would be fine. She refused to show me the wound, claiming it was nothing. In a daze I made us breakfast, and soon two of the three hired hands arrived.

I met them on the porch. I had to feign surprise on learning that Nate, the hardiest and smartest of them, was dead. Late last night his family had awakened to what sounded like a woman shouting amidst neighing and bellowing in the barn. Nate took his musket and went out. After a while, a single shot brought the rest of Nate's people on the run. The deathly silence that now reigned in the barn made them warier as they entered than if the uproar had still been going on. The livestock, as if just awakening from profound slumber, were staring indifferently toward what was left of Nate. He lay limbs outstretched in star shape, with blood and bits of flesh reddening the hay in a great circle around him, as if he'd exploded. The beast had vanished, leaving no tracks, no scent for the hounds, no trail of blood if the one shot had been good.

We all stared at the ground a moment. I peeked back toward the house, and sure enough, a curtain wavered. The other attacks had left no traces either, and every kind of trap in the woods had failed. Nobody knew what to do.

I told the men not to worry about me for the next few days and paid them for the rest of the week. I also gave them an extra week's wages for Nate's family. When I needed help, I said, I'd come around.

Bridget had bandaged her shoulder and was burning the blood-soaked rags in the stove. When I announced the men's departure, she said, "Timely."

I took a deep breath and let the question just tumble out. "Why Nate?"

She regarded me tenderly as she said, "Their talk was causing you distress. Your happiness must always come first, and your peace of mind."

And those other victims?

Bridget shrugged. "If they would take me in their dark and secret places, and all have tried, then it is allowed me to have them, for have I not shown that I am yours?"

But why kill at all?

"The abundance I bring you must come from somewhere. What is given must first be taken. Now that those two men have gone, see the good that has come of sacrifice."

Bridget wrapped her arm around my waist and led me to the south-facing window. I was speechless. The wheat and corn that had been seed two days ago were knee-high already. "Your fields will be blessed with many harvests this year." Bridget kissed me long and hard and stepped back as if expecting applause.

The only words I could manage were, "Why is all this happening?"

Bridget planted her fists on her hips and stared as if I were simple. "You put out the cloth and rushes, as if you cannot recall. It was you who offered me haven from my wanderings on the one night when I could accept. In former days on the feast of Imbolc, many were the invitations, and I could give only a little of myself at each house. But in this age, to chance upon any who do me honor is hard, as I rove among my people on this side of the ocean and that."

"So you love me purely on account of some straw by the back door? Suppose someone down the road instead of me had done the same? Would you have killed me by now?"

Her lips gently brushed my scarred cheeks and mouth by way of reassurance. "It was not anyone else who invited me. It was you. It is silly to worry about things that did not happen."

Silly? After five unguilty murders on her hands? How did I know I could trust her?

"Kindness is owed to friends, not strangers," she explained, tapping my chest with one finger for emphasis. She sighed. "Men can never understand. In Ireland, you know, I was a saint, while in lands not yet Christian across the water, the people called Brigantes addressed me as goddess of death and war. It amuses me that men must think me only one or the other."

I carried on as if sleepwalking in the days it took me to accept that I had a supernatural creature on my hands, or rather that I was in her hands. Bridget, meanwhile, remained my lover and helpmeet without apparent notice of my state of mind, as if I must have been happy unless I were obviously agitated.

By Saturday the wheat was ready to reap. And how to do this without calling in the men? Bridget was amazed at my lingering doubts about her. After dark, with full moon as sole light and witness, we entered the field, each bearing a simple short sickle. Bridget and I appeared to be working at the same pace, but time was different for her. I looked up from tying my second sheaf to find her starting her second dozen. As the moon set, we lugged in the entire harvest. The sight of it made me forget myself and rejoice in this foretaste of plenty, until I saw how Bridget glared at the cornfield, which at waist height was lagging unacceptably behind. Something ominous in her tone sobered me when she said, "Monday night, we will come back for the corn."

Sunday at bedtime Bridget wanted me, lulling me into supposing she was home for the duration. But afterwards, she rose from bed and hastened away, without even waiting for the appearance of my being asleep. And why should she have? What she did was no longer a secret between us; at issue now was only the extent of my complicity.

I lay awake knotted up inside, picturing what Bridget might be doing at any given moment. Families around here always scraped by at best, and now they were losing fathers, husbands, sons. Friends of mine they were not. Even before my smallpox, visitors were rare who were not paid labor. Yet they were helpless and in need, and they aroused pity if not fellow-feeling.

And at this rate, who would finally remain in the valley but Bridget and me, and where would her literal bloodthirst turn then?

I had no sense of dozing off, but suddenly Bridget was resting my head in her lap and trying to soothe my sweating brow with gentle fingers and a lullaby in some gruff, singsong language. Unable to find words as my eyes turned toward her, I could only hope that she had not killed anyone I knew. With that thought, I drifted back asleep.

I woke to Bridget's anxious gaze, her face inches away. She herded me from bed and to the window, where she proclaimed, "See? I knew what had to be done." Where yesterday the scarecrow had been waving at the house, today only a hand showed above the corn, as of a drowning man. By the light of waning moon that night we harvested, Bridget again doing the lion's share. And again the prospect of a fat year got the better of me, and I went to bed joyful.

Next morning, Bridget was up first to make breakfast, as usual. I snoozed a while longer, until a volley of crashes roused me from bed. I dashed to the top of the stairs and found Bridget starting to crawl up on all fours. I hauled her the rest of the way, and under the covers.

Her complexion was ashen, and her demands for water were hard to hear. When I held the ladle to her lips, she put her fingers to it. Her sleeves slipped down, and long, bumpy rashes in wheat-ear pattern crisscrossed her arms. She swallowed with difficulty and then croaked, "Examine the corn! Tell me how bad it is!"

Unsure of her meaning, and loath to leave her too long, I rummaged through the corncrib until I came to an ear that was striped with a wine-colored ergot on both husk and kernels.

I reentered the bedroom in time to see Bridget sit up and cough a gob of blood onto the sheet.

"Is it the consumption?" I asked. Bridget looked up from the blood with tears on her cheeks, maybe of suffering, maybe of mortification.

A glimpse at the corn was all she needed. "Take it out of the house! Out! Hurry!" She waved toward the window. I opened it and flung the cob across the yard.

"That was why the rows were so stunted," she moaned. "The rust, the rust. The moonlight was too weak. It hid all the sickness I was touching."

"But the ergot just hurts the corn," I said.

"What strengthens me, strengthens my plantings. What hurts them can hurt me."

"Will you be all right?"

She frowned as if at my feeble wits. "I cannot die." Mentioning her bandaged shoulder as warning to the contrary hardly seemed politick.

For now, she insisted, nothing mattered but to find all the tainted corn and burn it to cinders, and then sell the rest lest it had the ergot's unseen beginnings. Recuperation would take time, and until then, the sight of her would only cause me needless distress.

Several barrow loads of corn formed a heap at the center of the grassless patch between barn and house. As I circled around torching the edges, I dwelled on the curse of sickness that so routinely befell those closest to me, parents with the yellow fever, wife and boy with the smallpox, and now Bridget with something that should have done nobody harm. How to account for this ongoing thread in my life? Was it my falling away from the church, or my pride in believing I deserved better than my dullard neighbors?

By default, Bridget had become the one closest to me. But what bond of affection could be natural between myself and whatever she was, even without her disdain for human life? Already I pitied and cared about her up in the sickbed. Supposing she were to conceive a child—would my loyalty then not become a hopeless snare? I scuffed aside a few ears before they caught fire and stashed them under the seat of the wagon.

As soon as I was on the road with the salable corn, my breath began clouding up. Except on my own land, the valley was bitterly cold for late May. I had to throw the old seat coverlet over my shoulders.

In town, my thin clothing caused comment, while everyone obligingly assumed that my out-of-season corn must have been left over from last year. All talk revolved around two topics: the weather, concerning which the cold was bad but the drought worse, as no rain had fallen since late March. Bridget's effect on my crops had kept any dry spell from coming to my attention. And then there was the beast, which had struck again Sunday night, though luckily the victim was no one I knew.

I wanted to be among people a while longer. Human company was impossible at home, and maybe that alone made me crave it. I hitched the wagon by a tavern, where winter drinks were still the bill of fare. I took a flaming rum punch. In the mirror above the bar I could see some old gents whose palaver I could not help overhearing. They were a lean, grizzled lot, dipping their cups zealously into the bowl of now-lukewarm toddy at the center of their table.

They were discussing the "murderous beast," and one of them made me pause in mid-swallow by denying the existence of any beast at all. During his childhood, before the Revolution, a girl had died of consumption, but had returned as a night haunt to prey on her family. Those to whom she came in dreams wasted away. The girl, like the alleged beast, lived on blood. The valley's most learned men put a stop to the ghost by exhuming the body, which was still uncorrupt, and chopping off the head, burning the blood-filled heart, and jumbling the dismembered limbs and torso inside the coffin.

The rest of the old topers pounced on all the differences between doubtful reminiscence and present reality, but to me the similarities were striking enough. Bridget was no less a destructive spirit, and if bullets took their toll on her, then why not the drastic olden measures? And I had the advantage of not having to dig up the body first. I downed my drink and left.

My roadside stone wall showed its dim outline long after dark. The mild weather waiting on my side of that wall was gratifying, especially as the rum had come to weigh on me. No lights shone in the house. Guided by candle, my sole ambition was to creep into bed quietly. I was far too logy to try acting on my newfound knowledge of exorcism.

It turned out I was home too early rather than late. Occasional shudders shook the bed and warned that Bridget's fever had yet to break. As I lay beside her, she mumbled in what seemed the language of Sunday's lullaby. I was wary of snuffing the candle yet. Her eyes opened, but the way they squinted and widened at the emptiness over-head led me to believe she was dreaming. She panted as if running at full tear, and her hands and face twitched. It was like watching a dog or cat dream. Then her skin turned deathly pale and her eyes and cheeks sank, as if she were aging or decaying before my eyes. She kneaded the blanket, and in so doing her hands grew long and bony, her knuckles knobby like tree galls. She shook her head back and forth like a beast with prey in its jaws, and her eyes reflected the candlelight as if gold coins floated in them. She then raked at the covers with hooked claws instead of nails at her fingertips, the ripping sound setting my teeth on edge. Her reach went wider and wider. I squirmed as far aside as pos-sible, though not quickly enough. One claw barely nicked my elbow but hit bone, making me bite my wrist to keep from crying out. Here was the least bit of what Bridget's victims felt, and why she'd wanted me out for the duration. I was afraid simply to get out of bed and away, in case that amount of movement should cause her to turn on me. She began chewing, and licking and slurping, lips peeling back to show long outcurving teeth, square-ended but sharp-edged. Her dream-feast went on for longer than I could stay awake.

When next I knew, Bridget was on top of me, my face between her clamping hands. Then she was kissing me with cool lips, and whispering that she was well again. Sheer relief moved me to respond to her.

Rum, late hours, and Bridget's night changes left me unsteady in the morning. I cut myself shaving, the blood spot still wet on my cheek when I sat down to breakfast. Bridget was humming and bustling about the kitchen, as if yesterday had never happened, apparently unaware of what I'd seen by candlelight.

She joined me at the table, and my stomach began to churn ominously at her announcement of good news. "I can tell about these things," she said. "I have conceived your child." She squeezed my hand and leaned forward to kiss me, apparently believing me too overwhelmed to show more enthusiasm. In any case, even as she rhapsodized about how wondrous our child would be, her focus narrowed to the blood on my chin. She could not look away from it, as if she had become two selves oblivious to each other, one looking, the other talking.

She was chattering about someone to "carry on" for me, and I'm sure she hadn't meant to imply that my life would be of less account once I had fathered her child. But I would have been a fool not to anticipate the day when none but myself remained to sate her thirst, or the day when fever changed her again. Nothing said in her own defense could have changed my mind, now that a picture of what to do was forming.

Tonight after moonrise, she announced, we would sow the second field of wheat. I just nodded. While she cleared the table, I remarked a desire for pea soup, as we'd need a hearty supper to last the night. She immediately set to soaking the peas, and I reminded her not to skimp on the salt pork and pepper.

By late afternoon the kettle was bubbling and the aroma filled every room. Upstairs and down, all was bright and orderly. The comfort had grown on me, and I had started looking forward to the trappings of prosperity. But today it all had to end, and nipping it in the bud was bitter. I could not stand thinking about the bleak years to come.

Bridget was off bringing the cows from pasture. I fetched a tainted ear from the wagon and brushed the rust into the soup. The red floated on the green like nutmeg until I stirred it in. Then I sniffed deeply and tried a spoonful, satisfied that this last seasoning was undetectable. I replaced the corn in the wagon.

We ate at dusk. Bridget was still aglow at future motherhood, and I just let her talk. I seldom looked up from my bowl except to nod or make sure she was still dining briskly. If she had the same quickening effects on herself as on the fields, then I was acting none too soon. Perhaps tomorrow the innocent child in her would be obvious, and I would falter, to all intents lost.

Rising from the table she stumbled, and I broke into a sweat. No, she must not fall sick in the house. I strode to the window and reported seeing the moon. She leaned against me, feeling nothing amiss yet, I gathered, as she nuzzled my cheek. "My zealous man," she murmured, "what could ever hold you back?"

I told her I would get what we needed from the barn. She said not to hitch up a plow, but that a harrow for each of us would do. In with the harrows I smuggled an ax. The weight of three tools should not have made my arms tremble, but it did.

From the barn door, I watched Bridget come outside. I felt like a leaf afloat on the current, helpless to stay the onrush of events underway. At first Bridget strolled with the usual air of control, but out in the moonlight she reeled, arms thrown out, as if clubbed from behind. She regained her balance an instant before staggering forward, hand at her throat. The timing could not have been better, and my own excitement perhaps hinted at how Bridget felt before a kill. The well in the middle of the yard was the nearest thing for her to lean on, and as she crashed into it I started toward her. Out in the open field, this would have been much trickier.

She clutched the rim of the well, elbows bent at right angles, her back arched and heaving. She was retching into the well, her long wild hair veiling her face, her slim neck exposed. I approached her more nimbly, refusing to accept that I was committing murder because Bridget, whatever she was, was not a person. Her love for me was not in question, or all that she had done for me, but it was the cost of her services that egged me on. I too much feared forsaking my kind for hers.

With one hand I gripped the ax handle and let the harrows slide to the ground. The clatter made Bridget shudder, at which point the ax was swinging up. Without a thought I brought down the ax before Bridget lost her ideal chopping-block pose. The stroke was good. Her body was pushed back onto the ground by the force of blood gushing from her neck. Her head was down the well, which angered me. So much work loomed already in disposing of Bridget, without having to remove a source of poison from the water. From the house I fetched a lantern. I held it over the well and frowned into the depths. To my surprise Bridget's white face shone in the black water, eyes wide and mouth open in what seemed most like disbelief. The face sank slowly, as if unwillingly, and after it disappeared I backed away, determining to take care of the body first.

Six feet of grave, out behind the barn, took hours to dig. I dragged Bridget's body by the ankles to the grave. Dismembering her was bad enough; I could not bring myself to chop out the heart and burn it. Dropping in the torso backside up and then piling the limbs in a jumble would have to serve. I imagined this would pass muster with the old toper back in the tavern. By the time the grave was filled I felt fevered and nauseous, whether from the stress of the task or from the rust that had certainly been in my soup too. The well would have to wait till morning. And so ended May.

I woke with fierce chills around noon. I was still queasy, and worse, the rust must have affected my eyesight, making me blink away curling embers every few minutes, changing the outlines of familiar objects so that they flowed and took on the shapes of things that belonged in other rooms. In this state I returned to the well. Where the blood had spilled, ants and flies and yellowjackets had come to drink, and now they lay frozen. Squinting down into the well, I saw the sun reflect off ice.

I rummaged up my winter coat and, from the hearth, a bucket of live coals. Altogether, three bucketloads went into the well, and then I lowered the pail through the twisting smoke and vapor. It clunked against floating objects and needed a lot of finessing before it submerged. I brought up only chunks of ice and steaming coals for a while.

The work went on until my fingers were numb and almost too swollen to bend. Though every pail that did not contain what I sought was more merciful to behold, I swore at it for forcing me to try again. I was working mindlessly by the time something yellow, and no bigger than a cake of soap, rolled onto the ground. I poked it around with my foot, before recognition made me jump a little. No matter how many times I blinked and rubbed my bleary eyes, what still remained was the head of the old tabby cat that had come that February night. It was frozen hard, with soaked fur and charred spots in places. I knew, without putting it to myself in any articulate way, that this was the closest to a trace of Bridget I would ever raise. I buried the cat head in the unplanted wheat field. Afterwards I inspected the earth over Bridget's body. It was curiously sunken already, but no, I did not need to learn anything more.

Thereafter, cold and drought and hunger forged a temporary bond of sympathy between myself and my neighbors. Once again I submitted to overwork and maddening boredom, with less than ever to show for it that frigid summer.

No one ever knew Bridget had been here, and since her mortal status was that of friendless transient, I have never feared human penalty for what I did. The guilt has been bearable, with the greater good to justify me in the long run. But with the passing months, and then years, I could not abide the gnawing loneliness. Given a second chance, I do not know what I could have done differently—but would I have been able to kill again?

She claimed she could not die, and even though I seemed to put the lie to that, I have gone through dwindling youth and middle age putting out the rushes every February first. If she reappeared, would she forgive me? Who can say? On the other hand, I am all too aware of what would happen to me sooner or later, if someone else happened to spread the rushes instead.

Midnight Call

Leave it to Walpurgis Night. Something had to happen. The concierge woke her after midnight. Banging on the door fit to splinter it. "Your cat is dead!" he shouted for the whole floor to hear.

Emma in her nightgown opened the door. He continued without lowering his voice, "Your mother call just to tell you that. Ask me to tell you right away. I tell her it is very late here."

Emma nodded and closed the door. Jesus, Mom! You couldn't let it wait? Poor kitty! Her sweetest little friend. Not that he didn't have his beastly side. How many mouse heads had he loyally dropped at the foot of her bed? Just the same, the cat had been as dear to her as anyone ever had been, and who else had ever loved her in return?

And who ever would? The question, as usual, cost her hours of sleep that she could ill afford. Especially tonight. Tomorrow was going to be a really big day. Maybe the biggest of her whole thirty years. What the hell did her love life, or lack of it, matter right now?

Underwater archaeology had been all she'd wanted to do since high school. Back in Florida that connoted Civil War, colonial-era piracy, conquistadors at best. But here in Brittany it meant money for work she'd have traded her right arm to do.

Come dawn, the boat was halfway out of the harbor of Gavrinnis before steam began rising from thatch roofs in the village. Everyone drank deep of coffee and had little to say, nothing to betray the import of the occasion. A British diver said he was sorry to hear about Emma's cat. She winced and said she was sorry he had.

The gulf around them had been rising little by little for millennia, since after the last Ice Age. And on its shores five thousand years ago had thrived a stone-age culture with a passion for raising massive slabs into monuments and tombs, centuries before Stonehenge or the pyramids. Back on the island of Gavrinnis, the Er-Lannic, a figure-eight of maypole-high stones, was already half-submerged under the inexorably rising sea. How much older, then, was the dolmen three fathoms below, discovered last summer by a scuba-diving tourist?

To find out, the French government had taken bids from archaeological firms. A contact at the winning firm had called Emma. And here she was, joining the pick of divers from two continents, all of them eager for any insights into so alien and labor-intensive a culture.

And when the moment came, wet suit or no, the cold water made Emma shiver. She assumed the others were equally grateful for the directives on this first dive: look, measure, video, photograph, come back. Half an hour could tell them how much metal piping they'd need for gridwork over the site, to ensure methodical excavation.

Emma forgot the cold, forgot herself when their lights swung through the murk and hit their prize. Out of the mud and weeds it pushed like a giant mushroom, with a causeway of slabs leading up to the cap. It was big enough for a chapel at least, or a rustic deity's temple. The causeway would be the roof of a long, uterine passage, and under the cap would be a chamber, holding bones, symbolizing rebirth? How apropos, Emma mused, for May Day, ancient holiday of second chances, lucky starts.

Everyone swam for the entrance, batting aside seaweed, barred from a glimpse inside by what resembled a millstone. A spiral carved at its center slyly broke into concentric circles out to the edge. The obstacle made for anticipation rather than disappointment. Before the fall of Rome, thieves or zealot Christians had violated almost everything megalithic in France. This promised to be one of the great exceptions.

Emma's colleagues crowded the plug stone, recording, touching, and to all intents ogling, it seemed to Emma. A good time to video the rest of the structure. Behind the fronds she made out support stones like broad backs, whose closed ranks shouldered the capstone. At the far end, though, appeared a gap wide enough to shimmy through.

She did it, without second thought till she was inside, and then she resolved to make a quick sweep with the camcorder before anyone missed her. Flouting the buddy system like this would win her no points. But who could've resisted?

Seen from inside, the support stones evoked the same foreboding she'd felt in other dolmens: of a confrontational presence, ready to chase her out if she gave inadequate reason to stay. Particular aspects of this chamber overrode those qualms, though, and captured her attention. Surprisingly, the silt hadn't built up in here at all, despite the gap that had admitted her. The mud floor looked hard and flat as pavement, and she zoomed in on it with viewfinder. Soapstone spheres the size of pinballs, little red clay and amber beads, and stone mushrooms that could have been earrings all caught her eye. Maybe they had never been touched in thousands of years, even if they seemed freshly scattered around like toys. She stopped taping a second. Was it her, or had it grown warmer in here?

No time to ponder, she reminded herself, just scan and go. She focused on the walls. No square inch was free of sprawling, angular, mazelike design, the most obsessive and mesmerizing she'd ever seen, resembling nothing so much as circuitboards. How could anyone have put so much work into a place like this without at least imagining it served some worldly good?

The designs drew her in as she panned over them, making her pensive. Funny, how she felt less alone in here, among relics of hopelessly obscure antiquity, than among the population at large and even her coworkers. How had she fallen into this nowhere life, as if high labyrinth hedge kept her from emotional release? Loneliness never seemed to afflict those around her. Remembering the cat, she felt tears well up. Had Mom done everything to save him? She sure hadn't done whatever Emma had needed in childhood to help her deal comfortably with people.

A ripple in the water distracted her. She swung the camcorder back and forth but caught nothing. Must have been a sardine or the like. Look at that ceiling, though! Cupules, holes big enough to fit the soapstone balls, were thickset in an eye-shaped band from wall to wall, with lines cut between them, like a guide to points of interest across the Milky Way. She committed them to videotape and shimmied out without further ado.

Sure enough, a couple of divers were waiting, greeting her by jabbing fingers at their watches. She checked her own. My God, how had forty-five minutes gone by? She was practically out of air. Whatever else it was, May Day was not the time to martyr oneself for science.

Still, everyone was happy with the footage of her trespass. She'd found the only way in all right. But what was blurring the edge of the picture every so often, like a disturbance in the water? No idea. She had only noticed it once, herself.

The chamber provoked other questions in short order. What had kept it from silting up? How had the incised designs, and for that matter the dolmen itself, withstood punishing ocean current for ages? Nobody could say, but everyone was too grateful for relatively easy excavation to care. Let the oceanographers figure it out.

The grid went up around the dolmen, and inside, the slimy floor was parceled into shoebox-sized divisions, to be painstakingly examined one by one.

Emma felt less alone, for as long as she worked on the ocean floor. Not that she was hitting it off with anyone on the team. It was nothing she could explain. And back on land, her sense of isolation rebounded stronger than ever.

Emma's crowning find was a slate disc, with bore-holes suggesting use as a pendant. Its central motif was an overlap of three progressively larger circles, surrounded by radiating lines. Seen one way, it brought to mind a spider; seen another, an alignment of three planets. In any event, nothing like it had ever been found in dolmens that had already been burgled or purged. It was enough to justify the whole undertaking, even if it served only to render the builders more mysterious.

That evening the concierge greeted Emma, "I hope no more death in the family." He handed her a letter from Mom. Before opening it, she bought a bottle of hard cider, "cidre brut" according to the label. Her room was pretty much a booth, with scant room to squeeze between creaky bed and wobbly little table. Between table and door was a sink. Shower and water closet were down the hall. But out the window, Emma had the quay, the beach, the gulf, the staticky hiss of ocean beyond, the thick-strewn stars.

Mom got right down to acting the gadfly. Was Emma warm enough? Was the hotel clean? Shouldn't she consider a normal job with some security and benefits, where she could meet a man to take care of her? Don't judge them all by how your father was! Well, no problem with that, since he had been elsewhere before she was five. No mention of the cat, but the postmark predated midnight call.

Emma rose from the table, sloshing cider from her glass. She drew toward the window till her breath fogged it up. She yearned for what she felt on the sea floor, inside the dolmen, that sense of belonging or contentment or whatever. She caught herself calling out to it, as to a sympathizer.

Emma's eyes widened as if registering something. Huh? Nothing had crossed her field of vision. Nothing her consciousness could glean, anyway. Maybe she was getting a reaction to that cider.

Never mind, it was late. She slept a couple of hours. Woke up startled, disoriented. She wasn't home? The cat wasn't asleep at her feet? Her heart sank. But wait. Stealing over her, as if it had only shied away a second, was the same serenity that the cat had always imparted. Nothing she could see, hear or feel accounted for it. But did that matter? Emma drifted back to sleep.

Every bedtime, that sense of well-being returned, like a slowly unfolding presence. Her late-night fatigue made it easy enough to accept, and come morning, it faded like a dream.

Then Mom's next letter arrived. The phone call hadn't been enough. Headlong maternal duty somehow dictated Emma's need to know in detail the cat's suffering, how much better off he was now. Emma went to bed feeling hopeless all over again. In fitful half-sleep she heard herself calling the cat, and with no one to hear her, then well, why not?

She woke what seemed seconds later, and that sense of well-being, stronger by tenfold, filled her like air in a balloon, threatening to send her aloft. Warmth was rising from something curled up with its back to her, bulky as a bear, with thin, bristly fur. And it was purring, but not like a cat. There was a hard, rapid-fire clicking in it, and no pause for breath. And the warmth was like that she'd felt when first in the dolmen. A mosquito buzzed by Emma's ear and lit on her shoulder. She couldn't help flinching, and that dispelled the purring, and the presence. Sleep was a lost cause after that. She had no memory of swatting the mosquito, but in the morning, there it was, dead beside her pillow.

Days, she worried. Beyond token teamwork and sociability, she and the others were on different excavations. To them, every informative particle from the dolmen was wonderful; she wanted insight only into her dead-of-night companion. They were speaking more freely about themselves; she could never broach what was on her mind.

Nights, worry just switched itself off. She went to bed weary, knowing what would happen, but giving it no thought, as if that were part of its influence on her, or so she speculated. The visitor, when it briefly woke her, was always less skittish, more manifest. It drew ever closer, but not in the sense of approach in three dimensions. No, little by little, night by night, more and more of it was present, a mood in the air, a fleeting texture, a flash of motion, and now it was showing piecemeal volume and mass.

All the visitor did was snuggle up with her, nothing more, apparently craving only contact, innocent affection. The contentment it radiated was irresistible. And come morning, Emma was all the more afraid, recalling bristly fur, musky warmth, an occasional dreaming shudder that shook the bed. But squint all she would, nothing of the visitor was visible yet.

Meanwhile the dolmen floor was yielding no skeletons, no urns, nothing to indicate a tomb. Two of the more intriguing finds only reinforced Emma's sense that she was on her own dig with its own pressing interests. Out of a milk-white stone had been fashioned what looked like large earrings or else adornments for a cloak fastener. They formed a pair of fantastically long, hooked claws. At the end of each digit hung a head, with slit eyes and downturned mouth. There was also a polished stone bowl, the size of a pet's water dish. What resembled a pair of multifaceted insect eyes bulging from the side lent the bowl the likeness of a hollow head. In each facet of the eyes was a head like those dangling from the claws.

To the others these items were mystifying; Emma felt cold dread at possible glimpses of her midnight caller. And she alone gained a clearer impression of the dolmen builders, since only she surmised the artifacts' basis in observation rather than fantasy. The boastful abundance of stylized trophy heads bespoke no gentle folk. At the least, they took vindictive joy in self-defense. Nor did their unearthly helpmeet seem to rouse revulsion or even fear. Those who kept the images of those claws, those eyes, near their flesh would not associate them with harm. Emma's visitor had been their friend, their loyal servitor.

From whoever summoned it, apparently it craved only affection, approval. And Emma had to admit she'd summoned it. The cat's death had triggered her attack of loneliness on Walpurgis Night, when the Invisible World traditionally loomed close, and she had called out for relief down in the dolmen, on May Day, when wishes legendarily found their most receptive audience. This particular dolmen, whether built the right way or in the right place, was a gateway, and Emma had beckoned at the right time. And then from her room she had beckoned twice again, hadn't she?

What could she do now but endure in silence for the rest of the dig? What could she say? She needed nobody's help doubting her own sanity. At best she could speculate on the nature of the beast, whether it had undergone translation into later pantheons, or if she had struck the unwanted truth about Cupid and Psyche, or if here was something H. P. Lovecraft could have named.

The visitor seemed to sense Emma's hapless acceptance and exploited its sporadic solidity in celebration. Pens and bottles were batted off the table, to roll back and forth across the narrow floor for what seemed hours. And hearing a fly or mosquito made Emma's heart race. Clumsy, invisible pursuit always included collisions with walls, the table overturned. Once, a chair collapsed and, after much scrabbling at the knob, the door flew open, with thumps and crashes afterwards in the hall. At breakfast next morning, the concierge stood on a chair and threatened to evict the whole crew at next complaint of drunken excess in the hall. Whoever had hidden the broken chair in the broom closet should, especially, beware. Emma gulped and lowered her eyes toward the concierge's chair, wishing for its timely collapse.

The last day of the dig, one more find was freed from the mire outside the dolmen, an arm's length from the gap in the stones. Had the chamber been a tomb after all? A human femur and tibia, detritus-crusted, chomped open in places, brought a general response of mild shudders and raised eyebrows, of what struck Emma as intellectualized titillation. She, however, blanched and bolted below deck at first sight of the bones on board. The others, she was sure, must have looked at her with pursed lips, as if questioning her stability. Maybe that recent midnight commotion should be laid at her doorstep. After all, you always have to watch the quiet ones, who keep to themselves . . .

Emma had the option of helping with the lab work in Paris, analyzing soil cores, reconstructing potsherds, mapping the site. She begged off, pleading homesickness. The bitten bones made Emma even leerier of her night caller, and never happier to board the plane back to Florida.

What more did she care to know about the dolmen builders?

She moved back into her cottage, former servants' quarters, on the family orange farm. She tried not to think about the cat, or about the night caller. It took days to relax, to conclude that the entity lacked the wherewithal to trace her all the way home. Its actions, after all, had borne out her take on what the drooling, pigeon-eyed demons of Hieronymous Bosch would actually have been like. Assuming the reality of such creatures, what had ever recommended the churchly dogma of calling them fallen angels? Why even accord them the intelligence of Lovecraft's scheming monsters? Emma had seen no reason to put her visitor's I.Q. on a par with that of dogs or cats. Telling herself this over time gave her peace of mind.

Basking in solitude, letting nothing weigh on her mind, the mix of sea air and citrus, the mild funk of old wallpaper and wooden beams made her glad to be home. Mom could be a pest, but there was little Emma hadn't learned to let roll off her back. Only once in two weeks did she regret that the cottage had no phone, when Mom dragged her away from whatever she had been reading, to take a call in the main house.

It was her contact at the firm that had sent her to France. He asked how she'd made out over there, what she thought of her co-workers, and other concerns so general that Emma couldn't doubt he was tiptoeing around talk of her own aloof, erratic behavior. After an awkward pause, he got to the point. Had she heard about the concierge? Well, he was dead. The help had found him a few days after Emma and company had cleared out. He was in her room. Last seen going up to investigate noises. How had he died? Heart attack, maybe, they weren't sure. Of course Emma wasn't implicated in any way, but what did she suppose could have happened? Emma recoiled from the phone a second, as if the entity were popping from the receiver. She blurted, "It's a shock to me. I don't know."

It was a shock all right. Her guilty dislike for the concierge, no doubt, fueled feverish nightmares in which she, as the devil, set Bosch critters on the concierge, who reprised the temptations of St. Anthony. His foremost tormentor, wide as a window, was her erstwhile cat. Emma recognized him despite his beak and coxcomb and knobby carapace. So according to her subconscious, she'd hated the concierge enough to play his evil scourge, to want him dead. But worse, she woke with fresh sadness about the cat, oh no! That accounted for far more stress.

That morning, Mom dropped by with a bill from the vet. "This just came," she said as Emma unfolded it. "He was your cat, so I think you should take care of it."

"Fine," Emma said curtly. "What's this line that's been x'ed out?"

"Oh, they must have gotten a little mixed up over what to charge. When I talked to the vet at first, he said an operation might help, so I told him okay, but next day I changed my mind and just had him put the poor thing under. After all, he was old and the operation would have kept him alive only another year or so. And besides, the vet wanted almost a thousand dollars!"

Emma's eyes were full of tears, a lump was big in her throat, and cheek muscles were clamping her lips tight.

"Now don't tell me you'd spend that kind of money on a pet!"

"You could have saved him and you didn't!"

"Now honey, don't be unreasonable. It was only a cat. Sometimes I think you have no kind of handle on real life at all."

"Suppose we just put you under if you took sick?"

"Well, if you feel that way maybe it's time you moved out of here and started paying rent on your own. In fact, I wish you would. I do believe it would be the best thing for you."

"Sure, why not add insult to injury?" Emma cried and stormed out of the kitchen. From the bedroom window she saw Mom trudge back to the main house a minute later.

The placid surface of Emma's last two weeks was broken. That night she lay unblinking in bed, bathed in sweat and despair. Mom, above and beyond bringing up Emma all untutored in social skills, seemed an especially loveless creature at this point. Her callousness toward the cat was bad enough. And then at that juncture, to tell Emma to move out, when what she needed was some apology, some reassurance, any sign of love! Emma had grown up here. It was the only home she'd known. To pull that out from under her, and force her focus onto a world where loneliness seemed more than ever a glacial wall between herself and any kind of fulfillment, that felt like a spike between the ribs, that was unforgivable. Her pity and sadness for the cat felt renewed in full, the cat who'd felt the utmost brunt of Mom's cold-heartedness.

The electric fan whirred on the nightstand beside her bed, below the window. Its old top-heavy motor was wont to back it slowly across the stand. Emma's eyes had closed a minute. A crash made them open wide in alarm. The fan had fallen to the floor, coming unplugged, the blades rasping to a halt. Oh well. It would have to happen just when she was starting to relax and doze off.

Picking up the fan and plugging it back in, she looked out the window. Mom, with dour expression, was playing her flashlight across the yard, heading toward the trash cans. Must have heard some animal scrounging in them. Emma's just-awakened awareness made the scent of oranges almost sickeningly strong.

Back in bed, she tried willing herself to drift off again, but instead she kept wondering why the fan had fallen at that moment. Fallen, or was it pushed?

Emma sat up, alarmed all over again. She went back to the window. No sign of Mom, but the flashlight lay on the lawn, its beam casting a half-circle, like a bright cave mouth, on the main house wall. She heard crickets, frogs, and nothing more, until a clicking as of teeth surprised her from behind.

As she turned, a smell of wet fur and chemical bitterness hit her. In the shadows at the doorway she could, at last, make out glinting details of the thing whose love had crossed unimaginable void and, more tardily, ocean. Fangs like those of a wolf spider bobbed excitedly. Claws like those of a mantis flashed and swung something in a wide arc. Gee, Mom, he followed me home, Emma found herself thinking. Can we keep him?

The visitor, with an anxious twittering sound, let fly its little burden toward Emma's feet. While it was still rolling, Emma recognized grey hair, a strong chin, the curve of plucked eyebrows. A prize, Emma realized, just to please me! A prize of the one who'd been making me unhappy!

"Mom!" she started screaming and sank to her knees, at the edge of where the blood had spread. "Mom!" Meanwhile the thing that loved her stood there, chirping nervously, as if wishing it knew what was wrong and what it could do to please its mistress.

Damn the Wheelwright

The wheelwright married into our clan. Damn him. I've heard that beyond the Southern mountains, the bride goes to live in the husband's village. That would have been better here for all concerned. Especially the wheelwright.

Not that I'm against new blood, a fresh face, now and then. Learning the ways of a stranger should be plenty to slake a normal thirst for novelty. That was certainly the case with cousin-in-law Knub. Some of us at first were in awe of his flashy amber beads, his face full of blue tattoos. Which to me looked like he'd caught his head in a burning basket. A tasteful circle around each eye or cross on each cheek was certainly decorative enough for the rest of us.

And though he never said directly that nothing here was good enough for him, people would fidget and seem to shrink as he spat question after question at them. Why didn't we use plows? Why did we still grow wheat when everyone else had switched to barley? And why slaughter so many cattle in the fall, when we could winter them over with hay? Hard to answer him, when nobody knew what plows, barley and hay might be. If he'd really wanted us to benefit from these alleged godsends, why didn't he just tell us what they were in the first place?

I wanted to shake those people dazed by his interrogations and say, Look, we have nothing to be ashamed of here. Our pigs are roly-poly from all the acorns they get in our woods, our cows give us milk enough to bathe in, our crops never fail. In my entire life, circumstances have never demanded the sacrifice of a child. I don't think we've ever really sacrificed anybody. If we had, we'd probably have been more tough-hearted than to be intimidated by the likes of Knub. But clearly the gods bear us no ill. Even if we worship them in nothing but an old wooden henge. Sure, in the far West someplace they've taken to raising huge stones on their sacred acres. How pretentious!

And besides, those are the thickly settled places where people aren't safe except behind towering stockades, inside which they're always robbing and murdering one another anyway. Here, on the other hand, we all get along for the most part, and we count no neighboring village an enemy. Life is so peaceful and regular around here that I knew someone who almost lived to be sixty! Why shouldn't we leave well enough alone?

But no, Cousin Hinda had to get fixed up with a wheelwright. And planting and herding and basketweaving and leatherworking just weren't for him. He had to be a wheelwright. Never mind that we didn't need any wheels. Somehow he had to get us to need wheels, or else what were we good for?

I stand by my statement that we all get along for the most part. However, if someone got along less well than the rest of us, that would be Groit. Always trying to make himself a bigger man, heedless of the impact on others. He's in charge of all the ceremonies at the henge because he wants to be, and that's fine. Less for the rest of us to think about. And he's welcome to swagger and show off all he wants, as long as he knows better than to tell others their place. From hosting and visiting those like himself in other villages, he's amassed a hut full of bronze doodads and ornamental axes, if you like that sort of thing. In a place like this, Groit can never get so big that he'll be anything other than harmless. But the wheelwright reckoned otherwise.

Ever since moving here, Knub had contended that the village should feed and clothe his household in return for a steady supply of wheels. And he rightly assumed that Groit, if anyone, had the surplus to spare and the vanity to stoke. But the big man, to his credit, was not so readily led. When Knub dropped in on him, their discussion became known to the village at large thanks to the orphan girl Groit had taken in to do housekeeping, and who stood high in our affections for her skill at eavesdropping.

Knub's first appeal was to village security. Very many days to the South, he intoned, one mighty tribe had learned to fix two wheels onto a kind of basket, which in turn was pulled by horses. A warrior stood in the basket, and with a number of these bizarre assemblages, this one mighty tribe had overrun another mighty tribe. Would Groit be no less than a hero if he prevented that from happening here by having the wheel-and-basket things built and on guard in case of invasion? Groit responded that he would likelier be called a fool. He had heard of no such mighty tribe in all his travels, and they sounded too far away to worry about. And he knew that none of us on so flimsy a pretext would ever agree to training as warriors, let alone standing in strange war-baskets.

An appeal to pure piety fared no better. Did we or did we not want to please the sun god? According to Knub, villages in the know these days celebrated every major religious festival by rolling a flaming wheel down a hill. After all, the sun was shaped like a wheel, it rolled across the sky, and as it turned so turned the seasons. And naturally the sun would shine warmly upon whoever fashioned this reflection of itself to admire. Groit demurred on practical grounds. If the sun god received this extra attention, then what would Groit have to make or set on fire to keep the gods of thunder and death and water from getting dangerously jealous? Besides, the sun was in happy balance with the other elements. Meddling with that could only be risky. As was rolling anything aflame through forest and pasture. If that were even possible, as our territory had no hills to speak of.

Finally Knub wielded his masterstroke. In a word, wagons. Was Groit content with his position and bronze baubles, or would he rather be a big man among big men? And make his word law among the little men? The more wagons he had for transporting farmhands and harvest, the more ground he could cultivate. He could take on so many dependents and work so much land, given enough wagons, that he could store immense amounts of wheat, so much that his fellow villagers would find it easier to work for him in return for wheat than to grow their own. And at that point, he would truly be a chief. In control of the staff of life, and thus of everyone and everything in the territory.

But the wheelwright was far from finished. He assumed that we were at least cultured enough to hold processions on holy days. Groit, to be sure, was never prouder and bossier than when managing a procession. So he was humbled to hear that nobody actually carried holy images in their arms any more. Statues rode in wagons. Much more impressive, to gods and men alike. And that old wooden henge of ours. What were we thinking? We were lucky that divine lightning hadn't leveled it yet. The day was fast approaching when henges of anything but stone would be sheer sacrilege. But if Groit were religious leader enough to suitably inspire the labor pool, then wagons would give him access to slabs of reputable girth and the means to bring them back. No big man around here had ever made his people put in the kind of work involved in raising a henge of stone. Imagine the prestige!

The wheelwright, damn him, was dangling so much self-aggrandizement that Groit couldn't help but grab at it without a second thought. How to account for the likes of either man?

The orphan girl had to smirk as she went at Groit's behest from hut to hut. Summoning us to the sacred acre on business "too profound to reveal through a helper girl." Groit's own words, of course.

Within the circle of posts and crossbeams, we tactfully squinted and nodded at Groit's utterances as if they were news. As he put it, warning had come that the gods were weary of our lackluster forms of worship. Our henge and our processions were shamefully out of date. He threw a fatherly arm over Knub's shoulders. The two of them were standing atop the oak altar block at the center of the henge. Luckily, Groit proclaimed, our newest member of the Crow clan could guide us out of spiritual crisis. Our two goals were simple: to build a wagon for the upcoming procession of the Feast of Dead Souls, and to replace the rotting old posts around us with stones, which we could accomplish with more wagons.

I could not have been the only one stifling a resentful groan at this point. Apart from the wheelwright's selfish passion for being a wheelwright, and Groit's own well-known passions, we all knew there was no reason to replace the posts. Exactly that which I'd called the height of other people's folly, and which we supposedly knew better than to embrace, was being inflicted on us from a quarter which allowed no debate. How infuriating! Especially since our backs, and not Knub's or Groit's, would bear the strain. But Groit officially spoke on behalf of the gods, and who dared second-guess their will?

At least Groit, to the general satisfaction, was the first to know hard labor and unexpected frustration because of Knub. The big man could demand our divinely justified services, but Knub was in charge of making the wheels, and nobody was about to obey him. And so Groit himself, along with sons, nephews, and in-laws, had to fell trees and shape wood and otherwise give Knub the assistance that resulted in a stack of wheels that reached up to the eaves of Groit's hut.

"Now how soon will we see a wagon?" Groit asked of the wheelwright.

Only then did Knub spring the trap. He snorted haughtily. "I can only make wheels. You have to send at least a week to the South for specialist woodcarvers, bronzesmiths, gluemakers, painters. A proper wagonwright team. But they'll come at my say-so, and if you make them happy, you'll have your wagons in plenty of time."

Groit bristled, but what could he say? To berate Knub for failing to mention what wagon-building really entailed would only put Groit's own ignorance in a starker light. He had instantly gone from providing for Knub and Hinda to providing for a mob of hungry Knubs. But he was as averse as anyone to crossing the gods. And they had evidently decreed in favor of wagons by letting the work get as far as it had.

To fetch the wagonwrights from their several villages, Groit sent a man from the Crayfish clan who owned only a few pigs and no cattle, and who couldn't afford not to work for food. In the long run, if Groit had his way we would all be in the same position as his lackey, so I sympathized with the poor man but cursed the fates at his safe return. Which was also the day we saw our first wagons, and they were indeed amazing. We heard their unearthly creaking and rumbling as they entered the meadow below the village, a stone's throw from the edge of the territory. Even from there, the sunstruck red and green and blue on the sides of the wagons were dazzling. And up close, the decorative spirals and pinwheels and spider webs were more remarkable yet. This was also the first time most of us had seen horses, and these big stallions, shiny black and tossing their manes, were about as impressive as the wagons. I, for one, briefly forgot the trouble that was also arriving.

As the four wagons drew near our huts, our messenger leapt from the foremost as if he could not part company fast enough. Without a word to us or even a glance at Groit or Knub, he ran home. But nobody gave him a second glance. Too diverting were the peculiar tools and mysterious clay pots and sundry unnamable items that jangled and clunked together as the wagons rolled over gullies and stones. Less wondrous were the men in the wagons. Despite their exotic red or yellow cloaks and drooping mustaches, they came across as scrawny and dingy. Yet they looked around disdainfully, as if entering a hog wallow. When Knub stepped forth from the standoffish crowd, the wagons finally grumbled to a halt. And when Knub greeted the newcomers with words I'd never heard before, they finally cracked ungracious smiles.

In coming days, the wagonwrights completely failed to endear themselves to us. They kept to themselves, and if ever they needed anything they shouted at the nearest passerby, as if nothing were more important than to run their errands. Even Groit rated no warmth from them, despite feeding and lodging them and promising them hefty parting gifts of grain and cheese and dried meat. Their sneers never softened, whether we offered them kindness or sneered right back at them.

And the dinginess that seemed to infest their persons was soon dispersing through the village, as a new variety each day of smoke or dust cloud or just plain stink. The once-green commons was their work area, scorched and discolored by the smelting of bronze and boiling of glue and mixing of paint. Hammering and sawing and squabbling rang out from dawn till dusk. Nobody set foot on the commons any more, no matter how long a detour was involved.

So avidly did we avoid our unwanted guests that seeing two finished wagons in front of Groit's hut took us by surprise. Groit acted well-pleased, though he could hardly have failed to notice that these were smaller than the builders' own wagons, with paint duller and thinner, and without any eye-catching designs. For the first time, too, I wondered if Groit had clearly established how many wagons he was expecting. The stack of wheels behind the wagons seemed little shorter for the eight that had been used.

But whose problem was that? Straightaway, thanks to Groit, we had our own worries. He clapped officiously to draw our critical eyes from the wagons and proclaimed that the day was young and mild, which augured well for our first journey to retrieve slabs. Near the village where he had grown up, only three territories to the East, was a field with big rocks galore. We could be there and back in a week. In plenty of time for the Feast of Dead Souls.

"If we're not dead souls then ourselves," someone muttered.

Groit winced. He dared not let doubts weaken his god-given influence. Which meant sidestepping the issue. He bellowed for one of the wagonmakers, who along with Knub were sitting on stools watching us from within the wasteland of our commons. One of them at last stood up, stretched lazily, and ambled over. He regarded Groit blandly.

"Can we not use these wagons to carry stones?" Groit demanded.

"Sure you can put stones in them," said the wagonmaker, as if a child should know that. With a smile that was beginning to look superior, until Groit resumed his spiel. At which point the wagonmaker ambled back among his own.

"We will be welcome in the three villages on our route. For this task I will require only bachelors, who may soon have cause to thank me, as many women in these places are seeking husbands. And how could you fail to impress them, pulling the sacred wagon behind you?"

We bachelors then realized how much work we were really in for. The wagonwrights had horses, but we had none. They had always seemed like more trouble than they were worth. Till now. So just like that, six of us including myself were handed ropes which were threaded through eyeholes on a pole jutting from the front of one of the wagons. Groit explained that the other wagon was reserved for the procession, and while we were away it would receive suitable adornment from the wagonwrights, in order to win all possible divine approval. At no little added expense to himself in cheese and meat, selfless Groit pointed out. And then our big man bid us embark, to save his dignity from further compromise as children from the Crayfish clan ran up to our wagon and viciously kicked its wheels.

The prospect of finding wives may have been more than empty come-on. But after long days of struggling across rocky ground and rushing streams and muddy sloughs, all of us but Groit were dead on our feet, fit only for eating and sleeping. Or at most, gawking horrified at each day's new blisters and rope burns on hands and shoulders. How were we supposed to manage a wagon full of stone later? The villages hosting us could almost have been our own, hut for hut, except that their commons were grassy and fragrant. Nonetheless, the local big men, Groit assured us, were so enamored of our wagon that they wanted him to send the wagonmakers their way. The outcome of our trip would prove of more benefit to those villages than they would ever realize.

All boded well at first. Groit's memory of the field ran true. It was just outside his home village. Too many boulders bulged partway from its grass for sowing to make sense. Above the field rose a wide hill, from the middle of which beetled a ledge of the same gray rock as lay scattered below. Groit's friend, our host, accompanied us. Perhaps both big men had a reputation for hatching schemes to be avoided. In any case, no friends or relatives of either man joined us.

At first Groit skipped among the prospective henge slabs as merrily as a crow after the fall slaughter. But he soon perceived that no stone bore much likeness to a pole. The best that came to hand was shaped rather like a sheep head. But it stood higher than any of us could reach, which Groit favored, and it was leaning almost upright against the ledge face, which we favored, as it thus seemed easier to tilt into the wagon.

None of us had ever seen, let alone handled, stones of this size. Still, hadn't the wagonwright made plain that we could carry stones? When the local big man saw us back the wagon up to our chosen rock and tip the wagon up on its rear wheels to receive it, he expressed concern about how strong the wagon was. Two men with upheld arms strained against the skyward dragging-stick while Groit, with florid gestures, bragged of the bronze wheel-rims, the further bronzework that kept wagon and wheels in one piece, the extraordinary glue that held the painted planks together, and the wagonwrights' incredible brilliance in general. Once he had shown off this masterpiece of craftsmanship down to the last sliver, he stepped back, arms folded grandly. The other big man arched his eyebrows but said no more.

Meanwhile, we other conscripts pressed as best we could between the slab and the ledge face and pushed. As the slab began to give way, we roared triumphantly and pushed harder. It went over suddenly, followed by an unpleasant, splintering crash. We were flabbergasted; Groit was horrorstruck. Groit's politick friend assumed an air of silent detachment. The dragging-stick was, if anything, straighter up in the air than before, but without human assistance. The rock had gone through the floor of the wagon. Leaving not enough for a man to stand on. The side boards flared out like gasping gills. The rock, in flattening the rod between the rear wheels, had bent the wheels inward, so that the stone sheep head now had wooden ears. "That sheep has jaws like a wolf," someone mumbled.

This seemed that much funnier to me on realizing that Groit's plans for a henge of stone were now at an end. Even if twenty wagons were waiting back in our village. So much for Groit's version of the will of the gods. Red-faced, he demanded to know what everyone found so amusing. "You have not been married into our village long enough to have seen a true crisis," I said. "You've heard of tears of joy. Well, at times like this we have laughter of sorrow." Everyone looked Groit in the eye with a confidential nod, and laughed harder. The local big man, casting his gaze here and there but never at the scene of destruction, appeared embarrassed. Maybe for Groit's sake. Maybe for having anything to do with the proceedings himself.

If the women on our route had seen any of us as prizes before, they must have changed their minds as we trudged back with our two-wheeled, splay-sided wreck in tow. Just the same, the return trip was much more to our liking. We weren't too tired this time to enjoy local hospitality, though Groit had little to say, beyond alluding to a near-fatal, wagon-crushing rockslide, obviously the work of malignant tutelary spirits.

On our return, the commons was vacant, and in front of Groit's hut sat the second wagon, with a mere straight line painted along the sides, sloppy dots above and below. "Where are the wagonwrights?" Groit yelled at his household. "They must repair the rockslide damage to this wagon!"

"They said they'd decorated your second wagon as you'd insisted, and that they were done," replied Groit's wife. In a quiet manner that belied any quiet in her heart. "They said they had to go. They couldn't take it here any longer without beer. Whatever that is."

Rather than go indoors for less restrained words from his wife, Groit, choosing to give rather than get, paid a visit to Knub. Who had to be called several times before coming out. "Did you think this was what I wanted?" Groit greeted him. "Only two wagons, and one smashed to pieces already?"

Knub, playing at the put-upon innocent, said that the wagonmakers had fled in the night. Long before anyone was the wiser. Groit scowled. And how, he wanted to know, could they have sneaked off when their wheels were so loud as to have been heard when coming over the horizon? Nobody wanted to take Knub's side, but neither did anyone want the wagonmakers back. "Knub is right!" a bystander shouted. Others pitched in. "We must have been drugged or enchanted. And by now they have put themselves out of reach. Someplace far away, with this beer that they spoke of. Let them be. Pursuit might be dangerous. Suppose this beer is some kind of fierce protector?"

"So, Knub, you did not know your friends as well as you claimed," Groit grinned vindictively. "Or did you know they were versed in magic or some other trickery?"

Between admitting himself stupid or else in cahoots with sorcerers, Knub had to take the first choice or face worse consequences. But was this repayment enough for the humiliation Groit had endured in three territories?

"Take heart, Groit," Knub implored. "You still have a beautiful wagon, the only one for many days in any direction, just in time for the procession. You have come out ahead in these dealings."

Groit stared longer at Knub, and finally scratched his chin thoughtfully. He said nothing else, but turned and strode off.

When suddenly the days wane shorter and the wind drives with slashing edge from the North and the new moon after the harvest begins to wax, then whoever tends the sacred acre must find in the stars the signs that fix the day for the Feast of Dead Souls. Thereafter, winter darkness is in ascendance, with frost and snow in the offing, and those who are dead and cold and in darkness must be propitiated by sacrifice, lest they tarry at the fall slaughter and put their poison touch on the beef. When nature dies down, our world more closely resembles that of the dead, letting the dead more easily walk upon it. A fearsome prospect, and whatever esteem Groit enjoyed was based on his role in keeping the dead at bay.

Before the Feast came the procession, wherein our image of the god of death was borne around our borders, gathering incoming spirits to the sacrifice. Everyone hale enough would march, shaking rattles, shrilling with bone pipes, pounding on skin drums, and defiling at last into the henge. There, the unseen dead were supposedly so thick around us that our most sensitive celebrants would shiver or shriek or sometimes faint at claiming to feel cold spirit breath or fingertips. Not that ill-behaved children had never been caught trying to give the more gullible a touch of the supernatural. In any event, little at this point could delay the climax of the ritual. An ox was poleaxed and hastily quartered, and as its blood snaked toward the toes of onlookers, an orderly but prompt retreat to the village took place, leaving the dead to partake as they would, with the god of the dead presiding atop the oaken block. Thus could we hold the fall slaughter and a feast for the living, usually free from ghostly taint. Thanks to the wagon, though, this year would be different.

In the days before the Feast, Knub proved himself little chastened by the big man's anger. Based on what the orphan girl heard, the wheelwright still took Groit seriously only as a potential benefactor. And otherwise must have believed Groit nothing more than a bumpkin among bumpkins. Knub saw nothing audacious in calling on the big man, and may not even have noticed Groit's unpromising reserve, so anxious was he to get on with his newest ploy. Wasn't it a shame, he asked, seeing that stack of wheels out front going to waste? But not to worry! Without resorting to outside help, Knub could use them to make Groit a bigger man than he ever had been, that incident with the rockslide notwithstanding. Groit's brow furrowed at this point, but he said nothing. Knub wanted the big man to reconsider the war-basket idea. Why be satisfied as big man of just one village? Groit would probably not even have to strike a single blow to dominate the surrounding territories. Merely ride in with a squadron of rumbling, arrow-swift war-baskets. And demand tribute and labor in exchange for peace. Our modest sacred acre would become a magnificent center of worship for every village within Groit's purview. The big man's power and wealth would be unlike anything ever seen in these parts.

Groit made mildmannered reply. He reminded Knub that the village had no horses. Knub promised to acquire some himself. Groit admitted liking the sound of that, especially as we, "his" people, had lately seemed lax in our piety. It was high time we renewed our religious commitment, and high time we got in step with the rest of the world, before it was too late. Let those who wished divine favor build and man the war-baskets.

Knub, with widening grin, could hardly contain his glee. But Groit cautioned him that other matters needed attention first. "As you must know, the Feast of Dead Souls is almost upon us. To do our wagon justice, and to make its introduction memorable, I have ordained great changes in the procession. First and foremost, the people will not march this time. Instead, you will guide the wagon in its circuit of the territory, and with you shall ride our god of death. All the wheels will you take as well. Since they will be attached to bringers of death and war, they will in this way be consecrated to the god of death. The gathered people shall await you in the henge. Imagine their wonderment as they hear the wagon approach from afar, and then as they see it racing up to them. Then you shall proffer me the god's image and the sacrifice will commence. And, oh yes, one more detail. Since the people will have to get used to horses soon, I want you to acquire one immediately for the procession, one that is trained to pull wagons. How long should that take you?"

A week, the wheelwright guessed. Groit said that would be fine.

Knub was actually gone for ten days. Not until his return did Groit announce that the Feast was fated for the morrow. Knub riding in on horseback was worth a long look, as nobody till now had seen a man atop a horse, but the horse himself was hardly imposing or warlike. Dust-colored and dwarfish compared to the wagonwrights' stallions, he looked around apathetically and resignedly took tufts of grass from children. Hard to imagine him taking any part in a battle-charge. Knub confessed that he had been able to do no better with the bronze items that Groit had provided for bartering. But Groit replied cheerfully that his bronze had been well-invested.

Meanwhile, who among us had not been aghast on hearing that Groit still took the wheelwright seriously? That disastrous expedition with the first wagon should have presented lesson enough. But apparently Knub had to fall still further from grace.

A few of us in the Crow clan had not been content to wish that Knub simply would not come back. He had been too lucky so far for that. But luck was like water. The enterprising could channel it. Groit himself had professed that pride mattered more than peace, both here and with our neighbors. Yet that pride was never greater than when he presided at the sacred acre. If wheels were to bring a holy occasion to ruin, then wheels would be anathema ever after.

And so we discontent few put on dark hoods and cloaks on the eve of the Feast. At moonrise, when all others were asleep, we convened at the henge, where the eastward-facing wagon was waiting to set out. Our byword was stealth, but we did poorly at concealing our jitters. While two of us watched warily all around, I and one other lay under the wagon, chipping away with our flint hatchets at the rod that connected the two front wheels. Between us we hacked halfway through in a dozen places and at as many angles. Before we could attack the rear wheels, hoarse whispers from the watchmen bid us stop. What they called devilish laughter had risen from somewhere afield. Perhaps nothing more than an owl, or a raven awakened by our work. But in case man or ghost had discovered us, hasty departure seemed only sensible. What we'd already done would surely suffice once the wagon started crossing bumpy terrain. We scattered home one shudder short of a panic, but well-pleased with ourselves.

At dawn we were back at the henge with everyone else, to see Knub off. The horse had been bound to the dragging-stick, and another cord stretched from Knub's hands into the horse's mouth. In the back of the wagon were four stacks of the unused wheels. And beside the wheelwright rode the oaken god of death, with skullish grin and fleshless ribs and double-ax at his side. Along the sides of the wagon were fastened the ghost-baiting rattles.

Groit, in his inevitable proclamation, vowed that none would ever forget this Feast day, even if not everyone grasped its full significance. Knub had undertaken a sacred trust, upon which hinged not merely the success of our fall slaughter but the well-being and fame of our village. This was the closest Groit came to brooking the business of the war-baskets. But of course that would have been old news anyway, thanks to the orphan girl.

Lastly, the big man commended Knub for bravely traversing land still unfamiliar to him at a time when any number of ghosts would be flocking around him. Trying conditions, indeed. To speed him along, Groit had personally overseen the planting of stakes every several paces over the entire circuit. Knub was always to steer just right of these. "May you find favor with all the dead around you," Groit concluded.

With that, Knub nodded solemnly, flicked the cord going into the horse's mouth, and shouted some strange word at the horse. The horse plodded forward, and the wagon jerked into motion, creaking ominously, rattles clattering.

Then the people retired to their homes, under instructions to return when the sun touched the Western horizon, in order to cheer the wheelwright's approach. I, for one, felt divinely blessed when no one noticed the little wood chips on the ground where the wagon had stood.

For the first time in memory, no procession filled this day. Many went back to bed till the sun was at its zenith. Some huddled miserably on their stoops or around their hearths, starting at every noise, convinced that ghosts would soon swarm thick as flies without proper procession to restrain them. I was in the minority trying to keep busy, cleaning or making repairs around the hut. And sometimes, from deep within forest or across the plain, carried faintly the rattles and groaning wheels of the wagon.

In late afternoon, households began showing up at the henge. Everyone appeared uneasy, whether at the chance of ghostly trouble today, or at the prospect of war-baskets and war soon enough. Waiting by the oaken block, both Groit and the ox wore stolid expressions. The sun was going down and the wind began to rise. The only able-bodied villager missing was the wheelwright. Exasperation soon crinkled the big man's brow. Who, besides we four of the Crow clan, would not assume that Knub must have come to supernatural grief?

The wind brought a faraway cry from the West. All at once the crowd broke and ran toward what was obviously Knub in trouble. They followed the great curve of stakes onto the moor, while Groit strode along behind them, not deigning to exceed the measured pace that befit his office.

Between the moor and the river lay a bog. The procession, of course, would have crossed the river at a ford, from which a path led around the bog. The stakes, though, led right into the bog. This caused no talk at the time because of the general rush to find the wheelwright. Anyone growing up here knew the safe trails of solid ground through the bog, but as Knub had proved, these were not for the novice. He and the wagon were both half sunk in putrid-smelling mud, and sinking deeper as we watched. This came as no surprise, but the rest of the scene beggared belief. I marveled that the wagon had come as far as it had, since off in the distance a few crows sat and pecked idly at the front wheels which, many paces apart, leaned against broken lengths of the wheel-rod. And insofar as wagon, stacks of wheels, and Knub were all enmired, how to account for the horse, dry and free of the ropes, munching swamp grass on a nearby hummock? And how to account for the equally bone-dry god of death, staring skyward, on the same hummock?

In the moment before Groit caught up with us, Knub had sunk down to his chest, to which he was forlornly hugging one of his wheels. Plainly this was not working to his benefit. Cousin Hinda led the chorus imploring him to let go of the wheel. He seemed not to hear, until Groit pushed past the crowd and called out, "I have a rope! Unhand the wheel and I will throw you the rope!"

"The wheels are my life!" answered Knub. "And soon they will be everywhere! You will see!"

"Forget the wheels! Live among us as one of us! The wheels are not worth dying for!" At this point I understood, as Knub must have understood as soon as he was in the mire, that rescue had nothing to do with forfeiting the particular wheel in his grasp.

"I am a wheelwright!" Knub roared, only head and neck above the mud.

"It is almost too late!" Groit shouted. "Let go of the wheel and pull your arms free while you still can!" Whether or not people realized the choice Knub really had to make, they joined in begging him to reach out. He held onto the wheel and stonily faced his would-be rescuers.

Hinda turned away as Knub's mouth and nose went under. His eyes widened, and then he sank from sight quickly. Aunts, sisters and mother consoled sobbing Hinda. They went back to the village, while the rest of us completed our obligation at the henge. Not that ghosts felt like a pressing concern at the moment, when death itself had been so close at hand. Groit had taken the ox's tethering rope to the bog, but the ox hadn't known enough to try fleeing for its life. Maybe neither ox nor Knub truly realized the trouble they were in until it was too late.

Good to know, at least, that the big man's ambitions knew some bounds of decency after all. And that he had obviously come around to making our village wheel-free, one way or another. As for how Knub and broken wagon, but not horse or death-god, had wound up in the mire, perhaps the four of us in the Crow clan had not been the only concerned villagers. Then again, during the Feast of Dead Souls, was intervention by a higher power any less likely?

Hinda was soon over her loss. She had to admit that Knub hadn't been much of a husband. Nothing on his mind but wheels all the time, as far as she could tell. Life was too short to mourn very long over a husband who really was not working out.

We sent a messenger to Knub's family to break the bad news. Couched in terms of tragic accident. But all the same, you never know how the bereaved will take it, especially when there is no corpse to be seen. The big man of Knub's home village sent the reply. Condolences to Hinda, as was to be expected. And then the offer of another bachelor wheelwright in his village to replace the one she had lost. We were all agreed that the only tactful course was to say nothing and hope that the question never came up again.

The Road to Schwärmerei

By boarding time it was mostly they who filled the seats in the waiting area, and who stood gabbing merrily, oblivious to anyone trying to get around them. When Syd felt a nudge at the forearm he'd been resting on the back of his seat, he withdrew, even though the name-badged matron whose arm now rested there was, after all, invading his space. And worse, her queenly look prompted him to mumble, "Excuse me." With peripheral squint he sometimes noticed heads cocked his way, as if cold crow eyes were sizing up a bright trinket. But when he stared back, their looks turned presumed-upon, smoldery. Syd couldn't quite make out what kind of cutesy mascot adorned all the badges.

Once airborne and at cruising altitude, the mass loosing of seatbelts was alarming, like cardboard in bicycle spokes. Syd glumly saw at last how deep he was in apparent company picnic. Out of two hundred-plus on this Boeing 767, at least two-thirds were up and socializing, saying nothing he could pick out over jet drone, but shrill enough to make him dread these seven transatlantic hours.

At the end of Syd's row, a corn-fed patriarch, with Ahab beard and bald pate, had planted himself. He stood hobnobbing with the aisle passenger, and Syd detected an archetype of sorts in pencil holder and glasses case jammed into sport shirt pocket, and lip of trusslike money-belt jutting over waistband, in the shadow of potbelly. The name-badge mascot was still out of focus, maybe with Viking horns or rabbit ears, maybe with hockey stick or T-square, maybe with none of the above.

The giddiness in eyes and chatter bespoke more than getaway anticipation. Syd knew from his own ancient history where these symptoms pointed, though for this crowd full of mutual reinforcement, cure seemed unlikely. And they, no doubt, felt at their happiest and best in the throes of their enthusiasm, whether for Jesus or *Star Trek* or

Hummel figurines. Of the nature of these converts he had no inkling, but make no mistake, true fulfillment flowed solely from whatever they had in common, for that was always a condition of *Schwärmerei*. And who to say it better, mused Syd with unregenerate political incorrectness, than the Germans, with 1,500 years of going overboard between sack of Rome and Third Reich?

Syd sighed relief as Ahab beard finally sauntered off to block some other row. Bathroom had become top priority, and though red lights ahead signaled "Fwd Lavs Occupied," intrepid Syd zigzagged like a pinball past the laughing gaggles, braced for waiting in line. Oddly, the little sliding panel on one bathroom door read "Vacant," though the overhead light still insisted otherwise. Syd nudged the door, heard no protest from within, and entered shrugging.

Brrr. Kinda cold in there, but then again, didn't these toilets empty into subzero sky? More bothersome was the latched panel, broad as a doormat, above the toilet. He blinked, clueless as to what lay behind. Circuitry, emergency kits, spare parts? The prolonged sight of it made him antsy, in the event turbulence pitched him against it and all hell somehow broke loose.

Happy to escape the washroom without incident, Syd again marveled at the ubiquitous name badges: on oldsters, kids, society dames, strapping rednecks, all in comfortable leisurewear. And from so much diversity came one bloc, one group mind that seemed to think it owned the plane. At the outset of stop-and-go trek back to his seat, as tots raced back and forth and pensioners tugged at overhead compartment items, Syd caught his first snatch of conversation, without seeing who spoke: ". . . a mistake, but it's all right now I guess." "Just a case of too much too soon." The tone was ominous, but no way could it have been Syd under discussion, so his mind roved elsewhere.

His last obstacle was a fine-boned Nordic lady, with lines of post-forty written plain on her face, but who filled maternity dress to bursting. They had to sidle past one another, and their stomachs unavoidably brushed, though hers, firm as an apple, seemed to nuzzle unnecessarily against his. And he could have sworn her eyes flashed and her lips blew a swift kiss at him. But none of his nonplussed backward glances at her were returned.

At this point, the flight crew was pleased to announce complimentary wine service. Syd and the rest of his row soon lowered their trays to receive little bottles of red wine and plastic cups. Syd longed for something stronger, but saw nothing else on the cart. And since it was free, after all, he felt inhibited about speaking up and disrupting well-oiled procedure. He unscrewed the cap and poured. Any darker and heavier, and it would have been a liqueur. Syd felt a tingling to either side of his molars. The label read "Champs d'Elysée." What kind of hack name for a wine was that? Still, "Produce of France" it was, so he sighed and enjoyed. Everyone else, seated or standing, was duly downing theirs. The alcohol's first rising warmth softened the brunt of sudden certainty: whereas the bulk of passengers had initially struck him as loopy, now the same seemed true of the flight, or maybe of the airline itself.

Syd's travel agency, despite framed posters of glorious beaches and cathedrals, had the ambience of a hard-nosed brokerage. His travel agent could have been any beefy, humorless businessman. And was that arch of eyebrows judgmental when Syd requested the rock-bottom fare, peak season or not, with destination secondary, be it anywhere but a war zone? Syd had lately come to sense that people, whether checkout clerks, barbers, or doctors, tried getting rid of him as quickly as possible. In happier youth, he had been either more likable or less observant. As middle age loomed, his income was marginal, his wardrobe drab, and his manner blasé. But these were scarcely grounds to begrudge him however much Europe he could afford while he was still young enough to enjoy it. The agent recommended a charter on "New Spirit." When Syd asked, sensibly enough, why he'd never heard of them, the agent huffed with a take-it-or-leave-it air that nothing else was as cheap, and that they'd suffered no bad press yet. Hesitation on Syd's part would apparently mark him as a waste of time and hence respect. With all the brusqueness he could muster, Syd okayed the booking.

A little logy from his first "Champs d'Elysée," Syd blinked as a second was plunked onto his tray. He grasped the tail-end of announcement about impending dinner service. Standees traipsed back to their seats, many giggly, several couples seemingly burlesquing a chase. Some, Syd swore, were not in their original seats, and other formerly occupied seats remained empty.

Then the no-less-mystifying business of dining was upon him. The cellophane around his silverware ripped only after a violent tug which left him self-conscious, and his cramped tray offered no good place for the lids from salad and entrée. Capping his frustration, his elbows invaded neighboring airspace unless he ate like a mantis, arms bent sharply and pressed to his sides. And still, between turbulence and tiny-pronged fork, accidents happened. Luckily, those spatters of apparent chicken curry blended right in with his yellow shirt.

The rest of Syd's row was digging in without visible hardship. Elsewhere, though, others seemed to be copying his pose, until steadier focus showed hands folded in prayer. Prayers over, they attacked their food as fiercely as mandrills. With renewed intensity, Syd tried pegging the "mascot." Failing that, he gulped more wine.

While the tingling behind his molars ebbed, his look happened to linger across the aisle. A big-eyed redhead with heavy makeup was licking the mouth of her own empty bottle provocatively, snaking her tongue as far inside as possible. With a jolt he realized she was gazing straight at him. No sooner had blushing Syd lowered his eyes than the gangly yokel in the aisle seat snatched the roll off Syd's tray, remarking, "Seeing as how you're leaving this . . ." Syd could only gawk at him until the thief summarily whispered, "Waste is a sin, you know." The man between them was studiously minding his own business. Were these Puritans or libertines, or something else altogether that rendered such polarities moot? Syd still had four joyless hours to figure it out.

For the moment, though, the heavy wine in him was like a center of gravity, pulling his errant awareness down, down, into fitful dozing. Chat and laughter were filtered through a dreamy haze of dislocation, turning the cabin into a cocktail party, an Italian wedding reception, an Oktoberfest. Syd languidly despised the exuberance rattling his rest, with sole consolation that joining in was not expected of him.

Then even this was wrenched away with a tap on his shoulder. The seat between them was empty; the yokel was leaning so close that Syd could smell his carroty breath. "Some of us had a little game in mind, down by the big screen. Thought you might be interested."

"Don't like cards," Syd mumbled and closed his eyes dismissively. When he reopened them the barest slit, the yokel was gone.

Before Syd could drift off, the announcement for inflight entertainment hit him like reveille. He lowered the sliding panel over his window, as per general request, and shortly the cabin was dark as a mineshaft.

Squirming, he tugged loose his headset, with no idea how long he'd been sitting on it. Even before takeoff he'd scorned the bland music channels in his armrest, whether pop, country, or chamber. But what the hell, this as much as dinner was part of his hard-earned travel experience, and not to be wasted. Anyway, how to nod off with image bombardment at every blink?

He thumbed to the right channel on armrest pushbutton just as the lights dimmed and the screen lit up. A CNN world events recap preceded a longwinded infomercial about milk that stayed "fresh" at room temperature for months. Syd shuddered, and then felt completely at sea with the ensuing public service short. Near as he could tell, it endorsed safe sex, while avoiding all mention of "condoms" or even "protection." Especially amazing was a scene on an airplane, where a leggy vixen, triggering lust with every toss of her hair, primly refused the clumsy gropings of the unassuming, sweater-vest kind of guy with whom Syd identified. Over a freezeframe of this tableau, a screen-wide black X flashed for emphasis. Syd fidgeted lower in his seat, worried that here was warning both to and about him. It was unclear, though, why having sex with him on this plane was off-limits.

Syd furtively gazed hither and yon. Caveat or not, nobody was paying him more mind than before. No, of course not. Just possibly, squinty window-seat angle had contributed to his wild, myopic take on the scenario. Surely one of those long-empty seats toward cabin center, with head-on view of the screen, was worth the effort of relocating.

On his way, a short girl with frosted perm and tortoiseshell glasses grabbed his forearm from across empty aisle seat. "Todd!" she exclaimed and smiled invitingly. Was she really batting her eyelashes?

"Sorry, I'm not," Syd said without pausing, so that her hand slid away. Funny though, she seemed not at all taken aback about her mistake, as if she'd wanted him beside her, never really believing he was "Todd." Well, maybe she was desperate to meet someone. Syd half regretted killing a chance for some forward female company, but punchy as he was, conversation would have been hopeless.

Anyway, those seconds of stimulation were far downstream by the time headset was reinstalled. And the new view proved a disappointment after all in terms of honing dull wits. Syd lapsed in and out of cognizance repeatedly during the pre-credits sequence, which seemed to prefigure the kind of lovey-dovey family comedy that the airline must have naively believed would offend no one. No surprise there. But then, with a saccharine orchestral swell, the title loomed, and it was *Will You Sleep with Me?* An incredulous blink later, and it was gone. Restoring his senses clearly hinged on more than line of sight. He closed his eyes with renewed determination to nap, but minus the wherewithal to doff earphones.

Choppy, crazy-quilt dreams weighed on his shallow sleep until broadsides of music or sound effects jarred him awake, mostly to trite domestic calamities involving freckly kids and white-bread adults, but sometimes to green snakes or black frogs springing jack-in-the-boxlike from unlikely places such as car hoods or soda machines. During a musical sequence whose bogus Andrews Sisters chorus seemed to be "You are your own voodoo dolly," Syd gave up his last perversely stubborn cares about what was going on and sank disgusted into hardier sleep.

When Syd next came to himself, less leaden than he'd felt in hours, his eyes happened to light on his erstwhile window seat. The sliding panel over his window was back up. In through the pane, which was suddenly elastic, thrust a claw large enough to encircle his head. Its dead blue flesh within rubbery glass sheath whitened with frost as the outstretched talons groped around the seat, plucking at the upholstery, and straining to pat the farther armrest back and forth. Syd's eyes widened and a cold stone seemed to sit in the pit of his stomach. Making a sound never occurred to him. He was too absorbed to see how anyone else was reacting. He didn't even know if the movie were still running. Grudgingly, the claw withdrew, and the last talon caught on the pane and pulled it out a little. Syd ogled while the pucker in the glass slowly flattened out. His fear began to babble out of him only when the sliding panel inched by itself back over the window.

Syd rubbed his eyes with the heels of his palms, and then the movie was yacking in his earphones again. His consciousness was brackish as ever, but he had the certainty of being awake now, of snapping out of a dream. Sweat odor hung heavy around him. Dammit, the long-sought sleep deep enough to shut out his surroundings had only subjected him to what his unconscious had been making of those surroundings. Talk about demonizing these people! Still, however little their good opinion mattered, he grimaced to think of anyone within smelling range of him.

Obligingly, no one was sitting within three seats in any direction. But during his look around, the curtains for the first-class section, many rows forward, parted, and Syd's gaze lingered on the woman stepping through. She must have been fifty at least, with glossy post-facelift skin, but thoroughly slinky with black stockings and clingy black dress and long, wavy black hair. Lust trembled a little deep inside Syd's drowsiness, until her glare homed in on him despite the distance between them. He tried lowering his focus nonchalantly, as if she'd crossed his line of sight but was never under his scrutiny, of course. When next he looked up, she was gone.

At that instant the cabin lights went up, surprising him. The end-credits of the long-neglected movie gave way to blank screen. Syd debated removing to his original seat, before someone came to oust him or fill his own empty place. That silly, mean-spirited nightmare, which might have given him pause a dark minute ago, was fading fast in the brightness, especially with passengers raising their window panels, revealing both dawn and Europe on the horizon.

People were now quiet, subdued. Hearing none of the badge-wearers' baleful chatter and bustling, Syd relaxed, and down came the guard so entrenched that he'd grown oblivious to it. And then the yokel approached, head weaving side to side gooselike until he spotted Syd and jerkily leaned over him. "Friend, I'm so glad we got your attention!" he blabbed, as Syd gaped uncomprehending. "Veronique's really something all right, but she's not for the novice."

Syd surmised that Veronique must have been the woman in black.

"Abby's available, though, and she'd really like to talk to you."

No sooner was the name spoken than the short girl with the glasses, three rows down, popped up her head and turned around. "Hi!" She flashed Syd a big smile.

Oh, why the hell not? Syd felt like he'd been flushed out of his warren, but he didn't care. That little current of desire was still pulsing deep down. They'd be landing in an hour or two. Whatever these people were about, any touchy-feely on the girl's part was fine with him. He just wouldn't sign, let alone use, his real name for the duration.

He sat beside her, pleased to see the yokel saunter somewhere aft. He introduced himself as Cy, and offered only the vaguest generalities about himself, but this seemed not to discourage her. He noticed her fingertips brushing the back of his hand, then stroking it, then settling upon it. He swallowed and wondered if his face was red. Neither his aura of old sweat nor a fresh outbreak seemed to phase her.

She flashed that big smile again and brought her face near his as if to kiss him, but pulled back at the last second. She whispered, her breath warm in his ear, "Have you had the wine?"

He nodded and she asked, "Did you watch the movie?"

When he said he had, more or less, her look grew more probing and earnest, but enticing all the same.

"Can I stick this in you? It's hardly big enough to hurt. And then I'll do whatever you want." Between thumb and index finger, Abby was slowly rolling a tiny silver nail, with a dainty tiny chain hanging from the head end. Worst of all, her eyes were glazed with that repulsive *Schwärmerei*.

"What?" he asked, his mood in pieces.

"It's just symbolic, really," she wheedled, "a token of good faith."

Abby seemed surprised when Syd's hand jerked out from under hers, and her tone grew pleading. "Didn't you ever have a passion for anything?"

"Yeah, sure," Syd faltered, unable to come up with anything zippy on short notice, but confident in saying, "Back when I was old enough to drink, but still just a kid."

The godsend announcement of momentary breakfast service gave Syd the out to excuse himself and bolt back to his window seat. He regretted the need to crawl over the man sitting beside him, but was thankful for any barricade against Abby. He stared out at wan predawn until the food cart pulled up.

Syd lowered his tray in synch with his neighbor. Taking stock of him for the first time, Syd regarded him with respect, maybe even as someone to look up to. He could have been the same age as Syd, but that was hard to pin down. He was dressed simply, in dungarees and light blue button-down shirt. He had wire-rim glasses and hair combed down in short bangs. He could have been artist, math professor, or historian. Deep in a Lawrence Durrell novel, he seemed impervious to all onboard antics, as well as to the standard annoyances of flying. His impassive face was free of oil or sweat; his shirt was dry and crisp. No importuning zeal was likely to well out of him. Best of all, he wore no badge.

Isolation and loneliness suddenly assailed Syd. This maiden European trip was a big deal for him, and these seven hours of shunning his fellow creatures had felt needlessly bleak, not the way he'd want to look back on it.

While they partook of croissant and coffee, Syd grew more eager to speak, but nothing came to mind that wasn't fatuous on reflection. Finally, as attendants were coming around to pick up, Syd heard, "Oh dear."

Syd, at a loss for words, met his neighbor's eyes. "Dropped my spoon." The tone was apologetic. "Might as well be down a crevasse." Syd checked the floor between their trays. The spoon was in easy reach, next to his foot. "Worse yet, I'm afraid," the man continued as Syd caught the spoon between two fingertips. "In the process, some milk landed on your jeans."

"I hadn't even noticed," said Syd, returning the spoon. "I'll just take some wet paper towels to it. I was about to get up anyway." As the cart paused at their row, Syd good-humoredly recounted all the dining tribulations he'd noted during dinner. He concluded, after putting his tray back up, "You must fly a lot, to be so cool all this time between one thing and another. Especially with all the religious kooks, or whatever they are, on this flight."

The man's brow furrowed and he frowned coldly but said nothing while putting up his own tray, to reveal a sweater vest folded double in the seat back's net pouch, and a badge at the base of the sweater's V-neck.

Pretending he hadn't seen the badge, Syd sprang up and said, "Well, guess I better go work on that stain." He avoided the man's look while squeezing by, and en route to the lav admitted miserably that maybe not all the badge-wearers were weirdoes like Abby. And now he'd either have to change seats or apologize, putting himself in the best light by explaining how one bad apple in the congregation was impaling strangers for a turn-on.

Syd did his last-minute best to regard these people with deference, which was much easier with most of them sitting quietly, apart from a few gaggles near the restrooms. The same lav as last time was unoccupied. Syd hoped to hear some enlightening conversation before closing the door, but something about "the hard way" held no insight.

More clearheaded than he'd felt since boarding, Syd took one glance at the mysterious latched panel while undoing his fly, and realized it must have been a platform for changing diapers. He chuckled at how obvious it was, and then the panel flipped down with a slam and something cold, foul, and leathery clamped over Syd's face, muffling and blinding him at the same time.

Wherever rail pass took Syd that month, whether Roman ruin, Alpine lodge or Riviera café, the locals were put off by his despairing eyes and heavy arthritic manner, so out of keeping in a young, trim American. Had anyone not shied from him at first opportunity, a few steady seconds would have shown the ends of a long needle barely protruding from opposite sides of Syd's head, skillfully thrust so as to effect only the desired change in attitude.

And not until the plane home, in fact, did Syd begin regaining any *joie de vivre,* warming, and then positively beaming, to find himself among his own enthusiastic people at last. That hateful word *"Schwärmerei"* was as good as lanced out of his memory.

McEveety among the Leisure Elect

M cEveety had been dead only a few years and wasn't used to the setup yet. Despite his appearance and habitation, he still hadn't gone all the way native, not in his mind. He was dark and dirt-poor, yes, but he hadn't inclined yet toward either standard response to island economy:

> *Tendency #1.* Become huckster, guide or servant to the tourists. Eke out a steady subsistence. But never catch up on all the calories the constant hustle costs you. Sometimes frayed, malnourished nerves snap. Seemingly pointless murders and arson flare up. The winged troops of the undeclared occupation enjoy easy berserker targets. Their armed presence finds easy justification. First and foremost, protect the tourists!

> *Tendency #2.* Conserve energy. Lounge in the shade. Be like the opportunistic crocodile. Heavy eyes full of hunger and heat. But devoid of sense, as if eyes were drainage systems for emptied minds. Until street commotion presents a situation to size up. Launches you into the baking light of day. The disputants may be locals, or tourists, or some of each. You play hero or villain, whichever secures what the situation offers, whether money, goods, or prestige. Not that boredom or bad moves won't lead to the same amok end as Tendency #1.

McEveety, on the other hand, was no less fixated on imposing order now than he had been in life. He carried no memories of mortal flesh, of course, no inkling of the sins he eternally expiated (who ever said the afterlife would have to be fair?), but earthly personality impressed reflexes on the soul nonetheless, and these had to wear out in their own good time. Hence McEveety crowded his shack with drift-age and rusty scrap for assembly into useless wholes, or he arranged seaweed strands into tablecloth-sized gridworks and set big striped slugs into the matrix at eye-bending angles.

This was how the life of a world-class CEO echoed away. McEveety had been wont to shape Third World underclasses into cheap labor, recking little that work conditions made short work of the laborers. In Central America, South Africa, the Philippines, McEveety had rejoiced to see his factory serfdoms outlast civil regimes. From corporate Sinai he descended to vacation among "his" people, who never guessed what particular Anglo yokel strolled and gawked among them. Except that at any suspicious native approach, he whipped silencered Mauser from under Hawaiian shirttails and preemptively riddled theoretical assault with hushed lead. His net worth, of course, settled any worries about local jurisprudence in case of the inevitable bad call.

In consequence, he found himself where everyone went: one place, but definitely heaven for some and just as definitely hell for others. On this nameless Caribbean isle of souls, none recalled death or judgment or even realized this was no mortal place. It was just that the elect went tourist class and the damned went native. From the day anyone appeared in allotted role as man, woman, or child, steady-state economic status was an unquestioned given. Nor was it in them to see themselves as saved or damned. Guardian angels wore the guise of occupation troops from a nameless mainland, and always put on a courteous, low-key act lest the distastefulness of martial law mar eternal holidays. The leisure elect were as blissfully oblivious of their own harpy role as their earthly equivalents had been.

These elect, in Raybanned droves, did the work of devils on McEveety every day, barging into his shack and blinding him with flashbulbs, insisting he pose with them, throwing him useless foreign change to keep him from feeling exploited, never letting up with stupid questions or remarks. "Ever wake up with a scorpion in your bed?" "Smells like low tide in here." "What do you do all day?" "When you get sick you must have a lot of quaint folk remedies." It was seldom worthwhile to do more than answer in brief or stare listlessly through the questioners. In terms of conserving energy, it was like waving away the flies: wiser to give up.

Even in his pre-assimilated state, McEveety understood that daily harassment would be his inescapable lot for some unthinkable, heat-bleared duration. He was spared the irony of recognizing former coolies in some of his wealthy white-nosed visitors, but he fidgeted with subcutaneous resentment when anyone mentioned how their factories had financed their getaways. All the tourists carried trumped-up memories of mainland lives to which they'd never return, not that this ever penetrated leisure-addled heads.

One morning, hunger sent McEveety skulking into the mainland-owned orange orchard. To calm his nerves while committing pilferage, he shaped a game of annexation with the rationale that momentarily guardless acres were in inexcusable disorder. He planted reeds every meter or so, squaring off an area five trees by five trees. Then he proclaimed, "I take this land in the name of the nation of myself, make it my sovereign colony and enjoy the abandoned fruits thereof." Without further ceremony, he leapt like a salmon again and again, batting oranges off branches and stuffing them into a lobster trap found on the beach.

He chased one rolling orange to the impromptu border, stopped, and caught only his breath as the orange kept going. Here was a moral quandary: Should he null-and-void his own pretext for trespass by an arm's length? And into his nose flowed a gooey-sweet smell that swamped the orchard citrus scent.

McEveety looked up from the ostensibly forbidden fruit, rising to a stance of authority even before his eyes met the newcomer's. The sandals and white socks, the baggy shorts that emphasized knobby knees, the red mesh shirt, the Shriner's Post painter's cap shading a turtlelike face goggling turtlelike with surprise, all bore out the instant nasal assessment of a tourist at hand. The tourist's bemusement ran too deep for encounter with a native to explain it, as if his unconscious depths had been shaken by sudden transplantation into the orchard from out of nothingness. Of course, neither he nor McEveety was equipped to entertain that idea. "I am the owner of this place," McEveety announced, affecting hauteur and folded arms.

"You couldn't be," stated the tourist. Membership among the elect included some share of the intuition of angels, but tact was not part of the programming.

"Well, no matter, since I may also ask what you are doing here." McEveety arched an eyebrow.

"I'm just a-strolling around, getting to know the place. The gate was wide open, so I came in. What of it?" McEveety, to his embarrassment now, had sneaked in over the pink stucco wall without even a thought toward checking the gate. Each of them took the Shriner at his word. Why not? Even if the Shriner were feeling disoriented, he had no inclination to examine his feelings. They were there purely for him to indulge, and for the locals to suffer.

Meanwhile the Shriner had put on take-charge airs, which McEveety had learned to read as symptomatic of career military. He ground his teeth at the grating resonance they set up with his own vestigial mania for control. Best to put the newcomer on the defensive before he got too bossy. "Now I suppose you're going to tell me all about how your years in the service taught you to walk in anywhere and handle anything. Well, you couldn't handle being me."

"Is that so? Listen, chum, I went through situations in combat that would've turned your bowels to soup."

McEveety shrugged floridly. "You chose the army. You could have run away or gotten a discharge after your first tour of duty."

"So how about you? Why don't you just hop a boat out of here?"

It would have been impossible for McEveety to clear his eyes of that film of despair which kept the damned from going anywhere. But there was no need to look for it. McEveety had a litany of unhappy endings ready, spilling out like a slot-machine jackpot. "No way out. Paddle out to sea, the soldiers flap up and divebomb you. No nation would take us even if we could afford to migrate. Beat the odds, smuggle yourself onto another island or the mainland, nothing would change." This was common knowledge, though it remained for anyone to trace collective opinion back to firsthand account.

The Shriner insinuated as much, provoking McEveety to sputter with the indignation of a hooked fish. "I will tell you of someone whose only crime was trying to survive, never mind trying to escape. One morning I beheld a suicide hanging from one of the cedars by the beach road. His leg was crooked, he was missing most of his fingers, and his nose was gone. It was as if by violence he had turned into a leper. The groundskeeper from the estate behind the trees appeared with a wheelbarrow and said he was supposed to get rid of the eyesore. It was the soldiers' job, but they were too slow. So the estate owner wanted to make them come pick up the corpse at his house and get a scolding.

"I asked how the body had become so mutilated. The grounds-keeper shrugged and said he had seen someone in town a while ago who might have been this man at the beginning of his troubles. A bossy tourist had called the man over and made him pick up some suitcases. The tourist's wife was buying something at a booth and turned around to get some money from her husband. She saw this man with their luggage and yelled, 'Thief! Thief!' Before her husband could shut her up, a soldier swooped down with his rifle and shot the man in the shin. The groundskeeper knew nothing more, and said he had to hurry up because his master would beat him if the soldiers arrived before he could take the body.

"Farther down the road I met an old woman, hobbling and gasping for breath. She grabbed my arm to steady herself, and asked if I had seen the hanged man. I pointed backward and asked if she knew what had happened to the man's fingers and nose. She sobbed, and sorrow like a great weight bent her double. No, she could only tell me what had happened to her son's hands. Maybe it was not her son I had seen, she asked as if begging me to make that true. Then, still holding onto my arm while waiting to get her strength back, she told me about her son's hands. After the shooting, fever and infection had come, and when the fever finally broke, neither his head nor his leg was right anymore.

"He became a diver for the coins tourists threw from the docks. He could move better in water than on land, and his simple head had fewer things to look out for there than on the streets. This was not as bad as begging, even if many of the coins were mainland and good for nothing.

"But one day the lame man came up from a dive and in front of him was a boat adrift. The people in it called down to him to look and see if seaweed was tangling up the propeller. His ears were full of water and he thought they were asking him to pull out the seaweed. He went down and tugged it loose and the propeller began to spin. On the docks they said his fingers looked like leaping minnows as they flew out of the water in all directions, and that the poor simple man giggled at this. A couple of soldiers swooped down and took him away before the sight of him could upset the tourists.

"Then I made the old woman go her way by saying how likely it was that some soldiers would come and remove the hanged man's body any minute now. I had only walked a little farther when an oily little man came along, nervous and whiskered like a shrimp. He grabbed my arm, but could not meet my eye for more than a second. Before he could speak, I told him the body was hanging safe and sound up the road. Then I asked about the body's third mutilation.

"He looked at me sharply and stepped back as if from an accusation. Why, he himself was the only one who had tried to help the poor bastard! He had seen the soldiers chase this man from the square for offending the tourists, begging with his fingerless hands. How unfair it seemed to harry a man because he could not hide what was forcing him to do what he was doing. Out of compassion, or so he claimed, the quick-eyed man found the beggar and offered him livelihood.

"All the fingerless man had to do was hold things, not in his hands of course, but in shirt pockets, trouser pockets, wherever. The quick-eyed man was a pickpocket who worked the crowds in the square. He was limited by what he himself could hold, but with someone else as stashkeeper, he could filch enough to support two. The quick-eyed man seemed proud of his finesse, and impressed with himself for thinking of a fingerless man to help him make a living with his fingers.

"It worked well until the pickpocket's rivals saw what he was doing. If too many followed his example, the wave of theft would bring the soldiers in scourging droves. And the pickpocket was already taking much more than his share.

"The quick-eyed man always met his helper under a certain plane tree at the edge of the square. But one day the fingerless man was lying in the shade of the tree as if asleep on his side. The pickpocket shook him and finally rolled him over. In the middle of his face was a red hole, with blood all around it, as if his nose had burst. He and the thief could no longer work together. A man with such a wound could not even approach the square without being cast out like a pail of scraps by the soldiers.

"This last disfigurement shocked the poor man back to his senses.

He could see how hopeless his life had become. The thief had last seen him on the edge of town gazing up at some cedars.

"I asked if the thief wanted to fetch the body and give it decent burial. He snorted and asked what good that would do. No, it was rumored that enemies had pinned a note to the body blaming him for the recent excess of theft. His shifty eyes shied from mine once more and he hurried along.

"So you see, thanks to you tourists, an innocent man cannot survive, let alone better himself." Naturally McEveety could not know that no native here could qualify as innocent. Nor could he ponder the niceties of someone in damnation sinning yet further by committing suicide. How many degrees of damnation were there? Where do you go from damned? McEveety sneezed.

The Shriner shook his head as if dispelling daze. "Well now, I've been patient so far, but how was any of that my problem?"

"Because everything here is for the tourists, of course!" McEveety was growing annoyed at the Shriner's thickheadedness. "Everything that is built here serves the tourists. The hotels, the stores, the playing fields. There is no room here for farms, for factories, for anything to help us feed ourselves, to make our lives better. There is no sense, no order to how we must live."

The Shriner planted his feet more militantly. "So what do you expect me to do about it?"

McEveety couldn't understand why the Shriner insisted on provoking him. With that attitude, how could they reach any face-saving accord? "You live in luxury, we live in shacks. You flaunt how well-off and happy you are. You rub our noses in our poverty without even seeing it yourselves. We beg and you don't listen. You treat us like children or shun us like lepers. And what you spend in a week could make one of us comfortable for a year."

The Shriner was getting fidgety. He smacked his lips as if chewing caramel. McEveety felt spurred to angrier heights. "All you do is play, and we are lucky if we get the chance to work like horses. You eat in restaurants where the luckiest of us get to wash the dishes. And meanwhile we cannot even walk down the street without seeing you stuff yourselves at your cafes."

The Shriner's beebee eyes drilled into McEveety's. "What do you want us to do? Give away all our money? What business is it of ours? After you spent it all, then what? You'd be back to zero. We'd just be throwing it away."

There was no way to puncture the Shriner's arguments. This was all the more insufferable because McEveety knew he was in the right. The disorder, the imbalance of life on the island only grew clearer and more hateful by the second. A maddening headache, sharp as an awl, was making McEveety clench his teeth.

"Now if you'd kindly point me the way to town, mister," the tourist was saying. "I'm kinda turned around."

Oh, so you want to go back to town, do you? A scheme began to form like a pearl around the irritant of McEveety's headache. The Shriner followed as McEveety strolled to the gate by which the Shriner had claimed to enter. McEveety started up the road away from town. "You sure this is right?" the Shriner asked.

"As right as anything," said McEveety. "How long will you be staying here?"

The Shriner shrugged.

"Don't you have to go back to your job?"

"I'm on indefinite leave with pay."

The unfairness of that! This son of a bitch was getting paid to do nothing, and among people who, thanks to this tourist and his kind, could do nothing to help themselves in their own land. McEveety's headache was making his ears ring, making him deaf to the birdsongs in the trees, to his own footsteps on the gravel road. He had to allay this pain somehow. He looked at the tourist as if for help. "It is disorderly, so few rich, so many poor." McEveety's tone was pleading, as much for the Shriner's sake as his own, giving him a last unspoken chance. "You are not even of this place, yet you own it."

The Shriner, trying to make out where the road went, shrugged again. This cold indifference to so much misery, and unfairness, and worst of all, disorder, cemented McEveety's resolve to start changing things, to start restoring balance. On a one-to-one basis. Only by so deciding could he feel his headache start to ebb.

A junked car lay by the roadside. McEveety pushed the Shriner in its general direction.

"Hey, watch it!" warned the Shriner.

"What kind of car is that?" McEveety asked. He knew that people on vacation were seldom at their brightest.

The Shriner impatiently turned to look. And with a speed that surprised them both, McEveety grabbed the back of the Shriner's head and slammed his brow against the roof of the car. Stunned, the Shriner tried to stand, and McEveety let him get just far enough to put some force behind another slam against the roof. After the third time the Shriner was out cold, face blood-webbed. McEveety dumped him inside the doorless car, found a shard of windshield, and drove it through the Shriner's throat. Some fever had hold of McEveety, and he couldn't slow down now.

He stripped the body and put on the Shriner's clothes, hat and all, pleased at only getting a little blood on them. His own clothes he shoved beneath the car. The pressure of the Shriner's full wallet against McEveety's backside was the grandest feeling he had ever known.

McEveety set off toward town. His headache was gone. His fever had broken and his mind felt clear, as if he were over some disease whose symptoms had been headache and the compulsion to do violence. The only cure had been to give in. Come to think of it, he had sneezed earlier, hadn't he?

The clothes did not fit. This annoyed McEveety. As he walked, he tugged at shirt hem to lengthen it, pushed up hat brim to keep it out of his eyes, pulled shorts up over navel, flexed toes to try stretching tight sandals. A blister rolled back and forth under instep before he had reached the shanties outside town.

Ah, but to go as one of the tourists, to whip out that fat wallet until it was empty, it was such a mouth-watering prospect. To taste some pleasure in life! The idea was too big to leave room for doubts in his mind.

At the town line, shadows overtook him from above. The gears of his mind stuck fast, so that the fairness or unfairness of it all was lost on him as three white-winged soldiers landed on the road ahead. They faced him just this side of the town line, denying him even a last view of his Promised Land. With bland looks they did their job, swinging automatic rifles to their shoulders. No, the tourists mustn't even get a chance to see you decked out as a travesty of themselves. It suddenly occurred to McEveety, pull out that wallet, try to offer the soldiers some money for mercy. But there was no time. He could feel himself burst even before they fired.

Meanwhile the Shriner, like any other casualty among the elect, found himself back among the orange trees as if nothing had happened.

But the consciousness McEveety regained was that of a dog. And still full of rancor from his last life, he bit a tourist the day he was weaned. The soldiers shot him again and he returned as a flea. The flea got as far as the tourist hotel before pesticide powder in the carpet got him. At last he came back as a bacterium, one of the germs from whom the natives, inhaling, caught deadly ideas. The damned inevitably became more damned, but there were limits. There was no need to be damned beyond the microscopic. The island had infinite room for those ultimately fallen spirits of the air.

And the saved, heeding the call of adventure, were always ready to island-hop, from that first resort on through the infinite chain of tropical paradises, through chartered-cruise eternity.

The Judgment Birds

One ongoing violation. That was soon Arlen's take on New York. He couldn't watch David Letterman without sirens drowning out punch lines. Or hear the radio because someone's boombox outside was louder. Every 7 A.M., seismic bells from a nearby nunnery woke him, and why did they ring twenty-nine times? Then by noon, some outpatient on the corner was screeching indecipherable laments. Never mind car alarms, fights, breaking glass, firecrackers, gunshots. Life had never sustained so grating a tone in the hills back home!

Still, he and Bethany were cheerfully resolute. They'd lucked into this snug fifth-floor walkup, right in the East Village. Their bandmates had settled in Park Slope. Country music was hot, and nobody had doubts about the band's glorious future. Back home, they gigged every weekend. Won popularity contests in the local weeklies. But paying the rent was the height of hometown success. And Nashville felt so slick and pompous. So Arlen and Bethany had scrimped enough to afford a New York year on part-time work, or on none at all if fortune cooperated.

Meanwhile, they had the view. Behold two bridges, Verrazano and Williamsburg most likely, and that hulking black citadel of a co-op where Cher and Iggy Pop were rumored to live, and uptown, the Empire State Building. You could practically give tours by pointing out the window!

For Arlen, though, brick scenery hardly made up for the dearth of nature. Forget Bethany's glib truism about taking the rough with the smooth! Parks were just lawns with too many people standing on them. In the Village at least, nature had been driven indoors, as if the landscape were inside-out. Spider plants, Norfolk pines, and cactuses crowded tenement windows, pressing to break out, sometimes spilling onto fire escapes.

Even the birds had more presence indoors than out! In their eaves nested starlings, with inroads into the wall above the couch. Mornings they sang on the fire escape, and they clattered and scolded at all hours behind the plaster. Back home, starlings were trash birds, but here Arlen felt like warden of a wildlife preserve. Though God knew what unseen havoc they were wreaking!

The band was Bethany and the Bird Dogs. They rented hourly practice space at a Canal Street studio. After two months, they felt ready. Their favorite country bar, Kevin's Cabin, gave them an opening slot, a modest guarantee, and the sense that Kevin was doing them a big favor.

By this time, Arlen's opinion of New York had changed. It was like Christmas, he now told himself, bearable to the point that it didn't force itself on your attention. The looming view, which at first seemed a poor parody of mountains, now partook more of barrier reef or marine canyons, with their currents of traffic, and their social food chain of predators, prey, bottom-feeders, drifters. Even the starlings brought to mind fish darting from coral hideout.

The Bird Dogs' New York premier boded well. Some dozen regulars, other musicians, and dj's from college-station country shows filled the tables. Kevin, in his usual plaid flannel and NRA cap, was as friendly as running around running things allowed. Standard c-&-w fetishes adorned the room: potbelly stove, Walker Evans photos, strings of chili-pepper lights. The one surprise was a stuffed buffalo sawn in half and appearing to crash through the wall stage left, steam puffing from snout courtesy of some plumbing ingenuity.

The band opened with Hank Williams, Merle Haggard, Porter Wagoner covers. Couldn't go wrong there. Applause emboldened them. Bethany took the mike and led into their originals. But now what? Confidence crashed, burned. People were exchanging looks, covering their mouths, or letting a laugh burst out. Sometimes eyes widened with disbelief at those turns of phrase Arlen cherished most. Sometimes it was the way Bethany leapt octaves or warbled up to hit a high note. He could have sworn someone mentioned Tiny Tim. These fucking snobs! Back home, Bethany was a star. Peers were jealous of Arlen's lyrics. What did these jaded Yankees know about the real thing?

There were empty tables when the Bird Dogs ended amid scattered applause. They had an extinguished look. No one approached them as they broke down their equipment, and they said nothing to each other. They recalled nothing afterwards about the other bands. Only at last call did Arlen shake off band-wide funk to collar Kevin. A guarantee was a guarantee. With cash in hand, the evening wouldn't be a total loss.

Unsmiling Kevin offered advice instead of money. Work on the writing. Lose certain, say, vocal affectations.

Who the hell did Kevin think he was talking to? Arlen wondered aloud why audiences here were so stuck-up. As if they'd know true country if it coldcocked 'em. In the South, people knew quality when they heard it.

Kevin's tone hardened like a lawyer's or a landlord's. "Listen, Arlen, that naïve nightingale stuff might play in the hills. But in New York you do New York country. People expect something different here. You gotta maintain your credibility."

You gotta what? Here was obvious impasse, so Arlen simply asked for the money again.

"Look, Arlen, people left during your set. You lost us money. It was my mistake, okay, buddy? The night wasn't what we were counting on, you know?" Kevin offered a much-reduced sum.

Arlen saw red. "That's not what we agreed on!" he shouted, drawing troubled looks from bandmates across the room.

"Now if you're gonna make this a big deal, I'm not sure you'll be able to play here again," Kevin warned.

"Well if you're gonna stiff us anyway, why would we want to?"

Kevin sighed and counted out three twenties. The Bird Dogs played elsewhere, but never more than once. By no stretch could they keep calling Kevin's response atypical.

Bethany wavered between vanity and reality. Maybe she should simplify her style. Maybe they should only do covers. Arlen's tireless railings against know-it-all Manhattan audiences were beginning to wear on her.

Was Bethany weak? She had to rally, so Arlen harangued her. Strength filled him as he spoke, more strength than he'd ever experienced. He was off like wild horses, and the horses knew the way! If he were lighting into Bethany as much as encouraging her, well, how could that be helped? Was she selling out? Giving up? They had to stick together! He was writing new songs. The band was honing its chops. Don't forget, we're the real thing! Was Bethany looking at him like he was scaring her? The look came and went too quickly to pin down. When Arlen finally let up, he flashed to Hitler sitting down after a tirade, but how could he help what random shit bubbled up from his subconscious?

The starlings were a perpetual distraction. Whenever Arlen sprawled on the couch, notepad in hand, bird cry shattered his concentration. Whatever he wrote down seemed to translate simultaneously into birdsong. Yeah, he couldn't help thinking, that does sound like Bethany, doesn't it? She does kinda hiccup into that range. That trill of hers does go through your head like a dentist's drill. He banished these unkind musings, but wondered if pushing them to the back of his mind only lodged them more securely. Meanwhile, the birds kept digging away, apparently as unhappy as any other New Yorkers with their allotted lebensraum.

Arlen lobbied for a band meeting after losing two weeks of rehearsal to lame excuses. Those guys flaked out to watch the Country Music Awards on TV, for chrissakes! Why hadn't they just moved to crummy Nashville in the first place? Making them agree to come over was an exhausting feat in itself, as if he'd set his shoulder against the whole city's apathy. To see everyone in the apartment felt like no less a triumph than rolling a boulder up five flights.

He gave his pep talk 100%. Don't take a rocky start so hard! You have to take the rough with the smooth! That fevered enthusiasm was back, those wild horses were running, and when he gave them their head, nobody could look away! But then the vote was 3-2 in favor of indefinite sabbatical.

Bethany took Arlen's side, with resigned eyes that bespoke wifely duty more than conviction. That rankled him. It wasn't good enough! To the others he was barely polite as they finished their beers and left.

Bethany wouldn't have minded staying in touch with them. Better than no friends at all. But Arlen never wanted to see those quitters again. From whom else could Bethany have contracted this lethargy? Arlen doggedly worked on new songs, but without a band, it wasn't the same. He toyed with recruiting new players. But after the Bird Dogs' disgraceful slink from the scene, he couldn't face the rest of the musical community.

Then even Bethany turned on him. Arlen was reading in bed while she sat on the couch writing a letter to some aunt. He heard the birds scratch and squabble before settling in for the night. His eyelids grew heavy, only to snap wide open as shrill whistling suddenly assailed him. He dashed into the other room. Bethany was twittering along with the birds, looking hideous, with vacant eyes, puffing cheeks, and rosette lips. The imitation was too good for Arlen to derive any whimsy from it. Wildness in his eyes silenced her. "Don't ever do that again!" he screamed. "You scared the shit out of me!"

"Fuck you," Bethany said.

Thus began the first of Arlen's many nights in neighborhood bars. Somehow, Bethany's birdsong was a capitulation to everything going against him. A shift away from him. He preferred the noisy company of strangers from whom he expected nothing, and who shared his craving for too much noise to hear themselves think.

Arlen offered to take Bethany drinking too. It seemed their best bet for rediscovering common wavelength, but she never took him up on it. Instead, on logy midnights when he aimed apartment key at keyhole, he could swear that faint bird calls alternated with one much louder bird voice inside. Bethany chatting with her only friends? Good God! But when he walked in, she was always in the bedroom, greeting him, damn her, with the same whipped, unresponsive eyes as everyone else on the street. If she was conversing with the birds, Arlen didn't really want to know.

The bar-hopping phase ended when someone from another country band recognized him. Arlen regarded him as someone from another life, a virtual ghost. They went through motions of polite conversation, despite Arlen's rising hackles and inner chill, until the ghost asked, "Have you been playing out lately? I really liked your guitar style, I must say."

"Thanks." A hot updraft was chasing the cold out of Arlen's hollow innards. "What do you think of my wife?"

"What do you mean?" Hah! She was still a conversation-stopper, wasn't she?

"You son of a bitch!" Arlen doused the jerk's fancy Western shirt with beer and stormed out. He ran the three blocks home. He never turned around to see if anyone was giving chase or had come out to watch him. Afterwards, he stayed in nights.

Bethany took a job at some department store. She rated less respect for immersing herself in the mire. But Arlen had to admit, cabin fever lost half its force in halved company. He cooked, he cleaned, he read, he played CDs. Remarkable the way something always claimed his time. The view he shunned. Looking outside seemed to put the weight of the sea on his head. Foggy days, when the Empire State Building stood at half-height, at least fostered the illusion of less city out there.

Whenever Arlen had to go out, the streets seemed intent on rejecting him, like foreign matter from veins. He hated how bicycles zoomed out of nowhere and came within hairsbreadth of clipping him. He hated how cars turning corners braked at the last second, though he crossed with double blessing of crosswalk and ticking Walk sign. As if every right and courtesy common elsewhere were subject to constant challenge here. He hated how pedestrians barged across his path with never any eye contact or an "excuse me," as if he didn't exist. And the sight of people spitting on every available surface sickened him. Why, he pondered, do people stay here? What was there to like here?

At the same time, Arlen was not homesick. Small-town drawbacks were still vivid. Nor could he help groaning aloud at visions of the journey home wearing sackcloth rather than laurels, one more wannabe defeated by the big city. But where to go?

Staying and going were equally untenable. The quandary made him sit as if catatonic for measureless spells. Usually the birds snapped him out of it. And every time, they were louder, weren't they? Closer to breaking through. Unresting familiars of the city which ceded no satisfaction or peace. Sometimes he wondered if his negative attitude was a psychic magnet, drawing bad experiences, and if his growing animosity were courting really major backlash. But that was putting the cart before the horse, wasn't it? New York was the irritant, and he the innocent reagent. Moreover, that was magical thinking, which everyone knew was ridiculous.

Even getting a pound of coffee at the corner bodega pitted him against panhandlers and a delivery truck that blocked the sidewalk, forcing him into traffic. But it did inspire him to pen his first lyrics in weeks, two verses before he ran out of steam:

> Death to bad drivers
> And the bicyclists swift
> And all the New Yorkers
> Who get me miffed

> Death to the slobs
> Who spit on the street
> And all of the yuppies
> Who dress too neat

He didn't ask for Bethany's input. Her sense of humor lacked his mordant edge. Not his fault if she always came home depressed, good for no more than moping in front of the TV. Spending so much time outside, she was turning into a humorless New Yorker herself.

One night he asked point-blank, "Do you accept this place?"

She frowned as if the question left room for interpretation. Then ignoring it like any typical rude New Yorker, she said, "Our savings account is almost empty. I can't do this all by myself, you know. You have to find a job, too."

What? Go out and deal with those people, those streets, from morning till night every day? Whose side was she on? She was lost to him. An extension of the ongoing violation he'd called New York in the beginning. When would he learn to trust first impressions? Trust in nothing but himself?

Bethany spoke on, but Arlen's ears felt hot and muffled, stuffed with cotton all the way to the eardrums. He understood nothing. Was Bethany actually using words? Then right inside his head, as if projected there without agency of ears, birdsong, in sync with Bethany's moving lips, boomed at him.

"Stop that!" he screamed.

It looked like she was asking him what he meant, but he heard only starling racket.

Something deep inside Arlen pounced at Bethany, and he was dragged along behind it. As if by wild horses. She was against the wall beside the couch. He was slamming her head against the wall, again and again, bellowing, "So you want to be with them? You want to be one of them? Go on and join them!"

He had no idea how long this went on. He wondered if he was trying to put her outside through the wall. But at some point his hands were at his side, and at eye level, as if floating cloudlike, was a sticky red blob.

Arlen's ears were wide open at last. In fact, it sounded as if someone were holding a seashell up to them and he could hear faint surf.

He gaped at dead Bethany on the floor. He hadn't meant to do that!

A pinhole appeared in the wall above the blood, and another, and another, till it looked like the wall had some kind of pox. All at once, a saucer's width of plaster crumbled and fell. Arlen found himself face to face with the starlings. A dozen at least. Eyeing him cold and murderous, as if they were antibodies. Antibodies he'd been antagonizing for months.

This town ain't big enough for both of us! Now what made that line pop into his head?

The birds all shot from the hole at once.

That week, the rent was due. When none was forthcoming and nobody answered the phone, the landlord sent the super to inquire. At the first whiff from under the door, she ran and called the police.

The landlord, the super, and two cops broke in and put handkerchiefs over their mouths. Nausea and confusion both hit hard, but it was the confusion which lasted. On the floor lay Bethany's untouched body. Arlen's bones, though, had been stripped and scattered like something the sea had rejected, shreds of cloth trailing like seaweed. Through a saucer-wide hole in the wall, cool air entered, but did nothing to dispel the stench. No one pretended they would even try making sense of this one.

Instead, one of the cops looked out the window. "They had a real good view," he said, as if all this carnage were all the worse for happening despite a nice break like that. Everyone else nodded.

An Office Nymph

Warner alone in the office. Same as many other nights. Phony constellations, each star a light bulb, take and lose shape on surrounding high-rise walls. Second-to-second configurations fill in to make overachiever nightlight pegboards.

Warner derives sweet melancholy from being alone together with all other night toilers. His world feels whole. Full and stoppered like a bottle. Comfortably snug. Held tight by sex surrogate of career.

Nonetheless, something missing craves appeasement. Something missing in his idea of the world. In what he gives the world. Something with no respect for the pure liquid medium of his contentment. Invisibly fruitful within it like bacteria. Uncompromising, unabsorbent in it like a gallstone.

Hours later. Warner's body has assumed the topography forgotten below cityscape. Back stiff as a hill. Eyes, lagoons clogged with sand. Between his legs, estuarine ebb and flow. Subject to something unapprehended and remote as a moon.

He goes to the window. Searches all other lit windows for a woman's silhouette. Imagines her facing him. Becoming aware of him. Establishing a symmetry. Generating a field, charging the air, between them with romance and sex urge.

No luck. He turns from the window. More mindful of the emptiness he has reached into. Standing on the edge of it. No bridge across. He paces back across the office. Scented pages from a glossy magazine catch him in passing. Warner flips pages. Pauses at pictures of temptresses. Throat suddenly dry.

He goes to the water cooler. Drinks one cup. Then another. Eyes idly probe waters of the blue-tinted tank. A water nymph swims in them. Naked body the length of an open jackknife. Temptress eyes meeting Warner's, sizing him up. His eyes, open portals to the void left by unfulfilled carnality. The circumference of this void intersects the circumference of the void in his idea of the order of things. The water nymph has entered and fills the common gap.

Warner naively thinks: Cities today blot out topography. Mythic creatures have lost old secluded haunts. Are forced to find new ones in places like after-hours offices.

The nymph treads water. Shrugs at him. As if at his theorizing. He is tired. Overridingly horny as only minds in isolation can get. Vulnerable. He wants her. His state of mind overshoots her size. Her minuscule gills. The shock of her sudden manifestation. She presses up to blue-tinted glass. Flattens and rubs her body up and down, up and down it like a climber up and down netting.

Warner thinks fast. But only along trajectory of desire. Realizes: His schematics of reality were incomplete, since she had no place in them. Maybe way to bring him and her together also exists. Only waiting for ripe time to enter his awareness.

He plants fingertips on glass. A circuit closes. Weight, size, and barriers lose meaning. He leaves his gravitational field. Enters hers.

Next day, Warner's coworkers arrive. Find lights on. But no Warner. Until one of them goes to the water cooler. Where Warner's body drifts. The size of a candy bar wrapper. Without even his tie loosened or fly open. After corrective measures, in balance at last. Between the x-axis of the physics he knew, and the y-axis of the physics he didn't. Meanwhile, a water nymph explores bay waters.

Another Psychic on Comp

You know, Mr. Wenoff, we don't get many applicants in Brooks Brothers suits."

"Are you implying I should know enough to look poor if I expect to collect benefits?"

"I'm sure you simply wanted to look your best."

"Coming here dressed like this should convey to you how far I've fallen."

"I see you've put down 'Screener' as last employment."

What is this affinity of psychics for telephones? A generation ago they had all those "psychic hotline" numbers, and now the Screeners. Maybe it's something about being okay with voices in the air, whether from the receiver or the ether. But bring this up, and they accuse you of calling them crazy. Now how can we clear the air of misconceptions if they're too touchy for dialogue?

"What 'Screener' means to the public is painfully apparent. A pampered, shiftless indulgence of the rich and powerful. Battening on delicacies while lounging by the phone all day in opulent boardrooms or sitting rooms or the limo in between. Exerting oneself only to say, Pick up the phone, Let the machine get it, or Turn off the machine."

"But you're saying that's not how it is."

"It's true, you do rate some deference. Much can be riding on you. Your predictive powers are like a fragile mechanism in a black box. Nobody wants to shake the box and upset the workings. Still, the job is exhausting. Often nerve-wracking. However sharp you are, you never sense an incoming call more than a second ahead. And then the pressure's on, to augur within three rings. Every call puts a Screener's credibility on the line. And when you're on duty it's day in and day out, as if you're an indentured servant or a virtual extension of the answering machine. You come to take posh surroundings for granted, but nothing is yours."

Maybe that's why he keeps squinching around, like the room's about to ooze sewage. Sitting all uptight like a folded-up umbrella, perched on the edge of his seat, like he wants to touch as little as possible. Who does he think he is? Try staring at these walls every day for thirteen years. Cheapo pine-box paneling, corpse-blue paint. More like a cheap movie set than a real office. Smell of wet corduroy, rain or shine. He must really feel like he's hit bottom, coming in here. Elitist jerk.

"How long were you with your last employer?"

"I was with Mr. Fitzroy seven years. Do you know of him? Realtor, developer. Very active civically."

"And were you laid off or fired, or did you resign?"

"I had to quit. I know this can disqualify someone, but there were extenuating circumstances."

"Well, I'm here to listen, Mr. Wenoff." *Listen and laugh, in your case.*

"You see, until the very end, my relationship with Mr. Fitzroy had been typical. A Screener may be an employer's most constant associate, but he eschews details of that employer's business and personal life. These would only clutter his intuition, and out of respect, Screeners never pry. Our interactions were cordial and reserved. Fitzroy's name might catch my eye in the papers, but current events seldom hold my attention. What time is my own I spend on rambles in the country, or on a shady bench in the park, observing and reflecting. My most pleasant evenings tend to be with a book or a DVD. But other people's money seems bound to interfere with the simple life, sooner or later."

So you'd prefer not to sweat at all like the rest of us, eh? Even that mumbo-jumbo passing for work finally got to be too much. And now you just want to bum around like a country squire at taxpayer expense. Rambles in the country, indeed. We'll see about that.

"Does this have any bearing on how you came to be here, Mr. Wenoff?"

"Yes. Wealth cannot leave well enough alone, wherever it can further itself. Caring nothing for the cost in quality of life to others. That is how I came to be here."

"No need for agitation, Mr. Wenoff."

"Pardon me. I will always have mixed feelings about what I had to do. Beneath the aloofness between Screener and employer, trust and confidence are still key to any long-term relationship. Turning upon Fitzroy crippled my own belief in myself, my ability to work for anyone."

There you go. These guys are not to be trusted. He admits it himself. It follows that someone calling the shots for the Fortune 500 has way too much power himself. And yet he's taken at his word. He could be out for himself, or a phony, or a bum, and who'd be the wiser? What a racket!

"How did you turn against him, Mr. Wenoff?"

"You're familiar with Windmill Park? I don't know if there ever was a windmill there. Maybe the name has some bearing on the quixotic nature of the place, since it's not even officially a park. More like a glorified vacant lot, with old picnic furniture and upkeep provided by the neighborhood. Very charming and informal, and whoever the legal owner was, his chronic negligence of the property as good as gave it to the people. He was obviously getting along fine, letting it be.

"My last moment of contentment was in that park, a breezy Sunday, watching some dogs chase an old paper bag, when a scruffy youth handed me a flyer. Generally I would have considered this an imposition. But he said, 'If you care about the park, please read this.'

"The flyer was an invitation to a community meeting in a church basement, for purposes of brainstorming. The plat that contained both the park and the adjacent Victorian row houses was suddenly on the market. The owner, already a multimillionaire, had rebuffed all attempts at discussions with tenants or park users. The prospective buyer was unknown, but insiders at City Hall were sure that some hundred luxury condos were in the works. The kind of money involved made the zoning variance a laughable formality. I did my best not to get upset. The publishers of this flyer might have been alarmists. Grandiose housing schemes often fall through for numerous reasons. Still, walking back to my room at Fitzroy's, I was shaking with indignation to think that this entire neighborhood had no say in its own survival, just because of one callous patroon's legal entitlement. Property as theft, indeed."

Oh brother, head in the ground or someplace else the sun don't shine. And I thought all the Commies were dead.

"Please, Mr. Wenoff, get on with the facts."

"Well, Monday morning, Fitzroy and I stayed home. He was expecting a call. Just before noon, it came. Let the machine get it, I said. Our hours at the kitchen table with newspapers and coffee had been so pointedly casual as to make them feel unnervingly portentous. And on hearing the voice of the caller, Fitzroy showed his true colors. He stared at the phone with the intensity of a dog sizing up its quarry. The caller identified himself and said something like, 'Hello? The plan was, you'd be home. We have to talk. Whatever's going on, call me a.s.a.p. I'd like to get this done.' Fitzroy was ecstatic. He practically cackled. 'Now I got him. I could have met his price. It's twice what anyone else could offer. But now he's afraid I'm blowing him off. And he's alienated every other potential buyer. Thanks to you, now he'll negotiate or lose out altogether.' His overbearing glee made it impossible not to grimace back, until it came to me that the caller's name rang a bell because I'd seen it in yesterday's flyer from the park. Lost in his own gloating, Fitzroy never saw my change of expression.

"Better for him had he been cool enough to see the blush heating up my face. Maybe a collision of professional and personal ethics comes sooner in most lives. For me, completely unprepared, it was like handling a first sailing lesson while the boat was capsizing. Any move of mine to save the park meant opposing my employer. I'm no 'joiner,' so I wouldn't have exposed Fitzroy as the buyer at any grassroots meetings, not that impromptu democracy could have helped. Any reprieve for the park was up to me alone, and the need to commit myself could arise at any second. The greater good, I knew, called for betraying Fitzroy. But seven years of loyalty wouldn't die so easily, even if they now seemed clearly on the side of selfish opportunism. Every time I told myself, 'No, I can't do this,' it was with one choice in mind, then the other."

Jesus, is it noon already? How long can he go on? I'd say something. But let him keep digging that hole.

"Fitzroy had scarcely managed to reseat himself with his *Wall Street Journal* when the phone gave off that meaningful vibe. This was the call all right, and the first ring put me in a cold sweat. The voice of someone tiny, deep inside my cavernous self, fought to be audible, and it said, 'Don't tie up the line with a call that will bring no good.'

"My Delphic phrasing surprised myself as much as Fitzroy, who whispered, 'Don't even keep the machine on?'

"I shook my head desperately, aghast at realizing how short-lived my deception had almost been. Fitzroy regarded me closely, but stopped the machine on the third ring. As if hunger must have prompted my flaky mood, he fixed hefty sandwiches, and to keep him from doubting his assessment of me, I ate. We then waited in vain for another call, while afternoon wore into evening. I buried my nose in a book, sneaking occasional views of Fitzroy pacing restively, finishing a bag of corn chips by grabby handfuls, tapping out 'Bolero' with his fingertips on the toaster oven. I felt like a fugitive on the run in spirit but not yet in body, a backstabber whose every minute under the roof added insult to injury.

"The cook's arrival ousted us from the kitchen. We reset ourselves in the den, in overstuffed chairs to either side of a little telephone table. The chairs faced a big-screen TV. Fitzroy liked to wave the remote like he was flycasting. All through the six o'clock news he squinted intently, as if expecting word about the callback. The cook brought supper on trays during *Jeopardy*. I don't remember what else we watched—"

"That's quite all right, Mr. Wenoff."

"Anyway, there we stayed until the eleven o'clock news. I had never taken the liberty of studying Mr. Fitzroy so keenly before, not in all my spotlessly discreet years. I was starting to feel like a wildlife observer. Sometimes he seemed to be drowsy like a gator, sometimes grimly tasting the air like a lynx. But when the late-breaking lead story came on, Fitzroy's face turned chalky, so wrathful as to seem stylized, like a Kabuki mask. A prominent businessman had been booked hours ago on assorted counts of extortion, money laundering, et cetera. For the first time I beheld the owner of Windmill Park. He glared impenitent at the lens as if it were somehow to blame. This morning's unanswered call had been Fitzroy's last chance in a long time to cut a deal with him. He was being held without bail as a bad flight risk.

"Without a word Fitzroy left the room. And that was the last I saw of him. All that was mine fit easily in two suitcases. I'd needed few things of my own these seven years. My note on the fridge door said only that I was resigning, effective immediately. For personal reasons. Fitzroy would interpret that however he would. Probably it appeared I was taking the only honorable course after costly incompetence. Career seppuku. Maybe it even seemed to Fitzroy that I'd saved him the mortification of being there during the arrest. In any case, I'm unaware of any attempts on his part to contact me.

"I took off that night, sliding my key back under the door, going by cab to the nearest motel. I was up all night, bouncing between shame and elation: I'd saved the park and made a difference for the better in the world; I was also a traitor to my craft and my trusting employer. And I'll never be in a position to claim credit for the good I've done. No one but you has ever heard this story, and I doubt anyone else ever will."

And he doesn't think we'll use it against him? Maybe he's a little loopy in conjunction with his psychic powers. Or maybe he really is a babe in the woods. Either way, no one ever volunteers all this personal stuff.

"If that's all, Mr. Wenoff, I'm afraid we'll have to cut this short. You've heard the expression, The poor you will always have with you. Well, the rich you will always have with you too. Better get used to it."

"About my claim—"

"We'll have to get back to you. Okay for next Wednesday at 10 A.M.? Good. Come straight to this same office. Here's a card to remind you. Now, I have other business waiting."

"I understand perfectly. And I feel sure you won't abuse what I've confided to you. You've been most obliging, letting me get all this off my chest."

He trusts me? What? How naive can you get? How the hell does he think this works? I have to contact his old boss, and when I do, all will be revealed, I guarantee.

Anyway, good riddance. I'm starving. Oh God, look at the time. He wasted half my goddamn lunch hour. Ah, the sun. I'm free. For the next thirty minutes, anyway. Dammit, looks like the line at the coffee shop is coming out the door. Weird about that Wenoff character, so sure I wouldn't use his story against him. First thing after lunch, Fitzroy's first on my list of things to do. Hey, doesn't that guy in the truck see me? Slow down, you idiot! Hey—

Towbear to Hell

All these smart people have dumb bastards in 'em screamin' to get out. You think I'm kiddin'?

Last week I was talkin' to a guy right here in the cafeteria. At this very table. Smart guy, went to college, grad school, you name it, but he's doin' the same shit now I'm doin'. So I ask him why his finger's bandaged up, and he says he cut the tip of his finger off slicing asparagus. And I said, "You weren't cuttin' toward yourself, were you?" And he says, yeah, he was, but he had a lot on his mind. A lot on his mind, a little off the knuckle.

That happened to you too lately? Oh, that's why you got the Band-Aid on. Well, I guess it must happen to a lot of people.

But I knew this other guy, he was so stupid he got eaten by the vampires on the third shift. The ones everyone knows about who works nights long enough. You must know who I mean.

Anyway, this was another one of those smart guys, went to college, don't know what he was doin' here in the first place. Asked him once what he did before comin' to the post office, he said somethin' about starting a telescope-making business but it folded. Ha ha. Wise ass.

I keep this in my wallet. Found it on break here one night back when he was around. Thought it was only a used napkin at first, almost threw it on the floor when I noticed writing on it. It's a letter. Here, read it, it must have been written by that college boy I was tellin' you about:

> Dear Amy,
>
> Forgive the stationery, not that you've ever known me to try impressing anybody. Sure can't impress anybody with what I'm doing now. Glorified stevedore on the so-called "docks," filling trucks up or emptying 'em out. Piles of *TV Guides* on freight skids, hundred-pound

bags of supermarket circulars, stuff like that.

The working floor inside is like a set from *Brazil,* all these dense thickets of indescribable machinery you have to blaze a trail through. It's all dirty industrial chaos. Always wash your hands between handling mail and eating, that's one thing I've learned. I've been here a month and still get lost twice a week. There's always this buzzy tickertape-on-feedback sound of factory production, just loud enough to set your teeth on edge. And when the overhead belts are on, they squeak like rats in the rafters or bird souls in torment.

Judging by the miserable old faces and neurotic young ones, there are plenty of human souls in torment too, but for every one of them, there are three in confusion. For being a communications resource, the P.O. is Misnomer and Doubletalk Central, like a bastard branch of the military. E.g., I'm "casual" labor, which means graveyard shift six nights a week at half of union wages, no coverage or benefits, doing the heaviest work, and then 'cos I'm a temp, I'm back on the street in six months, square one again. So really, "casual" amounts to "slave." But it'd be worse if I were "part-time flexible," which equals up to twelve-hour shifts six nights a week, and you have no idea what your reporting time is for more than a day ahead. The pay is good, but it's "flexible" only in the sense that you're constantly bending over backwards.

Then there's the ever-mystifying patois for the names of things, some of them pretty picturesque, like "towbear" for the big orange rolling bins you throw airmail into, or "silver bullets," which are shiny new versions of towbears that only take mail going interstate by truck. On the other hand, there are "g.p.m.c.'s," which are wheeled containers made of vertical steel bars and about the dimensions of a china closet. I've no idea what "g.p.m.c." stands for, but they're also called "cages."

Well, I think of you a lot while you're sleeping

(which means you'll just have to take my word for it, I guess). Hope grad school's still to your liking. Lemme know when you're coming back East next, or at least send me news next chance you get.

Love,
Howie

What a space shot, huh? I mean, you have to wonder how much he was thinking about her to forget his love letters in the cafeteria, not that he didn't have legitimate distractions. It's funny, but didja ever notice how the best-lookin' babes here come in around midnight? Don't know why that is, but of course the one who lover-boy got the hots for would have to be a day-sleeper, which is the polite term we use to their faces, if you get my drift. Everyone could tell he liked her, the way he stared at her after she walked by, or how he'd say anything to her for the sake of talking even when it was plain he didn't have anything to say.

Don't get me wrong, Roxanne was one foxy vampire. It was obvious what he saw in her, maybe not so obvious what he didn't see at first if he didn't know what to look for. I mean, why not give the guy the benefit of the doubt? She was older than he was, just enough so that every extra year was a plus in terms of how she'd learned to flirt and dress and carry herself. Experienced without going downhill yet, you know? She wore black, had a tight little figure like she worked out a lot, and had an inch of scar on her cheek that only made her look more exotic. Haven't seen her lately, but you know who I mean? Freckles, blue eyes, small features, kinda French, kinda Irish, nothing big or sharp about her face, so it seemed easy to get up close to her, safe to start something. Kinda the way the girl next door would look in that old soap opera *Dark Shadows,* you ever hear of that? Where everyone was really a werewolf or something?

What might've saved Howie was what he considered his own worst luck. The supervisor out on the docks was named Tyrone, he's retired now, he kinda had it in for Howie, probably just because he was a college type. Tyrone came from somewhere down South, acted like he came from halfway between *Dukes of Hazzard* and *Night of the Iguana.* Fat, loud, foulmouthed, bad breath, never bathed, changed his shirt twice a week, smoked fat stinking cigars, called everyone who didn't outrank him "boy." And like every other boss here, as you must know, the only way to do things right was his personal own. And Howie could never get it right, not that Tyrone would ever let him. In fact, Tyrone had him written up a couple of times for insubordination. Strike three and Howie would have been out on his ass.

It was only a matter of time, Howie knew it, and that's what must have made him really start putting the moves on Roxanne. I was sitting right here and happened to see him go into action. She was sitting by herself at that corner table, and he came in and asked if he could pull up a chair. She seemed to think about it a minute and then said okay. I couldn't overhear everything they said, but after a while Howie mentions he's thirsty and tries to dig up some change for the machine. He's short, so he asks her if she has change for a dollar. She said no, but he was welcome to the rest of her drink, there was about two-thirds of it left and she promised she was clean. She got up and went back to work, and he looked pretty smug till he took a big gulp and went for his handkerchief, which didn't soak up too much. It got all over his hand, all over the table, and I could hardly keep from busting out laughing as he ran to the men's room. It was blood, of course, and was he surprised!

But wait, this gets better. He'd seen her dinking from the cup, right? And he was smart even if he had no common sense. Still, I always felt he put two and two together a little too quickly, like maybe there was a sick little kink in the back of his mind all along, like this was something he was secretly looking for. A sexy little vamp to nibble on his neck. Or maybe he'd just gotten desperate waiting around for the likes of Amy. I doubt she had what he really wanted anyway.

So instead of being scared off by Roxanne's little joke, Howie started following her around like a hungry puppy. Hinting all the time that he knew all about her. He'd have been the only person here who didn't. Offered to take her out for Bloody Marys after work, offered her blood oranges from his lunch bag, you know, his idea of the subtle approach. She wasn't having any but she kept being nice to him, never told him to fuck off, which is what it would've taken.

Meanwhile, Tyrone-wise, the b.m. was about to hit the fan bull's-eye. Tyrone had been out on sick leave a few nights, and the substitute super had his own order for lining up the g.p.m.c.'s for the late dispatch to the different city stations. Howie didn't realize Tyrone was back yet, so he lined up the cages according to the substitute's way. Tyrone saw it and threw a fit. "All right, which one of you goddamn idiots put these g.p.m.c.'s like this? I've told you boys a hundred times, and this time there's gonna be hell to pay. Speak up now, who's responsible for this?"

Everyone else on the crew made their excuses, which left only Howie, who was off doing something else for the moment. Tyrone couldn't have been happier. As soon as Howie came back, Tyrone lit into him. "Hello, boy, it is my goddamn pleasure to inform you that I'm writin' you up for the last time. The wheels are turnin', and you're gonna have to work fast if you want to screw things up here again." And so on.

Well, that talk of "working fast" hit home, and come break, there was Howie practically throwing himself at Roxanne. Telling her he wasn't going to be around much longer, and he really wanted to get together with her soon, or at least take down her number. She asked him, "You know what I am, don't you?"

And when he said yes, she said, well, she didn't really go out at all, but she liked him and did he want to have what she called a "dirty interlude" right there in the building? Since he was leaving soon anyway, what could management do to him? She promised she wouldn't drink very much. Only what he let her.

Their half-hour dinner breaks were scheduled for the same time, and she told him to meet her at the northwest corner of the docks, over where they do the airmail dispatch and then go home around midnight, so it's completely deserted after that. What's more, she told him to hide in one of the towbears, throw some empty mail sacks over himself and she'd come around. Then they could snuggle up under the sacks, safely out of sight, and if you know how skuzzy those sacks are, boy, that'd be a dirty interlude all right.

So there was Howie, about to get canned, but singing to himself, as light on his feet as if he'd won Megabucks. At 4 A.M. he clocks out for dinner and sashays back to the docks and gets into one of the towbears, covers himself with a couple of number three sacks, and waits. A few minutes later he hears somebody tiptoeing around, and he goes,

"Pssst."

The next thing he knows, the mail sack comes flying off from over his face, except it's not Roxanne, it's smelly Tyrone, grinning like some kind of fiend. And he told Howie something like, "Now if you ain't the sorriest fuckup I ever seen. Y'know, boy, no matter who the girls report to on the floor, I'm the real boss in these parts, if you catch my meaning." And he put out his fat cigar on the bottom of his shoe, and climbed into the bin. And like I said way back in the first place, there was one dumb bastard screamin' to get out where a smart person used to be.

Poor Howie. I don't know if Roxanne even got a taste of him. How do I know all this? It was going around the building for days. Best story in a long time. Anyway, Tyrone hated college kids so much he drove in the stake himself, to make sure he'd never have to put up with Howie again. That was that. Just the way things get done around here.

On the other hand, you seeing anybody these days? I can tell you're no well-educated dummy. You know Dawn who works Express Mail? She's one of them too, don't know if you were aware of that, but she's real nice, and lonely too, hasn't had anybody in a while. You want me to introduce you? C'mon.

No? Not right now? Well then. Would you happen to have a toothpick I could borrow?

The Christmas Clones

There they go again. Owner and clone. Clone of some loved one, of course. But the owner pushing, yelling, venting God knows what pent-up spleen. Simply because he can. Because the loved ones will never know. And therein, the beauty and ghastliness alike of the Christmas clones.

Not that they're really clones. Not exactly. But the name has stuck simply because it's too good to lose.

For myself and salespeople everywhere, it's enough to know that the clones were the active ingredient in degrading the merely wretched "holiday season" into a month of nonstop nightmare. Especially on a weekend afternoon, when five or six owners are always berating their clones within unseemly earshot. And then there's the unpleasantness of the clones themselves.

To my knowledge, though, I alone can blame the clones for creating my psychosexual dilemma. My coworkers can look forward to slackened pace and cessation of canned carols in January. Not I. Such-like relief I won't likely notice, wallowing in the mire of rotten choices. Do I humiliate, maybe even endanger myself with a phone call, or do I become a stalker?

So far this Yuletide, every other "person" at the mall seems to have been a clone. Based on my informal survey, mall clerks make up the only walk of life which wouldn't be caught dead using one. No mystery there. Not after even a single day's overexposure to those fixated eyes, ogling with uncouth hunger like those of pigeons or turtles. And the whiny, insistent tone. And the compulsive, cranelike stride. Hard to remember a time without the damned things. A measure, isn't it, of the rampant but logical success of the coldest, most cynical shopping incentive in the history of commerce? The one upside has been the abolition of every complaint and exchange department in the land.

For even the sappiest romantic must admit: however much you feel like one with your soulmate, only that soulmate knows for sure what had better be waiting under the tree. But God forbid that soulmate tell you outright what to buy, and so ruin the warm and fuzzy surprise attendant on the sporting chance that you guessed right. Science, no fool when it comes to seizing the quick buck, came to the rescue of romanticism. Enter the Christmas clone or, strictly speaking, "limited simulacrum" (which nobody says, of course; too highfalutin' and a tongue-twister besides). Like a baby duck imprinting on its mom, the clone knows only its owner. Is good only for demanding what it wants and where to find it. The embodiment of Christmas spirit! Ask any member of the board.

Interacting with loved ones at their nagging, greedy worst never seems to bother people. No big deal, weighed against the convenience, the fail-safe results, and the annual outlet for catharsis, an example of which is forthcoming. What, I daresay, should rate a double-take about consumerism on the march? Who knows where I'd be working if strip-zone desolation hadn't rolled over the countryside, starving out mom-and-pop operations on scenic Main Streets everywhere? What's the extra little ugliness of "limited simulacra"?

For the salesperson, though, the worst still awaits after the owner has gone. The clone is abandoned in the store, where it stands around blinking or roams the aisles gawking at merchandise. And then eight hours after issue, the clone, solid to the touch but chemically flimsy as a hologram, evaporates. The manufacturers assure that the end is painless. That the clone was devoid of any "real" consciousness in the first place. One minute, there stands a bundle of twitching avarice; the next, a fleeting, odorless cloud hangs over a heap of white smock, baggy white trousers, white slippers. Their standard wear. What's one more category of trash to sweep up? In a scant legislative nod to decorum, clones are allowed only "in season," and wisdom dictates ordering months ahead to guarantee receipt between Thanksgiving and Christmas Eve.

What recourse has the clerk but to secrete a Yuletide shell, so as to face with detachment even the clones of friends and relatives? And I had thought my own shell professionally thick. Till into Home Electronics stormed a flashy young success with Mr. Hyde airs. Whose sharkskin jacket, skinny tie, and sleek black hair (the classic look inspired by that classic decade of greed, the 1980s) could all have been cut from the same bolt. Thank God he was just passing through, hurrying his clone with curses and pokes. But the clone, on turning to whine about wanting something, made me weak in the joints and hot under the collar. Madeline, I mouthed in wonderment. Hadn't seen her, or thought of her, in the several years since high school. Nonetheless the crush I'd never had the chance to see through one way or the other was back in full force.

I sighed. In light of her evident marriage to the affluent creep, I wouldn't have been her type in the first place. And obviously he could give her what a clerk never could. But was she happy? Every so often, hubby reddened and grimaced and his fists clenched. As if about to wallop her. From here his words were only squawks and snarls. Never letting up.

More Xmas joy for the salespeople: that catharsis indulged by clones' owners, especially among the nouveaux riches. Rudeness, verbal abuse, a more or less discreet shove or kick now and then. And much worse, no doubt, in private. Payback for a year's festering grudges, on top of the expense and nuisance of that day's trip to the mall. Who are lowly clerks not to condone letting it all hang out? Who knows how many marriages these walking pressure valves have saved?

And who was I to knot up inside, at seeing Madeline so beautiful and browbeaten, so passive yet insistent, so unattainable yet plainly unwanted? Breaktime was coming up. I signaled my colleague that I was taking off. In the event of a customer, he'd have to hang up on his broker and earn his pay for a change.

I trailed faux Madeline and her abuser through Housewares, Toys, Cards (where he made her pick something out), Jewelry and Watches (where he bullied her into making up her mind), and Candy (where he smacked her hand away as she reached for a Toblerone). Finally he made her sit on a mattress in Beds and Bedding. She fumbled open the Toblerone he threw her. He hightailed it, the way some assholes would ditch a dog.

And then with no more sense than a clone, I got involved. When I beckoned at her, she stopped eating and rose. No recognition, no resistance in her remote full-moon eyes. Completion of Christmas list had meant depletion of willpower. Customers and coworkers averted their faces from us. Staring at a Christmas clone and its presumptive owner amounted to a newfangled taboo. I led her through the nearest Employees Only door. Squinted at boxes and pillows and blankets stacked up in the gloom, a bale of mattresses propped against the wall. Her weight had no visible effect on the stack of boxes where I had her sit.

Once I stopped directing her, she seemed unaware I was there. She lowered her eyes to the half a Toblerone in her hands. Raised it to her face, gobbled it down. Dreamily licked chocolate smears off her fingers. I sighed. For the second time in as many minutes. In deference to the real Madeline, why not let her clone evaporate in here? In the relative dignity of solitude. Leaving her here seemed safe for the few minutes she probably had left.

Her gaze came to rest in my general direction. Without apparent focus. Removing myself from this last eyeful of her was hard. I might never see even this much of Madeline again. God, she was gorgeous. Why not seize the once-in-a-lifetime chance to kiss her before she vaporized?

Protest I rightly did not expect. But neither had I thought she'd kiss back, make it last, grab hold of my hips. And before the situation getting out of hand could worry me, she intoned, "I want you." Holding on to me, she backed us into the upended mattresses. At the moment, sense of responsibility went no further than wondering how much later than usual I'd be coming back from break. Too eager and overwhelmed, I couldn't imagine anyone interrupting. After all, I could be spending my passion on a cloud any second now. Talk about a perfect fantasy coming true. How often does that happen?

Life would have been far simpler if only she'd vaporized in the afterglow. Instead, eyes still remote, she murmured, "I want another Toblerone." I told her to stay put while I got one. Nothing more welcome than the chance to run off and think. The clones had it in them only to voice the desires of their originals. So did the real Madeline harbor some ancient, secret longing for me? Stupidly or not, I let exhilaration put a spring in my step.

On my return, no Madeline to be found. Especially post-shopping spree, clones had no mind to disobey orders or form their own plans. Presumably she'd dissolved in my absence. But where were her clothes?

Good God, suppose this had been no clone? The implications were dragging me to scary depths. My total ignorance of the real Madeline was glaringly obvious. Had she impersonated her own clone to learn in the worst way what hubby really thought of her? Or had she, known or unknown to him, played her own false self by way of kinky game? Foolhardy or weird, one or the other she must have been. Or at the end of her rope with him, and now that she knew how much of an abusive swine he was, our storeroom encounter signified her intent to secede. Or else she'd conned me into playing some sick game. Temples starting to throb, I bolted from the storeroom. The red and green and gold of chintzy giant balls and chains and icicles hanging everywhere were painfully bright. Making me squint and grimace at every chance sight of them till the end of my shift.

Only another few shopping days till Christmas. No idea how many. Anyhow, few enough that the mall becomes a massive Sea World tank of turbid flesh, inducing mal de mer of dizziness and headache. And all the worse if you're an employee dealing with the haunted eyes, the driven, mechanical footsteps intercepting you, the shrill voices making themselves heard above the background seashell roar of everyone else trying to do the same. Often impossible to tell the owners from the clones at this stage. The light wherever you look is like that in an aquarium, so that it stings to focus beyond arm's length. Still I strain for a glimpse of Madeline. Knowing full well that the chances of that are just as poor as they are of getting her off my mind.

No sane pretext for phoning has occurred to me yet. My come-on would be awkward, to say the least: "You may not remember me from high school, but since your clone fucked me I decided maybe we should talk." However I managed to phrase it, that would be the nub, and it wouldn't do at all. And no comfort in belated realization that a janitor might have had time to pick up the clone clothes during my candy run. At this rate I may never know who, back in the storeroom, was exploiting whom. Damn those Christmas clones!

Awakening of No Return

Maybe it counts as a blessing, the way illness can dislodge its victim from the suffering moment and make vivid some time past, or imaginably to come.

For Acton, after unsteady shuffle to the bathroom, brushing his teeth before the mirror abruptly became the experience of brushing his teeth one brighter morning, age twelve. Not an important morning. But one that at arbitrary cue laminated itself over his sense of the present and was gone again in the blink of an eye. And late at night, squinting at his shaky upheld hands, he swore he knew how eighty-four would feel. But how old was he, really? And what was the date? He could put his finger on neither.

When a blinding rectangle of daylight outlined his drawn shade, Acton was still pondering predawn dreaming, wherein he confronted Bigness and Littleness in some purely tactile way, through no reaching or touching on his part, but by alternating impressions of these two extremes, between which he drifted. When he was better, he decided, he'd have to check some anatomical studies of the womb, to see if they might indicate points on a map of fetal recall.

By the time the shade and its framing light were the same dim amber, Acton bleakly considered dealing with the crusty soup bowls, teacups, glasses, and plates on the nightstand. For all that mess, he had nothing more substantial in him than saltines. Then he spotted a notepad sheet poking from beneath it all. Acton eased it out. An unknown hand had jotted, "A box is coming for you." Huh? Where had this come from? And what's more, where had everybody been all day?

In any event, the note was worrisome. Had he sent away for something? Would the mailman make him come to the door and sign for it? Could he even get to the door before the mailman gave up and shoved a yellow slip through the mail slot, in which case how could Acton get to the post office in his condition before the package was returned to sender? Would he even hear the doorbell in the first place?

More unsettling yet was the note's unaccountable arrival. Especially in this circumscribed setting, how could it, or anything unfamiliar, have lain there any time without his knowledge? "A box is coming for you." The longer Acton dwelt on it, the creepier it sounded. But it wasn't as if he were on his deathbed, for God's sake! In pursuing the question of who the writer could have been, his mind wandered. And then he was relaxing, spacing out.

Suddenly he knew how wasteful all his fretting had been. Of course a box had been coming for him. Nothing else had been on his mind all that summer. After hoarding every penny from allowance and garden chores and litterbugs' returnable bottles, he finally had enough for one of those deluxe Don Post over-the-head masks, as advertised in *Famous Monsters of Filmland.* Last-minute choice between Mummy and Mole People was hard, but Mole People won out by virtue of weirdness. Mom counted his bankroll and made out the check, with her usual caveat that mail-order places liked to cheat kids. He refused to believe it this time; he wanted the mask too much.

The ad said to allow three weeks for delivery. But to be on the safe side, Acton watched the front door every day after the weekend. Casually, intermittently at first. But by the end of three weeks he awoke every morning in a flush of anticipation, in spirit already as good as planted in the chair facing the front door. Mentally he had staged the moment of triumph dozens of times, hearing the mailman fumble with a box, rushing to the door before the mailman could ring or anyone else knew what was going on, claiming with his own two hands the coolest thing he had ever owned, all the more so because it was the first thing he had ever saved up and sent away for, the first thing that would ever truly be his. And opening the door for it himself would be the most exciting moment, the moment most fantasized about, in the whole process. And fantasy was what the moment would prove to remain.

First, Mom tried bursting the bubble by waving the cancelled check in his face, well into the fifth week. See? They took the money and sent nothing. As she said, a gyp-joint! Acton's faith was battered but not broken. He stuck to a wait-and-see policy, not letting himself get so worked up mornings. There must have been a mix-up, a delay, something. Surely a company that never made good on orders wouldn't still be in business after, well, however many years!

Then on Saturday morning, Acton came in to take his usual seat in the living room. Dad, home for the weekend, sat in the big red armchair, sorting through the mail which he'd set on the hassock. The mailman had been early for once! Dad eyed Acton sharply and asked, "Did you send for something?"

Acton stood there speechless. This couldn't be. Not on the one morning when he'd relaxed his watch!

"I said, did you send for something?" Dad leaned forward accusingly, as if Acton had done something wrong, as if getting or not getting what was rightfully his hinged on the whim of stern authority.

"Did it come?" Acton asked meekly.

Grudgingly, reproachfully it seemed, Dad dragged a box from behind the hassock and pushed it across the carpet toward Acton. "If it's yours, I suppose you can have it."

Acton took it joylessly. He felt like crying, but held back on suspicion that it might give Dad extra satisfaction. Almost two months he'd been waiting for this moment, and the old man had to spoil it on purpose! And now instead of basking in a sense of accomplishment Acton felt small, ashamed. He didn't even open the box that day. And didn't as long as it bothered him that there was no one whom he could have told about the way he felt.

Still, much bigger reasons to dislike Dad had come up over the decades. Best to rest and invest no more angst in ancient history. But wait a minute! Was he sick in bed again, so soon since that last time? Or had mere minutes passed since that cryptic note had come to hand?

His room was white and airy now, rather than stuffy, dim. A fresh breeze carried a trace of wisteria. Had someone seen to the room while he slept, or had he been moved? And the question remained, where was everybody?

Free of dishware, the nightstand surface appeared to be white enamel with black trim. Someone had cleaned up in here. So quietly that Acton's slumbers, or his ruminations, had gone undisturbed. But then, his hearing had become muffled, as with deep-lodged wax. Still, he discerned a current of footsteps and voices, like shadows of sound, from the hall beyond the heavy institutional door. And the nightstand wasn't altogether vacant. The same message, on a larger lined manila sheet, assailed him. "A box is coming for you."

He mumbled the words a little while. A box? Oh, of course! A box was how he'd wound up in the hospital. And the accident, well, that had been in the making for a long time, hadn't it? Back to those by-gone days of his damn Aunt Rose and her weekend visits. A later generation would have dubbed her an animal-rights nut, maybe. In Acton's childhood, any excursion with Rose behind the wheel occasioned a trauma of dread and pity, cumulative over the years. Seeing any kind of box or bag by the roadside prompted story after story about unwanted cats and puppies stuck into flimsy containers and ditched in high-speed lanes, where unwary drivers invariably smashed into them. The poor innocent things! Acton shuddered and blinked back tears every time. And grew up unable to overlook the potential horror in a box left sitting on the road.

And so it happened he was driving, amidst farms and forest, on two-lane blacktop that twisted to avoid low hills. The morning, dark and squally. Bursts of rain on the windshield made him weave his head from side to side, often without clue as to what lay ahead. The windshield wipers were only pushing the water around, as if the car surged across ocean floor.

There was a pause in the downpour as he steered around a sharp bend. In the middle of the lane was an overturned crate big enough for a computer or a TV or a whole litter of kittens. He knew even at the time that it was likely just imagination, but the box seemed to be coming straight at him.

His nerves, already embattled, were put to rout by this lowest of assaults. He yelled and swerved off the road. The car jumped roadside ditch and hit embankment head-on, rebounding at an angle and rolling ponderously onto its side. Acton shoved the door open and hoisted himself up, shaking blood from his eyes in time to see the empty box blow off the road and bounce weakly off the hood of his car, just before the effort of boosting himself waist-high into the cold rain made him fold up and pass out.

But that was all buried somewhere deep in the past, wasn't it? He couldn't be farther from such a tableau, here in the glassed-in porch overlooking the lawn sloping gently to the road, beyond which reedy marsh fringed the bay where bright sailboats skimmed. Who wouldn't feel euphoric at having such a scene to savor at leisure?

At the same time, though, he felt too weak, too used up, to leave his wicker chair. The blanket was heavy as a harness on his shoulders. Beside him on the little side table shaped like a citrus wedge, a sunbeam was warming his ginger ale. He didn't care about that, but condensation was leaving a wide, soggy arc on the "While You Were Out" memo sheet under the glass, making the ink spread toward illegibility. How and when had that gotten there? A wave of déjà vu broke his calm, and at the same instant wind rattled the windows, and sails on the bay wobbled like meter needles. Acton's hand felt flimsy as a November leaf as he pushed the glass aside and made out without surprise, "A box is coming for you." Acton squinted back and forth, almost ready to concede he just wasn't fast enough for 'em, whoever the damn messengers were. All the easy chairs, rockers, and sofas around him were empty.

For a while he stared at the sailboats cutting white semicircles in the bay as they tried tacking back on course. In that time his ponderings on the meaning of the note fell in and out of focus, until he fidgeted and something fell off the wide arm of his chair. He stretched his creaking neck to see what had smacked the floor. A box of matches? What could he have been doing with those?

Acton bent to get the box, and swinging his arm back to reach it drove all the breath out of him. Dizziness immobilized him a second, everything rippled before his eyes, and then a wave of despair, of desperation, pressed against him, only now it was a door he had to reach, and he couldn't. Smoke bleared his sight and stung his nose.

Behind him was the third-floor window, night chill still numbing his back. The walls to either side of him were half-eaten by flame. The way out was only six paces away, but whenever he took two steps forward, the heat pushed him back. It wasn't a matter of courage. He wanted to go ahead. He knew he could make it if willpower were all there was to it. But his body seemed to have its own say. It would not obey him once the heat stung his skin. And then he noticed red glow between the floorboards, and soon, wafer-thin sierras, as in those grow-your-own-moonscape kits from when he'd been a kid, were ad-

vancing along the cracks. To the left and right of him, knee-high lines
that had started at opposite walls were already meeting at room center.

Acton sat up straight, drawing in deep breath, surprised to find it
smokeless. The matchbox was still on the floor. He was all right now,
he kept telling himself, while the throbbing in his temples and the
tightness in his chest subsided. But the more he thought about the
burning room, the harder his heart beat. Definitely the scene was from
experience rather than imagination, but he hadn't the vaguest idea
when it had happened to him. Or had it yet to happen?

He closed his eyes and let all sense of the here-and-now fade out.
Then he tried backtracking, link by link, through recent memory, but
the series of impressions fit no chronological order, strung together as
capriciously as bracelet charms: the fire, the porch, the car crash, the
airy room, the mask in the mail. Nothing connected them but the note
about the "box." And worse, each apparent "awakening" into sick-
room reality was proven false by the next. In fact, right now he could
hear no wind against the panes, no occasional car on the road, nothing
anchoring him to the glassed-in porch. If he opened his eyes, he wondered, what next? No, don't do it!

Grasping at last how deeply he dreamed, Acton's first urge was to
snap out of it, rise above it, learn where he really was. But would the
truth really set him free? Each dip into his past had brought up graver
happenings. That last close call had been all too close. From what had
his memories been diverting him so far, if not something so much
grimmer, from which full consciousness would deny him retreat? Did
he really want to know what the box in the note ultimately meant?

"A box is coming for you." Eureka! Like a bolt from heaven, what
he had to do, all that he could do, occurred to him. "A box is coming
for you." What happy day did that refer to? Think back, to skinflint
Uncle Lou's bequeathal of a lousy cigar box full of change, but which
turned out to contain a rare 1943D penny that allowed for two years
without working; or think back to the bait box that fell overboard on a
solo fishing trip, necessitating a day of contemplating clouds and
waves, until the realization hit that this had been the one perfect day of
peace in a lifetime, at which point the box obligingly floated back; or
think back to when two prizes, instead of the usual one (they were little plastic prehistoric mammals), tumbled out of the cereal box, and

Dad said it would be dishonest not to send one back to the company, and Mom told him to shut up. Or else think back to any other happy day when a box came, and let that take shape, and be surrounded by it, and with any luck stay there and stay there and stay there unless another time yet more euphoric came to mind. He scoffed at the idea of anyone else doing any differently, and grasped at one idyll after another till the effort put him under.

A Vampire Heart

Fear of his own mortality hit Ambrose Lamouche his first day stamping out plastic St. Judes at the icon plant. Before the weekend, his job had been to seal magnets in the bases of dashboard Madonnas, but then the former Jude molder died suddenly during Sunday dinner from a hitherto unfelt brain tumor. Hence Ambrose was enjoying a promotion in a sense, in terms of reduced squinting, backache, and concentration. More pause for reflection, though, sank him into ever deeper funk at standing on a dead man's worn spot.

Depressing, the way it all went on, a dozen hot, carrot-sized Judes popping out of injection encasement every five minutes, as if it made no difference that it was this other guy Friday, and Ambrose now. The deceased was a nodding acquaintance, no more, but still, this relentless production without pause smacked of disrespect to living and dead alike. Ambrose felt more expendable than one of his mass-produced statuettes.

The fluorocarbon odor grew more stifling each time the machine puffed hot air at him. Equating himself with the dead man was all too easy, as if lingering in this oppressiveness, on the worn spot, feeling hopeless, made him as good as dead himself. A vivid sense of his own last moment arose, of how it would feel when he couldn't move or inhale or see, when his fingers and toes got cold and he went wild with rigored panic. No, he had to shake this feeling at any cost, this sense that made all the world a tomb. All these Patron Saints of Hopeless Causes hadn't done his predecessor any good, had they? Hell, Ambrose wasn't even Catholic! Paying mere lip service to the concept that multiple Judes should have protected their maker warned him of dangerous lapse toward the dear departed's way of thinking. Flash! Get too close to a dead man, and you become the dead man! It sounded right.

Out! It was imperative. Vile smoke some while later brought co-workers running to Ambrose's corner. Cracked and blackened little mummies of St. Jude rattled to the floor once the mold was released. No one from the factory ever saw Ambrose again.

Hoofing it to the bus stop brought no relief. The avenue was lined with thundering foundries and dye works reeking like crematoriums. The midday heat was like a monstrous hand shoving against Ambrose's every step. Outdoors and indoors felt no different.

To top it off, funeral limos and a train of mourners' cars, high beams ablaze, kept him waiting at the first corner. His knees wobbled and his jaw hung limp with a booster dose of that same choking despair from back at the machine. Every exposure to death, whether of stranger or loved one, sent a shock to the system, and the more death in your life, the weaker and more vulnerable to it you became, as when infection set into one untreated little cut. Your own death was the cumulative effect of all the deaths around you. Too much habituation to the idea of dying damped out the will to live. It was simple as magic and reducible to childishly simple formula: to avoid dying, you had to avoid death.

Then he noticed how the passing mourners were gawking in apparent shock or dismay at him. Ambrose saw this as terrible proof of his theory. For all the misery on their minds, they had to home in on him! Death in his face! He nigh well jumped out of his skin, horror-struck that it might be too late for him already. He backed away as from a python and hid in the nearest alley until he heard no more cars.

Truth to tell, Ambrose LaMouche would have held a wincing fascination for any stranger anytime. His eyes goggled hungrily, and his nose turned up at right angle to normality. Head sat on shoulders without mediation of neck. Without bending, he could brush his knees with his fingertips. Bow legs gave the impression that he was on the eternal verge of pouncing. As long as Ambrose was stuck with the rest of his appearance, this proved a blessing in disguise, since potential harassment shied away from him. Everyone knows you don't mess with belligerent weirdoes. Ambrose took the deference of bullies for granted, all unwitting of the intimidation projected by his own stance.

Keeping death at arm's length, though, was a whole other story. The easy part was holing up in his attic efficiency, shunning friends who were old and hence well deathbound, or even friends his own age, the better part of halfway there. For company, who could be healthier than the citizens of old TV sitcoms, despite the deathly cathode pallor they cast upon him? Watching anything else sounded too risky, and happily it never occurred to him that most of the casts in these shows were dead.

No, covering the rent was the heart of his dilemma. He'd be scraping the bottom of his savings by winter. He subscribed to the paper and scrutinized the want ads, vigilant for anything he could do that wouldn't rub against his esoteric grain. The funnies he also read, and the rest of the paper he ignored, except for the obits, which took up the same page every day. These he dealt with first, and who but a fool would not properly disarm his paper? Flipping through the booby-trapped section backwards, he found the hindside of the dangerous sheet and tore it out with aid of yardstick, crumpling it with nary a vampiric word seeing light. By association, the yardstick was taboo the rest of the time, and stayed hidden under the kitchen sink.

Soon the morning paper did literally lead him to the answer. When it landed on the sidewalk during the one downpour in weeks, Ambrose was fuming until he picked up the soggy tabloid and found himself facing the word "BABYSITTER" dominating a phone pole flyer. "Experienced BABYSITTER for Hire." He blinked runnels out of his poolball eyes and shivered with waterlogged anticipation at his new direction in life, in amassing life. Children! He smacked his lips. Richest in unspent years, and likely furthest off death's beaten trail! Babysitting wouldn't do, though, in terms of either income or child-yield.

Luckily the want ads were dry. The right something, he knew, had to be in there. And then his eyes stopped short at "Day Care Help." Why hadn't he thought of that before? He felt all keyed up, as if about to slake a mighty thirst. To steep himself waist-deep in all those children, to absorb all that combined longevity, he felt as if tomorrow could be the first day of living forever.

With redoubled urgency he hunted the want ads that and every day till an entry-level daycare position surfaced. A clean shirt, clean face, and he was out the door, as exhilarated and sure as an owl swooping at a mouse. Incredibly, he ran head-on into rejection, and for the first time in memory, the need for self-critique.

The daycare center looked and smelled like a cross between a hospital and a Lego fort. The spectacle of attendants herding children flustered him with the realization that he had no idea how to react to children, especially en masse. It would be like controlling a lot of birds or monkeys. The receptionist seemed taken aback at the sight of him, and before he could even finish asking about the job, she stated that they weren't looking for a janitor at present. Something was wrong here, and as he shuffled unsteadily out, he did see that no other man completing forms in the foyer looked anything like him. No, they were younger, sporting ties and jackets. And far from having a distinct appearance like his, they were hard to tell apart, like photos of men in barbershop windows.

Glaring into his bathroom mirror, he resented those men without whom he wouldn't have looked out of place, who were ignorantly thwarting his personal right-to-life program. He grinned like a clever fiend, and got even by making himself one of them. He bought non-prescription glasses to mask his ogle eyes, kept a neat beard to cover nature's sin of omission between chin and collar, and cultivated the habit of keeping his orangutan arms folded. Clothes, and loose trousers in particular, made the rest of the pass-for-normal man. He was convincing at a polite glance, though something non-Euclidean about the sum of his parts tempted a more probing stare. It wouldn't have helped. He had accounted for most of his physical singularities, and his extremely pug nose had to bear the entire brunt of suspicious curiosity.

Yet for a frustrating while, the malaise he aroused inspired excuses not to hire him. Flu season brought his lucky break when coughing children, adorable little disease carriers in Ambrose's view, left places shorthanded. Employers in desperation were looking wishfully at all applicants, not daring to assay a deep first impression. Ambrose ironically landed a job as a substitute at the address he had tried in the beginning, without incurring any look of recognition from the receptionist.

Ambrose got over his jitters about dealing with children by simply doing what he was told. And counter to obvious safe practice, he hovered whenever possible over his weak and sickly charges. They more than made up for their potential proximity to death by being all the easier to deprive of what Ambrose instinctively knew he was somehow taking. And of course before their ebb of life could threaten him, they went into home quarantine.

He had no idea what exactly he was doing or how he was doing it, but the basic math was manifest, that additional life for him meant life subtracted elsewhere. It also rang true that he could do what he was doing at least in part because of his willingness to do it. In any case, he rounded up the cranky, sluggish, and cold-looking children daily for snacktime, stories, and games, and within a week they fell, one by one, too sick for the facilities. Those few who slipped through his dragnet, he observed, didn't fall prey to whatever was going around.

Far from enduring any remorse, he luxuriated in his newfound fiendishness, as if learning how to save himself had also shown him himself for the first time. He felt as natural as a hyena loping beside a herd, and superior with a wisdom seldom reachable except via death camp or sinking ship, that any means of prolonging life amounted to a rag stuffed in the mouth of conscience. Pushing death away from his own person meant upping the level of death in his surroundings, making him in effect more deathlike to those around him. This was power to reckon with, and to emblemize his identification with death was his violently upturned nose, skull-like now that he thought about it. Through his death's-head nostrils, he imagined, he inhaled life from those who, after all, had it to spare.

His attraction to the susceptible children caused comment among coworkers and supervisors, but he followed orders competently and did nothing visibly wrong with those who would have gotten sick anyway. Still, there was something too eager in his approach to the children, too unctuous in his stance, like a dirty cloud looming over them. The children sensed something that made them draw away at his approach, but the instinctive dislike of five-year-olds was insufficient grounds for dismissal. At least during flu season. If only enough of the stricken regulars could return to work and render Ambrose redundant!

Meanwhile, Ambrose reveled in his bonus of life, finding further evidence of death-proofing in his conspicuous good health, despite all the illness the children sneezed into the air. Thus he accounted for the wild energy that kept him up for nights on end, thrusting him in his job-search formalwear onto the mean streets to flaunt his deathlessness. He stationed himself at key locations and yelled the worst names he could think of at toughs who loitered at exactly the right distance. Then he beat strategic retreat to nearby church grounds, where he shimmied up bigger-than-life statues of Jesus, Joseph, or strange Russian saints. He was ready on lofty shoulders when pursuit caught up, and as he yelled more abuse, his long reach broke stone fingers off outstretched arms. He cast them at would-be assailants, whose low threshold of freakishness always sent them bolting. Ambrose climbed down laughing uproariously.

Ambrose smoldered with a junkie's craving for pure nirvana the morning he first saw the frail boy he dubbed "Poster Child." His connoisseur's eyes bulged with greed at the child's weak, wobbly legs, whitish hair, and anemic pallor. There was less an impression of vulnerability than of nakedness, like that of a shivering, featherless bird. All the children gave Poster Child the same wide berth they gave Ambrose. But for all Ambrose's kindly show of doting, Poster Child's big sunken eyes regarded him with doomed indifference. Ambrose relished the prospect of upcoming days with his ultimate innocent delicacy, but broke into cold sweat, as if hip-deep in his own special bane, on learning the boy's name was Jude.

It was his past giving chase like a fissure opening toward him from behind, some secret agent of mortality on his trail, with implications of vast cosmic wheels of preordained action and reaction too ghastly to contemplate. He knew in his bones that here was a ticking incarnation of that same Jude who had functioned as his harbinger of doom back at the factory.

To kill the kid with an o.d. of kindness, make his noxious presence do its inscrutable stuff, what else could Ambrose do? Never mind that he was launching all-out spiritual assault against a toddler. He had to get Jude before Jude got him. Heart had no more place in the situation than if Ambrose were an old king oak depriving a sapling of light.

Next day he corralled some children, including Jude of course, into a game of hide-and-seek. If proximity and encounter were going to wear Jude down and out, then games that involved catching someone would take so much bigger a bite. As with everything else, Jude joined in with a martyr's resignation, as if life were an unbroken chain of dreary chores.

Ambrose used the rumpus room that doubled as cafeteria and that had a door, usually locked, onto the street. Today, though, halfway through Ambrose's count to one hundred, after most of the children had hidden, the dairy man came in by the front door, opened the side door with the receptionist's key, and started wheeling in the week's milk. Meanwhile, none of the children would share their hiding places with Jude and shoved him away. While the delivery man was loading up the fridge, Jude saw the open door and felt drawn. Outside! Where better to hide from everyone in a room?

Out on the sidewalk, he heard bells and hymns up the street. But he couldn't see over the milk truck and the parked cars. It was the Feast Day of St. Nicholas, and a grand procession was bearing his sedan-chaired icon, a big wooden Christ crucified, and crosiers loud with pendant sleigh bells. A priest in fur-collared windbreaker brought up the rear, leading the hymns by dint of megaphone. A couple of motorcycle cops rode back and forth on either side of the somber parade. Jude wanted to see all this, and mistaking the sound of the dairy man and his dolly for that of Ambrose in pursuit, forgot caution. He ran into the street between milk van and a parked car. Engine racket flared at him, there was a blur of motion and suffering, and then a white flash and a little snap as when the TV tube went. The motorcycle cop had no time to slam on the brakes until after the fact.

The screech stopped the procession which bunched up into confusion, only the plaster St. Nicholas enjoying clear view of the tableau from aloft. Everyone from the daycare center came running, choking on their hearts at the long red skid mark ending with capsized bike and broken child, as did the inner circle of paraders, as did the cops trying to hold back the crowd and radio for an ambulance.

Amidst his coworkers, Ambrose's even stronger reaction callously stole attention from the tragedy. He sucked hoarse breath as if stabbed in the lungs and raised his arms, making convulsive claws. He keeled over, and then spasms wrenched his limbs straight and shook his glasses off. His mouth bubbled with blood as he gurgled, "Gypped! Fuck!"

The autopsy would find blood clots and call it miraculous that they hadn't caused cerebral hemorrhage before then. What made one of them kick up at that special moment? Who can say about these things?

But at the time, the daycare receptionist, at the sight of Ambrose's naked eyes and storm-drain arms, blurted, "The janitor!" And even if she misstated the case, it was clear to herself and everyone around her that she knew what she was talking about.

Subway of the Dead

Convent bells, garbage truck, gunshots. Half an hour later, can't remember what woke me early. But here I am. Underground before my time. Waiting for the subway. Beating rush hour at least. Stale earthy breeze smacks me upside the head. Here comes my train.

Funny, it's a D, not an N. Didn't think the D even rode these tracks. But what the hell, it's going my way, right? Nobody else in my car. And several stops later, only a few.

At Prospect Avenue, aging yuppie gets on. Sits down across from me. But I see over his shoulder, as the train pulls out, that he's also still standing on the platform. Yes, him. Same face, suit, briefcase. At last second, I glimpse the man on the platform convulse and fall. Same instant, his double on the train nods off.

My thoughts race, with intuitive sprints of a mind still in fog of dreamtime. Train's too empty, even for this hour. Plus, it's the wrong train. The D? As in Mr. D? The big D? Suddenly I don't feel so good. Crawly critter in my stomach is stuck on its back, legs churning.

Life and death in the big city. Day to day, more live than die, of course. If people on a normal train right now represent the number who'll survive the day, maybe we on this D make up those who won't. Maybe. What do I know?

Woman two seats away also gives sleeping yuppie the leery eye. She too must have seen his doppelgänger go down. She's very pretty. Long blond hair, black velvet jacket, jade earrings, big blue eyes, lean face. Pale complexion in apparent inkling of something really wrong.

We both jump as something thuds and rolls at the end of the car. An old drunk dozing off has dropped his Midnight Dragon.

We stop at a station. Two guys dressed like subway cops get on. The doors stay open while the cops grab the yuppie, then the bum, by the underarms and drag them, arms flapping, to the bench on the platform. Neither wakes. The cops ignore the woman and me. Once they leave, the train goes.

This woman's not the type who'd deign to say "Excuse me" if she knocked me down. But now she asks what's going on. Implores, even. My best guess? We're on the doom train. Or our souls are, or spirits or whatever. And our bodies are back in the physical world, carrying on as usual. But if we nod off here, our bodies die there.

Instead of questioning my sanity, the woman acts as if I'm as good an authority as any. "And after they take us off the train? What then?"

I shrug. While whatever's been churning in my stomach suffers seizures.

Why not just exit the train? The urge to bolt exists, all right. But we never stop except to let on cops or passengers. At which point, only the doors in use open and close. We're scared of provoking the cops. And also of whatever's out there. Suppose we find our bodies, what then? Knock and walk back in? We don't know enough to go on yet. I, for one, am not giving up. But no denying, I feel trapped. My new friend summarizes our options. "We have to stay awake."

By now, only one other passenger among us. A church lady in wide-brimmed mauve hat and fur-trimmed green coat. She stares out window.

Certain ideas more readily come to mind in the face of nothing to lose. But not within hearing of church lady! The blonde and I make small talk to forestall sleep. Topics like jobs and home life already feel remote. Idle in the extreme.

Church lady leans back. Her eyes close. Next stop, subway cops collect her. And then it's just the two of us.

From where I sit, she's the last woman on earth. I lurch into seat beside her. "I have an idea. We can't let our life force weaken. We have to reinforce it. Make it shield us. Make love to me. It'll be like charging our batteries. We can use the life force as a prophylactic. If you get my meaning." Why not go for broke in the time left? It's not like I disbelieve what I'm saying.

Her first look says, Nothing doing. Then fear, despair, desperation cross her face. Turns out I'm not someone she wouldn't touch if I were the last man on earth. No self-deprecation intended.

It's cramped. We keep getting jostled apart. The tracks are bumpy.

Waves of worry make for stop-and-go. Ah, but still. Urgency, surrealism, even starkness of moment make for a certain exquisite edge. And as long as we continue, the train keeps rolling.

Yet all good things must end. I finish first. Pull out and look into her face. Trying to think of what next. But she's asleep.

Am I callous? Safety first is all I have in mind. Panic stampedes me to another seat. Don't want cops catching me with her.

Sure enough, at the next station they take her away. Nary a glance at me. Singlemindedness of angels, or robots?

Gotta find another means of self-assertion. Break the pattern in which I'm bound to be woven sooner or later.

Next stop, a hard body gets on. The type unable to walk right because macho muscle bows his legs and swells his shoulders. The simian strut. Devolution through fitness. At least he lacks a salon tan. He sits toward center of car. Stares at his feet.

That empty quart of Midnight Dragon rolling hither and yon inspires me. Sex served only as stopgap measure. But what about violence? What happens if you kill someone already as good as gone? If this guy underwent a second death, would the two cancel each other out? Send him back to his body, with him none the wiser? Maybe even stop the train, short-circuit the whole scenario, and restore normality? Worth a shot. I have nothing better to do. No crime, after all, in killing a dead man. Though truth to tell, I'm happy with this choice of guinea pig.

But act now! If this guy fades, the experiment is ruined. I stride to the end of the car. Smile affably at hard body as I pass. He scowls to let me know I'm a wuss. Returns to shoe-gazing.

I catch the bottle quietly in mid-roll. Stroll up to the guy. Hopefully now that we're down to astral selves, he no longer has the brawny advantage of me. I regard my reflection in the window, rushing darkness beyond, as I raise the bottle over my subject's head. Smile affably again. Bring the bottle down full-force.

Crack! Down he goes, in a burst of green shards, his forehead bumping back of next seat. I pull him by the hair, expose his throat. No point doing this halfway! Drive flaring jagged bottleneck through his Adam's apple.

I back off in surprise from blood gush. Disgusting! Astral body or not, what a mess!

I hightail it back to seat. Stare at my own shoes, innocent-like. And yes, train slows as station lighting brightens my feet.

But what's this? Platform is packed with people.

I am not reassured. Seems to me, if this were rush hour back in the mortal coil, more would've happened than the simple reappearance of commuters.

All doors open, to a torrent of humanity. Within it, the cops. They elbow through to me. Dauntless as harvesting machines. Officers, there must be some mistake! They grab me by the arms and pull me up. Out of my seat, off the train. Push me through unabating flood of dour faces. Slam me against platform wall. Ow! When I look around, they're gone.

No ebb in the human tide, though. This feels even more wrong than everything else today. Something to do with offing that guy? Maybe activities on the D do produce some effect, some feedback, in the land of the living. While I was having sex, no lives ended. When I killed, did death hit the city en masse? And then the cops ejected me lest I kill again. They look overworked enough.

My train left. Not one more could squeeze on. The platform is fast filling up again. But the crush is starting to slow. The stairs are passable at least.

I'm free to go. But I shudder to picture what my one little murder has wrought out there. I don't want to look.

What's more, the question of why I stay awake pesters me. Why me? Has this all been a test? Is the doom train a vehicle of my doom alone? Maybe death gives us each our own world to make into heaven or hell.

Force from behind knocks the breath out of me. I'm going forward. But not under my own steam. The cops have collared me. Drag me up the stairs. Officers, officers, was I less than pure of heart in fucking the blonde and killing the jock? I never said fun was everything!

People still flow down the stairs around us. The light from outside flickers. I smell smoke.

Hey! Officers! I'll wait for the next train! I'll behave!

Oh no, it's the old heave-ho! Flat on my face, knees well-scraped. Well, they can't make me open my eyes! They can't!

Graveside Friday Night

You don't want to see the guys who drink in graveyards at night. Say you did, how could you ever look them in the eye without telltale jitters? And they might seem paragons of normality like Lou, Morris, and Vinnie, forklift jockeys par excellence, devotees of the dog track and Nightly Number, staunch revilers of foreigners and queers. To see deeper stirrings from these personalities by light of day, you'd need lucky timing and the fortune that favors the brave to see you through your risky vantage. Take the slow Friday when Lou and Vinnie ran forklift races in seemingly bossless warehouse outback. They discovered the foreman taking inventory behind some boxes only by side-swiping a stack onto his head. And then of course they had no reason to assume he wouldn't revive by himself later. What? Wake him themselves and take the rap for some innocent high spirits? After he'd finally shambled out with no idea what had hit him, the boys drank to each other's common sense.

But for Lou, Morris, and Vinnie, cocktail lounges and sports bars were no place to spend Miller time. Their kindred souls derived no satisfaction where ceilings on their social conduct cramped their style. Rather, they knew every family plot off every dirt road in every second-growth forest in the state. Weather permitting, weekend evenings found them killing their high beams and stepping out of their vehicle and out of civilization as well. They eased eelishly through lonesome darkness as through their natural element, incapable of imagining anything to fear in those grounds at dead ends of habitual, footfelt paths. Dim graveyards existed solely for their drinking and recreational pleasure, and tombstones were purely therapeutic things against which to vent emotional steam. Nothing ever happened to convince them they weren't kings of their world, of course.

One Friday, Morris felt even more kingly than usual, thanks to the great rare fortune of a queen for the evening. His date was a lean, big-eyed blonde styling herself Joleen after the old Dolly Parton hit. Truth to tell, maybe Joleen wasn't fantastically bright, but she'd only been a week on the job and had no workplace friends yet to wise her up. And Morris could swing a kind of suave when the inspiration moved him and he chose to smile and watch his mouth and seem to listen.

So Morris told Joleen he could see she was a country girl, and at heart he was a country boy, and with her new in town and all, wouldn't she like to see the pretty country with his four-wheel-drive and then have a drink at a little place where he and some friends from work went sometimes? At a loss for any objections strong enough to back up a no, she said yes. He came by promptly, as promised, honking out front, in the nice cool 7 P.M. September dusk.

Morris's face was suddenly a little too big for his head, and behind the wheel he seemed shorter, as if for all his joshing and flirty talk some kind of sneakiness was making him more lowdown, more weaselish. Must be, she told herself, that he's awkward and nervous about making a first impression. When he pulled up in front of a Burger King and two guys piled in, Joleen's nerves lit firecrackers in her stomach, but she said nothing because she was too surprised to know what to say.

"You don't mind, do ya, darlin'?" Morris grinned. "Long as we're meetin' up later anyway, might as well get everyone together now."

Of course it felt completely wrong, the more so as the over-cologned newcomers, each twice the size of Morris, announced that tonight they were going to party. Joleen found a beer in her hand and heard twistcaps popping around her. The wave of their enthusiasm came close to lifting her up, and every couple of minutes she lapsed into taking their good ol' mood at face value. And then it was too late to do anything but worry, because the oldies station was too loud for her to make herself heard, and they were already too far down back roads for her to get out and walk, and they were all bellering along as the radio played, "Come along and be my party doll."

Joleen's poor substitute for escape was a hard stare out the side window, which served only to escalate her desperation. The roadside grew houseless, the road grew bumpy, and soon the ride grew rough as it only could on one-lane dirt surface. Joleen had no inkling where they were, aside from being in the middle of the woods.

Morris pulled over at a spot seemingly no different from any other. The men quieted down as they filed from the jeep and took some memorized route through the underbrush. Vigilant as if navigating by radar, they paid her no special mind as she stumbled along like a drugged victim en route to sinister ritual, half-full beer still in hand.

Joleen heard someone's empty bottle clink tentatively on metal, then heard the bottle smash. Suddenly Morris was giving her a hand over a low fence made of cold iron pipes, and he was telling her, "Watch your step, honey. Here's that little place I was tellin' ya about." They were in a graveyard, and her improving night vision showed her a dozen rows of slate markers and white obelisks, for the most part truncated or toppled. Slivers of glass sparkled in the moonlight wherever she looked. From some stashing place, Vinnie and Lou had grabbed some plastic chaise lounges, which they were unfolding around the sunken ashes of an old campfire in the middle of the cemetery. Joleen had an urge to laugh coming from parts unknown, and that scared her more than anything else going on.

"Yeah, that's the spirit, relax!" blustered Vinnie, leaning his long, doggish face over hers, doubly scaring her with the hint that she'd been laughing aloud without knowing it. His beer breath and cologne backed her weakly into one of the chaises, and Morris reclined in the one adjacent. "We are like the knights of old! We are like the Musketeers! And that's how come nobody understands us! They don't make good friends like us anymore. We'll always be together and we always share everything. Right?" Vinnie brayed.

"Hear, hear!" hooted Morris, and Joleen's breath stopped up in her throat at thoughts of where sharing everything would likely lead. And her date, as she gaped speechless at him, seemed all for it.

"Look what I got to share with youse and the lovely lady," announced Lou, whipping out a squarish fifth from inside his green nylon jacket.

"Yeah! Mescal!" yelled Vinnie as he grabbed the bottle. "I've never had this stuff before, but I hear it makes you see things. Lou, you're the best!"

"Hey, hey! Ladies first, ain't that right, boys?" called Morris as Vinnie thirstily unscrewed the cap.

"Morris, you are the chivalrous one. No wonder you're the one who always brings the date." Vinnie surrendered the bottle to Morris, who put it in Joleen's hands. "But me second, got that?"

Joleen tried getting a little swig over with, but the barest of gulps scorched her throat and warned that there was no such thing as a little taste.

She held out the bottle to Vinnie, who raised it and proclaimed, "A toast! To our lovely guest! See, Morris? You ain't the only gallant one. Sometimes you gotta think of these things to make a lady feel at home." He took a big swallow and smacked his lips.

"Yeah, next time I'll think of that," Morris mused. The bottle made the rounds again and again, and Joleen could feel it bringing on headspin despite her best attempts at token tastes. And it alarmed her to watch the men's emotional pitch rise and rise, their slurry pledges to her and each other growing mawkish-unto-tearful. Sobbing shook them as they cursed the godlessness, the disrespect for home and manhood, the breakdown of the family, all sending America and in turn, somehow, the rest of the world to hell. It suddenly became too much for staggering Lou, who like a shaman in fitful trance pounded bare fists without apparent pain on a granite obelisk. Nor did he seem to see anything amiss in attacking the last worldly evidence of one of his idolized American forebears.

"Don't mind Lou," confided Morris, still on the chaise next to Joleen's. "He just gets depressed sometimes." By way of reassurance he tried taking Joleen's hand, but she swatted it away like a big moth, desperate that nobody else see any first contact that might lead to the unthinkable. Morris happened to have the bottle in the crook of his other arm, and it seesawed nose-first downward. First things first! Morris caught at it and made a save, but sent all the more alcohol in a gurgling crescent.

Better for them, had they known the first thing about libations, whether offered unwittingly or not on unhallowed ground by over-wrought men invoking the past, no matter how oafishly.

But no, Morris just turned back to Joleen and snarled more angrily than a little spillage could account for, "Hey! There'll be hell to pay if you waste that! That's our whole supply!" But at least he was keeping his hands to himself. Meanwhile, that precious water of life was sinking below the topsoil.

The little incident had caught Vinnie's eye, and he had a disapproving frown for Joleen as he fetched the bottle from Morris. Another swallow was all the fine-tuning he needed to hit Lou's wavelength. "What does everybody have against us?" he broke down, passing the bottle to Lou, who was sniffling and catching his breath. "All we wanna do is have fun, release a little tension, live while we're alive. Why does everyone act like we got some kinda disease?" Frustration made him drive his fists down onto the top of a slate marker as if to hammer it deeper into the ground.

There was rote in Vinnie's passion, though, as if countless other graveyards on countless other Fridays could have heard the same oration. The men reminded Joleen of windup toys, doing things they had no idea of having done before. All sense of past was apparently buried in hangover forgetfulness, along with the memory of countless other dates like Joleen. What had happened to those "dates," she dared to wonder, and where were they now?

Then there was a pause in the action, as everyone looked up, mouths open, though expectant of what, nobody could say. The air had changed as before a storm, and they heard birds chirp and flap around in the dark. "We gonna get rain?" Morris finally asked as if that would be something incredible. The next second, restless birdsong was drowned out by the rush of a wind that shook the branches but came from no apparent direction.

"Whew!" Lou sniffed. "Rotten wind, huh? Wherever it's coming from, somethin' must have died there." He raised the half-empty bottle, but never took the swig to chase the dead smell from his nostrils. "The worm in the bottle!" he shouted. "It's halfway up the glass!"

"Well, the bottle got turned upside-down," Morris said. "The worm just stuck to the glass after Joleen here made me spill some."

Joleen set all her will to shrinking unto invisibility in her seat, not even hearing Lou say, "No, I swear to God the worm is crawlin' up the side!"

Vinnie snatched the bottle and decreed, "Well, you ain't the designated driver no more. And your worm ain't goin' no place either." He took a slug from a shallow angle that washed the worm into his mouth.

He crunched it and made a face as he swallowed. "Some bitter shit! I thought the booze was supposed to keep 'em from tasting rotten. Well, live and learn." He took another pull.

The wind was dying down by little fits and puffs and leaving coldness in its wake. Morris gallantly asked Joleen if she wanted him to get her a sweater from the jeep. She nodded emphatically, relieved to see his temper cool and to get some distance between them for a while.

Lou and Vinnie watched Morris take off down the thickety path, and then Vinnie handed Joleen the bottle and said, "Yeah, Morris is a good guy all right. He's our friend. He deserves a good woman in his life."

Leery Joleen said nothing, smiled, lifted the bottle as if toasting Vinnie's sentiments, and took a nominal gulp. Lou, leaning on the obelisk he'd been battering, agreed with Vinnie and added, "Not as if we're not good guys too."

Motion from the direction of the path made the three of them turn, and Vinnie presumed, "Morris sure moves fast."

But no, they glimpsed someone else beyond the iron fence, an old guy dressed in white, no, not dressed in white, but a dull white all over. The three of them concentrated on getting a better look at the newcomer, and with that he was gone, and Joleen's hopes of a rescuer from this ticking package of a situation rose and crashed in a second.

"Hey, this shit does make you see things!" Vinnie proclaimed.

"Could it of been like a cop or a ranger or something?" Lou asked, sharing none of Vinnie's enthusiasm. "He might've just ducked behind something."

"I don't know," mumbled Vinnie, and with dampened mood, he and Lou listened to Morris clumping their way, and they relaxed only on getting a clear look at him.

"What's the matter?" Morris asked, tossing Joleen the sweater. He stopped and went goggle-eyed. Two rows of tombstones behind Joleen, a little old hunchbacked lady with hair in a cable-thick braid down to her knees was shaking a fist at Morris and mouthing something. She was dull white, head to toe. The others turned as Morris gaped, but then she was gone.

Vinnie read Morris's face and said, "See what I told you? Now Morris is seeing things too."

It was true, the men had chanced to make the right moves for a conjuration, but as wireless receivers of the spirit world they were too drunk, profane, unbelieving, and self-involved to bring awakened ghosts into more than a few seconds' visibility at a time. Nonetheless the groggy spirits were taking in the whole tableau all right, and they were not happy. The vandalism! The vulgarity! The drunkenness! To suffer this they'd been called up?

Once one of the unwelcome mortals noticed something out the corner of an eye, the others would turn and stare, whether at cussing biddies, bawling children in pairs or threes, palsied patriarchs with killing looks, or sour-faced farmers pointing the way out. But no sooner had mortal focus gathered on inaudible ectoplasm than it winked out. And then someone else would turn toward another peripheral revenant.

It began to feel like a game. The men had too much mescal courage to imagine they faced more than hallucinations, and Morris, playing the gallant lest Joleen take fright at harmless bogeymen, started winging stones through them the second they appeared. "See? Don't be scared, babe, these things can't bother you none. Hit 'em with a rock and they blip out just like in a video game. Just our imagination playin' tricks on us, that's all." It looked like fun to Lou and Vinnie too, and soon they were even breaking off layers of weathered grave slate and scaling it Frisbee-like at the apparitions.

Joleen alone wasn't laughing. To the trauma of being lost in night woods with three soused apes of men, the addition of a ghost show only hardened the state of shock encasing her. And as for the figment nature of the men's target practice, Joleen was the only one still sober enough to perceive and worry about the white figures' old-fashioned clothes, like those of the townspeople in Westerns or something. It took her a long time to find and say the words, "I think we should get out of here."

Nobody was listening. But by that time, at least, Vinnie and Lou had grown bored with ghost-pelting and were plugging away at the rest of the bottle. Morris, by way of reassuring Joleen, still carried on, aiming at phantoms to which Vinnie and Lou kept their apathetic backs.

Morris's chivalry, though, did not go unnoticed. Vinnie repeated his earlier comment about sensitive Morris knowing how to make a date feel at home.

"Well, if we got the chance we'd be just as good," Lou pointed out, handing Vinnie the bottle.

"And it's high time we started getting lucky too," Vinnie declared, taking a swig for emphasis. "You know how long it's been since either of us had a date?"

"I dunno," Lou shrugged. "Months? What's the use of thinking about it?"

"Hey, it's not like we're gettin' any younger," Vinnie warned, his tone growing plaintive. "We gotta do something."

"Like what, huh? What do we do? How come Morris has all the luck?" Lou lamented, picking up Vinnie's desperation while he grabbed back the mescal. Morris meanwhile was still preoccupied cooing sweet nothings at half-gone Joleen and taking potshots at outraged spirits.

"Yeah! Why him and not us?" Vinnie demanded, glaring in Joleen's face, and then shouting at her directly, "Hey, whydja go out with Morris instead of one of us?"

On realizing she was being addressed, Joleen stared glassy-eyed at stormy Vinnie. Sensing that the situation had reached a new plateau of danger in no way helped her find words to mollify the threat.

"Why can't we be loved?" cried Vinnie in the melodramatic anguish of drunkenness. "Why'd you pick him?" he bellowed, while Lou loyally chorused, "Yeah!"

Vinnie pulled down his fly and exposed himself. He brandished his manhood like a jackknife. "I don't understand you. I want to open you up and see what's inside."

Morris turned from his marksmanship and spoke up, "Now that's no way to talk!"

Joleen's eyes finally convinced her body of the peril her mind had been screaming about all along. Terrorized into motion again, she sat up and looked around frantically for something to heave at Vinnie's crotch. But she was too frantic to focus, and instead, without giving it the least thought, obeyed her nervous system's orders to get up and run.

Momentarily too overcome by the drama of his own gesture to try stopping her, Vinnie watched her crash into the underbrush in the general direction of the vehicle. "She's getting away!" shouted Lou, breaking Vinnie's self-inflicted spell. They both took off after her, with

Morris joining in but confused about his role. Was he with her now or with his friends? Thinking far enough ahead to when they caught her seemed impossible.

Meanwhile, indignant Yankee phantoms were alarmed at the prospect of the mortal trespassers exiting unpunished. Vinnie's self-exposure and what it portended were affronts beyond endurance. Not that Joleen's plight had struck a sensitive or moral chord in defunct Swampy souls. It's just that they were prudish to the hilt, and they weren't going to let anyone get away with offending them like that!

That's when they summoned me up. How long have I been here? I'm a part of this place. How long is that? My vibes got under the first settlers' skins and were part of the reason this spot seemed right for a cemetery. My healthful presence was part of the reason nobody lives around here anymore. The newly deceased were always taken aback on finding me below them, but the interred and I have come to be the best of neighbors. Both they and I tend to sleep most of the time.

But now they'd awakened me, and I was grumpy, and famished. I wasn't so drowsy, of course, that I couldn't pick mortal minds and size up the situation instantly. Here were three foul bastards hot on the trail of an innocent, helpless girl, and it was plain to her, whether it was to them yet or not, what would happen when they caught her. Of course I wasn't going to let things reach that pass.

I yawned and stretched my limbs. The men stopped cold and turned as if they'd heard a hundred dog snouts gabble at once, and they wouldn't have been too far off the mark. With the darkness and undergrowth between me and them, they couldn't get a coherent impression of me, but they saw enough to send them scrambling again. That's when they learned, even if too late to save them, not to make light of, and certainly not to ignore the dead. I doubt they expected I could reach them without giving chase. With no bones to hold my arms back, though, they could have reached much farther yet. As I reeled the men in, I sensed the girl was off their minds completely, and their fear on top of their lingering hint of lust made for just the right flavor accents.

The hysterical girl, however, was not at all off my mind. Hearing the screeches and gurgling behind her, she indulged visions of all the men's previous "dates" rising from secret graves, like the Yankee codgers, and taking diabolical revenge. But as she quickly learned, things just don't work that way. I lunged out and took her too, of course. What did I care about her being hard done by? I wasn't sensitive or moral either, no more than my main course's idolized family-value farmers. And I was hungry, damn it all, though I knew she'd have a gamey taste from being in shock so long. Those bluenose Yankees called me up to do a job, and I was too cranky not to do it.

You don't want to see the people who drink in graveyards at night. Especially not the ones I've seen first.

Dappled Ass

Clear the streets of centaurs! This is my mission in life, futile or not, and almost one hundred percent unactualized.

At first there were only a few of them. A novelty, barbarically splendid. The sight of them conjured postcards of whatever little island they came from, in the Aegean or Caspian. Somewhere thataway.

Then someone opened the floodgates. And the rest, as Shakespeare said, smelled of horse piss. They did bump the bicycle messengers out of business, and for this I was grateful. In fact, they scared all bicycle traffic out to the 'burbs. And why? Because they were bigger, more aggressive, and more oblivious. In other words, everything wrong with the bicyclists, only worse. And there were more of them.

Like the bicyclists, they followed vehicular mode when it suited them, and acted as foot traffic the rest of the time. They'd hop from gridlocked street to crowded sidewalk and scatter citizens in their wake. They'd obey traffic laws when necessary, but otherwise, pedestrians beware! Crosswalk right-of-way meant nothing to them.

The cops tried hiring them as auxiliary mounties. But I heard that none ever got through training. Gunfire spooked 'em, and nobody on the force knew enough Centaurese to get the technical stuff across.

So what's a beleaguered walker to do? Lowdown times call for lowdown means. You don't want to be seen doing anything, of course. That's not the guerrilla way. And hard to enjoy the fruits of your labor if you get caught, or worse, hurt. What's more, the city has a million eyes. This has pretty much limited my operations to dirty looks and muttering under my breath at every near-miss.

But when opportunism knocked, I answered. Our six-limbed scofflaws are always in a digestive bind, you know. Scant choice of dining facilities. Even the most willing restaurateur wouldn't have the space. So the centaurs must resort to stands and pushcarts. But thanks to nature and nurture alike, the most available foods tend to be least edible. Careful or not, every centaur chances into fast-food suffering sooner or later.

At least in this respect I'm more than a match for any horse's ass. Come one lunchtime when I had no patience for deli crowds, I made for the gyro wagon at the corner. Craving kebab which would owe half its weight to onions, red pepper sauce, and sublime griddle scrapings. And hurray, no one ahead of me!

But as I entered hailing distance, a centaur bounded from the street and cut me off. With no hint he knew I was there. A step closer and he'd have broadsided me. Godammit, you horse's ass!

I glared at his dappled rump while he ordered. Falafel, extra lettuce, yogurt sauce in whole-wheat pocket. What a wuss!

The gyro man took my order while the centaur's pita warmed on the grill.

Our sandwiches were ready at the same time. I paid while the centaur was still digging in his fanny pack. Gyro man's eyes were downcast as he got my change. It struck me that both sandwiches were twins on the surface. Figurative little red horns were sprouting from my head. I nabbed the falafel, told gyro man to keep the change, and took off. In front of my building, I turned just in time to see that horse's ass put down my kebab, well, like a horse. Showed nary a sign of tasting it. Giddyap, you sucker! In me glowed that special glee reserved for the righteous, mean, and sneaky.

Well, what did you expect? Did my conscience call me petty? Cowardly, even? That was its big mistake. Cowardly is what I call those who throw their weight around with no concern for anyone else. Meanwhile, it's stupid starting a fight you can't win, however right you are. So, I just try my best to level the ground between myself and those whom it would be sheerest folly to confront directly.

In fact, my spiteful pleasure sat better with me than the soggy lettuce in that bland falafel. Fit for a horse indeed!

Around three, a call came from the lobby. Messenger here with a delivery. Could I hurry, please? Said yes, and took my time.

The messenger was a centaur, of course. And I'd know that dappled ass anywhere. He didn't look so good. Greenish complexion, glistening brow, foam on his flanks. Shifting from hoof to hoof as if badly needing a bathroom.

How I hated this! I wasn't renouncing my generalizations one bit. I knew they were right! But the generalizer still felt obliged to treat his generalizee as an individual. Dammit!

The desk man was being a pill as usual. Once my parcel was signed over, he asked the centaur gruffly, "You got any more business here?"

Ignoring him, I asked Dappled Ass, "You wanna use the bathroom?"

The centaur nodded desperately. The desk man started squawking. I cut him off. "This is a friend of mine." Deaf to further protest, I motioned the centaur to follow me. Fighting an impulse all along to grab some bridle and lead him.

There was a men's room past the elevators. A guy washing his hands scowled but said nothing. I opened a stall door and Dappled Ass backed in.

"Hold my tail!" he demanded.

"What?"

"You think I want shit on it?"

His distress was too urgent to argue with. I crowded in with him. His tail snapped up and I caught it. He hunkered over the seat as best he could. The sound and fury were brutal but brief. I was only too thankful he didn't ask me to wipe. I squeezed out of the stall before learning what, if anything, they did about this.

"You're welcome," I said as he clopped out. He regarded me blankly. Nobody flushed.

He was still shaky. Turned out he lived a short ways downtown. I hadn't really taken a lunch hour, so I offered to see him home.

He said okay.

Was I feeling guilty yet? Hell no. I was helping him, wasn't I? Would he have done the same for me? And as far as he knew, I was being selfless above and beyond.

His building looked like former warchouse. Made sense. Where else if not amidst big lofts and freight elevators? His place was on the third floor. I went up but didn't go in. His wife answered when he knocked. "You eat the wrong sandwich again?" She sounded miffed more than anything else.

If she saw me, she didn't let on. Before going in, Dappled Ass said, "Thanks for everything." Emphasis on "everything." Did he suspect me of the lunch switch? He'd given no sign of even recognizing me from the wagon.

A deafening thunder derailed this thought. Hooves overhead. Must have been a bunch of rowdy kids. Or is it colts?

Come to think of it, I went to an opening in this building once. Yeah, artists used to live here. A friend was telling me, artists had all these postindustrial spaces till the centaurs came. Then the scene cleared out pronto. What with centaurs holding midnight races, with the ensuing racket of an artillery barrage. Let alone the din of whole families cantering overhead day and night. One more neighborhood lost to the arts community. One more thing to hold against these horse's asses!

I hear talk about giving the centaurs their own traffic lanes, at least in midtown. It's supposed to work in other places. But they never even got around to bicycle lanes here. And I get as cynical as anyone else every time I see a centaur gallop down a one-way the wrong way. Or whenever one plays dumb after the police stop him for caroming into somebody.

Right now, nothing is making me dwell on guerrilla reprisals. Lending a hand still feels good. But would I be so quick to strike again? Well, that's up to the centaur, isn't it?

An Alternate History of Annette

October 1

Why demand a manse when this apartment more than meets my needs? The last couple of ministers, eyeing "statelier mansions," won only troublesome reputations with the trustees and short tenures for themselves. Why would a man of the cloth need more than a third floor anyway? Especially when it includes the whole attic for storage? I've met the neighbors, and they too are quiet, respectable professionals.

Students from the local School of Design used to live here. But renovation and tripled rents cleared them out, and to think nobody takes "divine Providence" seriously anymore! Why, the church is only half a block downhill and around the corner, and I have round-the-clock assigned parking next to the church bookstore. All to the good, actually, that my kind of people and I now hold the leases. The former youthful tenants were reputed to keep this gracious Victorian tenement looking like a haunted house.

In fact, hauntedness seems to linger like stubborn dust in the baseboard grooves. The van with most of my furniture arrives tomorrow, and so tonight I am camping indoors in a little wasteland of stark light, prickly-looking shadows and harsh echoes that spook me with every sound I make. Sitting on the floor in the bright circle of my desk lamp, I see the unfairness of consigning the supernatural to mansions and castles. After all, tenements and boarding houses have had much denser acquaintance with the miserable lives and deaths that supposedly anchor souls to the world. If I believed in ghosts, then the loud creaking of my weight on the floorboards and the foolish anxious flutterings in my stomach would seem like a collaboration between myself and the suffering of some long-gone tenant.

October 5

The ways of divine Providence must find a major intersection here. All this room at my disposal was starting to prove oppressive to my frugal frame of mind. But now I am in a position both to snatch a young life from crisis and to fill some space with fetching company. Due to sudden overcrowding at the home for runaways, where I am a member of the board, Annette (whom I've written about before) was about to be put out on the street. Technically she was over the cutoff age for occupancy, but since she was still too young to be on her own, we had let her stay on while there was room. She has her reasons not to go back to her family, and has been in this town long enough to call it home. So, the board and I decided it best to keep her from delinquency by letting her live here. Her room will be something fixed up in the attic, though she'll have the use of my kitchen and the run of the place too, of course.

And if I can get Annette to help with the housekeeping, so much the better. Never have I lived anyplace where the dust gathers so quickly. Every couple of days it dims the varnish and puts dry dregs on the bottoms of glasses. The undersides of pot lids have turned sticky as if from long neglect, and I cannot scour the greasiness from my frying pans. I cannot account for any of this, but will stop short of glorifying it with the term "unnatural."

October 25

I took Annette out to celebrate her eighteenth. The waiter had the nerve to ask if Annette were of age when I ordered our drinks, but I was swift to assure him, and he did not dare question my vestments. How unrealistic to think that someone her age wouldn't manage to toast a birthday one way or another! Or to imagine that a man of my calling would let her get into trouble! I am pleased to add, anyway, that Annette's deportment throughout the controversy was demure and sophisticated beyond her years.

She also surprised me with a telling example of what a small town this really is. It turns out that she knew the art students who lived in my apartment, and during her travels before the halfway house she had even stayed with them a few weeks. And if I wanted to make a case for an in-house haunt, Annette gave me more than enough material. One of the students was in the architecture program, which is apparently the school's most rigorous. Grading is tough, competition is nasty, and the workload calls for all-nighters more often than not.

Annette's acquaintance was one of those whose best efforts still earned only mediocre grades. Lack of sleep, the pep pills to keep him awake, academic pressure, and a sense of inadequacy all invoked manic depression with a vengeance. Annette moved out about the time he was becoming difficult, but later learned how aptly that semester's Final Project was.

Whatever it was, he closeted himself up with it in the attic, and none of his roommates saw him for days and heard only binges of profanity filtering through the ceiling at all hours. The passage of time insinuated that if he were making anything, it was not progress. His bouts with frustration grew uglier. He took to kicking and punching holes in the attic walls. One evening his roommates found the dish-drying rack on the kitchen floor, everything from it in bits. At that point they voted to have a talk with him. It was already too late. He wasn't in the attic, and it was a cold night in April for the window to be open. He and the foamcore model he'd been working on lay broken together in the alley below. To imagine what potential for grimness there must have been here as long as this was student housing! Thank God, that hard era is over for this address.

October 28

Maybe Annette is prey to superstition, but her growing reluctance to stay in the attic is understandable. Ever since she voiced her room's sad history, she has gotten little sleep there, as if some nervous energy from parts unknown were churning in her stomach, buoying her into a wakefulness just above the surface of sleep. She also claims the windows rattle without the help of wind, and that the holes in the wall reappear by night. The remarkable truth is, that in spite of new plaster and wallpaper, shallow indentations do remain and seem to deepen when seen from the right angle in the right light.

It has also been a trying time for her in regard to a boyfriend, someone just out of high school who waits tables downtown. She has apparently had him over a few evenings when I was at meetings, as recently as last night. Whatever they did before, and Annette was vague on this point, he became demonstrative much past her liking in this latest interlude, not at all himself she said, soon after they'd adjourned to the attic. She seems definite about breaking up with him, and I am loath to discourage her. How can a girl so young trust anyone at his impulsive age?

For now, Annette will sleep on the living room sofa until an alternative presents itself. I am also going to soft-pedal my disapproval of her affair with the waiter. To me it's far more important how much younger and stronger I've felt with her around, to say nothing of how immaculate she's kept the place. And she, in turn, has warmed to me considerably. Sometimes I think her deportment borders on shows of affection. I shall have to be more observant at these moments before doing anything, though.

November 1

The workings of the Lord are too mysterious for me. Or maybe Halloween was just living up to its arabesque image. Since it was a weeknight, there was little going on aside from the trick-or-treaters, whose numbers around here include the more shameless of starving art students. Nobody had come for a while as of 9:30, so we decided that was probably that. Annette, who'd done all the running up and down stairs, took a shower.

The second she turned on the water, the doorbell rang and I went down to get it. Before I opened the door, I saw that our candy bowl was empty and that the neighbors had taken theirs in. Even more exasperating, the late callers were students, acting half-drunk or high or something. Very giggly anyway. I sent them away, telling them if they were old enough to vote, they were too old for mooching children's candy. They looked taken aback as I closed the door.

No sooner was I upstairs than the bell rang again. I trudged back down, to find nobody there. Very well, I grumbled, you went without a treat, there's my trick. Uncannily, the instant I was back up again, the bell rang a third time. At this point I went downstairs all set to give the tricksters a piece of my mind. But they were neither down the street, around the corner, nor in the alley beside the house. I wheezed my way up, and sure enough, before I'd caught my breath, the bell rang once more. The shower was off, but Annette said she wasn't dressed yet.

Another long, insistent ring persuaded me that this might be someone else for a change, but I was wrong. Still nobody. Dizzy, weak in the knees, I had to steady myself several times on the last climb up. I was hyperventilating, and my heart was racing, so it seemed prudent to lie down.

I recall saying nothing memorable to Annette, who came out of the bathroom then in her bathrobe, but she claims I played quite the swain. And rather than find me too forward, she was charmed and not at all surprised to learn how suave I could be. She did, however, get the impression I'd rehearsed my lines some. What could I have said that allowed for such interpretation? What did we do on the far side of my forgetfulness? All I knew this morning was that I woke up in my own bed, and she was on the sofa.

All for now. Annette has just come in from the cashier job I got her at the University Club. She's knocking now on the bedroom door.

November 5

Annette and I are an "item." After getting off to our mystifying start, nothing could feel more natural. Each in our own way is completely giving to the other. She is devoted, even doting, though in a teasing, vampish way that erases any sense of an April-October relationship. Not that anything is intrinsically perverse about an age difference between lovers. My father was ten years older than my mother. I've ordained many a marriage where death would them part and not likely rejoin them for a long time. Why, doesn't every schoolchild learn that Edgar Allan Poe married his twelve-year-old cousin or someone like that?

Better that Annette be involved with me than someone young and irresponsible who wouldn't know how to take care of her. I am uniquely in a position to offer her a stability and security she's never known before. For her sake I am thankful she has a man whose vocation requires him to be trustworthy and wise.

I only feel old sometimes after we have made love, when she remarks something I have no memory of saying or doing, as if my mind cannot hold on once it crosses a certain threshold of passion. As on Halloween night, too much exertion seems to make for mental gaps.

November 10

I've come in a few nights lately to a thick, smothering smell which a little mental searching helped me identify as marijuana. On every occasion, Annette claims not to have noticed it, which I find hard to believe, and even on pointing it out to her, she shrugs. To her it never seems that strong, and she dismisses it as somebody's backyard leaf fire. Whatever it is, she insists, it accumulates too gradually for her to notice. I've had to let it go at that, until tonight when we were both home, and a whiff of the odor rolled past me. I came out of the study where I was working on a sermon, and found Annette watching TV in the living room. She returned what must have been my confrontational look until I asked, "Don't you smell that?" Another wave of it hit me then, and she nodded.

We walked around trying to sniff out where it was coming from, until Annette called from the kitchen that it was strongest toward the back stairs. What's more, it was traveling on a downdraft. "There, now do you believe it wasn't me?" she demanded. I apologized, but with some gruffness since this was too tense a moment for niceties.

We switched on the attic lights and tiptoed up. There was nobody around, and no smoke, but the odor was so heavy my eyes watered. It was also freezing cold. Annette found the window open in her former bedroom. Some kids, I extemporized, the downstairs neighbors' or whoever, must come up and smoke sometimes. But how could I ever brook the subject with the neighbors without sounding pharisaical, since everyone knows Annette's background makes her a likelier suspect?

November 13

Apparently Annette is slacking off on her housekeeping. At the same time it seems the attic smokers have desisted, but it could just be that some sharper, more constant odor is taking over down here. It is hard to pin down but coarsely unclean, like cat litter mingled with a dust cloud from a long-unopened closet. Along with it everything has become rancidly oily to the touch, especially our own skin, the way it would get after riding the train all day. It almost has the force of a third presence among us.

Mentioning to Annette that I've put her in my will should revive her enthusiasm for keeping the place more savory. The plan was originally to save the news for Christmas or some special moment, but timeliness sets its own schedule. Well, the laziest she could be would still leave her more deserving of shares in my estate than either of my ex-wives. If for no other reason, bless her for giving me excuse to leave them all the less. If my frankness is forgivable, alimony already gives them more than their due.

November 14

As I expected, Annette was both bedazed and overjoyed about being in my will, but turned defensive when I implied a lapse in her housecleaning efforts. She was still doing all she ever had, she maintained, and if I thought the place was getting stale, maybe she should donate her bequeathal toward some new furniture? It seemed politick then to save the discussion till later, as a couple of my fellow prelates joined us at our table in the University Club. Neither they nor anyone else know about Annette and me, nor do I feel it any of their affair.

They wondered if I knew that the student who had jumped from my attic had been working on plans for the church's new administrative wing. Moreover, the parents were considering an endowment for the school to create a suicide prevention program. They belonged to our denomination, and the dean at the School of Design believed they would be more forthcoming if we performed a first-anniversary memorial service. It was, in fact, the parents' idea. I averred my unwillingness to conduct any such undermining of church tenets on suicide. Were our rites to be a bargaining tool for secular ends? And furthermore, I had never heard anything to support the idea that the student's character was one we should honor. My colleagues seemed a little disappointed with me, but they needn't worry, since the final decision is not mine anyway. And I need not be the officiating minister on that occasion.

November 15

This morning I was trying to type my formal objections to the proposed memorial service, but had to stop every half-minute and relieve a pestering itch. I examined myself, and was shocked to discover tiny black dots below navel-level that crawled after I scratched. I felt sickeningly unclean, hardly able to stand being in my own skin, and then I grew furious. Annette! I'd trusted her. That very second, the phone rang.

It was Annette, in a towering rage herself, down at the pharmacy. She asked if I'd had any wandering itches lately. Before I could make my own accusations, she asked, loudly, what kind of pediculicide I preferred, referring to me pointedly as "Father." I entreated her to come home and yes, please, bring enough Rid for both of us.

Once she was back, it was impossible to settle anything. She adamantly denied seeing anybody but me, and I denied any outside liaisons too, of course. If her protestations were an act, I have to admit they would leave a third party hard-pressed to choose between her innocence and mine. Still, these infestations have to come from somewhere, don't they? My recurring urge is to take Annette over my knee.

November 18

The pot smoke, the open attic window, the parasites, all signs point to a slovenly undergraduate living unbeknownst among us. Is it possible a squatter sidles around the edges of our awareness and our absences? Or does Annette know about him? Is he some old boyfriend, like the waiter, whom she smuggled up in the beginning? Annette has refused relations with me the past few nights, and all the while I've wanted her with what feels like the desire of two men. Should I evict her? How can I even broach any of this? It could just be that the thought of the parasites has cooled her ardor for now. And if my speculations are wrong, she'll think I'm suffering from paranoia.

November 19

Rumor must be the most malleable substance known to man. This afternoon I bumped into the landlord downtown and we had a cup of coffee. He remarked how surprised he was that Annette would have stayed any length of time in my attic, let alone move back into the building. Well yes, I agreed, it must have been hard at first, since the unfortunate student had been an acquaintance. The landlord eyed me as if I were simple and told me that from what he'd heard, Annette and the student, whose name was Russ, had been together right till the end. The landlord didn't understand how she'd put up with his destructive fits and supposed that she must have really loved him. How, he wondered, could she stand returning to the scene of so much pain? The most rational answer, I suggested, was that he could not have had his facts straight. He only shrugged. How could the simple account Annette told me ever get garbled into such foolishness?

November 23

As per the directions on the bottle, we took our second week's application of Rid yesterday, and I did all the laundry. Ever since lunch with the landlord, I've been trying to forget his alternate history of Annette, but so far I can only force his words into brief truces, always broken when my mind wanders. This was the case when I was folding the clothes and discovered an undershirt in other than my size. The back of the label was marked "Russ." I must have been trying too hard to show no reaction, because an impertinent local accosted me, "Whatsa matter, Rev, got someone else's load?"

"I certainly have," I snapped and finished my folding.

When I confronted Annette with the undershirt, she acted as if thinking of a response were beneath her. "Your stuff always gets mixed up with everybody else's in a group home," she finally deigned to say. I replied that there was no point keeping the shirt if it wasn't hers, and threw it in the wastebasket.

"It was a perfectly good shirt," she said with more indignation than if I were just wasting some fabric. But she didn't dare retrieve it.

By evening our tempers had cooled and we were the warmest we'd been with each other since the morning we found the parasites. She thanked me this morning for being such a great lover, though as often happens I must take her word for it.

November 26

I've made a doctor's appointment for two weeks from now, and hopefully I will be all right till then. That was the soonest he could take me. My memory lapses no longer confine themselves to the bedroom, and at those times my actions seem no more sensible than a sleepwalker's. This evening I noticed a carbon of a letter I'd apparently written to the trustees. It expressed my agreeability to preach a memorial for the student suicide. At the top was penned, "Sent 11/25." What will they think of my sudden reversal of opinion? And how can I reassert my genuine feelings?

November 28

Good Lord! Who could have written this? And in imitation of my own hand?

November 27

I am in it so deep. Too deep. Up here working so long on this damn thing that I'm one with it, with my studies, with the four walls around me. With the architecture of the four walls in particular. The project's too hard. It's just not going to fucking work. My limitations and its limitations are one. So the problem's with the work, not with me. If I really believed that, I could hate it and not myself. But no, I hate it, myself, and the four walls with one all-purpose hate.

When I get too mad and want to hurt myself, I hurt the walls. At least everything then feels fair, right, balanced. To think I used to like myself. And I came here thinking I would love what I loved to do more if I learned to do it like a master. But try to make yourself master of anything, and it becomes a you-vs.-it situation, and now the only love I have left is for Annette.

November 30

It's perfect! The right person for the right retribution. Absolutely! The minister can trot around church property whenever he wants, and I know exactly where to set the kindling to make the place go up like fireworks. I have to say, this is more fun than I ever had in life.

December 4

First my diary disappears for a week, and now it returns along with news that leaves me almost too shaken to write. Based on my own incriminating words, say the trustees, they are having me committed. And I did not even see the November 30 entry until just now! To avoid scandal, they would prefer not to pursue legal action against me and my so-called corruptive influence on Annette and what they believe I was planning. Technically my commitment would have to be voluntary, and to get my signature they are trying to convince me that there will only be an interim minister while I am gone. If my alleged problems are resolved by therapy, the pulpit will be mine again on my release. They are not affording me much choice.

They assure me the apartment will remain in my name. And for the time being, Annette can stay on here. They are treating her as some kind of pawn of mine, when it is perfectly clear she must have betrayed my diary to them. And Lord knows what kind of hand she had in the forged entries! She and the squatter in the attic. Oh, to have been involved with an eighteen-year-old in the first place! I must have been possessed. Yes, certainly, possessed by an infatuation that made me forget the church's first teaching, that nobody is born innocent. Why oh why didn't I just evict her back when she stopped keeping the place clean?

The strain, the shock from this day makes it hard to breathe, let alone write. I am too tired to go on.

Hey, Annette! How could you stand that nasty old windbag so long? Never mind, soon it'll be just you and me again.

Love, Russ

P.S. Too bad they're taking him away already. It would've been a riot preaching at my own memorial service!

Tendrils in Formaldehyde

H ere's your drink. Now pay attention.

Bet you never thought of libraries as cutthroat operations. But let's say you opt for that Master's in Library Sciences, cram all that anal library jargon for two years, and warp your sense of priorities into caring about every least iota of abbreviation and punctuation on a catalog card. Wouldn't you graduate homicidal, itching to vent pent-up spleen on workplace inferiors and the public? Wouldn't the wasplike daily buzz of procedural details in your ears make you as vicious as any high-powered CEO? And once you're locked into a career, therein lies all the power you'll ever enjoy, so don't tell me you wouldn't play it to the hilt. Especially in a world-class metropolitan institution like ours! I, myself, know nobody more elitist and ambitious than my supervisors.

No sir, behind the prim, mild-mannered image, we have no more conscience than anyone else. Mine came out on my thirteenth birthday, as per standard medical recommendation. Wait too long after that, and they can cause blood poisoning. I've never actually seen the scientific literature to that effect, but everybody knows it's true. My conscience still floats safely in formaldehyde, little passion flower tendrils reaching where they can do no harm, on the souvenir shelf between my tonsils and some gallstones.

Every adolescent seems to have a nightmare where that little monster unscrews the lid from inside and leaps all slimy onto teen ear, whispering unto madness something like "Do good, do good." Of course, people do good when it's in their own best interests. Otherwise, dissolution and psychosis await the do-gooder. Civilization trundles on because it's in the individual's selfish interest for it to do so. And when it isn't, well, we all get away with whatever we can. But that's not news to you, is it? Sorry.

Now, that new girl at work. Deirdre. She must have come from a family of religious nuts or something. You could tell hers had never been taken out, from that unguarded shine in her eyes. Made you want to trip her. And I clearly wasn't the only one in Rare Books to feel that way. I mean, you could be sorry for her at first. Bad upbringing, no prior access to reality. But the cardinal rule for adults is that you take responsibility for yourself, right? Deirdre's jobsite hardships began on her first day, at everyone's first convenience.

We rank-and-filers have a lounge on the third floor. It's generally smoke-filled. Some bleeding hearts tried making tax-funded institutions smoke-free a while back, but the tobacco lobby easily crushed such infringement of personal freedom. Anyway, breaktime in the lounge may involve a quick game of cards, or a palaver about current events, or a round of Pig's Eye. That's where everyone has to answer a nosy question, and then face interrogation to see if they're lying. If someone blushes, that's when it's assumed the truth is out. Whether this is really the case or not is secondary. The loss of face can be permanent, and what starts in the lounge soon titillates the whole staff. It's a great game for forging iron nerves.

Pig's Eye was underway when Deirdre waltzed in. She sat at the card table, with no apparent appreciation of the match in progress. Not that anyone cared to enlighten her. "So why did you get married?" asked Virginia from Reference.

Frank from Conservation said, "For tax purposes!"

"That's a crock!" snarled Nancy from the Gift Shop. "Taxes always come out higher for married people. And you? Married? Everyone knows you're gay." Still, Frank got due credit for brazenness.

Maggie from Circulation answered next. "I snagged my Johnny because he got a good position here in Development, and that's where the money is. With any luck he'll be promoted to the point where I can get out of here and never work another day in my life."

"Amen to that," somebody said, but Maggie's flatfooted honesty rated no enthusiasm.

And then it was Deirdre in the crosshairs. Poor clueless Deirdre. "Why, I married for love!"

That got a good laugh.

"In a pig's eye!" sneered Virginia. It was the stock phrase for challenging a whopper, but everyone could tell Deirdre was telling the truth. And sure enough she blushed, as Virginia must have intended.

Discomfited Deirdre never knew what hit her, and the players proceeded without wasting more time on such a pathetically easy mark.

Deirdre's first cafeteria visit fared no better. The cafeteria's in the basement, off a drafty corridor, and Ol' Mr. Pissy, as the proprietor is known, pays the library a flat fee for the privilege of hawking overpriced sandwiches, junk food, and coffee. It's an incredibly lame excuse for food services in so prestigious an institution, but the Budget Office must have figured that midtown offered too many other snack pits for ours to merit any attention. What was in it for them, after all? My first day, I naively figured the fruit salad was safe, but it was rancid all right, and based on Ol' Mr. Pissy's hostility toward other dissatisfied customers, I preferred to say nothing and buy nothing from him thereafter. Instead, like numerous others, I brought my own brown-bag provender. This really stuck in the old grump's craw, but since his authority extended no farther than the edge of his counter, he could only glare in silence and we all knew it.

Her first morning, Deirdre was sitting at one of the cafeteria's nine tables, and I at another. The room doesn't tend to get crowded. A new guy came in, young, and more presumptuous than he himself realized. Deirdre glanced over as if recognizing him from Orientation. He had come in with a can of soda, and grabbed a straw at the counter before sitting down. That instant, Ol' Mr. Pissy hollered across the room, "Young man!" It took two hollers for the young man to understand he was being paged. He looked glumly at Ol' Mr. Pissy without speaking.

"You ask my permission next time before you do that!" Ol' Mr. Pissy roared.

The young man stared incredulous and then went back to drinking his soda.

Deirdre and the young man happened to leave at the same time. I had left a few seconds earlier. I could hear her telling him, "I can't believe he was being so stingy about one little straw!"

And he replied, "So what goddamn business of it is yours?"

I couldn't help a backward glimpse. The young man walked on with grim expression. She stood there looking like she was about to burst into tears. Well, what did she expect, rubbing in his embarrassment that way? Had she imagined the guy had use for sympathy because Ol' Mr. Pissy's outburst was *unconscionable*? I would have snickered myself, but didn't want to draw the angry young man's fire.

In the next few months, Deirdre grew more adept at curbing sociable impulses. Meanwhile, it turned out that her husband also worked at the library, in the Budget Office no less. Apparently it had been his brainstorm to replace the paper towels in all employee restrooms with ineffectual air driers, for the sake of saving one grand per annum. The executive johns, of course, retained their towel dispensers. Budget Office was certainly no place for a conscience, which made me wonder what he and she were doing together.

By this time, Deirdre's closest approach to friendship was with old Merkin, a middle-level Budget Office lifer she must have met through hubby. Only rarely did others speak to him who were not compelled by inferior rank or office-politics advantage. Merkin's eyes always goggled as if at scandal, and his Adam's apple seemed in constant struggle to outjut his weak chin. He had the smooth yet overwrought gait of those stop-motion Harryhausen skeletons from the '60s. His neurotic passion was for spotlessness. In the cafeteria he gathered wrappers off the floor, not that Ol' Mr. Pissy ever thanked him. Virtue was plainly its own reward. On entering the men's room, Merkin flushed every unoccupied toilet and urinal in succession. One day, returning from lunch-hour errands, I spied him by the freight entrance, avidly scraping gum off the wall with a plastic butter knife.

And indeed, from the outside looking in, such rewardless compulsions seem at one with the burden of a conscience. Both are equally unsightly. But if Deirdre had taken him for a kindred spirit, she couldn't have made a bigger mistake.

When last I spoke with Deirdre, we were alone in the elevator. We'd been waiting five minutes for it after a colleague in Serials who was already in the cage saw us coming and punched the Door Close button anyway. She seemed disproportionately miffed at such a minor incident.

"Doesn't anyone in here have a conscience?" she asked me.

"Looks like you're the only one," I said.

"Out where I grew up, they don't just surgically remove them like warts!"

I snorted. Oh sure, like this is purely an East Coast thing!

From then on, Deirdre averted her eyes from mine and, apparently, everyone's except for Merkin. Nonetheless, he along with her husband were about to prove their Budget Office mettle.

Deirdre called in sick a couple of days, and on reappearing, looked awful. Locks of hair peeled out various whichways in absence or defiance of a comb. Through the makeup on her cheeks ran the moist, braided channels of her tears. Her eyes were red, and lipstick on her teeth gave away a new penchant for biting her lip.

A recent round of Pig's Eye must have involved her husband or somebody else in the know, for by then, word had gotten around: he'd been cheating on his wife of six months with an undeniably toothsome supervisor.

On break, I took coffee from the corner deli to the cafeteria, savoring Ol' Mr. Pissy's dirty look, and I was lucky enough to be within hearing range of Deirdre's final tête-à-tête with Merkin.

"Of course he's having an affair with her!" he was declaiming in his usual sepulchral lisp. "What did you expect? It's the best possible thing for his career right now!" A gloat creeping into his tone made even me fidget.

She was already staring aghast at him, but then he added, "What's more, I'm the one who fixed them up with each other!"

Her chair scraped deafeningly on the floor tiles. She stood up and had to sway for balance. "How could you?" she gasped.

"Because now he owes me big!" He was beaming. Then a crumpled napkin on the floor caught his eye. He lunged for it and didn't see her leave.

Three days later, a memo went up on the bulletin board. Anyone wishing to deduct the hours from their Annual Leave could attend Deirdre's funeral next day. With a come-on like that, I doubt there were any takers. Especially for someone flaky enough to end it all over a simple little career move.

Still, the whole oppressive chain of events put me in the mood for a few drinks. So here I am, and where do you think you're going? As long as I'm buying, you sit and listen. A deal's a deal, conscience or no conscience. That's just sound business.

You don't suppose a goddamn conscience can grow back, do you? As in cases where the surgeon doesn't get all of it out? Scary thought, isn't it? Well, pal, here's hoping alcohol kills the damn things, if they do try making a comeback.

Ariadne's Hair

The night they brought the baby home, the Jacuzzi in the attic sprang a leak. This came to light because the baby, who'd been beatifically serene in the hospital, started squalling the second they opened the foyer door onto the front room.

Jill wasn't surprised. Indoors was much colder than in the foyer. The evening was fraught enough without one of Roger's screw-ups. "Didn't I tell you to turn up the thermostat?" She had to be strident to compete with caterwauling little Kenny.

Roger knew better than to show resentment at wrongful accusation. "I remember putting it at 70," he said evenly.

"Then you must have left a window open!"

He hadn't, of course, but to say so with authority, he had to check all over the house. At the door to the attic stairs, between piercing shrieks from somewhere below, Roger discerned what could have been the resonant drip of an old percolator. Next thing he knew, the weight of a long day was pressing harder on his shoulders as he gawked at the base of the Jacuzzi, from which a doormat-sized blob of water had escaped, quivering at its forward edge, with a pseudopod questing toward Roger's feet.

Was the leak in the shell, or the pipes, or somewhere too technical to guess at now? A squeak echoed in the broad, empty recesses when he twisted the drainage spigot on the filter. Nothing more to do than spread towels over the seepage, and hope the tub emptied quickly.

He gave a start at seeing his breath cloud. Beyond the tub, the window overlooking the driveway was open after all, wide enough to accommodate a sprawling cat. How had that happened? Too weary, he tabled the question and slammed the window shut. The stark ensuing silence felt bated, yet so long overdue. The howling had let up as if by magic! He trudged downstairs, troubled about window and tub, but only too happy to shut the door on them, literally, till later.

The Jacuzzi hadn't been their idea. The recent owners, amateurs who'd bought the place to renovate and resell for a quick fat profit, had somehow reckoned that a hot tub added value or class or something; former servants' quarters in the attic afforded the best available plumbing connections. Meanwhile, Roger and Jill had needed more than an apartment because their baby was coming. This was their one successful bid in the shark pool of today's housing market. The tony East Side was the only part of town good enough for them, and for raising their child. No room for debate there.

On parenthood per se, they'd been less of one mind. Roger had never said he didn't want kids, but left to his own devices he might never have gotten around to it. Jill, on the other hand, hadn't broached the subject in all their months of carefree dating. Then right after the honeymoon, kids were suddenly the deal-breaker. What deal? What else had he missed in the fine print? In any case, the days of "protected sex" were over.

Jill was nursing at the kitchen table, an arm's length from the stove. The oven door was open partway, and the heat whooshing out felt good. But whatever could have possessed her? Fires, deadly fumes, explosions reeled through Roger's punchy mind in a blurry montage. "Do you think it's a good idea using the oven this way?" he ventured.

"You're the one who left that window open!" She must have heard him up in the attic, and since she'd been right about the open window, she must also have been right to blame him for it. He wanted to assail her logic, but something of the lioness in her eyes stopped him.

Squirmy infant struck him as a dubious basis for Jill's queenly demeanor. Kenny looked larval, incomplete, not fully human. Watching him feed made Roger squeamish. He started voicing an excuse to step out.

"Why don't I go and get the digital camera and record the baby's first night home?" he asked haltingly, not sure how he'd finish his question till he heard himself do so.

She shrugged. Affirmative enough for him! He bolted out.

Taking snapshots was hardly of importance to her now. What in the world was more important than motherhood? Nothing, of course. The answer was so obvious that she never wondered when and from where it had come to her. How could Roger ever have thought differently? Already she could hear the ticking, faint at present, of the interior clock that would only grow louder till she was pregnant again.

She heard Roger clumping toward the kitchen. Lurching in, camera already between his face and her, he was flitting around like something that didn't belong in the house, something airborne that was in very imperfect charge of itself, that perpetually clicked and whirred. Jesus, would you please hurry up and be done with it? What he saw as a smile, she felt as a grimace. If he could just help put Kenny to bed, so she could get some sleep!

Roger snapped out of a dizzy spell in the middle of snapping photos. He was ridiculously beat, wasn't he? Ah, there was that fetching smile he loved so well! Through the lens, the obvious sharpened into refocus: that she was as pretty as one of those retro-'60s Target models on TV, even if she was the furthest thing from a hippie. Not that Roger was of an age to have seen real hippies first-hand!

Kenny, at last, was asleep, head pillowed upon Jill's breast, drooling all over it. Every so often, Roger had to grasp anew that Jill had really wanted to get pregnant, and that she wanted to nurse Kenny. He could just as easily have seen her going the opposite way, scorning both choices as repulsive. Calling them "icky," maybe. He sighed, and lowered the camera. Maybe he didn't understand her at all.

Jill heaved her uncooperative weight from the chair and lugged the baby upstairs to the crib, which was set up at the foot of their bed. Let Roger turn off the oven, provided he had the sense!

But Roger was busy reviewing his photography. What the hell? He squinted, blinked, held the camera at different distances, tilted it this way and that, to no avail. Had he been moving at every exposure? Had they? Had the lens caught reflections off the ceiling light? Was the camera defective? From shot to shot as in a flipbook, a milkiness progressed from left to right, coalesced as a crescent in front of the baby, paused there and grew gibbous like the moon, and elongated wormishly, its edges dissolving, as it exited the frame. Dammit! Roger deleted the lot. And no hope of a retake! His eye chanced upon oven door as he reached for the overhead cord. He drew an exasperated breath. If Jill weren't so very pretty . . .

Within the week, Roger was back at work, and Jill was diagnosed with postpartum hypertension. Roger taught at a decent elementary school in the neighborhood. He preferred the term "educator" over "teacher," which sounded so banal, even menial. And in general, dealing with children was much more productive with well-aligned desks and lesson plans to impose structure on the situation, on lumpish, prelogical minds.

Jill, in unmarried days, had worked her way up to middle management. She knew now, thanks to the baby, that she'd known nothing then of responsibility. The feeding, the diapering, the sleepless nights, visits to the pediatrician for him, visits to the obstetrician for her, on top of laundry and cleaning and other housework, demanded more dedication than any business career deserved. Case in point, she'd brought Kenny in for six extra exams in three months, worried because he tended to focus on thin air and track imaginary motions with his eyes. But the doctor found nothing amiss, and Kenny was otherwise barreling precociously past every developmental milestone, doing mother proud. And Jill would be fine as long as she took her pills and minimized stress.

In the matter of stress, Roger could have made himself a lot more useful. Oh, he was generally a sweetheart: giving, mild-mannered, unassuming, but at times these seemed like other words for unambitious, scattershot, dull. On Roger's salary, the mortgage here would have crushed them if not for her dad's liberality. Roger never stopped her from doing what she wanted, and maybe that was his greatest virtue. But what got into him sometimes?

School was out for April vacation. Roger might have stayed in and helped. Instead, he disappeared for hours on errands in the name of home improvement, never to any visible effect. And then he had the local Jacuzzi dealer send a repairman to look at their busted hot tub. Kenny was napping, so Jill listened in from the foot of the attic stairs.

"This ain't a Jacuzzi."

"What do you mean? Of course it is."

"You see the name Jacuzzi anywhere on it?"

"No, but the previous owners said it was a Jacuzzi."

"They can say what they like, but that don't make it a Jacuzzi."

"Well, what is it then?"

"How would I know? You see anyone's name on it?"

"No, but can you fix it?"

"I only fix Jacuzzis."

"So what are we supposed to do with it?"

"I don't know. Make a planter? Grow mushrooms in it."

Jill had to walk away before she screamed, not at the insolent non-entity of a workman, but at Roger for wasting energy on a white elephant they never, ever used.

Behind her eyes was a rising pressure, and in her mouth a chemical sourness, that she associated with her condition acting up. And in point of fact, she hadn't taken her meds today, had she?

The lisinopril wasn't where it belonged, on the top shelf in the kitchen cabinet. The childproof cap was on the counter, but where was the phial? Had the repairman at the door disrupted her in mid-routine? Maybe. Her diuretics were on the top shelf as usual.

Kenny was crying in the bedroom. Jill dashed up the back stairs and passed the attic doorway. The attic was hushed. Roger and the workman must have just gone down the front stairs. Yes, they were audible in the foyer.

The mobile of nonthreatening forest animals, clamped to the head of the crib, was bobbing merrily when Jill entered the bedroom. Beside the crib was her comfy chair, on whose broad wooden arm nearer the crib lay a facecloth, an Ann Taylor catalog, and the phial, lying on its side, several white pills bright against the varnished mahogany. She frantically stuck the pills back in the phial and pocketed the phial in her pullover. She scooped up bawling Kenny and shook out his blanket and patted one hand all over the little mattress. No pills. Had he swallowed any that might have bounced into the crib, that he might have pawed from the armchair?

She was too worked up to shush him or even look at him. She slung him over her shoulder, flew down to the kitchen, and snatched the diuretics from the cabinet shelf. She dumped out the contents of both phials and counted. They matched. Then she heard Kenny sobbing as if he had started that instant.

In the den, she collapsed into the rocking chair and rocked Kenny, and cooed at him, and sang "Itsy Bitsy Spider." But her eyes were elsewhere. Had she left the lisinopril there herself? When? She couldn't possibly be such an airhead, such a bad mom. Had Roger found the phial somewhere and put it on the chair for her? When? He'd been wrangling with the workman for ages.

Kenny's outcries had subsided, but he eyed Jill searchingly, as if she might vanish without warning.

Roger ambled in, hiding any scars of working-stiff clash behind an overly deliberate smile. "Oh, there you are."

How could he be so chipper? "What were my meds doing in the bedroom?"

"I don't know, honey. What?"

"Roger, this is serious!" She had to contain herself lest harsh language stir Kenny up again.

Roger stood gaping foolishly, as at a train that had shot past his platform. Even if the misplaced pills had nothing to do with him, her trust in him had eroded a little, in the face of his cavalier attitude.

Nor was Roger done displeasing her that week. God knew what kind of hassles he courted by heedlessly fraternizing with the locals. For months she'd watched them from the windows or more obliquely while en route to her minivan. They seemed a dreary, threadbare lot, fusty in tweed and flannel. They must have been what her parents called Swamp Yankees, and their entrenchment forced her to question how genteel this neighborhood really was. She smirked to picture them in leather pants. And come Saturday morning, Roger was strolling among them, on the déclassé occasion of multifamily yard sale.

She had to put her foot down upon sight of his first purchase. She was initially speechless when he showed off an "authentic reproduction of a quaint Early American cradle." It was black and ponderous and reminded her of an open coffin, on rockers, and with the wrong end exposed. It reeked of mothballs and festering Christmas decorations. Had Roger seriously considered putting a baby of theirs in this squalid thing? No. Scrub it till doomsday for all she cared, but no.

Still, some childish urge made him recount the story behind his piece of junk. Those guys who'd remodeled their place last year had bought it from an old-timer, a Mr. Wilberry or something like that, who'd loaded a couple of moving vans with his choicest antiques, and invited the neighbors to cart off the rest. A lady down the street fell in love with the cradle, but on finding she had no room for it, was resigned to a selling price of $50. So now the cradle was back where it belonged, where it had been used for generations. How about that?

Well, if Roger was so set on keeping it, he could store it in the attic next to the broken hot tub. That was more than generous. Anyway, Kenny would be outgrowing cradles in no time, quaint or otherwise.

Jill knew she'd ruffled Roger's feathers, and that he'd likely smooth them by retaliating somehow. Sure enough, out the next morning with Kenny in the stroller, Roger affected that telltale improvement in posture. Uh oh! He had his goddamn thinking cap on. "You know, Jill, if Kenny's too big for a cradle, he's ready to sleep in his own room." The voice of pure reason! And now she'd been drawn into his game, at risk of forfeit unless she answered dispassionately. How grossly unfair, when they both knew her arguments would come from the heart.

She hated to think of Kenny lonely and afraid in his big dark room. To say nothing of online horror stories about baby-monitor malfunctions right before choking emergencies. Deep down, all the same, months of putting herself a poor second to an infant had worn thin. She had the right to step back, to keep from losing herself, didn't she? The scent of lilacs in bloom took her back to last April, those final simple days before she tested positive. The sun seemed brighter then, as it did again this minute. Time to get the nursery in order! Let Roger think she was giving in, for once.

The nursery walls were a rich crimson, winsome in theory. In practice, the paint blushed faintly at night, dispelling full darkness, but muted broad daylight, inducing subtle gloom. On the positive side, Roger quipped, they'd never need a nightlight. Jill's complaints of "unwholesome" atmosphere in the nursery, based on shade of paint, were absurd. Nor was Roger in any position to shell out for a fresh coat.

Kenny, if his vote counted, didn't fuss about nights alone in the nursery, ruddy walls and all. That was a pleasant surprise, but unpleasant flipside was in the offing. Sometime in May, Roger awoke in the wee hours to excited babbling from the baby monitor. The monitor was on a nightstand over by Jill, but she was still dead to the world. Jill had been fretting for days because Kenny hadn't started talking ahead of schedule; he wasn't quite six months yet. Roger had given up reminding her that Einstein hadn't said a word till he was two years old. He'd read that somewhere. Too bad Jill was asleep! Kenny was never this vocal by day.

What was so stimulating now? Roger eased out of bed and down the hall, making do with meager street light through the windows. Funny, in the cascade of syllables, he detected inflection, emphasis, attentive pause, but not a single word. As if an exchange were underway in which meaning somehow sidestepped spoken content. Baby talk came of no familiar country, did it?

An oblong of weak light crossed the floorboards outside open nursery doorway. Shadow motions within it suggested swaying boughs or clouds racing past the moon. No wind was audible, but that was good. Their replacement windows were soundproof, as advertised.

Roger's efforts to enter stealthily were for nothing. One step inside, and contented chatter gave way to furious screaming. Kenny must have roused everyone on the block! And Roger, gritting his teeth and surveying the room, couldn't tell what had engrossed Kenny, what from outside had cast playful shadows. They were gone now. The wind must have died down. Yet Kenny's bereft gaze was fixed on the window, as if his center of attention had fled through it. Then Jill was at the door, saying nothing, but asking with baleful eyes how Roger had made this mess. To him, the writing on the wall said only: Kenny liked to be left alone at night. Fine! Jill awoke in the dark later that week, and made the same earsplitting discovery for herself.

The next evening, Roger and the guy next door happened to wheel their trash barrels to the curb at the same moment. Maybe some friendly damage control was in order. He waved and started down the street. The neighbor stopped in mid-turn and waited, without speaking. He must have been on the far side of fifty, rangy, with gray and reddish beard and ponytail to offset a crown several strands shy of bald. Antique wire-rims, gold earring, and faded T-shirt from some wildlife organization reinforced Roger's impression of aging hippie. Jeez, why would anyone look like that these days? The social die was cast, though, so Roger assayed an ingratiating smile. "Sorry if we kept you up at all this week. The baby, you know."

The hippie's teeth showed through his smile. Obvious that he'd never had braces as a kid. "We thought it was an air-raid siren. Really had us going a minute. Then we decided he must've seen the ghost."

What was that? Wait, this had to be some kind of graceless joke. He tried to sound good-natured. "Don't tell me you believe in ghosts."

The hippie squinted toward Kenny's room. "I take a genuinely scientific attitude. They'll be there or not, whether I believe in 'em or not."

Roger nodded, in lieu of balking at anything other than a straight "No."

"We were pretty convinced Ariadne had moved to our place, though. I mean, what kind of self-respecting ghost would haunt an attic with a Jacuzzi in it?"

Was that meant as a dig somehow? How did he know about the hot tub? Roger heard himself repeating, "Ariadne?"

"That's her name. Know how we found out?" The hippie proceeded before Roger could assent or not. "Back when this was the Ol' Wilbane Place, right before the philistines started in on it, the Missus and I were rummaging around in the attic. With Old Man Wilbane's blessing, you understand. On top of a bookcase I found a little heart-shaped box. I got it open, and there was nothing inside but locks of blond hair. Creeped me out. So I put the lid back on and walked away. Then my wife found the box of hair on her own and thought it was cute, so we ended up with it anyway. A few days later, old Mr. Wilbane was gone, and all the stuff nobody wanted was in a dumpster in your future driveway. I was standing out front here, right before dark, when a strip of paper blew out of the dumpster and landed at my feet. I picked it up, and it read 'Ariadne's Hair.' Spooky, huh? Helluva coincidence, for that one little piece of paper among all that trash to find its way to me. So we could reunite the label and the box."

"Well, that's something," Roger lied.

"I wouldn't worry about her, though. She never gave us any grief. Mostly wanted to hang around with her old possessions, photos and fancy hats and such. Stuff that by and large went into storage in our own attic. At worst, she'd do kinda kooky shit like misplace things. Hide the remote, or leave jewelry and keys in the middle of the floor. Made us wonder if she'd been senile toward the end."

Roger felt completely adrift. He wasn't averse to learning a little neighborhood history. But how had he wound up back in the Dark Ages with this guy?

Jill was glaring out the nursery window at him. What? Couldn't he have a conversation with the local nutjob? He waved at her. She immediately withdrew, but had given him an out all the same. "That's my wife. I better go see what she wants. Nice talking to you."

In the midst of Roger's hasty retreat, the hippie called after him, "Tell Ariadne hello!"

Even though Roger badmouthed the neighbors in front of her, every time he had anything to do with them, Jill found him a little less desirable, and took him a little less seriously. Father of her children or not. And what kind of father was he? Making a show of sociability with those Swamp Yankees, when little Kenny plainly needed more proactive parenting. It felt like betrayal of sorts. Kenny was starting to falter despite Jill's best efforts, and whatever Roger was doing.

Look at Kenny right now. Sitting on her lap, he didn't seem to notice her clipping his fingernails, or the chaotic dust sparkling in the sun through the front windows, or the commotion on TV in front of the sofa, or the rattle in his own lap. Instead, for the umpteenth time, he scrutinized a random point in midair, until his head slowly swiveled to scrutinize another point. And surely he should've outgrown more of his clothes by now, and uttered a few recognizable words. He was indifferent to his toys, and to his name, and to standing up by himself, though he certainly could. His interests just seemed to lie elsewhere. Plus, there was that late-night tantrum after she'd checked on him in the nursery, and now he was having those fits in the dark by himself. She dared not speculate on what it all might mean, and contemplated getting a second doctor's less off-the-cuff opinion before Kenny crawled any farther down a neurological road of no return. She was really scared, both of doing nothing and of knowing too much.

And what had been on Roger's mind lately? Someone two doors down had told him that the renovators were originally going to slap vinyl siding on the walls, but their realtor had threatened to bail if they did. Why did Jill have to know that?

Her eyes wandered. The glass-top coffee table had camouflaged a couple of empty Newcastles and clear plastic dessert bowls from last night. Bob and Nancy had been over. Roger and Jill were the first in their circle to have kids, and throughout small talk, dinner, and drinks, their friends had to bear with restive Kenny in his playpen, which projected halfway out of the dark alcove underneath the staircase. He shook the playpen bars and rocked relentlessly and gabbled nonsense.

But none of that was a big deal, and couldn't have explained why Bob and Nancy shifted uncomfortably all evening as if their clothes were damp, or they were stuck in a waiting room with no end in sight. They always said they liked children, so something about the house itself must been off-putting. Anyway, she doubted they'd be back. Nor had other friends been calling or coming over. She didn't care. She was too tired most of the time, and preoccupied with Kenny. Entertaining took so much energy. Let 'em all go.

Pleading exhaustion, Jill took off for a couple of weeks' relaxation at her dad's place in some posh suburb of Cleveland. Or was it Columbus? Either way, school was out as of mid-June, and Roger had an embarrassment of free time, while Kenny, at six months of age, was off the teat. Thus Roger, in Jill's gratuitously tart phrase, could "start pulling his own weight."

One especially nice afternoon, Roger was inspired to drag canvas beach chair and playpen out to the front porch. The porch was enclosed up to waist-level, and Doric columns rose from there to support second-floor overhang. He could read the newspaper in shady privacy, and Kenny, who'd had an unusually turbulent night, could catch up on his sleep.

Halfway through the editorial page, Roger, who'd also missed plenty of sleep on account of Kenny, began nodding off, till voices in front of the house jarred him back to life.

He quietly raised himself on the arms of his chair till he glimpsed who was talking, then sank back. Two women. In their fifties, like everyone else on this street, apparently. One lived directly across and was married to a history professor or something. The other, at a guess, was the hippie's "Missus." Both were similarly decked out in shapeless housedress, flip-flops, knee socks. Almost like members of some drab proletarian cult. He might have been attracted to them if they'd had any sense of style.

"Hasn't been so noisy there since poor old Ariadne went around the bend."

"Really? When was that?"

"You've been here how long now? Ten years? Such newbies! This must have been back in the '80s sometime. Ariadne was Mr. Wilbane's older sister. A spinster."

"We have a picture of her, I think. Her eyes look kind of disturbed. R. J. calls her the ghost in the attic."

"Well, it was sad. You could tell she was damaged. Had been for decades. Then one night something put her way over the line, and around midnight we woke up to this terrible uproar. You see that ledge on top of the porch, right below the second-floor windows?"

Roger pressed a little lower into the canvas and hoped the baby stayed asleep. They were talking about his house, and they'd been commenting on how noisy his boy was. How could he not feel resentful? And worse, he was trapped. Please let this anecdote be brief!

"Ariadne was standing on the ledge in the pouring rain, screaming her lungs out. Accusing her brother of killing her family and trying to kill her. And other things that were complete gibberish."

"So what happened?"

"Nothing. Mr. Wilbane stayed inside, pretending he didn't hear. Everyone else minded their own business. We didn't know what to do. We were worried about her, but we didn't want to interfere. You could see Mr. Wilbane sitting by a lamp in the living room, reading a *National Geographic* like nothing was happening. We went back to bed, and eventually it was quiet again."

"Was her brother really trying to kill her?"

"Oh no. That was just the dementia talking."

"But what was it that damaged her in the first place?"

"I don't know, exactly. Something about a child she had, or didn't have."

A pause ensued, so long that Roger began to relax, and was about to stand up when "the Missus" took up the thread.

"Then I guess we're lucky her ghost is so well-behaved, considering she must have had Alzheimer's or something. Is that how it works? If someone with Alzheimer's comes back as a ghost, does their ghost have Alzheimer's too? Oh, listen to me. R. J.'s got me half believing in this stuff myself."

Something fluttered loudly next to Roger's ear, as if it wanted to dive in. Startled, he jerked aside, and winced as the chair scraped. But at least he kept his head enough to stay seated. Above and behind him, in the sheltered corner where a Doric capital met the side of the house, was a cruddy-looking nest. A bird was feeding its raucous hatchlings.

What the hell! Those filthy creatures could easily shit on Kenny from there. And how much had they damaged the woodwork already?

"Look, can you see that? There's a robin's nest over there!"

"I see it! How adorable!"

The women's voices had become remote, as if filtered through a long funnel. A push broom lay between playpen and front door. Scattering newspaper pages, he grabbed the broom and sprang up, fiercely jabbing the pole end at the nest a dozen times, smashing it and everything inside, while the parent bird took hapless flight. Nasty debris tumbled down, and he batted off the clinging remnants. Mindful not to touch the toxic end of the handle, he flipped the broom over and shoved the whole sordid mess into the rhododendrons next to the porch steps.

Roger was peripherally aware of the women staring horrorstruck, and was perversely grateful that they'd shut up at last. Kenny was sitting up in the playpen and soaking it all in, including, hopefully, a sense of the vigilance that home ownership demanded.

Oh fuck! What was that in the playpen, practically at the baby's feet? Roger had been too zealous to control where the detritus was landing. He hoisted Kenny over the bars and hurried indoors. To the attic! With Kenny still under one arm and the cradle under the other, he returned to the porch. The baby would be nice and snug in the unjustly maligned Wilbane heirloom till Roger could scour the playpen. Good thing Jill wasn't here! He risked glancing toward the street. The women, to his relief, were gone. Jesus, ladies, get real, it was only a bunch of birds!

In the wake of this incident, Roger finally realized that as homeowner, he had to be more industrious in putting his own stamp on the place, and in keeping destructive forces at bay. "Home improvements" should mean more than "errands" to get him out of the house a while. In the middle of the backyard, one scrawny tree had survived the fixer-uppers' chainsaws. But why? All it did was clutter an otherwise multi-use space, where Roger could teach Kenny to play catch and baseball and soccer as soon as he learned to walk. The boy was in sore need of some male influence. Whatever else Kenny was developmentally, he wasn't robust or outgoing. Roger had to drill some competitive spirit into him before it was too late. The tree had to go so his son could thrive. He had landscapers chop it down and pry out the stump.

Out front, grass and more arcane plant life were coming up

through cracks in the sidewalk. Another insidious attack on property value! To guarantee roots-and-all eradication, he sprayed with the strongest commercially available weed-killer. The woman across the street was watching from her porch. She didn't say anything, but her expression was scathing. What was she, an eco-Nazi? He shot her a cold look in return before heading back in.

As for the front lawn, on close inspection, dandelions and much else that wasn't grass had made worrisome inroads. He rifled through the junk mail on the end table in the foyer. Aha, there was that special trial offer for "lawn care." Those chemicals they used couldn't be so bad, or they wouldn't be allowed to use them, would they? The answer, on second thought, was irrelevant to home enhancement. Soon a little square sign stood in the grass, warning people away for seventy-two hours. Well before then, someone had turned the sign around and scrawled a skull and crossbones on the blank side, and the words "bird killers." Roger could've confronted the obvious suspects, but why bother? They'd deny it, and he had no proof. He yanked out the sign before its time and tossed it beyond the curb. It looked awful, and it was vandalism, a violation. Who were these people to challenge his freedom of choice?

Jill came home with a lot to think about. She was taken aback rather than happy that Roger had shown so much domestic initiative in her absence. And evidently he'd hit upon some serviceable household routine: the place was pretty clean, and he hadn't broken the baby. But she was no longer on the lookout for what would endear him to her. Quite the opposite. During her immersion in Dad's higher standard of living, she'd reflected that people were supposed to be better off than their parents, weren't they? This clearly wasn't happening under the present arrangement. On her return flight, she'd struck up scintillating conversations, and traded business cards, with a passenger or two who'd made her feel scintillating. When had that happened last? She'd forgotten she could feel that way, and wasn't that a crime?

She was also coming to a more philosophical, even clinical understanding of Kenny. Medical expertise might never correctly label whatever was wrong with him. Her new in-flight friends couldn't agree more. Better for her to admit that poor Kenny had major flaws, and go from there.

She kept a mental logbook of his aberrations, as well as of Roger's missteps, over the summer. When she called across a room to Kenny, he came crawling, but not to her. His course always veered aside and he sat down nowhere in particular, reaching and mewling into empty space to be picked up. No less inexplicably, he camped by the attic door, staring at it, or worse, he tracked illusory motion across the hall and to the door, and then threw himself against it, bawling in frustration when he couldn't pass through after repeated tries. He accepted baby food from her, without enthusiasm, without eye contact. And based on comparable apathy toward his soiled diapers, toilet training would be a mammoth struggle. Moreover, he was giving the lie to her prediction of vigorous growth. He still fit in a cradle, he stood bandy-legged when he stood at all, and those couldn't be dark circles forming under his eyes, could they? Jill was shocked to find herself gaping into the crib and thinking "monkey child."

Roger sometimes noticed Jill gazing sidelong at him. At first surmise, absence had made her heart grow fonder. But shortly, no mistaking it. Her affections had cooled somewhat. This made no sense to the reformed, more on-the-ball Roger. No, he didn't understand her at all. With any luck, this phase would be short-lived. Especially because his cravings for her increased, the longer she kept him at arm's length.

And all this, just when Roger was warming to fatherhood, and when he could see that Jill was right. Kenny needed all the parenting he could get. But while Roger was upping his commitment, Jill showed signs of disengaging from son as well as husband, spending hours on the phone with some friend of hers, and sleeping late. Could Jill have picked a worse time to lay back? For one thing, what would happen next month, when Roger had to work again?

More pointedly, he was still smarting from the weed-whacker incident. Those landscapers who'd uprooted that trash tree out back had been mowing the lawn every two weeks. They never did a good job with the grass under the rhododendrons, though, no matter how often Roger mentioned it. In desperation, he bought a weed-whacker. The instant he turned it on, the sound of power told him, Yes, now something will get done, now you're taking charge. In a minute, the edges, for the first time, were neatly, properly trimmed. With a rush of pride he killed the engine, and from a window across the driveway, R. J.

roared, "Haven't you ever heard of noise pollution?" Rather than dignify this outburst in any way, Roger kept his head down and withdrew on stiff legs up his own driveway. Not so easy, to escape the underlying message. His little family, more than ever, had to stick together. It was them against the surrounding world.

At least he hadn't made marital relations worse by bringing up that ghost-in-the-attic yarn. If he had, then knowing Jill, she'd have found him guilty of believing it by virtue of paraphrasing it. And he didn't believe it! He wasn't a crazy old hippie. Nothing psychoactive lingered in his veins. Sometimes Kenny behaved as if something were visible to his eyes alone. But that was neural malfunction, frightening enough, and weird enough. No need to invoke the supernatural.

Roger was sole witness to Kenny's latest episode. Jill was on the phone, behind locked bedroom door. Dusk had stolen in. The only illumination was from the TV. Ninja Turtles won scraps of Kenny's attention, when he didn't aim more probing looks here and there.

Garish animation flickered in Roger's torpid eyes as if it were hearth fire. Then he blinked away daze and focused on Kenny, sitting in the middle of the Persian rug, laughing wildly, clapping his hands, bouncing with delight. The baby faced straight ahead, then up at the ceiling, then slowly left to right. Fascination was displacing the unease Roger knew he should be feeling. But Kenny was happy, at any rate.

Streetlight through the windows relieved the dimness only a little, while evening breeze gently flapped the half-drawn shades. The TV remote fell off the arm of the sofa and bounced off hardwood floor.

Kenny shifted immediately from joy to anguished tears, cringing, and shitting his diapers. He pressed his stubby fists against his eyes, but continued to react as though his fists hid nothing. His arms dropped away, and he flinched to one side and then another, howling each time, as if to avoid something that lunged and withdrew and lunged from a different direction. He tipped backward and then rolled over and fled on all fours to Roger, caromed into his khaki trouser legs, pushed between and cowered behind them, keening hopelessly. Roger sat stunned, deeply upset of course. But perhaps because Kenny had crawled to him, Roger felt a closer bond between them than ever.

Jill was watching from the foot of the stairs. She wasn't mad. She didn't say anything. She reminded Roger of someone in a lab coat, clipboard in hand. She opened the foyer door, and Roger heard something about "going out for a while."

Roger extricated Kenny from between shins and sofa, and set him on his lap. Whew! That diaper needed changing pronto. Kenny's agitation was peaking less often, and Roger credited himself as an agent of calm. He gazed into Kenny's impenetrable eyes and tried the radical step of adopting babyish point of view. As an educator, Roger knew that kids didn't yet see the world in rational terms. They couldn't know how it was put together, at least according to grownups' priorities. From his own childhood, he remembered accidentally eating yam and lamb chop in the same mouthful, and observing that together they tasted like toothpaste. How odd! Still, the childish conclusion was straightforward. People made toothpaste by somehow mixing yams and lamb chops. Little kids lived in a world of unbridled possibilities. Until they underwent indoctrination into the adult world order of cause and effect and social acceptability, who knew what they might see, or think they were seeing? But let's get real here. Eerie as Kenny's displays might be, Roger reminded himself they were a matter for neurology, and not demonology or whatever. He fetched the remote and switched from Ninja Turtles to news.

Jill had expected Roger and Kenny to arrive at an understanding. They were both misaligned with reality, each a millstone in his intractable way. Like father, like son, all right. After she'd saved Kenny's life, she figured that was ample show of benevolence, and she didn't really owe them anything more.

She'd sent Roger to pick up her meds at the pharmacy, one evening before supper. Her blood pressure was still high, and no mystery there. She had Roger shop for groceries, buy gas for the minivan, anything to get him out of the house a while. He couldn't keep his hands off her recently, altogether oblivious to their changed situation, regardless of how often or brusquely she gave him the cold shoulder. That was another thing baby and husband had in common, wasn't it? Both were unbearably needy.

Jill was cooking. Kenny was up in his crib. Jill emptied two big cans of stewed tomatoes into the saucepan, and frowned at the clutter already in the sink. She carried the cans out to the recycling bin on the front porch. As she turned to go back in, something clanged against the front-step railing. A screen window from upstairs had come to rest on the pavement. What the hell? She hurried up to the nursery, where Kenny was kneeling silently on the sill below wide-open window, arms raised, and nothing between him and the twilight air. She sprang over and plucked him off the sill, and he started screeching, of course. Little ingrate! She was ready to confess that she'd had it. What point being a mother to a child who never acknowledged that she was his mother? She let Kenny cry in the crib while she retrieved the screen and reinstalled it.

She mentioned none of this to Roger. That would've been like handing kerosene to an arsonist. Nowadays, before going out, he always nagged her about taking good care of Kenny. She didn't know how long she could chafe in silence at this. Roger was the flighty one!

Then Cliff from the plane came to the rescue. Said she could stay with him. In his spacious new condo down by the river. Maybe that wouldn't work out either. But what would come of staying the present course? Of another child by Roger? He was the problem. He had to be. There was nothing wrong with her.

But how to explain it all to Roger? She hadn't meant for things to happen with Cliff. Still, these things just happen. She'd get her stuff out of the house as soon as possible. So said the note under the cow-shaped magnet on the fridge. She'd written quickly while Roger was out with Kenny in the stroller. Her lawyer would probably compose any future messages. She chucked her overnight bag onto the passenger seat of the minivan and pulled out of the driveway. She wouldn't miss the house. Something about it had always rubbed her the wrong way. Some places were just like that. No point dwelling on why. Or heaping blame on Roger for insisting they buy it. She had to get on with her life. Her inner clock was ticking.

In a few days, Roger started emerging from shock and coming to terms with his newly upside-down world. He was overpoweringly alone, with contrary feelings of being boxed in and suffocating, and of being naked on a vast savanna. Old friends had not called in months, and he could turn to nobody in the neighborhood.

And what of Kenny when school started next week? Daycare wasn't an option. He was too young, and had his "special needs." An au pair? Not on his salary, especially after Jill withdrew half their sav-

ings, which according to her e-mail was "only fair," considering her father's open-handedness all along. Otherwise, she wouldn't answer e-
mails or give out her new phone number or address. Kenny no longer
seemed to enter into her equations, and what could Roger do on his
own, beyond waiting around for some solution to present itself?

Jill communicated once more, to warn him of the hour tomorrow
when she'd pack her clothes and some kitchenware. Instead of helping
her or clearing out with Kenny for the duration, he devised a middle
course. There were some broken sections in the pavement between
sidewalk and front steps. Roger mixed a basin of cement, and while Jill
filled suitcases and plastic milk crates or made trips to and from the
van, Roger declined even to speak when spoken to. Kenny was
strapped into the stroller in the shade of the rhododendrons, where he
and Roger could watch each other, and Roger concentrated on extract-
ing pieces of loose old pavement and spreading a new surface. After
he'd smoothed some wet cement, he took a twig and incised his name
and Kenny's and the year. Once Jill saw what Roger was doing, she
loaded the van via the back door, damn the extra little inconvenience.
That afforded Roger a vindictive little smile, as did Kenny's admirable
indifference to Mom, apart from casual interest in her as a moving object. Roger and Jill exchanged no parting words when she left.

Late that afternoon, Roger went to the supermarket. Quite a
chore, toting Kenny while he shopped, and getting the bags indoors
before Kenny took umbrage at confinement in the baby seat, and putting food away while keeping an eye on Kenny. This was when a
spouse would come in handy.

Roger was about to stuff the empty plastic bags in a wastebasket
under the sink when he heard something jingle. How embarrassing!
When had he dropped the keys to the Lexus into a shopping bag? He
pocketed the keys, and then his eyes fixed on the kitchen table. Near
the edge sat a red heart-shaped box, the size of his palm. It was light
enough to be empty, but rustled faintly when he shook it. He worked
off the lid. Inside were dozens of snips of blond hair, underneath a label that said "Ariadne's Hair." He felt cold in a way he'd never felt before, queasy and lightheaded, and short of breath. Had Jill put this
here? No, that made no sense.

The disreputable R. J. had made off with an object of this description from the attic last year. Had he broken in somehow to return it? As a macabre joke? As harassment? Roger wouldn't put it past him, but where were the signs of forced entry? Then again, what other explanation was there?

And come to think of it, where was Kenny? He was no longer crawling around on the kitchen floor. The back door was open. Roger swore he'd locked it a minute ago. Or had he brought the groceries in through the front door? He darted out back, onto the redwood deck.

Kenny had trekked halfway to the white lawn-chemical sign, the one beacon of contrast in the uniform green. Meanwhile, a bluejay was squawking on a forsythia branch that overhung the yard from next door, and a squirrel was skittering straight down the back fence. Dirty animals! Roger ran at the bird, waving in wide arcs, and then at the squirrel. If they got too close to the baby, they might make him sick, or bite him for all Roger knew! They fled, and he caught his breath and checked around for more trespassers. R. J. was watching from one of his upstairs windows, with mingled disdain and amusement. Roger gave him the finger, and was ashamed of himself in mid-gesture. Appalling, that he'd sunk to the vulgar level of this neighborhood! He snatched Kenny back inside without raising his eyes from the ground.

With Kenny on his lap, Roger sat at the kitchen table, eyeing the heart-shaped box, mind racing, and still red-faced at his lapse of decorum. R. J. had commented once on the hot tub in the attic. Did that mean he had an old key of the Wilbanes, or some other way in, when the mood to prowl arose? Not really. He and "the Missus" might have snooped around during an open house when the address first went on the market. Disappointingly, this use of reason did not in itself make the heart-shaped box disappear.

His thoughts kept reverting to the ugliness in the backyard. Wow, if he'd been R. J., he'd have been seriously offended. Maybe it was the guilt talking, but Roger had to concede, just because scruffy old R. J. was crazy, that didn't prove he was wrong about everything. That was logical, wasn't it? Why not grant the hypothetical possibility, however slight, of a ghost, and work from there? Anyway, had Ariadne ever existed at all, she was beginning to feel more real to Roger, now that they had some common ground of grief and loss.

The kitchen had become dark, but Roger was too busy thinking to care. For the sake of argument, ghostly activity, visible only to Kenny's unacculturated eyes, did explain his motor-level quirks, and his emotional quirks, in response to Ariadne's demented behavior. But no. Roger wasn't ready to accept the whole invisible world on the basis of one little box of hair. He stood up to reach for the light cord and flood the room with reality again, and at the last instant remembered to hold onto Kenny, who was sliding to the floor. And curiously quiet about it. He pulled the cord and was blinking well after the light stopped hurting his eyes. The box was gone.

It must have fallen off the table. He could find it later. Kenny had been remarkably relaxed since his scramble across the yard. As serene as he'd only been in the maternity ward. Easy to tell what was going on when Kenny was laughing or in tears. His placid surface of a face, though, was enigmatic on the order of sphinx or Mona Lisa. Was he contented, expectant, patient, resigned? And why? An impossible riddle! Roger put him in the crib upstairs. Let him nap while Roger microwaved supper. A can of chowder would do for tonight, and after Roger ate, he'd feed Kenny.

Roger flipped to one of the news channels as he sat on the sofa with his bowl. Plane crashes, suicide bombers, Third World famines, leavened with come-ons for relief from leg ulcers and erectile dysfunction, failed to spoil his appetite. Or anyone else's, as far as he knew. Roger sighed. Most kids had no choice but to deal with the brutality of life, grow callous to it in the service of survival. Was Kenny pursuing an alternative? If so, it too, sadly, had its share of drawbacks.

Roger's bowl was empty. He turned off the TV. Directly overhead, through the ceiling, a nails-on-chalkboard scraping was in progress, ending with a thud. Bowl and spoon clattered to the floor as Roger leapt up and to the stairs. Incoming streetlight and tenuously luminous red walls sufficed to show the crib tilting upended against a windowsill, open toward the night. Where was Kenny? Roger had to pause and swallow hard, or the chowder would have come back up. He lurched to the window and knocked the crib aside. Snips of blond hair were scattered along the sill. A whitish bundle lay motionless on the sidewalk. That couldn't be Kenny. People would be swarming out there by now if that were a body. The street was empty.

Roger heard crying. It was coming from the attic. Kenny! The attic door was open. The light wasn't working, but Roger didn't need it to climb two steps at a time. At the top, he let his eyes adjust a second, for fear of treading on the baby. He hadn't been up here in a while. The waterless hot tub had accumulated a lot of cobwebs. At last it was in a state that wouldn't deter a self-respecting ghost from haunting the place!

He traced the crying to the far side of the tub. Yes! There was Kenny, and he actually had grown this summer, hadn't he, because he was crammed so tightly into the cradle that he could hardly twitch. No wonder he was miserable!

Roger hesitated en route to the cradle. Stupid of him not to bring a flashlight. He could have grabbed one in the nursery. In this untrustworthy murk, he thought he could see the rim of the cradle, on and off, right through Kenny.

Roger started forward again, and stopped. The cradle was rocking by itself. That couldn't be happening. If he thought it were happening, it would establish that he had gone mad. Ipso facto. And whether Roger cared to see it or not, Kenny's arms kept bobbing through the sides of the cradle. So it was too small for him now, at that!

He glanced aside and back again, but the cradle remained in stubborn motion, reaffirming his insanity. Was he positive that nobody was rocking it? No sooner had he posed the question than the cradle began rocking faster, which did nothing to pacify the baby. In the darkness behind the cradle, Roger made out bits of an outline, like the imperfect erasure of a pencil sketch. The longer he stared, the more confident he felt that a dowdy old woman was taking form. Her intimations of a face were directed toward Kenny. Then she was regarding Roger, and he could sense triumph, or maybe fulfillment, even if there was too little of a face to read any expression.

Without knowing why, Roger wanted to laugh, but knew he shouldn't. Wouldn't be respectful. All the same, a revelation sprang to mind, and it was too entertaining to bottle up inside. "Just because I'm crazy," he chanted, "doesn't mean this isn't happening."

Holding back the inappropriate laughter became harder and harder, until it exploded from him. But as he'd suspected, it didn't change anything. Ariadne persisted in becoming more defined. Verging on opaque. And behind his laughter and Kenny's distress, were those sirens in the distance, or were they hallucinatory as well?

During his past 35 years as a writer, JONATHAN THOMAS has also worked as factory hand, artist's model, manager of a recycling center, postal clerk, concert promoter, library technical assistant, comedian, and copyeditor for medical journals and the Providence Art Club. At Brown University, he was a student of Lovecraft scholar Barton L. St. Armand. He has written comics scripts for *Eerie* and *Vampirella*, music journalism for the *San Francisco Weekly* and other newspapers, and lyrics for performers Angel Dean and Sue Garner, Shackwacky, Fish and Roses, Escape by Ostrich, Video Aventures (in France), and scumCrown (in Sweden). He has written and translated liner notes for the French band Etron Fou Leloublan, and has collaborated with film-maker/musician Frank Difficult on two projects in progress, *Cthulhu Rising* and *Color out of Space*. His fiction has appeared in *Fantasy Macabre*, *Ballpeen*, *Radio Void*, *Resister*, and *Symbol*, and Radio Void Press issued a collection of short works, *Stories from the Big Black House*. He has composed and played keyboards and miscellaneous percussion with the Amoebic Ensemble, the Panic Band, and Septimania. Thomas lives in Providence and is married to artist and singer Angel Dean.

Printed in the United States
205682BV00005B/28-75/P